Also by Elizabeth Benedict

SLOW DANCING

The Beginner's Book of Dreams

ELIZABETH BENEDICT

The Beginner's Book of Dreams

Alfred A. Knopf New York 1988

I wish to thank the Corporation of Yaddo and the District of Columbia
Commission on the Arts and Humanities for their generous support
during the writing of this book. For their time and thoughtfulness
I'm indebted to Tony Beilenson, Joe Cameron, James Corman,
Lani Guinier, John Hatton, and Mark Power.

E.B.

THIS IS A BORZOI BOOK
PUBLISHED BY ALFRED A. KNOPF, INC.

Owing to limitations of space, acknowledgments for permission to
reprint previously published material can be found on page 327.

Library of Congress Cataloging-in-Publication Data
Benedict, Elizabeth.
The beginner's book of dreams.
I. Title
PS3552.E5396B44   1988   813'54   87-40480
ISBN 0-394-55157-7

Manufactured in the United States of America
First Edition

THIS IS FOR NANCY, FOR NICHOLAS WHEELER,
AND FOR THE B.

The Beginner's Book of Dreams

The Packages You Take with You

THIS IS WHAT they will do, she and her mother. They will watch the skaters and then they will pray. From the landing above the rink they will watch the woman in the center of it spin on the point of one skate, the most perfect pirouette, and then they will cross Fifth Avenue and go into St. Patrick's Cathedral and light candles. Then they will cross Fifty-first Street and go to the Prime Burger for medium-rare cheeseburgers and French fries. They will share a chocolate shake.

This is what Georgia and Esme do most Sunday afternoons. Georgia chooses this time of day, long after noon, to avoid the Mass. She is, or was, some sort of Protestant. No one in her family paid much attention to the distinctions, to the houses of worship, the fine points of the holidays. Nor did they put much stock in where they were from. Her father, born in California. His father before him—no one had a clue. Georgia never saw a Jew until she was nineteen, and married one when she was twenty-two, Esme's father, Meyer Singer.

The man Georgia is married to now, Quinn Laughlin, says to her when they are alone, and when she tells the story in front of guests, "How do you know you never *saw* one?" "Because there weren't any in Redondo Beach, sweetheart. They were all in L.A." Her voice is unwavering and deep. If she has been drinking, the words are slurred. Sometimes, some nights, the liquor dulls the disgust in her voice. Other times it sharpens it.

This cold Sunday, almost Christmas, Esme stands on tiptoes at the bright red guardrail, looking down at the skaters, looking across to the beautiful tree. Their first Christmas in New York. She holds on to the rail; her pink angora mittens clash with the red. She is fat. Her pale pink tights keep her thighs from chafing and burning when they rub together, as they chafe and burn in the summer, in any damp heat. The woman in the center spins and spins. Another skater tries to imitate her and falls. Children hobble along the side of the ice in their scuffed rented black skates, gripping the guardrail around the rink. She has never seen snow.

She is obedient. She follows rules, instructions, her mother's wishes, her teachers' orders. But here, in the dark of the cathedral, the blues and reds of the stained-glass windows deeper than any she has ever seen, wishes, prayers, dreams, and memories become confused, become one. Georgia hands her a quarter and says, "Light a candle to remember someone you love." Other Sundays she says, "Make a wish," or "Say a prayer."

Today Esme wants everything. She cannot choose. She drops a quarter into the metal box and picks up a thin wooden votive stick. She points the tip into one of the candles that is already lit and then chooses the candle, in its small glass cup, the rows and rows of white lighted candles, that will be hers.

She looks up at Georgia, who is attentively lighting her candle. One Sunday when she looked up, she saw a single tear running down Georgia's cheek. Esme moves her lighted stick across the row and stops at the candle she has picked out. She holds the flame against the wick. She shuts her eyes and remembers someone she loves. Her father. She wishes. That when he comes to New York he will take her skating. That she will not be fat. That her mother will not get drunk again the way she did last week. Falling on her way up the stairs, mumbling to Quinn as he picked her up, "Goddam duplex, deluxe goddam duplex. Hear what I said?" "Funny, Georgie. I've got you. Let go of the bannister."

Esme holds out her palm. "Can I have another quarter?"

Georgia moves her fingers through the pocket of her wallet. "I'm all out of change, sweetheart."

Quinn is in television, an executive at one of the networks, in charge of advertising, selling thirty-second spots, package deals for sports specials. He gets tickets for Broadway openings, invita-

tions to parties at Sardi's, the Rainbow Grill. "Was a day—"
he loves this story, tells it often to guests, many of whom have
heard it more than once—"when a guy who took a date to the top
of Thirty Rockefeller—when they got off the elevator and he led
her to the right—to the Rainbow *Room*, instead of to the left—
the *Grill*—she knew he was a cheapskate." This year he has
been promised tickets to the Kentucky Derby.

Early Sunday evening in the duplex. Quinn mixes a pitcher
of Manhattans. Georgia fixes herself a Dewar's and water and
offers Dru and Ted Seaver macadamia nuts in a cut-crystal dish.
"God, Georgia, you look terrific. Doesn't she look terrific, Ted?"

"Georgia always looks like a million."

"Try this," Quinn says and hands Dru a cocktail glass.

"What else would you drink in Manhattan?" Dru says.

"We moved here so Quinn would have an excuse to make
Manhattans," Georgia says. "A better excuse. Cheers." She holds
up her glass, from which she has already taken several sips. "I
mean, who in the hell would name a drink after L.A.?"

It's true, she always looks like a million. That's exactly the
way Quinn had put it the morning they met, in an elevator at
CBS in L.A., in 1958. She was being tested for a pilot. She was
to be the pretty girl standing at the counter on a cooking show,
demonstrating techniques for dicing, mincing, and pulverizing.

She was sometimes mistaken for Lauren Bacall. "Except for
the boobs," Georgia would explain, looking down. "Georgie
didn't have any until she was nineteen," Quinn once added.
"They came with the Jews." They had been very drunk. Out of
earshot of the host and hostess a man had murmured to his
willowy date, "How long do you give *this* marriage?"

Tonight in the duplex. They are tall, stunning, recently married. They are introduced around town as "just in from the
Coast." It is 1962.

"Quinn, this is super," Dru says, taking another sip. "But
your place—" She casts her eyes around the large living room.
"Honey, it looks like Halloween. I mean, *black* walls."

"The decorator's a fag," Quinn says.

"They both are," Georgia says. "Sy and José. Interior Design, Limited. Sy, needless to say, is a Jew. José's Cuban."

"I thought he was a P.R.," Quinn says.

"He's definitely Cuban." She turns to Dru. "And very upper class. Even for a Cuban. Anyway, the idea is that the maroon wall-to-wall and the wooden beams—" she fans her arm through the air, guiding everyone's eyes toward the dark-stained wooden beams that cross the high ceiling—"offset the black, so to speak, of the black."

"What did you say their names were?" Ted says.

"Sy. Sy and José." Georgia says "José" with what she thinks is a Cuban accent, pretends to struggle with the "J" in a guttural sound, as if she is trying to dislodge a string of celery stuck in the back of her throat.

Esme is upstairs in her bedroom listening to a Beach Boys album and putting on lipstick that she stole the week before from Woolworth's. It's called Plum Love. She sits before the ornate vanity that was her mother's and applies the lipstick for the third or fourth time, dabbing her lower lip with a Kleenex, humming along to songs about surfer girls and cars. She knows all the words and has a signed photograph from Brian Wilson taped to the mirror of the vanity that is a foot taller than she is. She will turn eight-and-a-half in seven days, on the day after Christmas.

The record skips. She walks across the room to turn it over, looking back once or twice to the mirror. The lipstick is smudged, her cheeks are pudgy. She stuffs them with candy, ice cream, slices of pizza that she buys on her way home from school, that she sneaks from the kitchen, that she eats on the sly. Georgia had told her at dinner recently that if she lost fifteen pounds, she would be svelte. "What's svelte?"

"Svelte. Thin."

"Like your mother," Quinn added.

Georgia turned to him. "*That* was unnecessary."

"You brought it up."

"Now I'm going to bring it down."

"You can't have it both ways, Georgia. Telling her to lose weight and then—"

"I can have it as many ways as I want. And I didn't tell her to lose weight. I simply told her that if she did—"

"You live your life in the conditional tense."

"What is that supposed to mean?"

"If. It's your favorite word. If your mother hadn't. If your father wasn't. If Meyer Singer didn't."

"Leave her father out of it."

"Excuse me, Esme."

"What did my father do?"

"He didn't do anything, sweetheart. Quinn Laughlin has a wild imagination."

Georgia had reached across the table for the bowl of chopped broccoli. She scooped out a spoonful and was about to serve herself when Esme spoke. "Why do you always call him Quinn Laughlin?"

"What?"

"You never just say Quinn, you say Quinn Laughlin."

"I guess I never noticed."

"Maybe it helps you to remember," Quinn said.

"Remember what?"

"My name."

In her bedroom now Esme picks up the record from the turntable, blows on the needle, and wipes "Introducing the Beach Boys!" with her sleeve. She does not understand why Georgia needs help remembering Quinn's name. Esme has known his name since she was four. She knows the names of Quinn's ex-wife and his two daughters. The girls are Peggy and Linda and they are coming for Christmas. They are very svelte and live in Chicago. They have chiffon dresses and spiked high heels and teased hair and they taught Esme how to do the Mashed Potato. She knows their first names and their middle names and their confirmation names. They took her to church once and taught her how to dip her finger into the dish of holy water and cross herself. They showed her the confessional and said she could not confess her sins because she was partly Jewish. They told her Communion wafers tasted like ladyfingers and then they told her that they were just kidding. They told her that sinners went to hell and that she could shave her legs when she was thirteen.

She slips the record into its cover and counts her stack of forty-fives. Then she goes to the bottom drawer of her dresser, where she keeps all the things she is saving. Two autograph books, a cigar box of shells, a scrapbook in which she pressed an orchid corsage Georgia gave her, in which she pasted a photograph of her friend Elaine, the ticket stub from her first Broadway play, *Stop the World—I Want to Get Off*, a swizzle stick from Toots Shor's, a postcard from France, a letter she had just gotten from her father: *Business is about to boom, if that's all right with you! Love U, Daddy*. In the corner of the drawer, in a small plastic bag, is a handful of candy that looks like smooth rocks that Quinn had bought her when they were in Palm Springs the summer before, on the Fourth of July. With Dru and Ted and their kids they had watched fireworks from the patio of the hotel and Georgia had cried in the car on the way to the airport.

"Esmeeee." She hears her mother's voice, her mother's footsteps coming up the stairs. Esme closes the dresser drawer and stands up as Georgia enters the bedroom. She shakes her head and comes toward Esme, holding out her hand to Esme's mouth. "It looks like you've been painting your chin purple. What is that color?"

"Plum Love. Do you want to try it on?" Esme goes to the vanity and hands her the lipstick. "Audrey gave it to me." She speaks the lie quietly, she looks for the truth in it. Audrey Finch had helped her to get it. Audrey had a whole shelf of lipsticks in her bathroom, half of them stolen from the Woolworth's where she had initiated Esme the week before. Audrey had given her the idea, the nerve, the technique.

Georgia reads the label on the bottom of the lipstick. "Sure, I'll try a little. And after dinner I'll show you how to put it on right. We're going to a new restaurant. Something about a dove." Georgia takes off the cap, puckers her lips, and looks at herself in the mirror.

"The Sign of the Dove."

"How do you know that?"

"Audrey and her parents go there all the time. I went with them once. I told you."

"I guess I don't remember." She is leaning close to the mirror, getting ready to apply the lipstick. She says "Jesus" under her breath.

"What's wrong?"

"This damn haircut." She runs the lipstick along her lower lip, concentrating intently. She moves to her upper lip. Midway, still looking at herself, she says, "Let's get haircuts for Christmas. We'll try someplace new. Maybe Bonwit's." Beginning to apply a second coat, she says, "I'd love to see you in bangs."

"I'd look awful in bangs."

"You'd look beautiful in bangs." She turns to Esme. "Precious. Lovely in bangs, sweetheart. The girl who cut your hair last time, she—"

"I don't want bangs and I don't want dinner."

"Darling, you have to have dinner."

Quinn calls from downstairs. "Georgia. Esme. We're ready to leave."

"I'll stay here. If I'm hungry I'll make toast."

"You shouldn't eat so much toast."

"Mom."

Georgia moves toward her, runs her hand over Esme's hair, leans down to kiss her forehead. "Please come with us. You can tell me which dish to order. Which dessert is best." She wraps her long arms around Esme and pulls her close, rocking her as she holds her. Her mother smells of perfume, she smells of mothballs. She holds the girl tightly, desperately. "Please."

Esme disengages herself. "You should go now. Quinn'll get mad."

"The hell with Quinn," she says quietly. She holds her hands over Esme's ears, stroking the sides of her head with her strong fingers. Esme lets her. It feels good. Sometimes her mother needs her, sometimes she needs her mother.

"Are you going to get divorced?"

"We just got married."

"Why didn't you get married before? You haven't been married to Daddy since I was two."

"We wanted to wait." She plays with strands of Esme's hair, she runs her thumb over Esme's cheek.

"For what?"

"I don't know. We wanted to be sure."

Quinn calls their names again. Georgia lets go of Esme and then leans down to kiss the top of her head.

"Sure about what?"

"Esme, sweetheart."

"I'm just asking."

"You have so many questions. Are you sure you won't come with us?"

Esme nods.

"Then give me a kiss goodnight." She leans down to receive the kiss. Her perfume is sweet, her cheeks are soft. "We'll be home soon." At the door to Esme's room Georgia turns back and says, "We're not going to get divorced." She blows Esme a kiss and closes the door behind her.

In the car on the way to the airport in Palm Springs when Georgia was crying, Esme leaned against Dru and whispered, "Why is she crying?"

"Because she's sad to leave this beautiful town," Dru whispered.

Quinn had bought her rock candy and they had watched the fireworks and Esme knew, as soon as Dru spoke, that she was lying.

Georgia herself did not know why she was crying. She knew only that it was rare, unheard of, for her to cry when she was, as she was then, stone sober.

Soon after they leave for the Sign of the Dove, Esme goes downstairs and eats what is left of a bag of Pecan Sandies and three pieces of cinnamon toast. She looks for change in the pockets of Quinn's and Georgia's coat pockets in the front hall closet. With the ninety-five cents she finds she can buy three ice-cream cones and two slices of pizza. On the sly.

At the corner table they are drinking champagne, toasting Georgia's birthday a month after the event. She is thirty-two. She never thinks about herself. Everyone is on her list. The closet in her bedroom is crammed with Christmas presents for them. She shops at stores that deliver, that mail anything anywhere. She ignores the signs posted on every floor of B. Altman's: THE PACKAGES YOU TAKE WITH YOU GET HOME FIRST. She calls the salesgirls "Dear" and asks their advice about scarves, belts, costume jewelry, and hose for all the women on her list.

"That son of a bitch thought he could cinch this without me," Quinn is saying as he holds up his hand for the waiter.

"I've worked with him for years," Ted says. "That's not his style. If he's going to take you to the cleaners, he lets you know beforehand."

"Shit." He looks up at the waiter. "More sour cream for the potato." They are talking about a man at the network, the byzantine place with bureaus all over the world, who has just screwed Quinn out of a multi-year contract with Procter and Gamble. The figures are staggering, his rage unspeakable, though he does not tire of speaking about it.

They drink, eat rib roast, red snapper, Caesar salad. Dru describes the deck that is going to be built in back of their house in Malibu, the thirty-foot drop to the Pacific. For Christmas the children want horses to ride bareback along the beach; on weekends they see— "Oh, what's her name, the one we used to say would never make it, come on, Ted, you know who I'm talking about. The kids are always talking about her goddam horse on the beach."

"Lucy's the only one who gives a damn about the horse," Ted says. "All the boys want is new surfboards. Surfboards and wet suits, like every other bratty kid in Malibu. The people next door to us—" he turns to Quinn and Georgia— "their son is eighteen, and all, I mean, *all*, he knows how to do is surf. This kid couldn't get through one semester at Santa Monica Community College, flunked every class. You could take away his driver's license as long as you didn't take away his—"

"Sweetie, don't exaggerate."

"If we'd stayed in L.A., at least they might have learned how to read before they learned how to wax a goddam surfboard. By the time I was eighteen—"

"Bobby won't be eighteen for five years."

"And at the rate he's going he won't graduate from ninth grade."

"He doesn't do any worse than any kid in that school."

"That's exactly my point."

The maître d' interrupts. "I'm looking for a Mrs. Laughlin." Georgia responds. "There is a phone call for you. I think your daughter." She walks with him to the front of the restaurant. "You were easy to find," he tells her, motioning toward the phone. "The little girl told me I should look for someone who looks like Lauren Bacall."

When she returns to the table Dru is the first one to ask. "Is everything all right?"

"There were some strange phone calls. She's a little undone." She sits down and lights a cigarette. "Someone called a few times and then hung up."

"Wrong number," Quinn says. "Not like there was any heavy breathing, was there?"

"She didn't say."

"Christ, that kid can be skittish," Quinn says. "She's afraid to walk in the grass because she might step on an ant and kill it."

"She's very sensitive."

"What do you expect? You treat her like a cripple and she acts like one."

Suddenly she is sober, responsible, this woman who thinks nothing of leaving her child alone for hours at a time, who left her child alone for the better part of a night when she was five. "She needs me," Georgia says and stands up, reaching to the chair next to her for her coat.

"More of the same, Georgie." Quinn holds up his hands, giving up. "Bust up another dinner because your baby's nose is running."

"Let me go with you," Dru says.

It is brutally cold, the slack of the canopy moves in the wind, snaps back and forth like a sail, the sound of a whip cracking. Dru can see her breath. The city is awesome, frightening to her. Georgia is already at home here, she does not even button her coat. She stands on the curb scouting for cabs, raising and lowering her arm, fanning her fingers at the traffic. They have been through this before, the scene in the restaurant, a rift in the middle of dinner, one of them leaving early. It occurs to her that Georgia might have been lying about the phone calls at home, covering for Quinn; perhaps someone who shouldn't have had called for him. He was known to gamble. Dru would not put it past him to screw around.

In the cab Georgia looks away from Dru, out the window. She lights a cigarette and crosses her legs. "Fuck, I hate Christmas," she says. "I hate every minute of it." She is drunk, sober, stunning, cold. The skin between her breasts is cold. Her fingernails, curled inside her palm, are cold.

"All right, Georgia, let's have it."

Georgia turns to her. She feels a draft on her calves.

"Why didn't you let him come to New York by himself and break it off that way? Why the hell did you marry him?"

Georgia is silent for a long time. She wants to be enveloped in the smoke from her cigarette, she wants to disappear. The answer is easy, but she has never been asked to put it into words. "I wanted to get the hell out of L.A."

. . .

It would be wonderful to be a grownup.

She would stay up until the middle of the night.

She would wear a bra, put it on that funny way Georgia did, leaning over to let her breasts fall into the cups.

On Sundays she would read the comics in the *Daily News*, even though Quinn said it was low class, which she knew that she was not.

She would have a signature that was different from anyone else's, because they made you write a certain way in school and said you were wrong when you didn't.

She would say "Hello" that particular grownup way when she answered the phone.

She would take a lot of taxis and say, "Keep the change."

Her boyfriends would take her to the Sign of the Dove and help her out of the taxi. She would wear a strapless yellow chiffon dress with a built-in bra, to push up and out.

There was this way grownups had of saying things, moving, gesturing to one another, like they were on TV or in the movies, it was so mysterious, it was like magic. The way Georgia leaned down to put on her bra, the way Georgia gave a tip to her hairdresser. She folded the dollar bill into her hand and then went toward the woman, held out her hand like she wanted to shake it, and pressed the bill into her hand as if she wasn't supposed to be giving her money, always with that smile on her face, saying "Thank you sweetheart" so quietly like she didn't want anyone to hear. And they were all so different, grownups, even about the same things. Every day before school Esme walked Mrs. Frumpkin's poodle, and when she brought the dog back Mrs. Frumpkin said, "Did Muffy do number one *and* number two?" Georgia always said tinkle for number one. *Sweetheart, why don't you tinkle before we leave for the restaurant.* Esme's father didn't call it anything. He just said, "Do you have to go?" "Piss" was a word for tinkle that Quinn said when Esme wasn't supposed to hear. *I can't even take a piss in private.*

It was not pissing that made you pregnant, it was something like pissing that the man did and it happened in bed, and even when the man wasn't there, there was something he left in the sheets, something invisible, so that if Esme went under the covers on Quinn's side of the bed, she could get pregnant. The reason her mother didn't get pregnant was because she used Tampax when Quinn put his thing inside of her, which he sometimes did because sometimes in the middle of the night Esme went to their door and it was locked and other nights it was not, and when he put it there, that was private, and if you didn't put a Tampax in when it happened, you could get pregnant, but you could also get pregnant if you were in the bed, on Quinn's side, when he wasn't there.

Which is why, today, yesterday, on and off for weeks, Esme was sure she was pregnant.

Her condition and her fear were all her own, as private as the thing her mother and Quinn did when the door was locked.

There was a girl who was three and was pregnant. Esme had seen the headline on the cover of the *National Enquirer* at the candy store on Seventy-first and Second. Next to a photograph of a girl in pigtails:

NIGHTMARE OR MIRACLE:
THIS PREGNANT
3-YEAR-OLD.
*Doctors Can't Explain
the Mystery.*

When she is supposed to be sleeping at night, she pretends that her dolls are her babies. It is cold out and they are very poor. She wraps the babies in pillowcases. She knots kneesocks around their necks like scarves. They have nowhere to live and Esme's husband is in jail because he stole a gallon of milk from the Food Fair. He loves them all very much. Esme is certain of it, all alone in the cold with her babies, clutching them to her flannel bathrobe. They were so brave. They had endured so much. She would have to get a job. She wanted to work in a library or a store that sold greeting cards. She would take home books and birthday cards to read to her children. If she had a job, they would have enough money to live somewhere. Instead of sleeping here, in Central Park, on the cold hard ground, behind the Tavern on the Green. An artichoke Georgia had once made her eat there had made her vomit. That was why she told Georgia the restaurant should be called Vomit on the Green. Audrey Finch thought it was hysterical.

Audrey Finch lived in their building but not in a duplex, because her father didn't make as much money as Quinn. Audrey had the best mother. First of all, she did not call everyone sweetheart. Second of all, she let Audrey and her friends paint all over the walls of Audrey's bedroom with big jars of poster paint. She told Audrey that if she wanted to she could go to a boarding school in England called Summerhill, where you did not even have to go to classes or do homework unless you wanted to. "They don't have TV in England," Esme told Audrey. "There wouldn't be anything to do there."

"How do you know they don't?"

"My mother told me."

"How does she know?"

"Quinn told her. They don't have refrigerators either. And when you're in your house you have to put money in a box to turn on the heat. And even then sometimes it doesn't work."

"Well, I don't want to go now anyway. Maybe I'll go when I'm in high school. By then I'll have a boyfriend."

Esme hesitated a moment. "I will too," she said, wondering if her voice betrayed her doubt. "I might even have a husband."

"Oh, god, Esme, you are so dumb. Don't you know what kind of girls have husbands in high school?"

"What kind?"

"Pregnant ones. I saw a show on TV about them. No one likes them and they have to go away to a special house and knit all the time. Their husbands don't even like them."

Esme was speechless, fear swelled inside of her. Once you were pregnant you could not get unpregnant. Staying away from Quinn's side of the bed would not help. They would send her away. They would tell her story on TV, in the newspapers. Everyone would know. Everyone would say, "That's why you're so fat, because you're going to have a baby."

There were other confusions, misunderstandings of language or imagination. When she was four and played with Georgia's shoes, Georgia told her that someday the shoes would fit her, which she took to mean that they would shrink. When she was five her father said he had been to his sister's house and that everything in the kitchen, which was in the process of being refurbished, was upside down. She took this to mean that everything was on the ceiling. And many times, playing with her father in the ocean in L.A., he told her that he didn't need a bathing cap because he was bald. Then he told her a secret. True, he said, there was no hair on the top of his head, but that was only because he hid all of it behind his ears. It did not matter that she had never seen the hair there: her father did not lie.

So that when he told her, every time they talked on the phone, that even though she did not like living in New York now, she would like it soon, she believed him. She believed him when he told her that any boy who wanted to could grow up to be President of the United States, and that any boy who wanted to could become a rich man, and that soon, very soon, he was going to be one. She believed him when he said that you couldn't trust Nikita Khrushchev as far as you could throw him, and when he said that the doormen in her building were just doing their job, and thank god she lived in a nice building with a man to protect it, instead of a tenement.

What she especially did not like about the doormen was

that they would not let her skateboard on the sidewalk in front of the building. What she especially did not like about living in New York was the rack of tabloids and magazines at the candy store on Seventy-first and Second that she had to pass on her way to the counter to buy an ice-cream cone.

SHE WAS A LOVELY GIRL UNTIL HER STEPFATHER CHOPPED OFF HER HEAD.

I BELIEVED HIM WHEN HE SAID HE LOVED ME BUT THERE WAS MURDER IN HIS EYES THAT NIGHT.

MY BEST FRIEND STOLE MY HUSBAND AND NOW THEY WANT TO KILL MY BABY.

MY FATHER IS FROM ANOTHER PLANET: HE SHOWED ME HIS SPACESHIP.

Four days before Christmas at the candy store, she bought a *TV Guide* and a chocolate sugar cone with sprinkles with money she had taken from Georgia's and Quinn's coat pockets. Entering and leaving the store, she squinted and held her hands up to the side of her face, making blinders for her eyes, eliminating her peripheral vision until it was safe.

A Christmas Party

THE AFTERNOON BEFORE Christmas. Esme sits in a movie theatre before the lights go down, between her stepsisters, Quinn's daughters, Peggy, who is fourteen, and Linda, thirteen.

"I bet you don't know what the curse is," Linda says.

"I do too."

"What?"

"It's what happens when you don't go to confession. It's like hell."

"See," Linda says to Peggy. "I told you she wouldn't."

. . .

Georgia moved exuberantly, expectantly through the crowds that afternoon. She had just gotten her hair done, her legs waxed, a manicure.

She spent hours in Altman's gourmet shop, bought smoked oysters, French chestnut spread, cashews, paper-thin after-dinner mints from Belgium, and at a store across the street, a case, to be delivered, of French wine.

It had just begun to snow. Everything was possible, everything was as it should be. Clusters of gossamer angels hung from the ceiling of Lord & Taylor's first floor. Upstairs, Georgia bought each of the girls a diary, a cloth-covered blank book with a lock and key. It thrilled her to see the disheveled Santa Claus in front of the public library, the Salvation Army lady with her triangle, her collection pot, a bearded man with a trumpet.

She waited for a cab on Forty-second Street. Her bags weighed her down. It was windy, wet, as crowded as if they were giving away money in the place where she stood. She was jostled, ignored, her eyes were tearing from the cold. She remembered that when she was a child her mother kept a fading, flowery brochure from the Redondo Hotel, framed, on her dresser:

"Where the Spring is in the Summer, the Summer's in the Fall; the Fall is in the Winter, and the Winter—Not at all." The first lines Georgia had ever memorized. She repeated them now to herself.

It never occurred to her—this moment, this minute, was an exception—that her life was a falsehood, that she lived in a dream. The dream that the next man who asked her to dance, the next man who asked her to marry him, would be better than this one, better than the one before. She was supposed to have ended up somewhere other than here. Hailing a cab in this strange, cold city. Going home to a man who did not love her. The girl everyone had wanted to take to the War Bond dances. Georgia Stelle Bates. Junior-Senior Prom Queen, Redondo Union High, 1946. Third runner-up, Miss California, 1947. She had joined the Screen Actors Guild when she got a bit part in what was to be the 1948 remake of *A Star Is Born*. Her mother took this, the title of the movie, to refer to Georgia's bright beginning in show business, even after the production was abandoned.

Like a stagehand, a gofer on the set, like the bellboys at the Beverly Wilshire and the woman who gave out towels in the ladies' room at the old Mocambo, back then Georgia was often in the presence of celebrities. She had known not to gawk, had hoped, had prayed that she would be picked out of the crowd, given lines, given a part. But she did not take the dancing, singing, acting lessons, she never seemed to find the time to get an agent. She read the trades and showed up for auditions. She was paid SAG day rates for her many appearances in crowd scenes, sipping a glass of champagne on a dark terrace, crossing a street with a hundred other people, cheering in bleachers for horses, tennis players, pole vaulters. She modeled swimsuits, lingerie. Then there was television, the cooking shows, auditions for shows that were never produced, the pilots that didn't pan out.

She had been dying to get married, to be picked out of the crowd, given a leading role that would be easy to play. And then Meyer Singer came along with his bravado, his big ideas. She fell for every one of them. The house in Beverly Hills, the latest appliances, extra bedrooms, fidelity, more money than she knew what to do with. He would make his mark in business, in politics, success with a capital S. He convinced her that he had the world on a string.

The snow was light now, it hit the ground and dissolved, it made the crowded street glisten in the early evening. She touched her hand to her eye and felt her false eyelash loosening, coming off on the tips of her fingers.

"It's the second canopy on the right," she said to the cab driver as he turned off Third Avenue. She had to remember that her upper left arm was black and blue, had to remember to keep it covered in front of the children. Part of the dream, some damn dream, that Quinn would not do that again, send her flying that way. She had turned her face just in time to miss hitting her jaw on the corner of his dresser. Instead she fell against his shirt stand, landed on top of it as it fell to the floor. One of the thick wooden prongs jabbed her arm, and the black-and-blue mark formed around the scar from her childhood vaccination. "And a very Merry Christmas to you," she said as she handed the cab driver two dollars. The doorman helped her with her packages.

The girls were fighting over how much Hershey's chocolate syrup to put in the blender with the milk and the ice cream. "More," Linda said and grabbed the can, covered with chocolate finger-prints, from Peggy.

"It's already too much. Give it back," Peggy said and lunged for it.

"Quit it. My mother's here."

Linda returned the can to the counter top, scowled at Peggy, whispered, "Fortunately, I don't have to worry about pimples the way some people do."

"Hi, Georgia," Peggy said.

"Hi, darling. Don't tell me you're making shakes again. You

know what I could use, don't you? A nice, tall vodka tonic, that's what I could use." Esme switched on the blender and started to count to ten. That way the shake would be thick.

Georgia fixed a drink and planted it on the countertop, began to clear a space to prepare dinner. Peggy and Linda crowded around her. Esme stopped the blender. "It's ready," she said. "Get the glasses."

They were not listening. They were going through Georgia's things, shopping bags filled with cans, boxes, bottles.

"Look, it's from France."

"What do you eat this with, Georgia?"

"Put it down, jerk face. You're going to break it."

"What are *marrons*?"

"It's French, you idiot."

"Just because I don't know French—"

"Girls, please," Georgia said. "How was your movie?"

"*So* romantic. I loved it," Linda said. "Peggy did too. Esme was just scared."

"I wasn't that scared." She got the glasses herself, stood on the kitchen ladder, and opened the door to the cabinet.

"Then how come you had your hands over your eyes when he got stabbed?"

Esme stood high above them cradling three glasses in her arms. "There was too much blood."

"It's just ketchup. Isn't it just ketchup, Georgia?"

"Of course." She took the glasses from Esme. "Did you think it was really blood?"

"I knew it was ketchup." She stepped down. She wasn't sure if she had known that. "I just didn't want to see it."

Before the movie had started, Peggy told her that the curse didn't have anything to do with confession or hell. She said it happened once a month, just to girls, and you bled and bled for days. Sometimes you bled right through your dress. Sometimes you had to ask a girl in your class to walk behind you on your way to the bathroom and when you got there you didn't know what to do because there was blood all over everything. That was the awful part. The good part was that it meant you were a woman.

"Natalie Wood is *gorgeous*," Linda said.

"Is she really Puerto Rican?" Peggy said.

"I don't think so," Georgia said.

"Did you know her in Hollywood?"

"No."

"Who did you know?"

"No one very famous."

"She knew Marilyn Monroe. Didn't you, Mom?"

"I met her once at a party, when she was married to that writer. But that doesn't count as knowing her. You meet a lot of people at parties."

"How many husbands did she have?" Peggy said.

"I don't know. Three or four." Georgia took the bottle of vodka from the freezer where they kept it and splashed another shot into her tonic. The *Daily Word* tacked to the bulletin board caught her eye. She was several days behind. She turned to the entry for December twenty-fourth and pinned it back on the cork board. She drank and began to read: *Christmas Eve. The anticipation of a benevolent day, blessed with a multitude of meanings, feelings, and harmonies. On this day we strive to attain serenity and peace—*

"Why do you think she killed herself?" Peggy said. "I read in *Life* that it was because she had an unhappy childhood. If I was that beautiful I would never—"

"You won't ever be," Linda said.

"Look who's talking. Your eyes are way too far apart. Aren't her eyes too far apart, Georgia?"

"Her eyes are fine. But your mouth is on overdrive."

"What does that mean?"

"It means cool your heels."

"What does that mean?"

"It means it's time to shut up." Georgia turned and wiped

the ring of condensation her glass had left on the counter. "It's also time to start dinner."

"Mom, can't we go out?"

"We've eaten out every night this week."

"But still."

"When's Daddy coming home?" Peggy said.

"Late. He has to go to a few Christmas parties tonight, for work. I'm going to meet him after we have dinner. Why don't you check the TV *Guide* to see what's on tonight." The girls dispersed and Georgia slipped an apron over her skirt, pushed the sleeves of her sweater up her arm, the beige cashmere, the soft wool, the beautiful winter clothes she had bought since moving East.

There was going to be one party at Quinn's office, one at "21," one at P. J. Clarke's, god knows where in between. He had said he would call her later; they would meet at his next stop. It would feel good then, she would have had a bath, dabbed her thighs with Joy, taken a cab. A leading role that was easy to play. Drink in hand. Her husband would shepherd her through the crowd. They could cut quite a figure, the two of them. Oh yes, they had their moments.

Tonight he would lead her across the floor, hand dropping discreetly now and then to her backside, holding on, a promise for later. *You've met my wife. Georgia.* It made sense that the men adored her, less sense, on the surface, that their wives did too. Their jealousy was somehow confined to envying her beauty. She gave none of them reason to fear for their husbands' fidelity. She did not, as a matter of course, flirt. In public—at big parties, office gatherings—she rarely talked for too long to any man standing by himself. Her mother, just as striking in her prime, had schooled Georgia on these points from early on, with the desired effect that the men found her continually elusive and therefore intriguing, and the women found her—well, you wouldn't think so to look at her, but really, she was very down to earth. They often told her so. Told her that they hadn't expected it.

Georgia knew herself to be both beautiful and down to earth, and she aspired to nothing more, except to be happy, to feel all the time the way she felt after two or three drinks.

"Why can't we go with you?" Peggy said. The girls were back in the kitchen, a delegation. "We never get to go anywhere good. And we never see Daddy either. We hardly ever saw him the whole time he lived in California, and that was practically our whole lives."

"That's why you're here. That's why we invited you here for Christmas. Esme's been looking forward to it for weeks."

"So we can go with you tonight?"

"I'm afraid not."

"Why?"

Georgia looked from Peggy to Linda to Esme, who was examining the listings in *TV Guide*. "Esme wants you to keep her company. Don't you, sweetheart?"

She looked up and nodded. She was Georgia's daughter. She understood, without knowing she did, the value of certain falsehoods, the advisability of telling certain lies.

"Would you go upstairs and tell them that dinner's ready?" Georgia said later.

"Can I eat by myself in my room?"

"No."

"Why not?"

"It'll hurt their feelings. Do you have to tinkle?"

"No."

"Then why are you standing with your legs crossed that way?"

Esme went upstairs to look for them. She did not have to tinkle, she was just trying to squeeze her legs together, really squish them, to see if that would make them skinnier. The door to her bathroom was closed, there was a sliver of light beneath it. "How come it's wet?" Peggy said. Esme leaned closer, making sure her ear did not touch the door.

"I don't know."

"Let me touch it."

"Wait a minute. God, it really stinks."

"How can she stand it?"

"She can't feel it."

"I mean looking at it."

"She doesn't have to look."

"What about when he puts it on?"

"Maybe he doesn't do it in front of her. He probably does it in the bathroom."

"How many were left?"

"A whole bunch."

"You didn't count them?"

"No."

"You should have. That way we could look again tomorrow to see if they did it tonight."

"Maybe we'll hear."

"Did you ever hear before?"

"Just that time I told you. Mommy with the guy from Wilmette, the one with the sports car. They made so much noise."

"I can't believe anyone would do it with her. Do they come in different sizes?"

"Of course."

"Mickey Simmons said he measured his thing with a ruler and—"

"Did you hear that noise? Somebody's coming. Throw it away."

Esme stepped away from the door. She could barely hear them over the sound of the flushing toilet.

"It's sticking to my fingers."

"Let go."

"It won't come off."

"I hate olives," Linda said. She had a mustache of milk above her upper lip.

"You don't have to eat them," Georgia said.

"Georgia?" Peggy said. She was looking down, poking her pork chop with a spoon.

"Yes, sweetheart."

"Linda wants to know something, but she's embarrassed to ask you."

Linda glared at her.

Esme braced herself. Maybe it was about the wet thing.

"She wants to know—"

"I don't want to know anything," Linda said. "Just shut your trap."

"She wants to know why the clap is called a social disease."

The clap was probably a dance, Esme thought, like the twist.

"I never wanted to know that," Linda said. "You're the one who did."

"The reason they call it a social disease—" Georgia stopped. "It's a nice way of saying that you get it from other people."

"Get what?" Esme said.

The doorbell rang. Georgia smiled as she got up to answer it, crossed the dining room to the foyer. "Hello, sweetheart. Very, very Merry Christmas to you. Come in."

Audrey Finch had a puppy with light brown fur in her arms, and she carried it to the open dining-room door, standing in place as the girls clamored toward her. "My parents gave me one of my presents early." They crowded around her.

"He's so cute!"

"He's adorable."

"What's his name?"

"It's a girl. Look. She'll get thingamajigs like a cow."

"Can I hold her?"

"Let me."

"She came with a raincoat too. It has pockets and a hood. She's going to be as big as a collie, but not as hairy."

"Isn't she precious?" Georgia said.

"Mom, can we get one too? Please."

"You know Quinn won't have a dog in New York."

Audrey put the puppy on the floor and they watched her hobble across the carpeting. "My father said she was almost just born," Audrey said. "She can hardly open her eyes." They knelt in a circle around her, she was smaller than a loaf of bread.

"It's not fair. It's just not."

"I know it isn't," Georgia said. "I know."

Fingers splayed on the edge of the bathroom sink, Esme brushed Berry Red nail polish onto the nail of her middle finger for the third time. Her mother lay in the bathtub, bubbles up to her neck. An almost empty vodka tonic sat on the bathtub ledge, lipstick stains along the rim of the glass, a fleck of bubbles at the base. "So how did you know the planes wouldn't come when you were sleeping and drop bombs on you?"

"We didn't know. It was scary. But the worst part wasn't when you were sleeping, it was at night when everyone was awake, when everyone's lights were on. So they made us turn the lights off, and they turned the street lights off too. We got black shades to cover the windows. You weren't even allowed to smoke a cigarette on the street. If you were in a plane and you flew over California, all you'd see is black, like you were still over the ocean.

"My best friend in tenth grade was a Japanese girl. They lived in the house next to ours, on the beach. Her name was Keiko. She didn't know it, but her parents were sending secret messages to the Japanese. They were arrested and sent away. I never saw her again. I think she went to a concentration camp."

"In Germany?"

"No, in California. They sent the Japanese there during the war, to make sure they wouldn't do what Keiko's parents did."

"And they had to go even if they didn't?"

Georgia nodded.

"Kids too?"

"Yes."

"How do you do it so that the polish doesn't go under your nail? Look." Esme held out her hand. She did not like to think about children who got sent away, about parents who gave secret messages to the enemy.

"I'll do your nails tomorrow. After we open presents."

"Why not now?"

"I'm waiting to hear from Quinn. I'm going to leave as soon as he tells me where to meet him. And what if I've only done three of your nails?"

"And what if you're still naked?"

They looked at each other and smiled. Georgia leaned forward to turn on the hot water. She was conscious of each of her movements, hand to the knob, finger under the spray to test the temperature, elbows suspended in the bubbles. She was concentrating with the attention of someone walking a tightrope. She was practicing. She was a drink or two away from being sloshed.

"Mama, do you like New York more than you thought you would, or less?"

"I love New York, sweetheart. I always did."

"Even when you were eight?"

"I didn't leave California until I was nineteen. I'd barely left Redondo."

"Then did you go to New York?"

"I went to Las Vegas for two days with Dru. We thought that was the bee's knees, we might as well have been going to Paris. Dru had never even been in an elevator."

"Did you win lots of money?"

"We lost every penny we had."

"Then what?"

"Then we went home and Dru got married to Ted."

"When you met Daddy, did you think he was the handsomest man you had ever seen?"

"Of course. He was *divinely* handsome."

"Did he buy you lots of presents and tell you he loved you all the time?"

"At first he did. . . . It's always different at the beginning. Love is like the seasons of the year. At the beginning it's like spring. Then summer comes, then fall, then winter. . . . For some people the winter comes when they're old. Dru and Ted will be like that. They'll always be married to each other. But for other people—"

"You're going to get divorced, aren't you?"

"I wasn't talking about Quinn and me." She didn't know anymore what she was talking about. It was not the booze that had clipped the thread of her thought, it was the thought itself, it was the entire universe of people who would not always be married to each other, it was—

"Remember when I was six and I asked you what was behind a star and you didn't know?"

"I think I remember."

Esme lunged forward, dropped to her knees at the edge of the tub. "What happened to your arm?"

"What?"

Esme brushed away a patch of bubbles from Georgia's upper arm. "It's all purple. The whole thing."

"It's nothing. I just—I walked into the door. The edge of the door."

"How come it's turning yellow?"

"It means it's healing."

"If I touch it like that does it hurt?"

One of the girls was calling Georgia's name. "Daddy's on the phone!"

"It's just a bruise, sweetheart." Naked, dripping wet, she walked across the bathroom and took Quinn's long terrycloth robe from the back of the door, footprints trailing her on the cotton bath rug.

She picked up the phone on the night table. "Merry Christmas, sweetheart." She sat on the edge of the bed, legs crossed, rubbing them dry with the folds of the robe. "I was just getting dressed."

"Don't bother, Georgia."

"Partied out? Where are you?"

"I'm on the corner of—wait a second—" He sounded confused, incoherent. "Fifty-sixth and . . . something or other."

"Am I too late for the to-do at '21'?"

"You're too late for all of it, Georgie."

"What do you mean?"

"Your old man's got a big mouth."

"What did you say?"

He was silent for a minute. "Look, it was late by then, Georgia, all right, I'd had a few, everyone else had too. If you want to throw stones, go ahead, but—"

"Sweetheart, I'm not—"

"Do you want to hear or do you want to interrupt?"

"I'm listening."

"So there's Walters at the goddam company party doing his Santa act, the costume, the beard, the whole bit. Getting all the girls to sit on his lap, looking like a fucking clown. I went up and told him what he could do with Procter and Gamble and all the other crap he's been screwing me out of."

"I thought you'd told him that before."

"I had."

"Well?"

"I told you before, Georgia, it was that kind of atmosphere."

"What kind of atmosphere?" She heard noise in the background, trucks, sirens, horns. "Quinn? Are you there?"

He cleared his throat. "I had my hand on his collar."

"He's a big boy, isn't he? It's not like you—"

"But I did."

"Did what?"

"Christ, I wasn't trying to kill him, I was just—"

"You hit him?"

She waited for him to speak again, for the trucks to pass, the buses to stop. "He said this is the first time—" He spoke slowly, blandly, precisely, as if he were telling her the weather. "He said this is the first time he's ever canned anyone on Christmas Eve."

"Oh, Quinn."

"Don't say another word, Georgia. Don't open your fucking mouth to me again."

Before she could, he had hung up the phone.

What's a Family For?

"I TOLD YOUR FATHER no good would ever come of marrying *her*." Dot Singer, Meyer's mother, was speaking to Esme. "Lighting candles in St. Patrick's. I suppose she takes you to confession too."

"She doesn't go to confession. She's not Catholic."

"Then why does she light candles in a church? Never mind." She held up her hands, palms out, making a shield, and turned her face away from Esme. A caricature, a gesture borrowed from silent movies. "She wants to light candles, it's her affair. What I don't like is her dragging you along. My *shiksa* granddaughter. Not that it's any of my business."

Esme looked down at her lap, the skirt of her plaid jumper, covered with cracker crumbs. She knew it was not a good thing to be, but beyond that she did not know what a *shiksa* was.

"Dot, let her be," Goody Singer said. "It's her mother you're talking about. Her mother takes her somewhere, she goes. It's that simple."

"I've never heard such a story." Dot spooned two chunks of creamed herring onto her plate. "Tell me, who but *goyim* get fired on Christmas Eve?"

That was only the beginning of the story. There were parts of it that her grandmother did not know, that Esme would never tell anyone, even though all you had to do was look at Georgia to know what had happened, unless she was wearing sunglasses. She had worn the sunglasses that morning, four days after Christmas, when she took Esme to Grand Central Station to send her to New Haven, to send her away from Quinn, who was going crazy after coming home from what Georgia said was "a three-day drunk."

Goody held out his hand to Esme, palm up, as if she were on display. "Is it her fault? Does she need to be reminded? She needs to be reminded like she needs a hole in the wall." He withdrew his hand and turned to Esme. "More herring?"

She shook her head. "I didn't like it very much."

"What about toast? Toasted rye?"

"No, thank you."

He stood up and pointed his forefinger up into the air, signaling an idea that had just come to him. "Toasted Kaiser roll." He walked across the kitchen to the bread box in the pantry. "The best in New Haven. We'll make you a package to take home. Bring your mother something to eat." He returned to the table and eased a knife through the roll. "Take half." He looked at Esme. "Want the whole thing?"

"I'm not hungry anymore, Grandpa."

"Special rate for the holidays. No charge for lunch."

"Your grandfather. Everything has to be a joke with him."

He shook his head and looked at Esme. "She doesn't like jokes no more. Whadya gonna do?" He held half the roll face up in his palm. "Still fresh." She shook her head.

"You eat it," Dot said to her husband. "You get fat. Better on you than on her."

Goody looked at Esme and patted his stomach. "After we fatten up, we'll go to Shoe Town. You need shoes?"

Esme shrugged.

"Everything's discount. Next time, you bring your mother and she'll get shoes too. Name brands from the big stores. Two, three, four pair a shoes. However many you want."

"All these months you've lived in New York," Dot said, "and you and your mother didn't come to see us once. It takes a tragedy to bring families together."

"What tragedy?" Goody slammed a knife onto the table and looked at Dot. "He'll get another job."

"I'll give your mother this much. She's a looker. A real looker. Of course, I haven't seen her since I don't remember when. And I can't remember the last time I saw your father."

"Dot, we were to California in June. We saw them all. Esme, Georgia, Meyer."

"That's right," Esme said. "We didn't move to New York till September."

"And here it is, the end of December. Another year come and gone." Dot shook her head and tore off a piece of rye bread. "That's what happens when you get to be an old lady like me." She spread some chopped liver onto the bread. "You realize that you just can't stop it. You can't do a thing—" she bit into the uncovered sandwich—"you can't do a thing about the way time flies. I was in the beauty parlor the other day and one of the girls asked me how old my kids are. Forty-two, forty, and thirty-six, I say to her. My baby, your father, is thirty-six. That's when it hit me. About time flying. I tell you, it was like somebody threw a glass of cold water in my face."

She was taken around and introduced. To neighbors, strangers, the clerks at Shoe Town. "This is my granddaughter. From New York. Find her some shoes. The most important thing is she likes 'em and they fit good." To relatives, aunts, uncles, cousins of her father. "This is Esme. Meyer's daughter. Took the train up from New York. All by herself. First time. A regular world traveler. Her next stop is Paris, France." She met two of Goody's brothers, Meyer's uncles. They owned a restaurant supply company, one of the biggest in New England. They made sure there were utensils, chairs, floors, counters, coffee brewers, and menus with maps on them at over a thousand diners and restaurants. She met Meyer's sister Ruth, who lived in a beautiful house with sky-blue carpeting and a maid.

Meyer Singer was a ghost in New Haven. He had taken Georgia there twice, once before they married and once a few months before Esme was born. They had stayed for the afternoon. Meyer was in a rush to get back to New York. Meyer was in a rush to get back to L.A. Meyer was always in a rush to leave.

He had been back twice since then, once en route to Boston, and once for a funeral which—he would not have gone otherwise —coincided with a business trip to New York. "Haven't seen your father in years" was what Esme heard that afternoon, on her first trip to New Haven. "Don't know if I'd recognize him if I saw him right there in front of me. Is he still talking about politics? Could've stayed right here and *walked* into the state legislature, what with all the connections in the family. Nothing wrong with being a big fish in a little pond, for some of us Singers. But I bet you like it out there in California, don't you, honey?"

The first morning she woke up in New Haven everything was white. She had seen snow come down twice in New York, but it had not lasted, it had turned to rain. She stood with her grandfather at the big window in the kitchen and looked into the backyard. The sky was gray, dark against the white of every other surface, every other shape. The white was the pure white of clouds, of eggshells. The smallest thing could disturb the stillness.

In the driveway, her grandfather's car was buried in snow. Only the radio antenna rose above it. There were icicles hanging off the basketball hoop against the garage. "Your father, he threw balls in that hoop when he was thirteen, fourteen. Used to have a net hanging down. Don't know what happened to it." They had lived in the house for thirty-five years. Her grandfather told her that the trees out there, out back, were apple trees. When she came to visit in the summer there would be apples. They had apples, he told her, the way Carter's had liver pills. The way Newcastle had coals.

"My father has lemon trees in his backyard," Esme said.

"Lemons. Feh. Too bitter for me." He kept looking out the window at the snow. "Maybe your father, he'll come in the summer. It's too much out there in California already." He spoke slowly, as if to himself, to the iced window. You would think he did not have plans to speak again, it was that much of an effort.

"Too much what?" Esme said.

"Too much time. It's time to come back." This too he said distractedly, giving the impression he did not want to keep talking. He did not put much stock in the back and forth of conversation. He preferred to kibitz. Buttinsky, his wife called him.

If men were yentas, she said in front of him, to whoever would listen, that's what they would call him. But he was not a gossip. He told stories, about himself, his parents, his brothers, his children. They were stories, told in his slow, halting way, about mistaken identities, the eccentricities of fathers or sons, the errors of bureaucrats in foreign countries, hotel keepers who knew his name because he had been a regular customer for thirty years, a traveling salesman on the same route almost all those years. It thrilled him—quietly, the thrill was in his eyes, in the almost imperceptible movement of his lips in the direction of a smile— to give things to his children, his grandchildren. *You need money? Shoes? How 'bout a new coat? I ever hear you're going without when you're in want, I'll knock you one. Or else what's a family for?*

He had just turned sixty-four. At sixty-five—it was the company rule—he would have to retire. He had been selling knitting needles since he was thirty. His territory was the coastal states from Maine to North Carolina. With new clients, new stores, new management, they would look at his business card. "Singer? What, sewing machines?" "Like sewing machines but slower." Then he would untie the case of knitting needles, the sample, the rows of long shiny needles clipped to the black velveteen cloth, black to display the gold- and silver-colored needles to best effect. "Not the best needles for the money," Goody Singer would tell them, "but the best, period." He put fifty, sixty thousand miles a year on his car. He knew hotels, inns, backroads, diners, gas-station attendants. The ones who ran the hotels where he had been going for twenty years, the waitresses in the better restaurants, the ones who knew his name, who went back all those years, he hadn't told them he was finished next year. Off the road. Not that it was anyone's business. Not like next year was the day after tomorrow. And besides, what's to talk about? He was not a man who talked much, unless there was a story with a beginning and an end to tell, a story with a punchline or a moral. He talked to no one about the two things over which he grieved, the two things that made his heart hurt, as if someone were sitting on his chest, cutting off his breath: his retirement and his son Meyer.

"I want to play in the snow," Esme said. "I want to go out."

"You have boots?"

"Rubbers. To put over my shoes."

In a sudden movement he turned to her. "Whatsa matter, you dumb?"

She was alarmed. She hardly knew him.

"How come you didn't know it was going to snow when we were at Shoe Town yesterday? Didn't you see all them boots there? A real dummy. Like all my grandchildren. So dumb if you were a boy you would have to go over there—" he tapped his finger against the window—"to Yale. Get moving. Get your rubbers. Snow's already melting. Tell Grandma."

Goody paid a boy who lived across the street fifty cents to shovel the driveway and scrape the snow off the car. The boy wore a knit hat that covered his face, with slits for his eyes and mouth. As he heaved the shovelfuls of snow to the side of the drive, his breath billowed out of the mouth slit. Esme stood to the side of the car and looked down her nose to watch her own breath. When she was six she had wanted an older brother like the boy who was shoveling. Like Elaine Marsden's older brother who lived next door when they lived in the green house on La Cienega and had a girlfriend named Dawn who died in a car crash the day after she told Elaine's brother that she would go steady with him, and either before she died or after, it was one afternoon in the summer, he took Elaine and Esme in the car, his parents' car, for soft ice cream and the song playing on the radio was "Itsy Bitsy Teenie Weenie Yellow Polkadot Bikini." All of which made Esme certain that if there was ever a fire in her house in the middle of the night she would want to be rescued by Elaine's brother, who was so brave that he did not even cry when Dawn died.

She held her forefinger up in front of her mouth and blew. Her finger made the breath divide into two ribbons. It was like smoking a cigarette. Georgia had told her that she could drink coffee and smoke when she turned sixteen. By then Georgia would be married again. She might even marry Meyer again. He was going to be President and protect Americans from the Nazis, the Russians, and the Cubans. It would be thrilling to ride in a limousine and wave to everyone, her and her father. If he were President he could do anything. He could put Quinn in jail for what Quinn had done to her mother. S.O.B. stood for son of a bitch, and that was what Quinn was. She blew into her hands and then breathed in through her nose, trying to smell her breath. If it smelled bad, no one would tell her but everyone would know.

It smelled bad in the old people's home where Goody took her to meet his mother, her great-grandmother, Esther. "I can't see too good anymore, but you are, *kineahora*, a pretty little girl. We have lovely women in our family. You wouldn't know it to look at this one, would you?" She laughed and raised her hand to her chest. "Not exactly a spring chicken. You know how old I am?"

Esme shook her head. The room smelled stale, like bad breath, like feet. "Eighty?" Esme said.

"Eighty! Eighty, I could live on my own. Cook, clean, scrub the bathroom. I kept a beautiful house. Tell me, Esme, your father, he's in good health?"

She nodded.

"Some time ago, I wrote him a letter, and he must have thought his old grandmother was, you know—" She pointed to her head and chuckled. The skin beneath her eyes drooped and the skin above her eyes drooped. "Neither he or anyone in the family believes me, but we, the Singers, are related to Senator Goldwater. You see, formerly, his name was Gold-wasser, which, on my husband's side, may he rest in peace, was a first cousin by marriage. I thought this communication could help your father in his politics. With the influential side. I know how that aspect influences the political aspect. The family relation. You can't disqualify that. And tell me, who would want to? Nevertheless, your father didn't answer my letter back. Did you have lunch?"

Esme nodded.

"So you're not hungry."

"No."

"I wish I had something to offer you. Some peppermints. An orange. I can't eat sweets myself. That's a lovely thing you did, to come visit your grandparents."

"Thank you."

"All the way from California."

"Mama, she lives in New York."

"You live in New York?"

"Yes."

"Maybe that's why your father didn't answer my letter. I thought maybe he was busy. I sent it to the address Goody gave me in California."

"That's where he lives."

"Since when?"

"Mama, he's lived there for years. Years."

"Tell me, little one, you like California?"

"Yes. But I live in New York. With my mother. On Seventy-third Street."

"Oh. Nice?"

"Yes. It's a duplex."

"I'm sorry to hear that."

"Why?"

"They're so dark. We lived in one before your grandfather was born. With the bathroom down the hall. The infestation was everywhere. Like animals. It's a shame you have to live like that, in this day and age." She leaned forward, ready to tell Esme a confidence. "I'll be eighty-eight in two weeks. Before I sprained my ankle—" she patted her leg, drew attention to the Ace bandage that wound its way up to the middle of her calf—"I was one of the best dancers in the place. Goody, remember the afternoon the governor came?" She looked at Esme. "I danced with the governor. In the television room. We waltzed."

The attendant at the Esso station came to the window of the car. "Hiya, Pop," he said to Goody.

"Want you to take a look at something." Goody turned off the ignition.

"Oil?"

"Nope. Funny-lookin' kid." Goody pointed his thumb in Esme's direction, next to him on the seat. The man lowered himself, peered into the window. "This is Esme."

"I'll be a son of a gun." The man had black streaks on his cheeks, his forehead. "We were thinking for years he made you up."

"Who?" Esme said.

"Your old man."

"This here's Charlie Edelman. Him and your father been friends since they were this high." Goody held his hand up to the radio. "She took the train from New York. All by herself."

"What happened to your good-looking mom?"

"She's in New York," Esme said. She was not going to tell anyone what had happened to her mother.

"Then she's going to miss a heck of a New Year's Eve tomorrow night," Charlie said, still leaning down, talking to them through the open window. "Got any plans you can't break?"

"Not a thing," Goody said. "But let me check with the missus. She doesn't like being in the car New Year's Eve."

"Some things never change, huh?"

"Some do, some don't."

Charlie stood up, thrummed his fingers against the roof of the car. "Weather's something, inn-it?"

"Nasty," Goody said and turned on the ignition. He looked up to Charlie. "Listen, young fellow, could you do the back window?"

"Sure thing. You need anything else?"

"Nope. Got everything I need. Just about."

As Charlie walked away from the window, Goody said, "I still remember them two, this high." Again, his hand against the radio. "You couldn't keep 'em apart nohow. One time, I'll never forget, Mrs. MacGruder, the grade-school teacher, she said to me, 'Mr. Singer—' "

"Grandpa?"

"What?"

"Is Charlie rich or poor?"

"Not rich. Not poor. He makes a living. Right now, just one station. But this here's a good location."

Charlie walked back to Goody's window and knocked once on the roof, hunching down. "What's it gonna be?" he said. "We gonna see you tomorrow?"

"Do my best."

"Give a call."

"You open tomorrow?"

Charlie pointed to the sign high above the pumps: 31.9¢ OPEN EVERY DAY. "Only station in New Haven's open every day," Charlie said. "Gotta have something to separate you from the rest of the crowd. Used to think my good looks were enough." He smiled. "Bring your fannies over later."

As they drove out of the station, Goody said, "They were like this—" he held out his hand, crossing his middle finger over his forefinger— "them two." He put his hand back on the wheel. "Charlie took it worst of anyone. When Meyer left."

It was dusk. Her grandfather was silent for the rest of the ride home. The heater hummed, rattled, barely kept them warm. The sky was a patchwork of colors, bronze, red, broad stripes of gray left over from the dull daylight. As they turned onto the street where her grandparents lived, Goody said, "Maybe they'll get back together someday."

"Who?"

"Your father and your mother."

Esme opened her mouth to speak, to answer him, but did not

know what to say. He turned into his driveway. The gravel beneath the car crackled as the wheels dug into it. Suddenly, it was dark. When he turned off the engine, there was not a sound anywhere.

She pulled the door handle toward her and the door swung open. A light went on at her feet. She followed her grandfather down the driveway to the house.

Walking behind him in the dark, she felt his sadness and also her own. The cold, the snow, these old people, these strangers. If her father had stayed here, he might already be dead. That was what he had said to her when she asked him why he had left New Haven: *If I had stayed there, I would have died.*

Some Fun Out of Life

I WILL END UP one of those women like Heidi, Georgia thought. Bitter, broken, broke. Nothing to do all day long but call her lawyer, sue her ex-husband. No stories to tell but awful ones, lawsuits and countersuits, decrees and unpaid alimony. Or she could get onto the welfare circuit. You had to admit that *was* funny.

In the cab on the way to Heidi's on New Year's Eve, that was funny again, for a moment. They had all told the story a zillion times. Even Quinn had told it. The guy at the city office who had said to Heidi when she applied for welfare two months ago, "I've never had a client who lives on Sutton Place South." Heidi said, "You do now, babe."

"It's right here," Georgia said to the cab driver. The circular driveway off Fifty-seventh Street, the brass doorknobs polished so highly you could see yourself in them, the doorman's white gloves, the mole in the center of his chin.

The warmth of the lobby, the Persian rugs, the buttery leather seat in the elevator, someone to kiss tonight at midnight, someone to take care of you forever. Those were the promises.

"All right, sweetie, here's the line-up," Heidi said. She was pointing out the food on the dining-room table. "A barbecued chicken from Merit Farms, cole slaw from the Stage, four eggrolls from that Chink place we always go to on Third, Oreos and Coke for Danny, one bottle Mouton Rothschild that I charged to Ben's account, screw him if he can't take a joke, and three bottles of rot-gut New York State champagne. But don't worry, honey—" She touched Georgia's shoulder. "We won't be able to tell the difference by the time we get to them. In the meantime—" She picked up two tumblers from the table and took them to the bar in the corner of the dining room.

"Did you get a new table?" Georgia tapped her finger against it, clear glass, tinted gray.

"Where would I get the money to buy a table?"

"How come it looks—"

"I usually have a tablecloth on it. But they're all dirty and wouldn't you know, every single one of them needs to be dry cleaned. So the hell with it, until Ben forks over some money. And Danny gets a kick out of cleaning it with Windex and a paper towel." She untwisted the cap on a new bottle of scotch. "I just hope he doesn't grow up queer. You want water or soda?"

"Water."

"Rocks?"

"No."

"Are my cigarettes over there?"

"I don't see them."

"Sit down, would you, Georgia. And eat something, honey, please. Let me fix you a plate."

"Where's Danny?" Georgia kicked off her shoes. There was a hole in the toe of her stocking, the beginning of a run.

They sat down at the table with their drinks, they pulled the heavy glass ashtrays close.

"Lord sakes, Georgia, what you've been through the last few days. No one should have to go through that." She looked at Georgia and shook her head. "Not more than once, anyway." She pulled the plate of eggrolls to her. "I said to him, 'Make sure you put extra duck sauce in the bag.' Not one goddam duck sauce in the whole thing. But fifteen hot mustards. You don't want any, do you?" She pointed to the chicken. "Dark meat or light? Honest to god, you look like you haven't eaten in a week. Speak up. Dark or white?"

"Dark."

"Danny's out with Ben." She handed Georgia a plate and a linen napkin with an embroidered monogram. "Howard and I have this running debate about whether to tell Ben he can't see Danny until he starts back up with the alimony. Howard, in his divorce-lawyerly way, says if I keep the kid from seeing his father, he'll resent me." She lit a cigarette and dropped the burned-out match into the philodendron in the center of the table. "As if he doesn't resent me already." She leaned toward Georgia. "But really, honey, I shouldn't be telling you these things. I should be telling you you're in good hands with Howard. And you are. I've sent *everyone* to him. Nina Jenkins, Janey Sachs. These gals— Quinn looks like a prince next to *their* husbands. If you can believe that."

"He said Quinn and I weren't married long enough to get a good settlement." Georgia drank. She had been drinking on and off all day, on and off since Quinn had left yesterday morning.

"Yeah. You told me on the phone."

"Are you going to eat something?"

"I don't know. I was nibbling before you got here. I think I might just get sloshed on an empty stomach."

"Esme called just before I left for here. Her grandfather bought her four pair of shoes, it snowed, and she met her great-grandmother. And she was on her way to a New Year's Eve party at an old friend of Meyer's."

"Did you tell her Quinn split?"

"Yeah. The first thing she wanted to know was whether it meant that we're going to be poor. You won't believe what she wanted to know next. She asked if we were going to have to go on welfare, *like Heidi.* Wait, it gets better. After all of that, she says, 'Mom, what exactly *is* welfare.'"

They ignored the champagne. They drank scotch and smoked. They told stories they had told before. "I will never forget going to the welfare office. Godforsaken is not the word for it. But really, what was I supposed to do? Get a job at the A & P? I asked Ben. He said, 'No, I'd try Gristede's. It's more in line with your spending habits.' They pay him big money on Madison Avenue to be clever like that. I mean, all of a sudden, *sans* explanation, he stops sending money." She inhaled deeply. She pursed her lips, blew a smoke ring and then waved her hand through the air. He had not stopped sending money entirely, just the amount designated as her alimony. It had never occurred to her to get a job. Even if it had, there was nothing she knew how to do. She had gone to college for a year, intending to study art. Then she met Ben, then she got married. It was not until two months ago, when the amount of Ben's monthly payments dropped, that she had ever done her own laundry. Once she called Georgia to ask whether to put a garter belt in the dryer.

"Well, here we are, Georgia. Our very own New Year's Eve party. Intimate is not the word for it. But the way I see it is this. You're in no shape to go public tonight, what with that shiner, and the only party I got invited to was with the schnook with the false tooth that falls out whenever he decides to get sexy. Remember him?"

"How could you forget those teeth?"

"Those fangs." Heidi picked up a bottle of club soda and tipped it. "Looks like this has had it. Wouldn't you know. What time is it, honey?"

Georgia looked at her watch. "Ten-thirty."

"Where the hell is Danny?" She kicked off her shoes, then brought her legs up to her chair and crossed them Indian-style.

"That is *really* chic, sweetheart." Georgia leaned forward dreamily, pointing to Heidi's bare legs through the glass table top. "Looks like one of those glass-bottomed boats, where you look down and see all the fish."

"Did I ever show you my kimono? Ben got it for me in Tokyo. He thought it was *très, très* sexy. It has a fish design. Ben said fish mean something special in Japan. Here we have eagles, there they have . . . " She shook a cigarette out of the pack. "You have to see this, Georgia. Stay right where you are."

She put on the kimono, she put on Billie Holiday. She stood at the arched entrance to the dining room brushing the tip of the kimono belt against her lips. Barelegged, barefooted, she mouthed the words. "*When we want to kiss, we kiss, when we want to play, we play. In a happy setting we're getting some fun out of life.*" She winked at Georgia, she poured on the cheese-cake. She straightened up suddenly, tightened the sash, cleared her throat: time to play another game. She sat down at the head of the table and lit a cigarette. "What do you think?"

"About what? Your singing?"

"My kimono!" Heidi looked down and pulled on the lapel, pointing at the simple outline of a fish. "See the little fishies? You can tell they're Japanese because they have slanty eyes."

Heidi giggled into her hand. Georgia laughed a deep, full laugh that made her gasp. There was a pain in the middle of her back.

Heidi whispered, "Sweetie, are you all right?"

Georgia took short breaths, nodded faintly.

"That bastard."

Georgia sat back. "I think it's the bra."

"Why don't you take it off. This reminds me of the time—" Heidi drew hard on her cigarette. "The strapless bra. Remember that story?"

"Sweetheart, that was Dru's story."

"I thought it was yours."

"No, I must have told you about it. Those goddam strapless bras—like wearing a tourniquet around your chest."

"Wouldn't you have loved to be the one who found it on the freeway?"

"They hadn't even *invented* freeways in those days. It was something like nineteen fifty-one, fifty-two. We were driving Meyer's old Chevy Fleetmaster on some rinky-dink back road. Ted was the one who threw the bra out the window."

"I wished I'd known you then."

"How come?"

"I don't know. I always think that whatever happened before was better than now. Even when I was there and miserable. Like when Danny was six. Ben and I—you would not believe what it was like. Every day was hell. He used to do this all the time." She bent her arm in front of her and then swung. "He never actually touched me but he's twice my size and every time I saw his hand go up—god. But I sometimes look at Danny and think about how darling he was when he was six and how wonderful things were. Then I remember that they weren't. And then I can't believe that I could have ever forgotten." She pulled on her cigarette and let the smoke come aimlessly out of her mouth, her nostrils. "What time is it now?"

"A little after eleven. What are you waiting for?"

"Danny." She picked up an eggroll, looked at it, put it down. "A pile of money. A knight in shining armor. What are you waiting for?"

"Same thing. Same goddam thing I've always been waiting for. Howard said we weren't married long enough to get a good settlement."

"Yeah, that's what you said."

"What was it, five months. Six months. Some record." She flipped open the ice bucket. She dropped two cubes into Heidi's glass and three into her own. The shot of scotch she poured into her glass made the ice cubes crackle, like dry wood in the fire.

"Come on, Georgia, it's not like you were in love with him or anything. Do me another. Just a little one. You weren't, were you?"

"We were together for—" She poured the scotch for Heidi, she put the bottle down. "Five years. Christ, if we'd been married for five years, I could get a terrific settlement."

"You let Howard worry about that for a while. In the meantime, thank your stars Quinn left. Thank your stars he took his toothbrush back to L.A., because one thing you don't need is a wigged-out, out-of-work ex-husband who lives around the corner."

"Like what's-her-name with the chihuahua."

"Yeah. Like what's-her-name with the godawful dog." Heidi sucked on an ice cube and spoke with it clenched between her back teeth. "Just remember, sweetie, there's always the welfare office."

"Heidi?"

"Yes, Georgia."

"What exactly *is* welfare?"

"Enough of this talk about welfare." Heidi put her drink down emphatically, raised her hand, and fluttered her fingers for a moment, as if trying to get the attention of a roomful of people. She was quite drunk. "And enough of this talk about love. What is love, anyway? Danny asked me that the other night. 'Mom,' he says, 'what's love? And don't tell me it's just a nice feeling like you always say.' Like I *always* say. When's the last time you heard me say love was a nice feeling? Is it eleven-thirty?"

Georgia looked at her watch and nodded. "What a goddam phony."

"Who?"

"Quinn Laughlin. What time does the liquor store close?" Georgia noticed that it was becoming much more difficult to talk, harder to make the words come out in the right order.

"They stop delivering at nine. I'm not sure—"

"On New Year's Eve? Call them up. Tell them it's crap."

"What's crap?"

"I don't know." Georgia reached for the bottle and un-screwed it. "Want some?"

Heidi shook her head.

"Got something to tell you," Georgia said. She poured a shot of scotch into her glass. She took a cigarette out of the pack.

"What?"

"New Year's resolutions." She lit the cigarette, let it dangle between her lips. "Quit smoking. Lose five pounds."

"Georgia, if you lost another ounce."

"I'd be absolutely—"

"Divine. Miss Georgia Divine."

"Do you realize I'm thirty-two years old? I'm—"

"Honey, I'm thirty-five."

"Thirty-two years old." Georgia could barely hear herself. She would have to slow down. She took a sip, a dainty sip. There was only a little bit of scotch left in the bottle. "I married one man who was poor and told me he was going to get rich. I mar-ried another one who was rich and got poor six months after he married me. But I'm still here, aren't I? Even if I don't have anyone to kiss on New Year's Eve." Tears came to her eyes, she raised her hand to brush them away. The knot in her throat made it hurt to swallow what was left in her glass. "You know what my mother always told me was the worst thing about being alone —I mean, *the* worst. My mother, bless her heart—" The tears kept rolling down her cheeks. "And my father. Let's not talk about my father. The worst thing is not having anyone to kiss on New Year's Eve. At midnight."

"Maybe you can get some money from Meyer," Heidi said. "I mean, more than what you already get."

"My, My Meyer. That's what I used to call him. When he was going to be the first Jewish President of the United States. I think he married me because he needed a *goy* for a first lady. Half the time he forgets the money or doesn't have it. One of these days, Esme's going to find out. As far as she's concerned right now, he walks on water. How many cigarettes do you have left?"

Heidi picked up her pack and shook it. "Three." She looked more closely. "Four. What about you?"

"Two."

"Shit. How did this happen?"

"Call the liquor store and see if they're still delivering. Tell them to stop at the deli and pick up some cigs for us."

"They stopped delivering hours ago."

"Christ, Heidi. Don't be such a goddam pain-in-the-ass pessimist." Georgia waved her arm through the air, and then her other arm, an imitation of a ballerina. "It's New Year's Eve. The ball is about to drop. We could be in Times Square. We could be having *fun*." Georgia stood up and, to her surprise, needed to grip the edge of the table. She opened her eyes wide and then pushed herself away from the table with a little flick of her wrist. "If I don't get to the john in less time than it takes to say my name, I'm going to tinkle all over everything."

Heidi shrieked.

Georgia thought she was hearing things.

"Mother of god," Heidi said and thrust her hand to her chest. Danny was standing at the entrance to the dining room.

"What's wrong?" he said.

"When did you come in?"

"Just now."

"You scared the hell out of me. Why didn't you ring the bell?"

"Every time I ring the bell you ask me why I didn't use my key."

"Happy New Year, sweetheart." Georgia went to him, leaned down, kissed the top of his head. "Did your daddy take you to '21' like he always does?"

"Yes."

"Bless his heart. Bless yours too. You're getting so tall." She kissed him again. "Would you excuse me, sweetheart, I was just about to tinkle."

She crossed the living room and made a point of looking at the miniature grandfather clock on the mantel. It was twelve-oh-five. It was 1963. Or maybe it was 64.

Ripley's

THAT SPRING GEORGIA married again. It seemed, to Esme, to happen quickly, as if she had just turned around, turned her back on them for a moment, and then they were married.

His name was Chuck Abbott, he had come from Oklahoma. He arrived one night with a suitcase, Heidi's brother's friend. He had driven all the way and here he was. It would just be for a week or two. He would have gone to Heidi's except for the lawsuit that Heidi and Georgia explained—and their children repeated—had been going on for*ever*. They agreed it would not help to have a man living in the apartment while Heidi was trying to get her alimony back.

Chuck offered Georgia money, to help out. He was tall, gracious, young. She took the money, she gave him a set of keys, she called him sweetheart. He slept on the couch.

Audrey Finch called him Wood Chuck. *Hey, Wood Chuck, would you pass the ketchup.*

Georgia called him Chuckie, sweet. *Chuckie, sweet, oh, if I were your age again . . .*

He had come to New York to be a model, and maybe he would break into acting. He had a portfolio. He had the names and phone numbers of three agents and a woman who had been in two commercials and a soap opera.

One Friday night he and Georgia went to P. J. Clarke's and didn't come home. The next morning, when they did, they were married. They brought home a Sara Lee cheesecake for celebration and Chuck said that that was the end of sleeping on the couch for him. Georgia said she didn't need another wedding ring because she already had two and they weren't good for anything except hocking anyway.

"Chuckie, sweet, if I were your age . . . " Georgia blew him a kiss across the living room that morning and there was still smoke in her lungs from inhaling her cigarette a moment before and a faint trail of it accompanied the kiss.

If Georgia were his age, she would be twenty-seven.

An afternoon in the middle of May. Esme brought him his huge black leather portfolio, dragged it across the living-room floor. "Would you show them to me again?" The color photographs of himself in bathing trunks, tuxedos, Bermuda shorts.

They sat on the floor and he flipped through the big photographs covered in clear plastic. He paused at ones taken by water, sand, against a sunny sky.

"I really like to go on location," he said.

"What's that?"

"The place where it's supposed to be. The Coast, Greece, wherever."

"And if they say they won't take you on location—" it had a wonderful sound, it sounded like a wonderful place to go— "do you tell them to forget it?"

"If I were in the money I would."

"I thought we were already in the money."

"Sport, you have a good imagination."

"Are we poor?"

"No, we're just broke." He was examining a photograph of himself sitting on a boulder, modeling a pair of chinos.

"Till when?"

"Till some money comes in."

"When's that?"

"As soon as your mom gets a job. Or I get one."

"Maybe you and her could be in commercials together. She told me you can make five thousand dollars from one commercial. From the residuals. You know what those are?"

"Yes."

"So maybe you should."

"Yeah. Maybe." He was looking at a photograph. He was in tennis whites, holding a racket against his chest, ready for a backhand swing.

"Why don't you ask?"

He looked up. "Ask what?"

"If you can do commercials together."

"That's not how it works."

"How does it work?"

"E*sme.*"

"You don't want to get welfare, do you?"

"Welfare's for poor people, kiddo."

"And we're not poor, we're broke. Right?"

"Right."

"What's the difference?"

"Esme, please."

"You don't know?"

"It's hard to explain."

"Does my mother know?"

"I think so."

"When she gets home, I'll ask her."

"Do that."

"What were you modeling in that picture?" She pointed.

"The car. It was an ad for the car. We were on location. In the desert."

Esme was in love with him. Doing the simplest things, taking toast from the toaster, an ice tray from the freezer, crossing the living room in his pink Bermudas, he was so tall and handsome.

When she was seventeen she would go with him on location. They would go on Pan Am and have passports. He would take her to England to visit his grandmother, and they would go to Buckingham Palace. He would take her to the Riviera and to Las Vegas. He would be famous around the world, her Chuck.

Their lives were mysterious to her. She heard them talk about money, bounced checks, dunning letters, words she did not understand connected to words she did. He had a broker in Oklahoma who sent money every month, but it was not very much, it was just enough to pay the rent on the duplex. It came from a trust fund his grandfather had set up.

"If I weren't such a lazy bum," he said to Esme one evening, patting his cheeks with aftershave, preening himself in front of the mirror. "Good thing it didn't run in the family." He slipped a belt through the loops on his pants and turned to Esme. "Your mother is an expensive date." He pushed the end of his tie into the loose knot at his neck. "Good thing she got a job." Working the switchboard at Henri Bendel for eighty-five dollars a week. "Good thing your old man believes in child support."

"Have you ever been to L.A.?"

"Sure. Lots of times."

"That's where my father lives."

"Yeah. I know."

"I'm going there this summer, the day after school's over. He's sending me a plane ticket in the mail. I haven't been there since we moved. I was supposed to go for Easter vacation, but he was broke. Where are you going tonight?"

"P. J.'s. Where else do we ever go?"

She marked off the days on her calendar until school let out. It was an eternity, twenty-six days until the last day of June. The day would never come. She checked the mail every day for her plane ticket. She noticed something strange on the first day. It was repeated in the days that followed. All of Georgia's mail was addressed to Georgia Laughlin.

She asked about it at dinner. "I thought you were divorced from Quinn."

"I am, sweetheart. Do you want some more mint jelly on your lamb chops?"

"No."

"Chuckie, sweet?"

"No, thanks."

"Sweetheart, I know you don't like tomatoes, but would you try to—"

"I thought your last name was Abbott now, the same as Chuck's. That's how you wrote it on that letter to school."

"It is."

"Then how come all the letters are addressed to your old name?"

"It takes time, sometimes years, before people get used to using your new name. When I first married Quinn Laughlin—"

"Georgia. Why don't you tell her?"

"Tell her what?"

Chuck glared at Georgia. "It was your idea, not mine."

"I don't really think there's any need to—"

"No need to tell the truth?"

"That's not what I said."

"I told you it was a stupid idea, Georgia." Chuck flung his napkin on the table and got up. "Stupidest goddam thing I ever did." He stalked into the kitchen.

"Sweetheart, would you get me—" She stopped, turned her ear toward the kitchen. "Chuckie? Are you there?"

He did not answer. Georgia put her elbows on the table, put her face in her hands.

"Mom. Don't cry, all right?"

"I'm not."

"What does he want you to tell me?"

He slammed a door. He broke a tray of ice into the sink and a few cubes fell to the floor. He was talking to himself, mumbling, cursing. He called out, "For Christ's sake, Georgia, tell her. Get it over with."

Georgia took her hands away from her eyes.

"You're not really married," Esme said. She had said it without thinking, without knowing that she knew it.

"I thought it would be easier for you. Chuckie and I—" she lowered her voice, she leaned toward Esme. "He's so young, and just starting out, we both agreed it would have been a terrible mistake to really tie the knot, and it could be—"

"So you're not married?"

Georgia shook her head.

"Are you really divorced from Quinn?"

Georgia began to shake her head and then to nod.

Chuck appeared at her side. "What she's trying to say is that she's legally separated but she's holding out for a bigger settlement." He put a tumbler down in front of Georgia. "Chin up, sweetheart." He turned, crossed the room, and began to walk upstairs.

Georgia followed him with her eyes. "You're not leaving, are you?"

He stopped and did not look back. "No, babe, I'm just going upstairs." He took a few more steps and stopped again. "I told you a long time ago I wouldn't leave until I have somewhere else to go." His flipflops made a strange clopping noise against his heels as he took the steps up two at a time.

Georgia picked up her drink.

"How come you didn't get married?"

"The divorce isn't final."

"If it was would you?"

"I don't know." She lit a cigarette, tossed the match onto her dinner plate. It landed in the mashed potatoes.

"How come you don't know?"

"Deciding to get married isn't like buying a dress. It isn't like buying a car."

Esme sat back. "*That's* why you didn't get another ring."

"What?"

"You said you didn't get a ring because you already had two, but it was because you really didn't get married."

"Sweetheart, you don't have to keep repeating it."

"Were you really married to Quinn?"

Georgia looked at her. "You were at the wedding."

"But I don't understand why you wanted to marry Quinn and you didn't want to marry Chuck. He's so nice."

"Esme, it's not just—"

"Is it against the law?"

"Is what?"

"What you did."

"All I did was ask Chuck to stay here for a while."

"But why?"

Georgia took a long drink. She spoke softly. "I wanted company."

"If he asked you to marry him—"

"Darling, we've talked about this enough for tonight. Did you do your homework?"

"Mom, it's Friday."

"Would you like to visit Audrey?"

"She went to see her grandmother for the weekend."

"What about—"

"Don't worry." Esme stood. "I'll leave. I'll go see Pat."

"Pat who?"

She walked to the front door and turned around. "The doorman."

The worst thing was that this meant Chuck would be leaving soon. She could tell by the way he had put Georgia's drink down in front of her, by the way he had said, "Chin up, sweetheart."

. . .

By the middle of June it was muggy in the city. Chunks of soot blew in through the classroom window opened wide. In a burst of wind, the paper letter "P" taped to the wall above the blackboard, in script and block letters, snapped off and sailed to the floor. The teacher was telling them about the harmony of the solar system. They stood around a wooden model on a desk in the center of the room, and she made the little painted globes circle around the sun with a metal crank.

Venus was the planet closest to the earth, Pluto the one farthest away. There were gravity and inertia, and between them they made sure that the earth stayed where it should, turning on its axis around the sun. And if it were not for gravity, we would not be able to walk. We would float in the air all the time, the way the astronauts did when we saw pictures of them floating in their space capsules. The way we stayed on the ground, the way the planets circled the sun—these were truly splendid examples of the balances that nature herself provides, examples of the genuine order in the complex universe. Timmy Mullegan, whose father was a policeman, asked how close to the sun a rocket had to get before it would melt.

She was in a deep sleep that night, dreaming about drifting in space, about being weightless. She was floating between planets, she was on her way to Pluto, where she had been told there was a roller coaster. Her mother began to call her, to bring her back. Her father was on the telephone, her father wanted to talk to her. Georgia was touching her forehead, her cheeks.

It was not a dream. He was really on the phone. She had to get up and go to Georgia's bedroom to talk to him, and Georgia would hang up the phone downstairs.

"Is that you, Magoo?" he said.

"Yes." She was not completely awake. "I was sleeping." She sat cross-legged on the bed, nightgown bunched around her thighs. "Hi, Stu," she said as she began to wake up.

"Hi, Magoo."

Their special names for each other.

"Hi, Stu." She smiled. She was going to California.

"How's school, Magoo?"

"I guess it's okay. I can write the whole alphabet in script. Without stopping."

"I know. I got your letter."

"The plane ticket didn't come yet."

"I know, Magoo, that's why I'm calling. I've got some big news for you. Are you ready for this? How would you like to have a rich dad?"

"That would be great." She yawned. There were so many things she wanted, she said. The tree house at F. A. O. Schwarz, a three-speed bike.

"Before this is over, you'll have a bike for every day of the week." A deal had just come through, he couldn't believe the dimensions of it, he couldn't believe that it was going to be his.

"What is it?" she said. "What's the deal?"

"It has to do with imports and exports and a little country called Hong Kong. You ever hear of Hong Kong?"

"Yes."

"You think you'd like to visit your rich dad in Hong Kong?"

"I think so. When are you going?"

"A few hours. I wanted to let you and your mommy know I'd be away for a little while."

"How long?"

"A year. Maybe a little longer."

"But Stu."

"What, Magoo?"

"I thought I was going to see you. I thought—"

"Hey, what did I just finish telling you?"

"I don't know."

"What do you mean you don't know? I thought you gave me your seal of approval. You just told me how much you want that tree house and the bike. I thought I heard you say that was fine with you."

"I guess I did but I—"

"Magoo."

"Yes."

"Just remember this. If I had fourteen cents, I'd give you seven. Make it eight, because I love you. What's today, June fifteenth? By August fifteenth you'll have a round-trip plane ticket to Hong Kong. First class. And all the Chinese food you can eat. You got any complaints about that?"

"No, but—"

"Magoo, I'm counting on you to take good care of your mother. The two of you—you put together a list of all the things you want and send it to your daddy. Tell your mother to send it to my lawyer. She's got the address."

"But I don't understand—"

"Magoo, you've got forever to understand."

"What?"

"I'll call you from Hong Kong. What about one of those extra-special telephone kisses?" He made a screeching kissing noise into the phone that usually made her laugh.

She pursed her lips to return it but no sound came. She tried to speak.

"So long, Magoo."

"So long, Stu."

"I'll talk to you soon, baboon." He hung up the phone.

She stared at the receiver in her hand and dropped it into the lap of her long nightgown.

The phone began to make beeping noises, and she wondered if she was dreaming. She wondered why her father was going to live with Chinese people all the way on the other side of the globe.

It was the globe she was thinking of, the globe, the earth, the planets going around the little wooden sun painted yellow. She started walking down the stairs to tell her mother.

She stopped and then sat down because her knees were about to give way, because she could not stand up.

It was like gravity had stopped working, but instead of floating, she was about to fall off the earth.

"He's moving *where?*" Georgia said. She got up, took a rumpled Kleenex out of the side pocket of her flowered muu-muu and turned down the volume on Johnny Carson. She dabbed the corners of her mouth with the Kleenex, the way she did after she put on lipstick.

"He said Hong Kong."

"What for?" Chuck said.

"A big deal. A really big one."

Georgia shook her head. "I'd be rich if I had a nickel for every one of your father's big deals." She downed what was left in her glass and put it back on the coffee table, on top of the

June issue of the *Daily Word*. "Remember he used to talk about
being a senator or president or whatever the hell he was going
to do to save the world?"

Esme nodded.

"Remember that?" Her mother was drunk.

Esme nodded again.

"You're not upset, are you, sweetheart?"

Esme shrugged, shifted her weight onto her other leg. She
looked down. Her feet stuck out from under her nightgown. The
toenails of her left foot were painted bright orange.

"There's no reason to be. You know why?"

"Why?"

"Your daddy won't stay there. He'll be back as soon as this
thing falls apart. They all do, darling. When I first met him,
you know what he wanted to be?"

She shook her head.

"He wanted to be what's-his-name Huntington. He was
planning to *own* Los Angeles. He bought a few dinky lots in the
San Fernando Valley and thought that would make him a real-
estate tycoon. And I was dumb enough to believe him."

"What happened?"

"What happened? That's the sixty-four-thousand-dollar
question."

"Georgia, please." Chuck reached out and touched her hand.
"This isn't necessary."

She pulled her hand away. "Don't Georgia please me, I am
talking to my daughter about something that is extremely important and I will not—"

"What's so important?" Esme said.

Georgia turned to her. "Your daddy has his head in the
clouds, sweetheart. Your daddy consults *Ripley's Believe It or
Not* when he's trying to figure out what to do with his life, he—"

"*Georgia*." Chuck stood up and took a step toward her.
Esme stepped back. He grabbed Georgia's empty glass from the
coffee table.

Esme took another step back and felt her backside brush up against the knobs of the television. She must have hit the on-off button, because the room was silent suddenly. The silence was like a startling noise. The three of them froze, they looked at one another. Chuck strode into the kitchen carrying empty glasses.

"Mom?"

"What."

"Your eyelash is falling off."

Georgia touched her fingers to her right eye, her left eye. She shook her head. "I took them off before. What do you see?"

"It looked like something was coming off."

"Come, sweetheart." Georgia held out her arms. "Let's forget all these unhappy things. Say nighty-night to your kooky mommy."

Esme stood still, rear end against the television.

"Come on. It's just me."

"Say you're sorry."

"For what?" Georgia drew her arms in, folded her hands in her lap, against the big pink flowers of the muu-muu.

"What you said about my father."

"What did I say?"

"That he has his head in the sky."

"In the clouds, sweetheart, not the sky. Anyway, that's god's truth. It's about time someone told you."

"Maybe it's not true anymore."

"Come over here. Let me read you something."

Esme inched toward her. Georgia reached for the *Daily Word* and flipped through it. Esme moved closer. Without looking up, Georgia patted the space on the seat next to her and Esme took it.

"Listen to this. This will make you feel better." Georgia wrapped her arm around Esme. "This is today's prayer. See, they even write down the date for you. *I am never alone nor lonely. Always God is with me. Always silent unity is with me in prayer. You can never be alone. We know that there is power in united*

*thought and prayer. Those who pray together have a feeling of
oneness that dissolves any feeling of separation or—*"

"Georgia."

"*—aloneness. For anyone who feels—*"

"Georgia."

They looked up. Chuck stood across the room in his shorts,
his unbuttoned pink Oxford shirt, sleeves rolled up to his elbows.
"Why don't you let her go to bed already?"

"What do you know about children?"

"Nothing. Not a fucking thing."

"Now, where was I? Oh, yes. *For anyone who feels alone or
lonely, we are here, we are your friends, we care. As you join us
in prayer, know that you are one in spirit—*"

"Mom?"

"Yes, darling."

Esme stood up and smoothed her hands against her nightgown. "I have to go to bed now."

Georgia held out her hand and touched Esme's waist, her
hip. "Of course you do. Kiss, kiss." She tipped her head up and
puckered her lips. Esme kissed her, and with a very grownup air,
the grownup she would be when she went on the plane to Hong
Kong in August, she walked through the living room and the
dining room and up the stairs to her room.

There was a sudden noise downstairs, a glass hitting the
floor, shattering. She froze at the top of the stairs.

"Jesus, what—"

"Watch it, watch it, move away."

"But you're barefoot, you'll—"

"Get the broom."

"Don't move, darling, you'll—"

"Then bring me some shoes. Hurry up, for Christ's sake.
You want me to spend the rest of the night in the goddam
kitchen trying not to step on glass?"

Esme closed her bedroom door behind her and walked in
the pitch dark like a blind person across her room, stabbing the
air in front of her, feeling for chairs, the table, the toy chest, the

bed, the things she would leave behind when she was old enough
to run away.

After school the next day, she looked up "Hong Kong" in the
phone book. Beneath "Hong Kong Palace" and above "Hong
Kong Treasure" she found "Hong Kong Tourism Office." It was
on Fifty-eighth Street between Park and Madison. She collected
two dollars from her globe bank and her mother's and Chuck's
coat pockets and took a cab there. She explained the situation to
the Chinese woman at the desk.

"Very nice, father live in Hong Kong."

Esme nodded.

"We have many books, brochures with pictures, tours,
cruises. Which books you want?"

"All of them."

"How you take so many?"

"In a taxi."

The coins she was holding were moist, warm in her hand.
The buffalo nickels, the copper pennies with wreaths of wheat,
the silver quarters. At home in her room she would study the
brochures and pick out the things she wanted to see with her
father. She knew already. Pagodas. Rickshaws. Geisha girls in
beautiful kimonos serving plates of lobster Cantonese, spare ribs,
fortune cookies. It would be the happiest time of her life.

Between the Lines

THAT IS THE way it seemed to her the spring she was twelve. That Billy Maxwell was the knight in shining armor her mother had said she was waiting for. That Billy Maxwell had saved them. That if he had not arrived they would have—*There is no knowing what would have become of us,* she wrote in her diary. *Absolutely no idea, as we lived and breathed.* She knew there were second and third and fourth notices from the landlord, Con Edison, Bloomingdale's. One Saturday Georgia packed up the silver and china in cartons marked Jim Beam, Dickel Tennessee Sour Mash, Stolichnaya, stuffing pages of the *Times* crumpled up in balls between the plates, inside the teacups.

"Either we'll go back to L.A.," Georgia said, "or we'll hock all this crap at the pawn shop Heidi told me about on Ninth Avenue. Or—hand me another carton, would you, sweetheart?"

"When are you going to make up your mind?" Esme said.

"You know what the *Daily Word* says."

"What?"

"God's hands are good hands."

"So?"

"If you leave things in His hands—well, they'll take care of themselves."

That, precisely, was the setting for the story, for the arrival of the knight. Shortly after he arrived, Georgia and Esme took to telling the story as a duet, like best friends, like people married to each other for a lifetime.

"We were just sitting there on the floor—it was my job to crush up the newspaper and give it to Mom and she would stick it in the cartons—"

"And she handed me a fistful of these balls, my hands were black from doing this all afternoon, and there was her name in the goddam *New York Times.* If I'd turned my wrist I'd have missed it."

"It was the obituaries. She'd died—"

"But the weirdest thing was that we didn't know when. Esme had just been tearing up the pages and making them into balls, and there was no date on that one—"

"So we looked through the whole pile of newspapers to see what days they were from. We'd gotten them from the incinerator room that morning, this whole stack, it was this high—" her hand to her shoulder—"and they were from all different months."

"And I couldn't exactly call him up and say how long ago did your wife kick the bucket. We hadn't talked to each other in *years*. I didn't even know Billy Maxwell was still in New York. It's a wonder I even remembered his wife's name. Actually, it was his name that I recognized in the paper, before I saw hers."

"So she called the funeral home, she got the name of it from the paper, and she asked when Deana died—"

"I didn't just call up and ask when she died. I told them I'd heard something, and I wanted to send my condolences but I didn't want to embarrass myself by not knowing when—"

"They said it happened the fall before, in September. So she called Billy to say she was sorry. Then, just like that—" Esme snapped her fingers—"they fell in love."

"You're not going to believe me, but that isn't what I had in mind. I was just trying to be polite. It's not everyone you've known since your honeymoon."

"She means her *first* honeymoon."

"Both of our firsts."

"But that," Esme said, "that's a whole 'nother story."

The knight. In a three-piece pinstripe suit, cut with a little bit but not too much of a flair, befitting a man of forty who owned a seat on the New York Stock Exchange. It was the gray silk lining that shone, and the gold watchband, the watch thin as a half dollar. "He'll be here in seven and a half minutes," Georgia said to herself and in stocking feet tore through the apartment she and Esme had moved to the autumn after Chuck left. She was looking for her earrings, her eyeliner, the top to the cold cream. "Honey." She spoke to Esme. "Do try not to slouch."

Georgia settled in the bathroom in front of the special makeup mirror mounted on the wall, clear light bulbs all around the frame, with adjustments for NOONLIGHT, DAYLIGHT, TWILIGHT, MOONLIGHT, the dominant light of the occasion that you were making yourself up for. "And turn down the radio, would you, I don't want to have to ask you again."

"But it's Frankie, Mom. Billy's and your favorite song." "Strangers in the Night," the story of their affair, the way they had met on their first honeymoons in Acapulco.

Georgia smiled and ran the tip of the brush, the mink-smooth bristles, against her tongue and then around the eyeliner cake. "You're right." She began to paint a line above her lashes. "It is."

"Was it your favorite when you first, *first* met Billy?"

"God, no. It's a new song, isn't it?"

"Yeah, by an old fart."

"Don't make me laugh."

"You'd say yes, wouldn't you, if he asked you to marry him tonight?"

"Sweetheart, we've only been dating for a little more than a month. I think there's very little likelihood—" She stopped and leaned forward, looking into the mirror as she wrinkled her nose, the dial adjusted for MOONLIGHT. Just in case they went to the place in the fifties she liked so much with the tables out back, Chinese paper lanterns strung from the high wires that criss-crossed the patio.

"But what if he did? Just pretend."

"Honey, all I want to do is get through this summer without our usual catastrophes." She dug tweezers out of her cosmetic kit and began to snip at the skin just beneath her eyebrows. "I told you, didn't I, never tweeze the top of the eyebrows? Always the bottom."

"Yes." Esme sat on the bathtub ledge. "Always shave *up* the leg, never down." She imitated the singsong in Georgia's voice. "The pocketbook has to match the shoes, the lipstick has to match the nail polish. No black clothes after Memorial Day, no white after Labor Day. Ask boys questions all the time because that way they'll think you really like them even if you don't, and always bring mad money when you go on a date, in case the guy throws up or turns out to be a real goon and you have to get rid of him and pay for a cab."

Georgia smiled. "Who told you about mad money?"

"There was an article in *Seventeen*."

"Who told you to ask boys a lot of questions?"

"Winky."

Georgia turned the band at the bottom of her lipliner mechanical pencil to bring up the thin shaft of Real Red lipstick that she was going to outline her lips with. "That girl has more problems. She's really kooksville. I don't know what Billy's going to do with her. But what a love he is, what a prince, to take her in. Not that she doesn't help out, especially since Deana died. Winky is fabulous with those little boys."

"But she's Billy's sister, right?"

"Stepsister."

"So it's not true?"

"What's not?" Georgia drew a line along the edge of her lips with the care of a calligrapher, a cartographer.

"Should you or shouldn't you ask boys a lot of questions?"

"You should. Definitely. I'm just surprised Winky knows so much about the way to a man's heart."

"You think she's not old enough? She's twenty-one. You were already married when you were twenty-one."

"Twenty-two, darling. Anyway, age isn't Winky's problem."

"All you guys talk about is Winky and her problem. She isn't crazy, is she?"

"No, not crazy. Emotionally immature."

"What does that mean?"

"It means that she's a grownup but she acts like a child. You're a child but you act like a grownup. I was that way too, when I was your age. But skinny as a rail, like Winky. No hips, no boobs. Looked like a boy until tenth grade. Then I slayed them. *Slayed* them. Well, except for the boobs."

"If you got married to Billy, would she live with us?"

"At the rate she's going, she'll live with Billy and his kids until she's sixty-five. I don't know who else would treat her so well. Remember the first night we met her? I thought she'd bought out Bergdorf's shoe department. No one knows quite what to do with her."

"What do you mean, no one knows what to do with her?"

The doorbell rang.

"Shit." Georgia picked up the can of hairspray on the counter, shook it. "Sweetheart, would you get that? Wait, wait. How do I look?"

"You look fine."

"How's the length on this?"

Esme looked at Georgia's hemline as she backed out of the bathroom. "All right."

"Just all right?" Georgia posed. She slapped her hands against her cheeks—to bring out the color, she often told Esme. "It's fine."

"What about my hair?"

"Fine."

Georgia held her hands against her waist. "Are you sure the belt goes with the dress?"

"Ma, you look fine. You always look fine. Fine, fine, fine."

Georgia picked up her toothbrush from the ledge above the sink. "Esme?"

"Yeah."

"Always brush your teeth before a date. Remember that, when you start dating. In case I forget to tell you."

Esme shook her head and dragged her feet through the apartment, swinging her hips back and forth in an annoyed, strutting rhythm. She talked softly to herself, she screwed her face up to make it ugly, uglier than it usually was. "Fine, fine,

fine, kiss my behind. How do I look? Winky's a nut. Billy's a prince. You're such a pretty girl. Tweeze your legs, comb your eyebrows. Yakkity, yak. Yak, yak."

She flipped the top lock and opened the front door.

"Don't you even ask who it is?"

"Hi, Billy."

"Hi, Ez. Doorman gave me something for you." Jauntily, he slapped her shoulder with an envelope. "I think you grew some since last time I saw you."

"Last night?"

"Are you wearing heels?"

They both looked down at her bare feet.

She was five feet seven and a half, the second-tallest girl in the seventh grade, taller than all but three of the boys, two inches shy of her mother's full height.

She took the envelope from him. "How come the doorman had it?" It was from her father, sent special delivery.

"He wasn't sure. He said the guy who was on earlier today must have signed for it and then forgot to give it to you. Where's your mom?"

"Here I am, darling." Georgia slunk into the foyer and wrapped her arms around Billy.

They kissed.

From across the room Esme saw that their eyes were closed and their mouths were open wide as they pressed their lips together.

They did this all the time.

She watched to see if their tongues were really in each other's mouths, which it always looked like they were but she nevertheless found hard to believe.

There were many things she found hard to believe.

That Billy loved her mother as much as she was sure her mother loved Billy.

That she would ever be a size seven.

That Paul McCartney had slept with girls.

That she had gotten her period three days before and

Georgia had actually called up Heidi to tell her that now she had someone to share the giant-size box of Kotex with.

But she still believed that her father was going to be rich. She knew that it was just a matter of time.

She held his letter in her hand. She was going to wait until they were gone to open it. Billy draped his arms loosely around Georgia's shoulders and said, "Did you ask her yet?"

"I was waiting for you. You ask her."

Esme couldn't believe it. Billy was going to ask Esme for Georgia's hand in marriage.

"Let's sit down," he said.

They sat down in the living room and Esme decided that she would ask if she could have the empty bedroom on the third floor of Billy's townhouse on Eighty-first Street when they got married. She would ask if Billy would pay for her to go to private school, because she had gotten mugged twice on her way to homeroom in the morning, once the day she was supposed to buy a new gym uniform, and once the day the French Club was going to De Julio's Pizza for lunch, and both times her homeroom teacher, Mr. Gleason, who everyone said was a faggot, took her aside and said, "Next time you have to kick 'em in the nuts. You know what I'm saying?"

Billy reached across the couch and held Georgia's hand as he looked at Esme. "Winky and I wanted to invite you to spend the summer in Southampton. At the house. She'll be taking care of the boys." Ricky and Timmy, whose mother, Deana, had died. "Georgia and I will stay in the city during the week and come out on the weekends. Your mom wasn't sure you'd want to—"

"Sure I'd want to. Unless—"

Georgia turned to Billy. "You see, sometimes her father—"

"Sometimes I see my father. He lives in California. But I never know until—"

"He changes his plans *all* the time. That is, when we even know where he is. There was a stretch the year before last when we had no idea if he was even in this country. His parents, bless their little Jewish hearts, were on the phone with us every night of the week."

"Mom. That's kind of an exaggeration."

"Of course it is. But honestly. It was a nightmare."

She did not understand why her mother was talking this way. Leave it to her. Next thing you know, she would tell him that Esme had gotten her period. Next thing you know, she would tell him about Esme's special diet that the doctor had put her on, even though she was only two dress sizes bigger than the chart said she was supposed to be, not five or six sizes, not like the real tubs in the "before" pictures in the Ayds ads who took up two seats when you saw them on the bus.

"Esme, you don't have to answer now," Billy said. "Just think about it. We'd love to have you."

"What do you say, sweetheart?"

Esme glared at her mother and said, "You say, 'Thank you, Billy.'" If her mother did not quit acting so rude, Billy would never want to marry her. "I was just about to say it. You didn't even give me a chance to open my mouth. You think I don't have any manners, or what?"

Georgia turned to Billy and spoke in a low voice, like she didn't think Esme could hear. "I'll tell you later what's wrong." She was going to do it. She was going to tell Billy about the curse.

"Thank you, Billy," Esme said. "I'd love to go to the country this summer."

.   .   .

May 15, 1966

Dear Magoo,

It was great talking to you the other night! Leave it to your mother to have found Billy again. When we met him and his wife (Number 1) on our honeymoon, we thought they were just plain folk. I think it was wife Number 2 (the one who died) who helped him buy the seat on the Stock

Exchange. Would you believe they cost ¼ million dollars?
I don't even know how many zeroes that is! Business is
just starting to take off. Mort says it will probably skyrocket
by the end of the summer. If not, we will be rioting in the
streets with the colored folk.

In the meantime, Rhoda, Melanie, Johnnie & Your
Daddy send Love and Kisses!

Stu

Included in the envelope was a photograph of her father, in
bell-bottom jeans and a cowboy hat, and the people he had iden-
tified in other photographs as Rhoda, his wife, and Melanie and
Johnnie, her two children. Her father had married Rhoda last
year, but she hadn't come with him to New York when he came
last Christmas. He had taken Esme for a Shirley Temple at the
Rockefeller Center skating rink bar, because she did not want to
go skating, and to dinner with a man who was going to lend her
father money so that he and this man Mort could start this business that was about to start booming. It was a company that
manufactured little boxes so that you could open your garage
door by remote control, which was, her father said, a sure winner, a goldmine, a jackpot, his ticket to the top, his ticket out, his
ticket in.

In her bedroom, Esme read the letter twice. That day her
social-studies teacher had explained what it meant to read between the lines, and now Esme understood what it meant as she
read between the lines of her father's letter. Between the lines
it said that he did not have the money to send her to California
and that he might have it at the end of the summer, when business was going to take off, but it might not. Those were the words
between the lines, which was another way of saying that they
were invisible.

She put the letter in the second drawer of her desk, with all
of the other letters he had sent her. He almost always sent them
special delivery, even though he hardly ever had anything special to say. She was going to write him a letter and tell him it was

a stupid waste of money to send things that weren't special special delivery, particularly since he did not have money to burn and money did not grow on trees and if it was not for Billy she did not know what would have become of them, they almost got evicted the month before last.

She composed the letter in her head as she lay in bed trying to fall asleep. She composed one letter and another and another, wondering if she should really tell her father all the horrible things that happened when her mother got drunk and didn't have any money and called everyone she knew in California in the middle of the night and cried so loud you could hear it in the bathroom with the door locked and a towel stuffed in the crack, or whether there was some way she could let him know how it was without coming right out and saying it, whether it was possible not just to read between the lines but also to write between the lines. And if it was, maybe her father had been doing it all along.

The Best of Everything

THE PEOPLE NEXT door had a pony named Rutherford.

Down the street lived a woman who had once been married to a famous playwright. She herself was an actress, an heiress, old as the hills, Winky said, and never left her house, sent the Chinese houseboy to the village in a Jaguar to do her shopping. Her house was the biggest one on the block. Bigger than the McKnights' on Gin Lane, which had thirty-one rooms.

The house behind Billy's was getting a swimming pool. In the mornings Billy's son peered through a hole in the thick hedges at the yellow plow that dug up the earth. He was five. He wanted a plow more than a swimming pool.

The sun was bright, blinding, every day, except—the family joke went—some Saturdays and Sundays, the only two days of the week that Georgia and Billy were there. During the week, Winky took Esme and the boys, Ricky and Timmy, to the beach almost every day. Often it was to the one that was farthest away, the tip of the Shinnecock Inlet, going so far as a way of asserting a claim on the land that she did not have, showing off. *We're allowed anywhere in Southampton.* Which wasn't exactly true. Billy had been turned down for membership at the Southampton Golf and Country Club. Winky told Esme that she had no idea why. "I mean," she said, "it's not like he's Jewish or anything."

What a life this is, Esme wrote in her diary. *Fabulous. And so classy. Winky is teaching me about everything. And this house! The biggest one I've ever lived in. Winky calls it country elegant, which means that it is very posh but casual at the same time. I feel like I'm in a movie whenever I go up the stairs, the way they curve all the way around and the light makes the chandelier sparkle like a thousand diamonds.*

———

On the back porch, beneath the green-and-white-striped canopy, she read Winky's hardcover copy of *The Valley of the Dolls*.

> *"She felt herself responding to his embrace with an ardor she had never dreamed she possessed, her mouth demanding more and more. She couldn't kiss him deeply enough. His hands caressed her body, gently, then intimately. Yet her emotional excitement dominated all physical sensation. To have him in her arms . . . to be close, to feel free to kiss his eyelids, his brow, his lips . . . to know that he wanted her, that he cared.*
>
> *"And then it was happening. Oh God, this was the moment! She wanted to please him, but the pain caught her unaware"*—

"Esme."

> *"and she cried out. He pulled away immediately and released her."*

"Esme."
She looked up.
"I'm leaving for the city," Winky said. "I'm going to see El Shrinko at three and take the four-thirty back here. Flo's got the boys. They're in the village shopping. I'll see you tonight. About eight. Check and see what's on the Late Show, okay?"
"Yeah."
"Ta ta."

> *"All at once she knew—this was the ultimate in fulfillment, to please the man you loved. At that moment she felt she was the most important and powerful woman in the world. She was flooded with a new sense of pride in her sex."*

Esme listened for the sounds of Winky leaving and waited a few minutes. Then she went upstairs to look at Winky's clothes, as she did every Wednesday when Winky went to the shrink.

———

There was room to walk around in her closet, thick carpeting, the smell of mothballs and leather. Quilted hangers, suede mini-skirts the size of placemats, two tiers of blouses and skirts, an upper and a lower, and a stool so you could reach the ones on top.

She touched the sleeves, the collars, kilts of every tartan, the softest angora sweaters, narrow dresses with narrow waists, size fives and sevens, shelves of purses with dainty shoulder straps and inside pockets for mirrors and tissues.

She squatted to touch the rows and rows of shoes, hardly ever worn, so many pairs of slipperlike, butter-soft Pappagallo flats with tassels. Esme had had a pair of those last year; within a week they were stretched and scuffed, practically ruined. Georgia Laughlin's daughter, the prom queen's daughter—she should have gone to a camp for fat girls this summer.

When her father sent her the plane ticket to L.A.—she had sent him another letter the week before with Billy's address and unlisted phone number—she would go on a crash diet.

She stood on the stool and touched the lavender knitted top, the suede vest, the vest made of little round mirrors. Winky was svelte, Winky ate like a bird. "I had a weight problem until I started to smoke," she had told Esme. "These things—" flourishing a lit cigarette—"they saved my life."

Winky was scrawny, Georgia had told Esme, she looked like a boy. *I wouldn't mind looking like a boy,* Esme said back. *Someday you might mind,* Georgia had answered.

Now she looked at herself in Winky's full-length mirror. Her shorts were way too tight because she had refused to buy the next larger size. Her green T-shirt was hideous. Her hideous T-shirt. Her hideous self.

. . .

"Don't you think it's divine the way they met?" Winky said. "So incredibly romantic. I could listen to the story a hundred times."

Esme had heard the story a hundred times. Georgia and Meyer on their honeymoon at the Sheraton-Acapulco; Billy and his first wife, the one before Deana, on their honeymoon at the Sheraton-Acapulco. The two women are wearing the same dress one night at dinner, and sitting at tables adjacent to one another. There is embarrassment, a joke, an invitation to share a table, the beginning of friendship.

"And here we are," Winky said. There they were in the living room, the two of them, waiting for the Late Show to come on. "Just think. If your mother had been wearing a different dress that night. Did you ever see the photograph from then?"

"I don't know. I don't think so."

"It's in here." Winky crossed the room to the antique desk in the corner. She took something from the bottom drawer. "I found this last year, after Deana died."

It was a framed photograph of the four of them on their honeymoon, her parents and Billy and Billy's first wife, husbands and wives with their arms around each other.

"My mother has one of those," Esme said. "There was a photographer at the hotel that took pictures and gave them to everyone."

"I just had a great idea," Winky said and tossed the photograph onto a stuffed chair. "A fabulous idea. Come on." She tapped Esme's shoulder.

"Where to?"

"The third floor."

"What about the movie? It's going to start in a minute."

"This is better than a movie."

Esme followed her across the living room and up the stairs, the wonderful stairs that made her feel like a movie star. "What's there?"

"You'll see." Winky led the way. "Do you believe in ghosts?"

"Of course not. Do you?"

"I didn't until I was up here one night last Christmas." They reached the landing on the third floor and Winky felt around on a wall in the dark until lights went on all the way down the hall. "This is where Deana died. Exactly ten months ago."

"I thought no one was allowed up here."

"They aren't. Not since she died."

"Which room was it in?"

"That one." Winky pointed. "The one at the end. That was also where I saw the ghost at Christmas."

"Forget it, Winky." Esme turned and started to walk back toward the stairs.

"No, come on." Winky grabbed her arm. "That's not what I want to show you."

The corridor was long, uncarpeted, stark white walls, the feel of an abandoned dormitory. The floorboards creaked, there was a gentle thumping against the roof. "It's a squirrel," Winky said, "or a stray cat."

Winky walked ahead of her. She got to the end of the hall and pulled open the door. A light went on. She shrieked, she covered her face with her hands.

Esme froze. She felt pulses pounding in her wrists, the backs of her knees. The door opened out and faced her; she could not see into the room, all she could see was the band of light where the side of the door met the door frame. She could not move, except to watch Winky as she peered through her spreading fingers. She whispered, "It's gone now."

Esme could barely speak. "What is?"

"Nothing." Winky turned to her and smiled. She waved Esme toward the door. "C'mere."

Esme did not move.

"Come on, Esme."

"What's in there?"

"Love letters, silly. Here, help me carry them."

"What made the light go on?"

"It goes on when you open the door. Deana had the decorator do all the closets that way."

Esme stepped forward, peered into the room-sized closet.

It was empty, completely empty, except for a few shoeboxes on the floor. "Those are what scared you?"

"You take two, I'll take two."

"Did you say they're love letters?" The boxes were stuffed, they were heavy.

"Yeah."

"Whose?"

"The ones Deana wrote to Billy when she was dying."

"She would write them and leave them on the pillow for Billy to find when he came home." Winky swung her feet up on the living-room coffee table and looked at a small pale yellow piece of paper. "Listen to this. 'Be brave, my darling. I know that when the end comes you will take the best care of the boys. With all my heart I want you to find a new love, because I know I will always be your real, true love.' Isn't that the most beautiful thing you've ever heard? Poor Deana." She picked another from the box and held it out to Esme. "Here. Take a look."

Esme sat across from her and shuffled through the pieces of paper. Some of the notes were long, some were a line or two; the handwriting changed from large to small, upright to backhand. "Oh, my dearest love . . . thinking of you always . . . not afraid anymore . . . I used to believe . . . before I got sick . . . when your father called today I tried to sound as strong as I could . . . breaks my heart to think of Timmy growing up without even a memory of me . . ."

"What did she die of?" Esme asked.

Winky looked up. "What?"

"How come she died?"

"She had a weak heart. Oh, look at this, Esme, this is darling." Winky held up a piece of pink paper. There was a poem written on it, in squarish, boarding-school handwriting. " 'Every day my love does grow,' " Winky read aloud, " 'how I love you, my escargot.' They're snails, escargots. It's French."

"I know."

Winky read the poem again to herself and then put it aside, in a small pile of favorites.

Esme marshaled her courage, forced herself to speak. "What did you see up there, Winky?"

"Where?"

"On the third floor."

"Just the cousin of a ghost."

"What?"

"It wasn't a full-fledged ghost, like the one I saw at Christmas. It didn't last as long. And I just saw the feet." She picked up another letter, a long one, and read to herself.

"Whose feet?"

"A woman's. I guess they were Deana's."

"What did they look like?"

"They were beautiful. High arches, silver slippers, very Cinderella." She reached for her cigarettes, the matchbook. "I'm out of matches. Would you be a love, Esmeralda—" She looked over to Esme. "Good lord, you look like *you* just saw a ghost."

Esme felt her thighs flutter, her knees tingle. If she tried to stand up, her legs would not hold her. "You just said you saw ghost feet upstairs."

"You aren't going to tell me you took me seriously, are you?"

Esme did not answer.

"Well?"

Esme shrugged.

"You probably figure that just because I go to a shrink I'm off my nut."

Esme tried to move again, to make her shoulders go into another shrug.

"Your mother thinks that."

"How do you know?"

"The walls have ears."

Esme took this as another reference to the supernatural.

"You don't really think I saw a ghost up there just now, do you?"

"No," Esme lied.

"And you *don't* think I'm crazy, do you?"

Esme shook her head.

"But I did see a ghost at Christmas. I'm sure of that." Winky reached for her cigarettes again. "Would you go into the kitchen and get me some matches? There's a basket of them on the counter, by the blender."

Esme nodded and began to walk backward out of the living room, facing Winky, who was reading letters again. An unlit cigarette dangled from her lips.

Esme kept walking backward. She was afraid to turn her back to Winky. "Don't you adore these letters?" Winky looked up at her. "Aren't they absolutely fabulous? I'd love to be in love that way."

"Me too," Esme said and kept her eyes on Winky, which she would have to do for the rest of the summer, until her father sent her the plane ticket. Until she figured out some other way to get out of here, quick like a bunny rabbit. What her mother sometimes said to Billy: *Come over here quick like a bunny rabbit and give me a kiss.*

Every day my love does grow, how I love you—

If Billy loved Deana, if Deana was his real, true love, maybe he didn't really love Georgia. It was even possible that every time he kissed Georgia with his tongue deep inside her mouth he was thinking of Deana. But if the opposite was true, if he had just forgotten about Deana, then maybe he had never really loved her in the first place, maybe he had been lying to her, even though she, poor Deana who had died upstairs, even though poor dead Deana had thought that she was Billy's true love, his escargot—

Esme walked backward into the foyer table and accidentally bit her tongue, which accidentally made her start to cry.

Marriage and a Phone Call

ESME RECOILED, BUT did not want to, from her mother's embrace the following night, Friday night, at the kitchen door. She ended up kissing Georgia's cheek and hung her arm limply, for a moment, across Georgia's shoulder while Georgia held her tightly. The sensual, generous confidence of a woman in love. There was also, in the fullness, the unselfconsciousness of Georgia's embrace, a kind of apology. For how awful their lives had been before, before Billy, before all of this boundless splendor, this love unlike any other.

"Look who we found on our way," Georgia said. "Our favorite decorator."

"Hi, beautiful," Sy said and kissed Esme's cheek.

They stood in the big kitchen with shopping bags from the city in their arms.

"Hi, handsome," Esme said.

"Just call me the spy who came in from the cold," he said.

"The spy who loved me," Georgia said and looked at Billy and laughed.

"Did anyone ever tell you you look like your mother?" Sy said to Esme.

"Sy, what do you want to drink?" Billy said.

"Nobody," Esme said, "just you."

"And I'm nobody, right? Everybody knows I'm nobody. What do you think of my toupee?" He tipped his head to the side. "Can you see where it's attached?"

"He wants a gimlet, don't you, Sy?" Georgia said. "He's been talking gimlets since we got on the Long Island Expressway. Where's Winky? Where are the boys?"

"She's giving them a bath."

"Honey, let's go up and say hello to them."

"Just a second, let me get Sy his drink here. Hey, man—" Billy turned and tossed a can of peanuts to him—"catch this."

"Catch as catch can."

"What do you think of the kitchen?" Billy said. It was large, plain. The old cabinets had been painted a dull beige, spared the country elegance, spared any adornment at all, except the high windows above the sink, the view of the towering maple tree in the yard.

"It's got possibilities. Reminds me a little of a kitchen I redecorated for some friends in Connecticut. Pre-war—"

"What war?"

Sy laughed. "Korean."

"Come on, sweetheart, we should go upstairs and see them."

"You look like you need a peanut." Sy held out the can to Esme. "Take two, they're small. Have a seat." Sy straddled a chair at the kitchen table. Esme sat down next to him. "Your mom tells me you really dig Southampton."

"I guess it's all right."

"Just all right? Georgia, did you hear what she said?"

"We'll be right back," Georgia said and gave Billy the eye. "We have to see the boys. Don't we, darling?"

"Sy. Start with this." Billy handed Sy a drink and left the kitchen behind Georgia.

"Your mom's in heaven," Sy said. "Something, isn't it?"

"What?"

"The wedding."

"What wedding?"

"She didn't tell you? Shit."

"It already happened?"

"No. I think she said in the fall. They just told me today in the car. I thought she already told you. He gave her a hunk of rock you wouldn't believe. They were having a clearance sale at Harry Winston. Ten grand off the list price."

"Really?"

"Esme, honey, when are you going to learn when your Uncle Sy is making a funny?"

———

"Georgia, I screwed up," Sy said as she came back into the kitchen. "I told her. I thought she already knew."

"Let's see the ring," Esme said. "How much did it cost?"

"I have no idea. Want to try it on? It might fit your—"

"Yeah." Esme took it from her and pushed it over her fore-finger. "More than ten grand?"

"I don't know."

"Sy said it cost—"

"Never mind what he said," Sy said. "What are you drink-ing, Esme? How 'bout a Bud?"

"Sy."

"You're not eighteen yet?"

"She just turned twelve, didn't you, sweetheart?" Georgia took back the ring and picked up her drink from the counter. "She's probably the biggest twelve-year-old on Long Island. You know, it feels like she turned twelve ten years ago."

"Get off it," he said. "How can you only be twelve? You're as tall as your mom."

"*And* her boobs are bigger," Georgia said.

"Mom! For Christ's sake!"

"Darling, don't blush," Georgia said. "Thank the lord they're not peach pits."

"Mom."

"Georgia, leave her alone with your tale of woe." Sy turned to Esme. "You're the spitting image of your mother."

"Stop it." She covered her face with her hands.

"What are you doing?" He grabbed one of her hands play-fully.

"She thinks she's ugly," Georgia said.

"My sister should be so ugly," he said. "Your mother should be so ugly. Three years."

"Three years what?" Esme said.

"Come see me in three years and I'll tell you whether I was right."

"About what?"

"You and the guys." She didn't think that Sy knew about those things, because he was queer, because he used to live with José, and José was queer too.

"She'll slay them," Georgia said. "With her little finger. Can you believe those cheekbones? Can you believe that nose?"

"Just quit it, all right, both of you."

"Tell her your story, Georgia."

"Which one?"

"The one about your getting married?" Esme said.

"No, the one you told in the car today," Sy said. "About that man on the street."

"Forget him," Esme said. "When are you getting married?"

"At the end of the summer. You'll be the bridesmaid."

"Tell her the story about that guy," Sy said. "It was hilarious."

"She doesn't want to hear that."

"Yes, I do. Please, Mom, please."

"Sy, you tell it."

"She's walking down Madison the other day—"

"Lexington," Georgia said.

"All right, Lex. And this well-to-do businessman comes up to her and says, 'Got a match?' Georgia thinks he's okay, not some mad rapist, so she looks through her bag, pulls out some matches. He takes them and then he says, 'Look, I'm a man, you're a woman. Why waste the afternoon?'" Sy turned to Georgia. "Did I get it right?"

Georgia nodded.

"Isn't that something?" Sy said to Esme.

"I guess so."

"You don't think it's funny?"

"Sure it's funny."

"Maybe she didn't get it," Georgia said.

"Of course I got it." That was what you said to someone you wanted to go to bed with but weren't married to. "What did you say to him?"

"I told him I was busy."

"She said she was on her way to get her legs waxed," Sy said.

Georgia turned to Sy. "Isn't Esme's tan divine?"

"Heaven. Pure heaven. Esme has been heavenly since the day we met," Sy said. "Remember the day we met?"

"At Heidi's," Georgia said. "Remember, when we first moved to New York?"

Esme nodded.

"I'd just finished doing Heidi's living room," Sy said. "Then that prick ex of hers—what was his name?—decided he didn't want to pay the bill."

"You decorated her living room too?" Esme said.

"You couldn't tell?"

"Then how come she didn't get black walls like we did?"

"Esme, darling, lesson number one in decorating." Sy drank from his gin gimlet. "Lesson number one, know your client. I knew for a fact that Heidi Johnston would not dig black walls in her living room."

"Because she told you?"

"Esme, my sweet, what I'm talking about is something more in*stinc*tive. What you know about your client you don't learn because they *tell* you, you know it *before* they tell you. That truly is the—"

"Is that psychology, what you're talking about?"

"More like ESP. You know what that is?"

Esme nodded.

"Remember our Ouija board?" Georgia said. "Did we lose it or—"

"Here it is, this is exactly what I'm talking about, knowing your client without having to ask."

"Huh?"

"Black walls were Georgia to a T. Black walls, Ouija boards. All I had to do was *look* at your mother to know she was a supernatural kind of gal." Sy laughed.

"One of my husbands told me I was a witch," Georgia said.

"Which one?" Esme said.

"Not your father."

"Quinn Laughlin," Esme said. "Your prick ex."

Georgia smiled.

"Quick study," Sy said.

"Sy," Esme said, "what's lesson number two of decorating?"

"That? That's easy. Make sure the client has a lotta money. The more the better."

"And how can you tell?" Georgia said coyly.

"The rings on their fingers. And ESP."

"Georgia, hon," Billy said as he came into the kitchen, "have you seen my cigarettes?" Winky was right behind him.

"Didn't you buy a carton before we left the city?"

"I bought three cartons, four cartons. One for me, one for you, one for Wink."

"They must be in the car."

"I know I took a pack—"

"I'll go get them," Winky said.

"Would you, honey, thanks," Billy said and took a seat, scooped out a handful of peanuts.

"You know," Sy said, "I've been thinking about this kitchen."

"Let's do something with it," Georgia said. "Something groovy. You know what I'd love—"

"I bet black walls," Esme said.

"Black walls?" Billy said.

"Billy, don't you remember I told you about Sy and José and the black walls in our old apartment? Those crazy times."

"You're not going to do our place with black walls, are you?" Billy said.

"We've been looking at apartments," Georgia said. "There's a super new building on the corner of—what's the cross street again?"

"Sixty-third."

"Cigs for everyone," Winky said as she came in through the back door. She handed Billy a pack of Viceroys.

The phone rang. "I'll get it," Winky said.

"The place is huge," Georgia said. "How many rooms is it again?"

"Twelve, maybe thirteen. Not counting johns. Views like you wouldn't believe."

"From the johns too?"

"Esme." Winky held the receiver up in the air and waved it. "Your father's on the phone."

Esme had been watching the clock ever since she had gotten into bed at eleven-thirty. Now it was two-thirty. She got up to go to the bathroom and paused as she opened her bedroom door. She heard voices downstairs. She tiptoed out of the room.

If she had not been sitting at the kitchen table with all of them when Meyer had called, she would have told him why she had to get out of here. Because Winky was crazy. Because there were ghosts on the third floor. Because of the dead lady's letters. But he was in a rush, he had said, this wasn't a good time to talk. He had called to say hello, to ask if she was having a good summer, and to ask Billy a question about the stock market, could she put him on the line?

Now Esme stood at the top of the curved staircase in the dark hall and listened to the voices downstairs.

" . . . least he could have called me at the office," Billy said. "But I mean, there, in the kitchen, in front of everyone. Jesus. And after all these . . ."

Esme knelt to hear them better.

" . . . I thought your number was unlisted. Esme must have . . ."

"What did he expect me to say—"

"I thought you handled it beautifully. Under the circumstances."

"What nerve he has."

"You know. He always did."

"As if I had ten thousand dollars I wanted to piss away. If he were doing this the right way, he'd have asked me to invest in the company instead of just asking me to lend him the money. And even then—"

"You were such a darling not to say anything in front of Esme. Come over here quick like a bunny rabbit and fix me a drink."

The Darkest Hour

THERE SHE WAS in a cab between Esme and Billy, eight months after their wedding, thinking about love and how she always botched it. Just like stockings. You pulled too hard, put them on in a hurry, sat too far back on a bench, a wooden chair, you didn't even have to move and they ran, fell apart in your hand, against your leg, like a wet tissue. For a moment she envied those women who wore support hose, thick as argyle socks. Those women who didn't mind looking like spinsters, nurses. Those ladies with their varicose veins and their stockings that never run.

"If Sy is queer," Esme said, "then why is he getting married?" They were on their way to a party at his apartment, to meet his wife-to-be.

"Maybe I was wrong. Maybe he isn't a fag. Maybe he changed his mind."

"Maybe he always went both ways," Billy said.

"What does that mean, both ways?" Esme said.

"It means he likes men and women," Georgia said. It was unusually warm for April. It was 1967.

"What did you say her name was?" Billy said. "Elaine?"

"Adele. This is number six for her. Or seven."

"Maybe she likes fags," Billy said. "Some women do."

"How come she got married so many times?"

"I don't know, sweetheart. I guess she keeps looking."

"For what?"

"The Holy Grail," Billy said.

"What's that?"

"Never mind."

"Don't answer her that way," Georgia said.

"Is it dirty?"

"No, Esme. It isn't dirty," Billy said.

"Tell her what it is."

"You tell her what it is."

"For fucking Christ's sake, Billy. Do we have to—"

"Forget it," Esme said. "I don't really want to know."

"I'll tell you later," Georgia said, leaning over, whispering. Later, when she found out what it was herself.

In the lobby of Sy's building, Esme moved close to Georgia. She pressed the button to call the elevator. "When they do it, Mom, how do they do it?"

"Who, sweetheart, what?"

"Fags."

"Do what?"

"You know. It."

"Oh, that. Well, they—"

"Mother of god, Georgia, here, in the lobby!"

The door opened. "No," Georgia said. "Here. In the elevator."

Esme moved from room to room, Coke in hand, chewing on crushed ice, trying to make sure that he did not know she was following him around. The man in jeans and a workshirt and a psychedelic tie. He had brown hair, sideburns that came out to his mustache. He was at the center of a circle on the terrace. Esme leaned against the doorjamb of the sliding glass door, as close to the circle of people as she could get without letting them know that she was there.

"Tell that story, Janey," said a man wearing long beads, a bandana around his forehead. "Come on."

"You tell it."

"Isn't that our rule, honey, everyone tells their own story?"

"All right, all right." Esme moved a little closer. "It was nineteen-sixty-two, maybe early sixty-three. I was with Tim. My first husband. We got a cab in front of the Savoy Plaza, may it rest in peace, and the cabbie was just ecstatic. He'd just dropped off, guess who, Jack Kennedy, across the street. Picked him up like any other fare at the Carlyle, remember how he used to stay there? And when he realized who it was, he flipped. The fare

was eighty-five cents. Kennedy gave him a five and told him to
keep the change. The cabbie, he waved the bill in our faces, said
he was going to frame it."

Esme edged closer.

"But what Janey's not telling you," the man said, "is that
she was as excited as the cabbie."

"Where was he going?" Esme asked softly. A few of them
turned to her, letting her into the circle.

"The Plaza."

"How come?"

"Honey, that's anyone's guess."

The man she had been following around spoke. "You ever
see that Lenny Bruce routine?" He touched his mustache, he
took a swig of his drink. "He holds up the issue of *Life* with all
the pictures of JFK getting shot. Points to the one where Jackie's
scrambling toward the back of the limo. The caption says she's
reaching for a Secret Service guy to help the fallen President.
Bruce says, 'That's bullshit. All she's trying to do is get out of the
line of fire. She's trying to save her ass.' " Esme started laughing,
and when she realized no one else was, she slapped her hand
against her mouth. "Oh, I love it," he said. "Whose date are
you?"

"What?" She could not have heard him right.

"Just tell me something, what was so funny about that to
you?"

They were all looking at her. She was flustered, stunned.

"No, no, no," the man said, touching her arm, "I dug it
that you laughed. I really dug it. Where did you learn to laugh
like that?"

"Nowhere, I just—"

"Warren, leave the girl alone."

"There you are, darling," Georgia called from the doorway.

"You never told me whose date you are," the man said again.

"I've been looking all over for you." Georgia stumbled
through a group of people and threw her arm around Esme's

shoulder, leaned her head against it. "She's my date," Georgia said. "She's my most favorite best loveykins date in the world. Aren't you, darling?" She slurred her words.

"Georgia Laughlin," the man said.

Georgia looked at him, her brow furrowed, as if he had mentioned someone she was supposed to know but could not quite place.

He held out his hand. "Warren Gold."

"Well, hello, sweetheart, it's a pleasure to meet you. I don't mind in the least that you've been flirting with my daughter. You're not the first man and I hope to god you won't be the last. And furthermore—" She put her hand to her mouth and seemed to be considering something. "Would you excuse me, please, I think I have to tinkle." She turned and insinuated her way through the group again, smiling at everyone, saying, "Would you excuse me, sweetheart," and Esme followed close behind her. In case she fell over.

Warren Gold followed Esme into the living room and touched her shoulder, held on to her upper arm. "Let her go," he said. "She'll be all right." Georgia grabbed the arm of a man standing next to her and disappeared down the hall with him.

"I knew her," Warren said, "from before."

"Where?"

"I met her at your apartment. The place with the black walls."

"When?"

"Years ago. With Quinn—wasn't that his name? I was dating a girl who worked at CBS." He smiled. "I think that was how I got there. I guess you weren't there. Hey, look, about your mom."

"What about her?" she snapped.

She was waiting for him to walk away, to find someone else to talk to.

She would not care if he did.

He was much too old for her, and probably had a girlfriend. She did not know what she would do if he tried to kiss her.

"You know before and after?" he said.

"Before and after what?"

"You know, the pictures in the magazines. Ads for makeup or fat pills. Before the girl gets made over and after, but you can't recognize them? It doesn't even look like the same girl."

She nodded.

"That's what she's like. Your mother. When she's sober and when she's drunk."

"So?"

"Isn't she?"

"I don't understand what you're talking about."

"You don't understand?"

"I don't understand why you're asking me all these questions." She had hoped that he would ask her about herself.

"When I first started talking to you, on the terrace, I didn't realize you were her daughter. But I think that's why I noticed you. You look so much alike— You know, I don't even know your name."

"Esme."

"Like the girl in the story."

"What story?"

"The Salinger story. They must have named you after her."

Esme shook her head. "After a French model. Georgia read about her in a magazine or something." That sounded very grownup, calling her mother Georgia. If he kissed her, first he would put his lips against hers and then maybe he would open his lips and put his tongue in her mouth. "What's this story about?"

"A girl in England during the war. Very precocious. Too old for her years, but she has to be. She's an orphan."

"What war?"

"World War Two. I have the book at home. It's in a collection. I'll give it to you."

"Oh, my god, here she is!" Sy appeared at Esme's side, looped his arm through hers, looked up at her. "God, I love tall women," he said. "I just took off my shoes so you could be taller than me, Esme, darling. I see you've met Warren, the most lecherous man in all of the five boroughs." He turned to Warren. "Sixteen'll get you twenty, Warren."

"I haven't laid a hand on her."

"But you'd love to, wouldn't you?"

"I'm going to plead the fifth on that one, man."

"Esme, my love, this man—" he pointed to Warren—"is old enough to be your father. And besides that he's over thirty."

"Just barely," Warren said.

"Never, never, never trust a man old enough to be your father," Sy said. "If you don't believe me—" he pointed again to Warren—"ask him. And now, if you'll excuse me, I think I hear my charming wife-to-be calling." He bounded across the room.

"So, you're sixteen," Warren said.

She shook her head.

"Seventeen?"

She shook her head again. "Fourteen," she said. If she told him the truth, that she would be thirteen in two months, he would not even think about kissing her.

"Fourteen, huh?"

She nodded, a faint nod, a little lie.

"So you must have been about, what, nine or ten when I was at those crazy parties at your house."

"Yeah."

"What's your dad up to these days?"

"My dad?"

"Yeah, Quinn."

"He's not my father."

"I thought he had some kids. Maybe I got it wrong."

"He does. Two daughters. Little bitches. That's what my mother calls them. And just between you and I, the leaves don't fall far from the trees."

"The leaves. You mean the apples?"

"Yeah, the apples. That's what I meant. Anyway, everyone knows what an S.O.B. Quinn was."

He nodded. He started to laugh.

"Just what's so funny about that to you?" she said. That was what he had said to her on the terrace.

He looked at her hard. Maybe he was getting ready to kiss her. Or ask for her phone number.

"Esme." Billy's voice behind her was firm, urgent. "Let's go." He touched her elbow and tipped his head toward the back of the apartment.

"But, I was just—"

He glared at her and she understood. She held her hand up to Warren and fanned her fingers at him. "I have to go now. Maybe I'll see you. Around. Or someplace." She followed Billy down the hallway to a bedroom.

Georgia was sitting on the floor next to the bed with her legs crossed. Her dress was pushed up beyond her garters, and she stretched her arms high in time to the music. She waved her hands through the air and sang along with the Mamas and the Papas in a weak, wobbly voice, slurring words, skipping words, fooling around. *"Life can never be be be bop . . . want it to be be be bop . . . doodly bop bop bop . . . and the darkest hour is just before dawn."*

"Georgia, it's time to go," Billy said. "Esme, get her purse. It's over there."

Georgia kept moving her arms through the air, not in time to the music anymore, but as if she were trying to shoo away flies. "I'm not leaving. I'm having too much fun. I hardly ever have fun anymore and if I had more fun I wouldn't be having so much fun now. Do you love me, Billy?" She looked up at him, she could hardly speak. "Do you? Do I? Do-be-do-be-do. That's our song, sweetheart, strangers in the, uh, bathroom." She covered her mouth and giggled.

"Get up."

"No." She whimpered and pouted. "I don't love you, either. So there. I love my Esme. I love my mother. And my Dru. But I don't love you. And I don't love my father. Do you know what he did to me? Do you? Do you?" Her voice cracked. Tears rolled down her face. The mascara ran with the tears and made them a watery black. "He stole money from me so he could drink." She wasn't sobbing, she was sitting there, sniffling, talking to herself. "He stole the money my sister was saving to buy a dress for the prom. He hocked my mother's jewelry. And then he went away and never came back. Do you know how I found out he was dead?"

"Mom. C'mon. It's late."

"Do you know?"

"Yes. Everyone knows. Get up." Esme pulled on her arm, trying to pull her up.

"I was the only one home. A man came to the house." She pulled her arm away from Esme. "He said, 'I think I have some news about your father.' Then he took me to the morgue and showed me a body."

"Mom. Nobody wants to hear. We have to go." She yanked and yanked on Georgia's arm. "Billy, help me."

Esme pulled so hard, and Georgia was so loose, that she tipped over and curled up on the floor. Then she raised herself on her elbow and looked up at them. "You're so far away." Then she laid her head down and closed her eyes.

When she did not move for several minutes, Esme was sure it was because she was dead. She was afraid to bend down and touch her. "Do something," she said. "Billy, do something." He knelt by Georgia's side and touched her face. He touched her cheek and her head flopped in the other direction. "Billy, for Christ's sake. For fucking Christ's sake—"

"She'll be all right," he said. "She just had a little too much to drink is all."

My, My Meyer

MEYER ARRIVED THAT fall in a Rolls-Royce.

Georgia and Billy were not divorced by then but they were separated, she and Esme moved from the townhouse to a two-bedroom apartment in the Seventies off Third. *it really isn't so bad here just the two of us,* Esme wrote in her diary, *considering how awful it was in The House. she refuses to live on the west side because she thinks it isn't safe, even though i keep telling her we could get a really huge place for half of what the rent is here. i say i guess you'd rather keep complaining about the rent, and she says yes she would. then she says, you can get a cheap apartment in harlem too, that doesn't mean we're going to move there. she gets mad if i tell her to sell the diamond billy gave her, but unless you tell her what to do she doesn't do anything.*

They were not divorced but they were separated, and through their lawyers Billy had agreed to send her eight hundred dollars a month. Sy said to Georgia, "Someone up there likes you." Heidi said, "Don't hold your breath waiting for it." Georgia got a job at Bonwit Teller in the cosmetics department and brought home bags of free samples, lip gloss from England, body paint that came in tubes, tiny vials of cologne called Mist d'Amour and Strawberry Fields.

It was the thing Georgia did best, making the ladies on the other side of the counter feel special, beautiful, wanted. Especially the fat ones, the ugly ones, who had a special appreciation for her, because she always had something complimentary to say. *Who does your hair? That setting is divine—I've always adored sapphires. That's the perfect neckline for you.*

The thing Georgia did best, taking all the time in the world to help them match the eye shadow to the scarf, the face masque to the texture of the skin. They adored her, they sent their friends to her, she taught them to highlight their cheekbones, helped them pick out the right spot on the chin to paint a mole.

She was doing just that one afternoon late in September when she saw her daughter coming down the aisle between Elizabeth Arden and Charles of the Ritz. Margaret Lawrence was at her side, the new girl in Esme's class. She had just moved to the city from Vermont; her parents had been killed in a car accident, poor thing, and she had come here to live with her aunt. She was almost a head shorter than Esme, freckled, thin, tiny little breasts beneath her wrinkled workshirt with the sleeves rolled up. Hair cut in a ragged pixie, she looked like a waif. But that was the look this year, that was in, looking like a street urchin.

"Hi, Mom."

Georgia smiled broadly. She reached her arm across the counter and touched Esme's shoulder. "Hi, darling. Hi, Margaret, sweetheart, how are you? I looked up and all of a sudden there you were. What are you doing here?"

"Going to the movies."

"Hi, Mrs. Singer."

"My name is *Georgia*. And I love your haircut. Love, love, love it." She tousled Margaret's hair. Poor, poor thing, without anyone in the world.

Esme dug a telegram out of her pocket and put it on the counter folded in half, the big letters WESTERN showing against the yellow. "Look what came today."

"Miss, I hate to interrupt this—" Georgia's customer tapped her palm against the glass counter top, heavy rings on every other finger—"well, actually I don't—"

"You're absolutely right," Georgia said. "We were just about to pick out the right shade, weren't we?" She picked up the sample compact with the four rows of eyeliner cake.

Esme picked up the telegram and said, loudly, deliberately, to defy the woman with the rings, "It's from Daddy. He's coming in two weeks. He's driving. We'll be back soon," and moved Margaret down the aisle with a tug at her sleeve.

"I'm *so* embarrassed," Margaret whispered.

"How come?" They stopped at a tray of perfume testers. Esme picked up one of the bottles and sniffed the top.

"Because Singer's not her last name. I didn't realize until after I said it."

"That's okay." She sniffed another bottle, and another. "She's used to it. Everybody calls her something else." She sprayed her neck with something called Jasmine.

"It's really all right to call her Georgia?"

"Yeah."

"Are you sure?"

They wandered down a few steps to a tall display of blush-ons.

"Of course I'm sure. Don't worry about it. Here, stand still." Esme brushed Margaret's cheeks with a pinkish-brown powder. "It'll make you look like Jean Shrimpton. Suck in your cheeks."

Margaret obeyed. She looked in a mirror. "For goodness' sake, what did you do to me?"

"I guess I put on too much." Margaret rubbed her sleeve against her cheek. Esme pulled her arm away. "Don't do that. My mother'll give you a tissue. C'mon." Margaret followed her. Margaret did everything Esme told her to do. She liked Margaret all right but mostly she felt sorry for her. She didn't know which bus to take, she was afraid of the city, afraid in the junior high with the tough kids who panhandled, who said, "I'm on getchu you don't gimme none," when you didn't have a dime for them, the seventeen-year-old boys who were still in eighth grade and hung around on the first floor pinching white girls' asses. And she felt sorry for Margaret because she had to live with an aunt she hated, and her brother had died in the accident, too. *Poor Margaret,* Georgia called her. *Your friend, poor Margaret.*

"What do you think about this one?" Esme held up a scarf.

"It's all right. Why don't we go see if your mother can talk to us now."

"Did you ever steal anything?" Esme moved in a side-step, going the length of the counter, turning everything over to look at the price tags.

"No."

"Never? Nothing?"

Margaret shook her head. "Have you?"

"A long time ago." She picked up a bright purple leather wallet from a tray and undid the snap. "Lots of stuff."

"Esme—jeez—are you going to do it—"

"Don't worry." The wallet cost thirty dollars. She put it back down. "I wouldn't do it here." She picked up another one and wondered why her father had sent a telegram, why he hadn't just called from his house in Seattle, or from a pay phone on the highway. "Besides, my mother can get a discount."

"Did you ever get caught?"

"No."

"What did you take?"

"Just dumb crap. Lipstick, M & M's. Gum. It was this other girl's idea. What do you think about these?" Esme slipped on a pair of sunglasses. She looked in the mirror on the counter. "Who's that behind those Foster Grants?" She wrinkled her nose, twisted her lips in ugly shapes. "God, I wish I wasn't such a horse."

"You're not a horse." She gazed at Esme. "You're not a horse at all. You're—" She stopped.

Esme put the sunglasses down and noticed Margaret watching her, looking up at her, with a dreamy look, love and fear all mixed up together in the look. It was one she knew. It was the way you look at someone you adore and someone you're afraid of, afraid that they won't adore you back, like Warren from Sy's party, whom she had called four times and hung up on as soon as he answered the phone, adored him so much that she was afraid to talk to him.

"Let's go find my mother," Esme said and gave Margaret a little shove and turned away from her, which is what Margaret deserved for adoring her.

Leah Marks was new in the class, too, new to the city, exotic, shy. She wore narrow dresses made from Indian bedspreads that she had bought in England, where she used to live. She had spent last summer in Ibiza, she told Esme, and the summer before that in Ireland.

They lingered one afternoon after school in Georgia's bathroom, examining bottles and tubes on the narrow shelves. "Your mother really uses a lot of makeup." There was such scorn in her voice.

"It's her job. She gets it for free. Like this stuff here." Esme picked up a mascara and unscrewed the top. "I used to steal things like this from Woolworth's."

"Me too."

"Really?"

"Yeah." Leah opened a tube of body paint and squirted a line on the back of her hand.

"Ever get caught?"

"No." Leah rubbed it in and her hand was bright blue. She held it up for Esme to see. "If I had my parents would have sent me to a shrink."

"For stealing? How come?"

"Is this the only color she has?" Leah opened the medicine chest.

"I don't know." Esme helped her look. "Why a shrink?"

"My mother's a shrink for kids, so she thinks any kid who does anything weird should go to one." Leah picked up a prescription bottle and read the label. "Like she says that kids who steal things are really trying to steal love, and they should go to shrinks and their parents should too. What's Seconal?"

"Sleeping pills."

"Can I take one?"

"What for?"

"Just to see what happens."

"You'll go to sleep, that's what happens. My mother says they make you feel like shit the next day."

"I thought they make you high."

"Did you read *The Valley of the Dolls*?"

"No."

"It's all about sleeping pills. This woman takes some pills and sleeps for two weeks."

"On purpose?"

"Yeah. She wants to lose weight. In two weeks, she loses ten pounds."

"That sounds fucked up."

"Yeah, I guess so. Here's some more of that paint. It's red. Put it over the blue and you'll get purple." Leah held out her hand. "Hold it still."

"We don't have to do just our hands. We could do our faces, too." Leah noticed a small clear plastic box of false eyelashes. "Your mother really wears those?"

"Not so much anymore."

"My mother would *never* wear them."

"How come?"

"They're so bourgeois."

"She's a model," Esme said. "I mean, she used to be. She had to look beautiful."

"You can be beautiful without wearing *these*."

"Well, I guess you can, but it's—"

"Did you ever smoke pot?"

Esme shook her head.

"My brother goes to Columbia and he said he'd give me some when I go to visit him. You want to go with me?"

"Sure. Yeah. Where is it?"

"On Broadway. Near Harlem."

"He lives there?"

"Yeah."

"Is it safe?"

"Of course it's safe. My father says that the only reason you're afraid of black people is because they're afraid of you." Leah led the way out of the bathroom. "You want to go to Greenwich Village sometime?"

"You've never been there?"

"Not at night. Except for once with my brother."

"You know who goes there all the time? Cynthia Kreeger and Roberta Fein, in our class. They go to the Electric Circus."

"Which ones are they?"

"The ones who changed their names. Didn't you hear Mr. Young calling attendance that day and going, 'Just who the hell is Cleo and who the hell is Mars?' "

"That was them?"

"Yeah."

"That sounds fucked up."

"You say that about everything?"

"Just things that sound fucked up." They laughed. "I learned it from my brother. He's a Marxist."

"What's that?"

"Marx believed that the wealth should be redistributed. That everyone should get the same amount. That the ruling class should be abolished."

"Oh."

Leah picked up things from Esme's dresser and examined them. "Where'd you get your posters?"

"Different places. That one—" she pointed to Jimi Hendrix— "the headshop on Lexington. That one—" the Lovin' Spoonful— "I don't remember."

"Do you have any cigarettes?"

"My mother probably does. I'll go look."

"What's this?" Leah held up a framed bas-relief made of a dull marbleized salmon-colored plastic, showing a man pulling a rickshaw and some mountains and trees sculpted in the distance.

"It's from Hong Kong. My father used to work for the company that made them."

"It's really ugly." Leah put it down, leaned it against the wall.

"Yeah." Esme glanced at it from across the room and then looked away, because she was not sure what she should think of it now, whether she had made a mistake to like it. "I guess so."

"Did you ever go to Hong Kong?"

"No. I was supposed to but—" Esme shrugged. "Did you?"

"Yeah. When I was three. I don't remember anything except the hats." She held her hands above her head, making a pointed roof with her fingers, tips of her middle fingers touching.

"I have one of those," Esme said. "From Chinatown."

"Let's see. But first—" Leah held two fingers up to her mouth in a V. As they walked into the living room, she said, "In England doing that is the same as giving someone the finger."

"This?" Esme held up her fingers in a V.

Leah nodded. "A backwards victory."

"What?"

"This means victory—" she made a V with her palm facing out. "And this means fuck you—" a V with the back of her hand to Esme. "It also means I want a cigarette."

"Let's look here," Esme said. "She always leaves some in her purse." Esme opened the door to the front hall closet and squatted before the purses scattered on the floor. "Start with the ones back there."

"There's probably some money too." Leah stooped down next to her and picked up an alligator bag.

"So if there aren't any cigs, we can use the money to buy some."

"In England they call them fags instead of cigs."

"What do they call fags?"

"I don't know. I hope your mother doesn't smoke menthols. I hate menthols."

"That's what she smokes."

"Oh. Well, maybe I can get used to them."

"What's your favorite?"

"Gauloise. They're French. They smell awful and it takes ages to get used to them. Look what I found." Leah held up a small photograph of Esme in a clear plastic cover. Esme tried to grab it from her. Leah stood and looked at it more closely. "How old were you?"

"If you'd let me see the picture—"

Leah held it up for her.

"I think seven. Or eight."

"Whose pool?"

"Let's see."

Leah held up the picture again.

"It was a hotel we were staying at. In Palm Springs." Where Georgia had cried in the cab on the way to the airport, which Dru said was because she was sad to leave this beautiful town, and which Esme knew was a lie.

"My brother used to be fat too," Leah said, still looking at the picture of Esme in a bathing suit. "My parents sent him to a shrink because my mother said that kids who are fat eat so much because they need love. Because they're deprived." She handed the photograph back to Esme and stooped again at the closet door and picked through another purse.

"He's not fat anymore?"

Leah shook her head. She pulled out a handful of change and a fresh pack of cigarettes. "Wow. It hasn't even been opened."

They walked up Third Avenue to the Orange Julius stand on Eighty-sixth Street. "Look at her," Leah said, and pointed to a woman as they crossed the street. "That's the most bourgeois coat I've ever seen. Oh, vomit."

"Oh, puke."

"Oh, barf."

They pretended to gag, they laughed and laughed.

"What about her?" Esme asked and pointed. "The one with the sunglasses."

"Awful. Gross. The worst. My brother once went out with a girl who worked at the Orange Julius in Coney Island. He just did it because he wanted to find out what was in the powder they mix with the orange juice."

"What did he find out?"

"She didn't know. She told him it was a secret recipe and even if she knew, which she swore she didn't, she wouldn't tell him."

"Let me tell you something." Esme leaned close to Leah. "That is really fucked up."

They laughed and crossed Eighty-sixth Street against the light.

"I have a plan," Leah said at the counter of the Orange Julius. She whispered. "We'll get some pot from my brother and then we'll go to the Village."

"And tell everyone we meet that we're seventeen."

"Maybe sixteen."

"No, seventeen."

"What if we don't meet anyone?"

"We'll go somewhere else."

"Do you want a small or a medium?"

"I don't know. I never had one."

"Two smalls," Leah said to the man behind the counter and pulled out a handful of change from her pocket.

"What if you meet someone and I don't?"

"What if you do and I don't?"

"Maybe neither of us will."

"Then why are we going?"

"To have fun."

Esme adored Leah and did not realize for some time that the undercurrent of discomfort she felt in Leah's presence was fear.

It was not fear later that afternoon when Leah took Esme to her house, a house as big as Billy's. Downstairs it was dark, there were two kitchens. "How come?"

"One is part of the servants' quarters. My father is horrified that we have servants' quarters."

"Do you have servants?"

"Just a maid. She's been with us forever. She's like part of the family."

There were books in every room, walls of them, up to the high ceilings, next to the beds, in the bathrooms. There were photographs on the walls in the places where there were no books, walls of black-and-white portraits, each one covered with glass, metal clamps on the top and bottom to hold the glass in place. They walked through Leah's father's study. "Who took all the pictures?"

"My father. He's a photographer. Quite famous."

"Like who are those people there?"

Leah pointed to a wall of photographs, moving her arm down the row. "Katharine Hepburn, Garson Kanin, Huey Newton, Norman Mailer, Veruschka. The last one is a picture of my father that Paul Strand took. You want to see my room?"

The walls in her room were painted white. There was a mirror above the fireplace, Indian bedspreads on the two twin beds, a beige rug. There was hardly any color, any adornment at all in this room with high ceilings, beautiful wood floors. "My father's framing some posters we got in Florence last summer. I'm going to put one there—" she pointed to the wall by the tall window—"and one there—" the wall above her desk.

"What's your father's name? Maybe I've heard of him."

"Don Marks."

"Oh. I guess I haven't."

"This is a book he did." Leah went to the bookcase and pulled out a big hardcover called *The Writer's Life*. "Actually, he's done a lot of books but this is one of my favorites."

Esme took it and sat on the bed. The pages were heavy, as smooth as polished stones. A photograph on one page, a quotation from a book on the facing page. William Faulkner, Saul Bellow, Robert Penn Warren, Hemingway, Flannery O'Connor, Dylan Thomas. She turned to the title page, to the name Don Marks, and moved her finger over the letters one by one, as if they were engraved, as if they had a third dimension. She was daunted, intrigued, intimidated, as if by a sexual advance.

"It's beautiful," she said. She turned to the photographs

again, the quotations. "*One Christmas was so much like another, in those years around the sea-town corner now and out of all sound except the distant speaking of the voices I sometimes hear a moment before sleep, that I can never remember whether it snowed for six days and six nights when I was twelve or whether it snowed for twelve days and twelve nights when I was six.*" She looked hard at Dylan Thomas. His cheeks were fat, he was smoking a cigarette and the smoke was in the photograph, hanging in patches, clouds rising around his face.

"Everyone thinks alcohol killed him," Leah said. "But my father knows his doctor and he said it was heroin. He was actually a junkie. Have you read this?" Leah went back to the bookcase and took out *Manchild in the Promised Land*.

"No."

"If you want I'll lend it to you. It's about growing up in Harlem. It's one of my father's favorite books about black people."

Esme took the book when she left Leah's house that day, and another one called *On the Road*. In exchange, she told Leah she would bring *Valley of the Dolls* to school for her the following day.

"I think I'd like to go to a psychiatrist," Esme said to her mother that night at dinner.

"Did you say a psychiatrist?"

Esme nodded and pushed around the baked potato on her plate.

"Since when?"

She shrugged.

"What on earth for?"

She shrugged again. She wasn't sure. The idea had just come to her, almost as she had spoken it.

"That's ridiculous. Children don't need psychiatrists."

"Some people think they do. Leah's mother is a psychiatrist. Just for children."

"Who's Leah?"

"I just *told* you about her. The one whose house I was at today."

"You don't need a child psychiatrist."

"Why?"

"Because you're not a child."

"You just said I was."

"I don't care what I just said." She put her fork and knife down noisily on her plate.

"What if I go to a psychiatrist for grownups?"

"Esme, you're not going to any psychiatrist."

"What if I just go once?"

"What for?"

"To see what it's like."

"You could say that about anything." Georgia stood up. "You could say, Why don't I jump off the Brooklyn Bridge, to see what it's like." She stalked into the kitchen. "Why don't I lie down on the train tracks, to see what's it's like." Esme took the salt shaker and held it up high over her chicken bones, coating them with salt. "Why don't I set my hair on fire, to see what it's like." Esme started to laugh and covered her mouth with her hand. "People like Winky need psychiatrists," Georgia called out. "People with a few screws loose." Esme heard her cracking open a tray of ice, she heard the ice cubes dropping into the sink. "And you see how much good they did her." Now Esme held the salt shaker over the skin of her baked potato. "I'll be damned, did you hear me, *damned*, if anyone in this family is going to piss away money on a psychiatrist."

"Family," Esme said under her breath. "Some family."

Georgia came back to the dining room with a tall glass of scotch and water. "Everyone's got problems. Everyone and his mother."

"I didn't say anything about problems."

"And one more thing—" She wasn't drunk, she just wasn't listening; she was panicked. "The best thing you can do for your problems, I don't care what they are, whether you think your mother is a kook from the year dot, whether you think your father is a complete fink, the best thing you can do is forget them. Go to some shrink and he'll make you remember them. Then you'll *really* go crazy."

"Mom, all I said was that I was thinking about it."

"There's nothing to think about." Georgia took a long drink. "When you feel sorry for yourself—"

"I didn't say—"

"Just let me finish. When you feel sorry for yourself, just think of poor Margaret." She drank again. "Think of all her problems."

"For your information, poor Margaret has a trust fund. And she's applying to private school because she got mugged in the locker room and she—"

"That's enough about Margaret."

"You brought her up."

"I don't care what I did."

"That's for sure."

"What is that supposed to mean?"

"Nothing. Never mind. Pass the milk. *Please.*"

Georgia passed her the milk carton.

"That's all right," Esme said as she filled her glass. "When Daddy comes I'll ask him if he'll pay."

"Pay for what?"

"My psychiatrist." She was determined now to go to one, and now she had a reason for wanting to—her mother's resistance.

"You mean if he comes," Georgia said.

"He said he'd be here on the fourteenth. Today is the seventh."

"Your father says he's going to do a lot of things." She stubbed out a cigarette and lit another. "My, My Meyer," she said softly. "I wish you could see him for who is he is. Crazy man. Lunatic. The way he bought that trailer park in the San Fernando Valley just before you were born, you'd have thought it was the Plaza Hotel the way he went on about it. And that craziness in Hong Kong that was going to make him a millionaire."

Esme picked up the potato skin drenched in salt and held
it a few inches above her plate. She jabbed a knife through it and
drew the knife down and made two short ribbons.

"Esme. Please. I didn't raise you to play with your food like
an animal."

Esme slammed her knife on the table. "You think I think
he's perfect, don't you?" She stood up and stepped back. "Yeah,
well, I happen to know for a fact that he called Billy last summer
to ask for money." She took a few more steps back. "I happen
to know for a fact that he wanted ten thousand dollars and that
Billy didn't give it to him. I also happen to know for a fact that
his company made two thousand of those ugly things from Hong
Kong—" she pointed toward her bedroom, to the bas relief
leaning against the wall— "and no one wanted to buy them,
and I also happen to know for a fact—" She was close to tears,
she took a deep breath. She did not know what else she knew
for a fact.

"Sweetheart," Georgia said softly.

"That's not my name!" Esme turned and stormed through
the apartment. She hit her elbow against a doorjamb, gritted
her teeth against the pain, did not stop. She slammed her bedroom door behind her and stood for a few minutes in the half
light panting, almost as tall as the life-size poster of Jimi Hendrix
tacked to the wall that she turned to when she caught her breath,
next to the poster of a coffin that said BE THE FIRST ONE IN YOUR
BLOCK TO HAVE YOUR BOY COME HOME IN A BOX. She gave Jimi a
long TV kiss on the lips, lips tight together. She drew her arms
around herself the way he would have if he were there.

. . .

The picture of her mother in the morning. At the table with a
cup of coffee, the ashtray already full of cigarettes, a few dishes
left over from the night before, a wad of yellow candle wax stuck
to the center of the table from another night. "Your father called
last night when you were asleep. He wanted me to tell you he'll

be here on Friday. He's taking you to New Haven to see your grandparents."

Esme tried not to smile.

"He also wanted me to tell you that he's driving a Rolls-Royce."

"What?"

"That's what he said."

"Are you kidding?"

"No. I couldn't believe it myself. But he swore up and down."

"Maybe he was making it up."

"It wouldn't be the first time."

Esme held up her fingers in a **V**, which meant Fuck you and I want a cigarette.

The Dream Market

WHISKED AWAY, SHE thought, I am going to be whisked away.

Her anticipation assumed a shape, a texture, it kept her awake Tuesday night, Wednesday night, Thursday night, the Friday her father was going to come, the Friday that would not come. When it did, she would be whisked away in a white Rolls-Royce with cream-colored leather upholstery, and no matter how often Georgia said it from now on, it would not be true that Meyer was a lunatic, she could stick it in her ear for all Esme cared, she could cram it.

When the housephone rang Friday afternoon at four and the doorman said, "There's some people here want to know if they can come up. I said I'd have to ring first," Esme was certain he had made a mistake. What did he mean saying there were some people down there instead of one person, her father, who would be upstairs any minute now, who was here now, who was rich now?

As she walked across the living room to the front door, she stopped to close and lock the suitcase she had just packed to take to New Haven for the weekend. At the bottom of it she had put a list of her mother's shortcomings and worst offenses, ones she had written down in the middle of those insomniac nights, inspired in her ardor by *On the Road*, which she read then too. The plan was that if her father balked at her request to live with him in Seattle, she would present the list to him, one normal person to another, you could not argue with the facts, not three pages of them. *Dig this*, she would say to him, *and this*.

And this. Her father at the front door moments later dressed in a lime-green Nehru shirt, bell bottoms, a beard, and beads. Her father a hippie. A bald hippie, leading an entourage of hippies.

"Hiya, Magoo," he said and leaned forward to kiss her. "Where'd you learn how to get so beautiful and tall? This is

Tina—" holding out his hand to a slight woman in a floor-length Indian dress with long black hair streaked with gray, a cigarette holder without a cigarette, which she took out of her mouth to kiss Esme's cheek. "And this is Randy and this is Rich." Hands out to two teenage boys in jeans and workshirts, collars covered with peace buttons and love buttons and a green button that said DO NOT FOLD, SPINDLE, OR MUTILATE.

"Hey, how you doin'," the boys said in greeting, softly, without inflection, because it was not cool to say it louder or with more enthusiasm.

"Fine," Esme said. "Hi. I mean, I guess—come on in. My mother's still at work."

"She's working again these days?" Meyer said and ushered in the crowd.

Esme nodded.

"Where's the bathroom?" Tina said. "I've had to go since New Jersey."

"First door on the right." Esme saw the two boys sitting on the couch, hair all down their necks, bangs half over their eyes, talking quietly, as if they were making a deal, making illicit arrangements.

When she turned around, Meyer was gone. She found him in the hallway that led to Georgia's bedroom, found him looking over the wall of framed photographs.

"Who are they?" she whispered.

"You mean Tina? She's my old lady. The kids are hers. We're doing our thing together these days."

"Why didn't you tell me?"

"Tell you what, Magoo?" He turned to her and smiled. "Did I tell you you look just like your mother, and that's not nothing." He shook his head and looked at her with something like that gaze of adoration that she had felt from Margaret, poor Margaret, who had no father. Esme's father touched his fingers to his beard, the graying beard. *The short Jew and the tall, striking girl from Redondo.* Georgia had told her that they used to be called that, and Esme remembered it now, standing face to face, eye to eye with her short father, the short Jew, My, My Meyer, Your Crazy Father.

He turned back to the wall, moved from photograph to photograph, Esme at three, five, eleven, in color and black-and-white, fat, not so fat, short, tall, being told to smile, told to wipe the smirk off her face.

She did not know what could be read on her face right now.

Things never turned out the way you wanted them to, the way you dreamed they would. Disappointment had a sharp, sour taste, the taste of medicine, the taste of milk gone bad. She wished it could be kept a secret, that her father had become a hippie.

Or as much of a hippie as Meyer Singer was ever going to become. As much of a hippie as a man who wanted, as much as he wanted anything, despite his fondness for peace, love, flower children, despite his disdain for the system, for capitalist pigs, for the military industrial complex, he was a man who wanted, despite all of this, to be filthy rich. He wanted to be, in the Yiddish phrase his parents used to describe the wealthiest man in New Haven, *ungeshtupt mit gelt*. Stuffed with money. He wanted to be the man about whom that was said, said with admiration, jealousy, hatred, fear, truly, he did not care. In the meantime, he was a man people talked about for other reasons. Because he was forty-two and he did himself up like he was twenty. Because he was given to bragging of a peculiar sort. He bragged that he had smoked pot with Tina's sons, Randy fifteen, Rich thirteen. That in fact he had turned them on himself. That he had not been to visit his parents in four years. That his first wife, that he, a *nebbish* from New Haven—which is not the way he thought of himself, except in the context of having married Georgia Bates— that he had married a woman who could have nabbed Cary Grant, she was that much of a knockout, and depending on the company, he might say, *Or maybe she said knocked up, maybe that was why I married her.* A shotgun wedding was always good for a laugh.

"Let's hit the road, team," he said now.

"Back to the Rollsmobile," Randy said.

"You're going to love the car, Magoo."

"You're required to," Randy said. "Or else he won't let you ride in it." He turned to Meyer. "Right, man?"

"Right on."

It was like riding in an airplane, self-contained, separate from the outside; you were the object of envy, on your way to an exotic place. Here, ensconced in soft leather upholstery, windows tinted gray, the dash was a highly polished walnut. There were wooden tables that folded down behind the front seats, just like an airplane.

She sat in the back seat between Randy and Rich, trying not to take up too much space, to keep her thighs, her hips, from rubbing against theirs, these boys who might be her stepbrothers, since Tina was Meyer's old lady, which might mean that they were married.

"So you live in Seattle?" Esme said.

"Yeah," Randy said.

"With my father?"

He nodded.

"How long have you been doing that?"

He shrugged. "Like a few months. Since we left Paul's place."

"Who's that?"

"It's what we called this commune we used to live on in Oregon. Tina decided it was getting to be a bummer so we split. Then she met your old man."

"Where's your old man?" Esme was trying to get the hang of this, trying to get with it.

"Columbus, Ohio. Six feet under."

"What?"

"Dead."

"He's been dead forever," Rich said and tapped his finger on the window. "Hey, what's that?"

"Projects," she said.

"What kind of projects?"

They were clusters of red brick high rises surrounded by grassy yards and jungle gyms. "For poor people. Negroes and Puerto Ricans."

"We don't have Puerto Ricans in Seattle," Randy said.

"We hardly have any Negroes," Rich said.

"How come?"

"I don't know," Randy said. "I guess it's too far away. You into Scrabble?"

"You mean playing it?"

"No, eating it," Rich said.

"Shut the fuck up, Jack, would you?" Randy said.

"Name's Rich."

"Name's Toad."

"Yeah, I'm sort of into it," Esme said.

Randy leaned forward and pulled a traveling Scrabble set from a shopping bag.

"What's happening back there?" Meyer called out. "You guys digging New York?" They were inching along in rush-hour traffic on the FDR northbound.

"Yeah, Meyer, we're doing some serious digging back here," Randy said and jerked his head to the side to get his bangs away from his eyes for a few seconds, so he could roll them for Esme and Rich. "We're digging the poor people, we're digging the projects, we're digging the scenery, we're digging—"

"Stu," Esme said loudly, "how much did this car cost?"

"A small fortune," he said. "But it's a business write-off. Part of a little venture that's about to take off like a rocket. Like a fleet of rockets. Something so incredible I can't believe it isn't illegal."

"What's this Stu-Magoo stuff?" Randy said.

"When Esme was a little tiny thing just learning to talk, she couldn't say her name. She pronounced it Emmy. We started to call her Emmy Lou. Pretty soon, she learned about rhymes, wanted to play the rhyme game all the time. Remember the rhyme game, Magoo?" She nodded. "On her very own, she thought of all the words that rhymed with Lou. Like blue and Stu and Magoo. She started calling me Stu. Didn't you, Magoo?"

"I guess so."

"Here," Randy said. He put the box top to the Scrabble game on Esme's lap and put the magnetic playing board on top of that.

Tina turned around and swung her arm over the seat, a silver and turquoise bracelet on her wrist, rings on every finger. "We're business partners, your daddy and me." She smiled and looked at Meyer. "Isn't that so, baby, we're going to make a million dollars." She was not young and she wore no makeup. Georgia would call her a Plain Jane. Georgia would say, *There's someone who doesn't understand that a little makeup can go a long way.*

"For starters," Meyer said. "Then we'll make some real money."

Tina turned back to Esme. "You know what they say, don't you?"

Esme shook her head.

"You have to have money to make money."

"Yeah, I guess I've heard that. This man my mother was—" She swallowed the last words. This man my mother was married to knew all about making money. He knew that lending Meyer Singer ten thousand dollars was a lousy investment, he knew it was for the birds.

"But we're going to do it differently," Tina said. "We're not going to get hung up playing all the games. And we're going to have *fun*. It'll be just like playing Monopoly."

"What a coincidence," Randy said. "Monopoly and Scrabble. Our life is one big toy store."

"One big game show," Rich said and picked a handful of letters from the bag on the floor. "Our whole life. The whole time we've been living it. The Price Is Right. Let's Make a Deal. The Dating Game." He arranged his letters on the holder on his lap. "This hand eats the big one. Trade 'em in for what's behind curtain number three. Trade 'em in for an Oscar Mayer wiener."

"What grade are you in?" Esme asked.

"He's in third," Randy said.

"I thought so."

"Ninth," Rich said and scowled at his brother. He looked at Esme. "What are you in?"

"Eighth."

"He's tenth." Rich pointed to Randy.

"How come you're not in school now?"

"It's Friday night."

"I mean, this week."

"So what's the verdict from the back seat?" Meyer called out.

"Groovy," Randy called back. "We're feeling very groovy, aren't we, guys and chicks?"

Rich rested his hand on his thigh and gave his brother the finger.

"That's what I like to hear," Meyer said.

"So how come you're not in school now?" Esme repeated.

"Because we're taking this trip."

"Isn't it illegal?"

"What, taking a trip?"

"Not going to school."

"Hey, Meyer—" Rich's voice rose. "Is what we're doing illegal?"

"What the hell are you doing back there?"

"We're not going to school." Rich laughed. "Because we're taking a trip. A magical mystery trip. Lucy in the sky with diamonds. We're flying high with Lucy in the sky."

"I forgot to tell you," Meyer said. "I'm stopping at the police station in the next town. We're all under arrest for taking this trip."

"It's illegal not to go to school in New York," Esme said, "even if it isn't in Seattle. There are people called truant officers and they're in charge of—"

"So don't sweat it, Esme, move to Seattle," Rich said. "Take the rest of your letters. You get seven. Randy, if she lived there, what school would she go to?"

"Northwest. Next year, either Livingston or Wilson. Pick a letter. See who goes first. I got an 'E.' "

"Seattle's great. Seattle's the best. Better than Paul's hippie-dippy comune too. Man, that place stank."

"New York's pretty good too," Esme said. "I hated it when I first moved here, but I didn't know anything. I was only eight then and not very sophisticated. I got an 'X.' That means I go first."

On the other side of the Triborough Bridge, Meyer began to explain the business venture for which he had bought the Rolls-Royce.

"They're starting a company," Randy interrupted, "he and Tina are starting a company that conducts contests."

"Everyone loves a winner," Meyer said. "You've heard that expression?"

"Yeah."

"What do you think about this one? 'Everyone loves to win.' That's our motto. First, we're going to publish a magazine that lists contests all over the country. Each of the companies that holds the contests pays us to be listed in the magazine. We come up with this dynamite product, dynamite advertising, distribution, in no time the circulation's up to a million. You're on line at the supermarket and you reach for *TV Guide* and our magazine. You follow me?"

"Yes."

On the Scrabble board on her lap, Randy made the word S-E-X.

"Second, we start a contest of our own. Like the Irish Sweepstakes. Something big, something annual, something that becomes a household word. And guess what the first prize is going to be."

"A million dollars," Esme said.

"Guess again."

"A Rolls-Royce."

"How'd you guess?"

"She thinks just like you do," Tina said to Meyer and smiled. "I can see it runs in the family."

"Your turn," Randy said and touched her knee, touched the cloth of her denim bell bottoms with a firmness that surprised her, that made her wonder if the S-E-X had been meant for her.

"Magoo, how does the whole thing sound to you?" Meyer said.

She looked at Randy. "Great." He was looking down at his letters, bangs like blinders over his eyes. She turned to her father. "How much would the magazine cost?"

"Fifteen cents. A quarter."

"I'd buy one. Heidi would definitely buy one."

"Who's that?" Tina asked.

"A friend of my mother's. She used to be on welfare. Her son runs away from home all the time. He didn't come home last time. Heidi thinks he's in San Francisco. But she's pretty fucked up herself. She takes a lot of uppers. Anyway, the reason she'd buy the magazine is because she enters contests all the time."

"Didn't I tell you?" Meyer tapped Tina on the shoulder. "Didn't I tell you about the dream market? Thousands, hundreds of thousands of dreamers out there, that's who we're going for, the ones—"

"The things people do to their children, honest to god," Tina said and lit a cigarette. "You know what my philosophy is, don't you, honey?" She looked at Meyer and then at her children, who were shuffling through Scrabble letters to see if they could make dirty words. "My philosophy has always been, just let them do whatever they want, don't put a muzzle on those kids, let them say whatever they want, because that way they won't have anything to rebel against. This poor boy, running away, his mother probably held the reins so tight he couldn't even breathe, and when that—"

"She wasn't like that," Esme said. "She didn't make him do a lot of awful things. I've known him since I was eight, and he always wanted to leave—"

"Hey, Meyer, what's that over there?" Randy said. "That building?"

They looked to the right. "Yankee Stadium."

"Fuckin' A."

"There it is."

Randy touched Esme's leg again. "You ever been there?" She shook her head.

"What's a matter, you don't like baseball?"

"Not much."

"I can dig that. I don't know too many girls that do. I knew a girl in Oregon that did. Remember her, Rich? Rhonda Clark? Fat Rhonda."

Rich nodded. "A real fat mama. One of her thighs was about as big as—"

"It's my turn," Esme said loudly, to change the subject away from fat girls. "It's been my turn for—"

"—big as a refrigerator."

"—my turn for a long time, ever since—"

"—just fucking huge. Buck teeth too. A real dog."

"Here's my word," Esme said and used the "S" in S-E-X to make S-M-A-R-T.

"So, it's something else, isn't it?" Meyer called out.

"Who you talking to, man?" Rich said.

"Esme Singer, the gorgeous chick in the back seat." He turned to Tina. "As opposed to the gorgeous chick in the front seat."

"Chicks are for kids," Rich said.

"You wish," Randy said.

"What's 'something else, isn't it?' " Esme said.

"The contest business. Any way you slice it, this is an idea whose time has come. Totally unique. I mean, have you ever heard of something like this?" He did not wait for her answer.

"That's because there isn't anything like it. Not yet, that's what I keep telling Tina. Not yet, right, baby?"

"Right, baby," she said. "Right as rain."

"What's that?" Randy said and tapped the window.

"Yonkers Raceway," Esme said.

"Why don't we go to the races?"

"Yeah, let's go to the races, Meyer," Rich said. "Let's do something *we* want to do for once. Instead of just driving and driving and driving. It's driving me crazy."

Tina turned around. "No one drives anyone crazy but themselves. If you're bored, it's your own fault. You certainly didn't learn it from me, because whenever I feel the slightest bit bored, I mean the tiniest bit—"

"Ma, I didn't say I was bored, I said I was going crazy. I'm also hungry. In case anyone cares."

"I sure don't care," Randy said.

"We'll be there soon enough," Tina said.

"And my mother won't let you stop eating for a minute," Meyer said. "If that doesn't drive you crazy, nothing will."

"As long as there's food on the table, you won't hear me complaining."

"That's her favorite kind of victim," Meyer said.

"What kind?" Rich said.

"Captive. Hungry. She plies you with food and lays trips on you at the same time."

"What are you talkin' about, Meyer?" Randy said.

"And that's nothing compared to the trips my father can lay on you. He's the one you really have to watch out for. He'll kill you with kindness and then wonder how come you died."

"Like what kind of trips?" Rich said.

"Killer trips. Don't you think there's a reason I haven't been to see these people in four years?"

"What time are we going to get there?" Randy said.

"Too soon," Meyer said. "Too soon for my taste."

"Then why are we going?" Esme said.

"Because—" he stopped and thought about why they were going—"because every so often you have to make an appearance with certain people. Or else you'll never hear the end of it."

That was one of the reasons they were going. One of the other reasons was that Meyer wanted to hit up his millionaire uncle for a loan to get his new business started. He knew the value of a personal contact. He knew that showing up with his wife and children, not to mention the Rolls, would be the kind of collateral that would impress a man who was impressed with all of that middle-class baggage.

"Magoo? There's something we have to let you in on here." She leaned forward.

"It's in the nature of a little white lie. Itty bitty, when you get right down to it, when you think of the big lies they tell us every day, the corporations, the politicians. What I'm getting at is that it would make it a lot easier for my super-square folks to deal with this scene if they thought Tina and I were married. If you get my meaning."

"Esme," Rich said, "you ruined all the letters." She looked down. In the center of the board was F-U-C-K-F-A-C-E.

"On a personal level, Magoo, you don't have to say anything," Meyer said. "I already told them we're married. I just wanted to let you in on it."

"Sure," Esme said quietly.

"What?"

"I said sure." But she was not at all sure.

"It would just make it easier all around," Meyer said. "The way I see it, who needs more hassles with these people than there's already going to be?"

"Sure," Esme whispered. "Yeah." She nodded her head and looked out the window. They drove past a shopping center, a gas station, a fire station, a string of billboards.

"Whose turn is it?" Rich said.

"I don't want to play anymore," Esme said.

"Me neither," Randy said.

"Is everything still groovy back there?" Meyer called out.

"Yeah," Esme said.

"When are we going to get there?" Rich said.

"When we get there," Meyer said.

"And not a moment before," Tina said. "My goodness, isn't this pretty. Finally, some trees. Isn't this spectacular. Look, boys, it's fall here. Meyer, look over there, that patch of trees with the red leaves."

"She likes fall," Randy said quietly to Esme, "because we don't have fall in Seattle. She's been watching for fall the whole drive." He turned and looked out the window. He played an imaginary guitar in his lap and tapped his foot in time to the beat.

She sat in the car, the marvelous car, with her father and these people she was supposed to pretend she was related to. She remembered the list of her mother's failings, the worst things her mother had ever done, the moronic things she did every day, every night, including fucking some guy she went out with two weeks ago last Thursday, fucking him loud enough so that it woke Esme up in the middle of the night and she thought her mother was being murdered, until she got up and crept into the living room and saw them on the couch in the dark, dark enough so that they didn't see her.

She did not know what she was going to do with the list now, because she did not want to live with her father, with Tina, with these boys, with anyone. She had lived with so many people already, she had been related to so many people, but not really related. She had been related the way people are when they fuck, they're pressed together and then they let go and it's like it never happened, it doesn't even show afterward. Her mother looked the same the next morning as she looked every morning. There wasn't a trace of that noise, there wasn't anything that gave her away.

Esme closed her eyes now and counted up all of the stepbrothers and stepsisters she had ever had. It was like an accident, all of them ending up together in the same house and calling it a family, and then they would call it off, like stopping a movie in the middle, like stopping the car before you got to where you were going, pulling up on the side of the road and saying, this is it, trip's over, visit's up.

Randy leaned over to her and whispered, "Ever get high?"

She moved her head, first a nod, then a shake. She shrugged. "Almost," she said.

"I'll turn you on when we get there," he whispered.

Then he touched her thigh with his hand, actually pressed his palm against the leg of her pants and held it there for a moment, squeezed it, let go.

She stared at the place he had touched. Or maybe he hadn't. Maybe she had made it up. She reconstructed the event, went over it four or five times. She had to stop herself from doing to her leg what he had done to her leg.

Do it again, she wanted to say. Do it for a long time this time, so I can be sure it really happened.

Now That Before Was History

THEY HAD BEEN born in the same month but different years. She was about to turn sixty-nine, and he, seventy. To their younger grandchildren, and great-nieces and great-nephews, they were ancient, as old as anyone could be. Their children simply wondered how, meaning when, they had grown so old, and who, meaning which one of them, would take care of them when they could no longer take care of themselves. They excluded their brother Meyer from the running, as they had come to exclude him from all other family affairs, excluded him so thoroughly that his name was not even brought up as a possibility and then dropped; it was just left unsaid, like a curse they were afraid to invoke by its mere mention.

Now the Winesap apples fell from the trees behind the house on Howard Street where they had lived for more than forty years, fell into the bushel baskets they had placed here and there on the lawn, fell onto the hard ground and were left there to be picked up and taken away by the cleaning woman's young son. *The shvartzes*, Dot Singer called them behind their backs, as if that were their surname.

"It means Negroes," Esme whispered to Randy at the dinner table that night, whispered over the din of three or four conversations.

All of the table leaves had been put in to seat three generations of Singers, including Meyer's brother and sister, several of their children, and Tina, Meyer's new wife, the newest Singer-by-marriage, who for dinner had pinned up her long hair into a stylish bun and put on white sailor pants and a navy-blue knit pullover. She had considered taking off some of her rings, the rings on each of her fingers, but instead had only moved one that looked like a wedding band from the middle to the ring finger of her left hand.

"In what language?" Randy whispered back and moved his foot under the table so that it touched Esme's. His attention, his proximity, made her feel giddy, giggly. She was thinking about what would happen when they smoked pot. Maybe this time she would get high; maybe she would hallucinate.

"Northern California, Oregon, and before that Dayton, Ohio," Tina explained to Meyer's sister Ruth. "My kids were born in Dayton. When my husband died my kids were little, eight and six. There wasn't much for a single woman to do there, so I packed up the car and we split."

"Split?" said Dot.

"You know, left."

"And you went where?"

"First to northern California. Then Oregon."

"And now Seattle?" Dot said. There was skepticism, opprobrium, in her voice, as if Tina's itinerary were evidence that she was a fugitive from justice, that her son had brought home a vagabond, her son who disappeared for months at a time himself, her son who had forgotten for four years where he came from and showed up now with love beads and a Rolls-Royce, a car, in Dot's opinion, that was strictly for *goyim*, or for racketeers.

"Yes," Tina said. "It's a wonderful city. You and your husband will have to come visit us. Maybe for Christmas."

"As long as you're happy," Dot said and reached for the gravy dish. She had suspected the worst, and it had just been confirmed. If she had once hoped to see her son return a changed man, a man with a conscience, with a clear sense of right and wrong, good and evil, the values she had taught him as a child, the values she had tried to instill in all of her children— All of them except Meyer had listened to her. All of them except Meyer had turned out the way she had wanted them to. "Far be it from me to tell another person what's going to make them happy. I'll tell you one thing, you don't get to be my age and not pick up a thing or two about human nature."

"Of course," Tina said.

"Life is full of lessons," Dot said. "Chock full. Like the other day at the B'nai B'rith, who should I run into but Esther Weidman's daughter Maxine, Maxine who went to high school with Meyer, and the first thing she wants to know is how she can get in touch with Meyer. Normally, I'd have to tell her what I tell everyone, Your guess is as good as mine. But it just so happens, I told her, that Meyer is on his way here—" She glanced down the table to make sure that he had really arrived. What she saw made her heart break. Her youngest child a middle-aged man. Her grown son dressed up like he was going to a love-in, a demonstration. "Your children can break your heart," she said to Tina. "Just wait and see. You young people—the illusions you have could fill a book." She spread her thumb and forefinger. "A big, fat book."

"I guess time will tell," Tina said.

"It certainly will. You can count on that."

"All things considered, my kids have been super," Tina said.

"Still and all, that's something you've done," Dot conceded. "Raising two boys on your own." Not that she had done a first-rate job, as you could see from looking at the two hippies at her table, putting away her brisket like there was no tomorrow.

"I keep thinking that the worst is yet to come," Tina said.

"I don't think it ends until they're graduated from college and married," Ruth said. "My oldest son just started Dartmouth and he's called us three times in the last week. The phone bills alone—"

"Yale wasn't good enough for him," Dot said. "He had to go to New Hampshire and help keep the phone company in business. But I don't have to tell you that when they get to be a certain age you can shout 'Fire' and you might as well be talking to the wall."

At the other end of the table, Meyer was describing his new company to his father, Goody, and brother, Herbert. "What we're going after here is the dream market, what we're going to be selling here is hope. You know what they say?"

"What?"

"Everyone loves a winner. And everyone loves to win."

"Meyer, you have to have a plan," Goody said. "You can't do nothing without one."

"Even if all you're selling is dreams," Herbert said. "Or was it hope you said you were peddling?"

Meyer looked at his brother and knew why he had stayed away all these years.

"Even knitting needles," Goody said. "You still need a plan."

He had stayed away because you couldn't say three words around here without getting bombarded with useless advice, with sidelong glances. Trust was a word that had never made it into their vocabulary.

. . .

It was like a dream. The way Esme was lying on the opened-up Castro Convertible in the living room under the covers long after everyone else had gone upstairs to bed, thinking, wouldn't it be something if he came down here and touched my leg the way he did today in the car, wouldn't it be something if he gave me a kiss on the lips at the same time as he touched my leg, now that would be something.

The way she was lying there in the dark with her eyes closed imagining a kiss and she heard the stairs creaking and thought, he's coming to kiss me and thought, no, I'm hearing things, but oh, but what if I'm not, what will I do, and she could feel her heart pound as she was sure it would if he actually touched her, and then he would know that she had never kissed anyone because if she had her heart would not be pounding like this, if she had she would know exactly what to do when he kissed her, but what would probably happen, what would probably happen is that nothing would happen, he would just touch her leg again in the car on the way back to New York, if he had even touched it in the first place.

So that when she opened her eyes and saw the outline of a

figure that looked like his at the bottom of the stairs, she thought, no, I'm seeing things, the way Winky had seen Deana's feet that night in the closet in Southampton.

"Are you awake?" Randy whispered.

She could not speak.

"Esme."

"Yes." She whispered, she was sure he could hear her heart. He was wearing dark-colored pajamas. "Did I wake you?"

She shook her head and moved up to prop her head against the back of the couch.

He stood at the side of the bed and held out his hand. "You mind?" he said quietly.

"What?"

"Here." He moved his hand closer.

"What time is it?" She could not think of anything else to say. She did not take his hand.

"It's time to woolly bully."

"What?"

He sat down on the edge of the bed and did what he had done that afternoon but now she was wearing a nightgown and they were in bed even though she was under the covers and he was just sitting there, touching her thigh, but now he touched it for a long time, now she was sure his hand was really on her leg, pressing and rubbing and kneading, so that when he let go, she thought, why did you stop, don't stop.

He turned around and lay down on his side next to her. He draped his arm across her waist.

"Do you think I'm too tall?" she said.

"For what?"

"A girl."

"How tall are you?"

"Five-nine."

"That's tall for a girl. But not too tall."

"I'd like to be five-five. Or five-six. I wouldn't mind that. I'll die if I grow any more."

"I'll die if I don't."

"How tall are you?"

He took her hand and moved it to the front of his pajama bottoms and pressed her palm against the material and what was beneath it. She did not know what he was doing, what had happened to this thing that was supposed to hang between his legs.

He let go of her hand and held the elastic waist of his pajamas and pulled it down. When she saw what she was afraid she would see, she shut her eyes and tightened her arm against her side.

"It won't bite," he said and took her hand again. "Here." He put her hand on it, and when she started to pull back, he clamped his hand over hers and moved it up and down. "Do that," he said. "Like this," he said and continued to move her hand up and down over the strange skin that was smoother than butter, hard as bone. "This way," he kept saying and moving steadily next to her. "Just like this, do this."

She was trying but she did not know what she was trying to do, or why. Suddenly he shuddered, flinched. He said, "Stop, stop" quickly, as if in pain, and pushed her away. She was sure it was because she had done something wrong.

"Randy?"

He exhaled hard. "Huh."

But now she was afraid to speak.

"Ju say something?"

"No," she said.

"I guess it's pretty late."

"I guess so."

"Time to turn in." He sat up and reached for his pajama bottoms, twisted around his ankles. "Tomorrow's another day." He swung his bare legs over the side of the bed and stood up, his rear end facing her, a pattern of shadows emerging across his buttocks as he squatted to pull up his pajamas. He turned and said, "Hey, g'night."

"G'night."

"Sleep tight."

She nodded.

"Catch ya later."

"Yeah," she said.

He walked across the living room in the dark that to her eye had become light, so that now she could see the messages on the framed needlepoint hangings over the fireplace, she could see Randy's hand brush against the end table as he walked away from her. When he was out of sight, the stairs began to creak from his steps the way they had before, and suddenly the word "before" assumed a resonance, encompassed a drama, stood for a moment in history.

THE WORLD IS SO FULL OF A NUMBER OF THINGS—she read the words her grandmother had stitched in needlepoint—I'M SURE WE SHOULD ALL BE AS HAPPY AS KINGS. She listened for the sound of his feet on the stairs. Maybe he would turn around and come back and lie down next to her on the bed again. Maybe he would put his arm around her and tell her that she was pretty and that he liked girls that were a little bit fat, that was okay with him, but what he really wanted now, now that he was so close to her, now that she really understood him, now that she had touched him there, now that before was history, what he wanted now was a kiss.

More than Fourteen Cents

I WILL JUST GET up and act normal, she thought. The way my mother gets up in the morning and acts normal after she does those things with men in the middle of the night.

With her eyes still closed, she turned over and drew one of the down pillows close to her, pulled it against her chest like a baby, like a boy's head. She opened her eyes and kissed it, ran her hand down the middle, caressed the corner.

Voices came from the kitchen. Her father and her grandfather. Fragments of sentences, the answer to a question she had not heard, the end of a statement lost in the whistle of the tea kettle.

" . . . foolish?" Meyer said. "Says who?"

"The reason for family," Goody said, "the reason is to help out when you're under the . . . "

" . . . I never said I didn't appreciate . . . "

" . . . Mother thinks—"

"Thinks what?"

"She doesn't know what to think no more . . . just not used to all the changes, so she sometimes carries on. . . . nice girl, Meyer, this Tina, nice boys she's got too. Nice of her to take Mother to the beauty parlor this early. Here, take a saucer. Not that one, this one here."

There was the sound of running water, voices muffled, an eggshell being cracked.

" . . . not asking you. Wouldn't ask you for that much."

"So you'll ask your Uncle Artie."

"I plan to."

"At least he'll hear you out, even if he doesn't . . . "

" . . . not looking for a handout. I want a loan . . . "

" . . . him sending money to Georgia all these years—" Goody pronounced it, as he always had, with three syllables, accent on the first. Jor-jee-uh.

"I never asked him to do that."

"Someone had to."

"Behind my back?"

"Big shot. We couldn't find you. I told you before, I'll tell you again. If the family doesn't take care of the family—"

"Since when did Artie take care of you?"

"I don't keep score, he don't—"

"Because you know if you did—"

"I don't know nothing about that. I know that when I retired from needles he said, 'Goody, you want to work for the company now, you say the word.' I say, 'Okay, here I am,' and he gives me fifteen, twenty restaurants the first month. Four percent commission, six percent if I'm over a hundred, and—"

"What kind of bullshit is that? Nickel-and-diming your brother. Like he's doing you a favor."

"You want a job? In a minute he'd give you one. Less than a minute. You know why? Because he's your uncle. Because—"

"I don't want a job. I want a loan."

"So you'll ask him. You'll see what he says. But let me tell you something, Meyer, you need that fancy-shmancy car of yours like you need a hole in the wall."

Their voices grew fainter, as if they had moved to the other side of the kitchen, as if they were talking into their hands.

Esme tiptoed across the room and pressed herself against the doorjamb, ear toward the kitchen.

" . . . not impressed . . . that's what he'll tell you . . . throwing around money like there was no . . . "

" . . . didn't cost me a dime . . . not even mine for Christ's sake . . . a friend of Tina's . . . investor in the company . . . whiz, a real whiz . . . simple principle, go where the bucks is . . . "

" . . . between the car and the . . . stinks, Meyer, like rotten fish."

"Psssst!"

Esme froze.

"Psssst! Up here."

She peered around the doorjamb and up the stairs. Randy

stood at the top on the landing wearing jeans, no shirt. "C'ma, c'ma, c'ma, c'ma, c'ma, c'ma, wild thang." He grinned. "You make ma heart sing." He tapped out a beat on the bannister; he scratched his bare stomach.

She held up her hand to him, fanned her fingers. "Oh. Hi." As casual as she could be. Like nothing had happened.

But he kept tapping "Wild Thing" with his fingers.

She made his heart sing.

That was what he was trying to tell her, that's why he had picked that song.

"Where'd everyone go?" Randy bounded down the stairs. "Woke up and it was deserted. What's for breakfast? Where's Grandma? Where's Gramps?"

She slipped her arms into a workshirt. When she turned around, he was gone.

"Morning, Meyer, morning, Grandpa," she heard him say. "Where's everyone at? What's cooking?"

"Good morning to you, young fella," Goody said. "You'll catch cold, no shirt. Drafts all over the place."

"Don't sweat it, Gramps, my flesh is drip dry, wear and tear in any kinda weather. As long as we're together. Right, Meyer? Can you dig it?"

She heard her father laugh.

She heard the contempt for Goody in Randy's voice. She heard nothing in his voice for her.

Like nothing had happened. Like it had meant nothing to him that he had come to see her in the middle of the night that way.

She buttoned the workshirt and tried to pull it away from her body, so that her breasts, her bulging breasts, would not show.

"Where'd Rich go? Where's Mom?"

"Little ride," Goody said. "Took Dot to the beauty parlor over'n West Haven. Sit down. Meyer, put in some toast for him. You want juice. Here. Here's juice. How are you this morning, young fella? Sleep good?"

"Real good."

"Good. Here. For the toast."

"Thanks."

"You need shoes?"

"What?"

"Shoes. You need shoes?"

"Right now? You want me to put on my shoes?"

"Good morning, Magoo," Meyer said as Esme came into the kitchen.

"Good morning, Stu," she said. She did not look at him. She pulled on the front ends of her workshirt, she tipped her head slightly forward to let her hair cover the side of her face.

"How's by you, Magoo?" Meyer said.

"Okay, Stu."

"Sit down, sit down," Goody said. "Next to this fella here. I didn't hear what you said your name was."

"Where'd you get that name?" Randy said. "Esme. I never heard it before."

"It was her mother's idea," Meyer said. "She had a whole list of kooky names. Actresses, singers. Hedy. Myra. Marlene."

"What if she was a boy?" Randy said.

"What if she *was* a boy," Meyer said and smiled at her. "She'd be a helluva cute guy."

"Her *name*," Randy said.

Esme held her head down again to make her hair fall over her face.

"Cary," Meyer said. "Her mother wanted to call her Cary. After guess-who."

"What'd you want?"

"George."

"No. Come on, really, Meyer."

"What's wrong with George?"

"It's like Joe. It's like a piece of wood, a two-by-four. No-where."

"That's why they made her a girl, so she wouldn't be nowhere," Meyer said. "How many pieces of toast do you want?"

"Two," Randy said.

"Magoo?"

"One."

"What about you, young lady," Goody said, "you sleep good too?"

She nodded.

"What's 'a matter, you can't talk?"

She shrugged.

"The bed all right?" Goody said.

"Huh?"

"Grandma says some of the springs are busted. Not in the center of the bed. Around the outside."

"It felt okay to me."

"Just one person sleeping in it, I guess it's okay. You want cereal or eggs?"

"Neither."

"Just toast?"

"Cinnamon toast."

"I'll have cereal," Randy said.

"Good appetite. What kind? We got—" He got up and went to the cabinet. "Wheaties. Corn Flakes. Shredded Wheat."

"I hate Shredded Wheat," Randy said.

"Make up your mind," Goody said. "Quick."

"Maybe I'll have eggs instead," Randy said.

Meyer put a plate of toast on the table.

"Have some cereal," Goody said.

"You want eggs, make your own," Meyer said.

Randy rolled his eyes and Esme tried not to stare at his bare chest, with its handful of curly hairs.

"Don't get up," Goody said.

"I'll do it," Esme said and started to stand.

"Sit. Eat. Both a you," Goody said. "Eat now. We get shoes later. After breakfast. When the rest of 'em come back."

"What's he talking about?" Randy said.

"Shoe Town," Esme said. "He likes to take us there. Because it's discount."

"Cut-rate," Goody said. "Big-name brands marked down. Boots. Sneakers. Everything. Last year—" Goody looked at Esme. "Tell him about them shoes your mother got last year." Without waiting for her to speak, he turned to Randy. "Last year we took Georgia to Shoe Town. First pair of shoes she tries on, she says, 'I like these, they fit good,' I say, 'you like 'em?', she says, 'yup, I like 'em,' I say, 'good, buy three pair just like 'em. So you won't run out.' "

"But she didn't," Esme said. "She only bought one."

"One shoe?" Randy said.

"One pair."

"How come not three?"

"Because she only has two feet," Esme said.

Randy smiled and she was certain that he would like her more now.

"When everyone comes back, we'll go to Shoe Town," Goody said. "They sell socks too. Good socks."

"Is that all we're going to do here?" Randy said. "Buy shoes and socks?"

"Wiseguy," Meyer said and sat down at the table with them.

"I'm still hungry," Randy said.

"Then get up off your ass and fix something."

"Sit down," Goody said. "You want eggs or cereal?"

"I guess—"

"You're having cereal," Meyer said.

"He asked me which—" Randy pointed to Goody.

"And I'm telling you which," Meyer said.

"Look, if he—"

"Don't call him 'he.' "

"Jesus Christ, Meyer, for Christ's sakes alive, man."

"This ain't a commune, kiddo."

"What's that supposed to mean?"

"It means you can't do your own goddam thing just because you're in the mood to. Got that?"

Randy nodded.

"Now, sit down, all of you," Goody said, though everyone

but him was sitting. "There's Shredded Wheat, Corn Flakes, Wheaties. Breakfast of champions. Esme?"

"I don't want any. I'm on a diet."

"Don't tell your grandmother."

"Why?"

"She wants you should eat her food," Meyer said snidely. "She wants you should be fat."

"I already am."

"I should be so fat," Goody said, "and ugly too. That's some face she's got on her." He looked at Randy. "Isn't it?" Randy nodded. "A face only a grandmother could love."

"Grandpa, stop it."

"I don't know what I'd do if I was so ugly," he said. "Now, what about some grapefruit. That's what you want." He opened the heavy refrigerator door.

"Dad," Meyer said. "Enough already."

"You gotta have a good breakfast." Goody spoke to them from behind the refrigerator door. "Grapefruit. Apples. We got apples, we got nectarines, we got—what's this here? Fruit cocktail. Who wants fruit cocktail?"

"How about shrimp cocktail," Randy said and tapped his forefingers against the edge of the table like drumsticks.

Esme laughed.

"And eggrolls," he said. "And pizza."

"Cut it," Meyer muttered. "Now."

"No pizza for breakfast," Goody said. He brought two grapefruit halves to the table. "Here. Special spoons too. Don't need to cut the grapefruit, just use this." The tips of the spoons were serrated. "Grandma got them from somewhere. On TV."

"We have these," Esme said. "We also have special sugar. It's in the shape of little colored chunks. When you put it on the grapefruit, it runs and makes all these weird colors."

"Very psychedelic," Randy said and dug his spoon into the fruit.

"Actually, it comes from Bonwit Teller," Esme said. "My mother got it for free because she works there."

"Speaking of your mother," Meyer said, "have you heard from Billy the Kid lately?"

"I think she talks to him sometimes."

"Who's Billy the Kid?" Randy said.

"Georgia's ex," Meyer said. "Almost ex. Right?"

Esme nodded.

"Oh, him," Randy said. "The rich one."

"That's the one," Meyer said.

"The dirty cheapskate," Randy said.

"Says who?" Esme said.

"Meyer. Didn't you, Meyer?"

Esme looked at Meyer.

Meyer took a deep breath and stared at Randy, looking away from Esme.

"Finish your grapefruit," Goody said. "Hurry up. Before they come home." He stood by the table and pointed at the food.

"It comes with the territory," Meyer said.

"What territory?" Randy said.

"Eat your grapefruit," Goody said.

"I'm *eating*," Esme said.

"People get rich, they get stingy," Meyer said. "Hold on to their money something fierce. It's a law of nature."

"You going to do that when you get rich, Meyer?" Randy said.

"You bet your ass I am."

"You're going to keep it all for yourself?" Esme said.

"Me and a few other people named Singer."

"Oh."

"What did you think, Magoo? You thought I wouldn't give you any?"

She shrugged.

"If I had fourteen cents," he said, "I'd give you seven."

"I hope you make more than that."

He laughed. "You do, do you?"

She nodded.

"What are you going to spend it on?"

"I don't know. Clothes. Records. I guess posters."

"That's all?"

"College," Goody said. "Put away some of that money so she can go to college. Someplace good. Like Smith." He pronounced it Smit. "Where your cousin Sharon went."

"Magoo, when you get ready to go to college," Meyer said, "we'll be rolling in dough. We'll be *ungeshtupt mit gelt.*"

"What's that mean?"

"Don't talk and eat at the same time," Goody said. "Bad for the digestion."

The doorbell rang, a cute ring, five short taps on the bell, two long ones. Goody turned and walked out of the kitchen.

"Bad for the digestion," Meyer said quietly. "How do you like that?" He looked from Randy to Esme. "Believe that one and the next thing he'll tell you is that the sun sets in the east."

"What do you expect from him," Randy answered in the same low voice. "I mean, he's *so* old."

"You should have heard what he said this morning," Meyer whispered. "He says I need the Rolls like I need *a hole in the wall.*"

"Meyer, you goddam son of a gun, where are you?" The disembodied voice bellowed through the house. Then he was there, at the kitchen door, in a dark green uniform, a cap with an Esso decal. Her father got up and they went to each other and embraced, the gas-station attendant and the man in the brown-and-gold dashiki. "I never thought I'd live to see the day," Charlie Edelman said. "That's your Rolls-Royce, isn't it, you old son of a gun."

Esme lowered her eyes, kept her head down, as the two men hugged. She did not want to see her father, not because he had lied about the car or his marriage to Tina. Not because he called Billy a cheapskate. Not because he was a hippie and maybe even a crook, which were all bad enough. But because his eyes filled with tears as soon as he put his arms around Charlie. She could not stand it when people showed their feelings that way, especially people she was related to.

The Study of Perfection

LIKE EUROPEANS, LEAH'S family sat down late to dinner. Often there were guests—writers, photographers, psychiatrists, who wrote books, articles for the *Times* Sunday magazine. The next day Leah would tell Esme who had come, what had happened. "My parents had a huge fight about Becket," she told her one day. "But I think my father's right." On her own, Esme looked in the encyclopedia, the only place she knew to look. Becket, she read, English Roman Catholic martyr, archbishop of Canterbury, 1118–1170. The things they knew! Even Leah, who was only fourteen. She herself—her ignorance was overwhelming, insuperable. The evenings she spent at their house she prayed that no one would speak to her, no one would ask what her opinions were. She had none. Like a stone, like an idiot.

A Wednesday night in March. Leah's father, Don, had just come back from Paris, where he had gone to photograph the last days of Les Halles for *Life*. In the living room before dinner, he showed them—Leah, Esme, a friend of his named Will Kluger—some of the shots the magazine had not used, contact sheets, black-and-white prints. A plump woman leaning into a stack of crates, ears of corn, bins of carrots, a flower merchant weeping, the Métro tunnel with the tile sign that said LES HALLES. Much more than the end of an era, Don said, the market that had begun in 1135. You might as well demolish a religion, a country, a people.

"Well, we're in the process of doing that ourselves," Will said to Don. "And we took lessons from the French on that one, didn't we?"

It was 1969. Will had brought a petition for Don and his wife, Abby, to sign, another petition. *An end to U.S. imperialism in Southeast Asia . . . innocent lives . . . the urgency for Congress to act . . .* The list of names was twelve pages long. It was just the beginning, he said. Or maybe the end. He was soft-spoken, a tall, burly man, always smoking an unfiltered cigarette, shrouded in smoke, like the smoke in the picture of Dylan Thomas that Don Marks had taken.

Will stubbed out his cigarette and picked up a photograph. He lifted his glasses from his nose and drew the picture close to his face. "This is it," he said and extended his arm to see it from a distance.

"What?"

"What Cartier-Bresson means when he talks about *le moment décisif*. 'A supreme moment captured with a single shot.' How many did you take of this scene?"

"I don't know."

Will continued to look at the picture. A little boy leaping into the air to catch an orange. "Wasn't he the one who said that if you took two hundred pictures you'd be lucky if one of them was any good?"

"I think those were my words," Don said and smiled.

"Two hundred?" Leah said. "How come so many?"

It was the question Esme wanted to ask but would not dare to.

"Just consider it a given," Don said. "When you get really good, the odds get better—one out of every hundred and fifty."

"But why?"

"In a random group of two hundred women, how many do you suppose will be breathtaking? Not just all right, not just attractive, but genuinely magnificent?"

"But if the two hundred pictures are taken by *you*," Leah said, "then it's not a random group."

"The point is that it might as well be," Don said.

"He's right, Leah," Will said. "Not just about taking pictures. About any kind of creation." He looked again at the picture of the boy leaping. "Think of poor Mrs. Tolstoi writing out *War and Peace* seven times."

"They're not bad, are they?" It was Abby's voice. She had just appeared at the entrance to the living room in dark pants, a Mexican blouse with brightly colored embroidered borders.

"Not bad at all."

"They'd make a marvelous book."

"Who could you get to write the text?"

"Why not Daddy?" Leah said.

"No, I think we want a real writer."

"Let's talk about it downstairs," Abby said. "Dinner's ready."

"What about Queneau? Raymond Queneau."

"That's a thought."

They rose, picked up their glasses, their cigarettes. Leah and Esme led the way down the stairs, the narrow staircase in the narrow house, its elegance so underdone that it was shabby, an affectation—the walls of books, the upholstery on the chairs and couch worn down, worn through, the bare wood floors. On the kitchen counters, on the front hall table with the house keys and the mail were paperback biographies, autobiographies, Russian novels, prices printed on the back in pounds and pence.

Their lives are perfect, Esme thought as she sat down next to Leah, their lives are easy.

The cloth napkins did not match, the edges were slightly frayed. Leah had bought the tiny silver salt and pepper shakers at Bonnier's the Christmas before. On the wall near the table were two small framed molas.

"It's *cassoulet*," Abby said. "French peasant stew. I wish we could buy that coarse-grained bread around here. Leah, remember our bakery in Avignon?"

"Of course."

They tore off chunks of Italian bread and dipped them in the spicy stew.

"There's probably a place downtown," Will said. "Beverly and I go to a bakery on Mulberry Street. Around the corner from Puglia's."

"You know, Puglia's has the best *zabaglione* in town," Don said.

"There's a place we've been to—" Abby said.

"It's Puglia's," Don said.

"I thought it was—"

"No." He shook his head. "It's the one with the long tables. You sit next to strangers."

"They also have the best mussels *a raganati*," Leah said.

"No, the best are in Sardinia," Don said. "At the Café Salta."

"Okay, the best *here* then."

"Fair enough."

"I thought that place was called Luigi's," Abby said.

"Which one?"

"Puglia's. Isn't it the one with the fat waitress who puts the bottles of wine on the table and says she'll be right back with the nipples?"

"That's the one."

"How come I thought it was called Luigi's?"

"What nipples?" Will said.

"You know, like a baby bottle."

"Oh."

"They do have marvelous *zabaglione*."

"It's not hard to make," Abby said. "Marsala. Egg yolks. Sugar." She had long unpainted fingernails, an ornate silver wedding band that she twisted around her finger as she spoke. "It's as easy as pie. Which I've never understood. Pie isn't easy to make. Especially the crust."

"Maybe the expression means easy to *eat*," Will said.

Esme was trying to chew without moving her mouth, without making a sound.

"I'd never considered that before," Abby said.

"Well," Will said, "even if it is easy to make—Rilke wasn't always right."

"About what?"

" 'Almost everything serious is difficult and everything is serious.' "

"It's a wonderful thought," Don said, "but his logic is slightly off. It's not quite a tautology but it's—"

"It makes perfect sense to me," Abby said. "Everything is serious. And almost everything is difficult. That's all he's saying."

"That's quite a lot, don't you think?"

"I guess it's a bit dire."

"Just a bit," Don said.

Esme's fork slipped out of her hand and fell in her lap. She was sure they would ask her what a tautology was.

"Here, have some more," Abby said. She passed the clay pot of *cassoulet* to Will. "Esme, Leah, have some more."

They talked about Solzhenitsyn, Eldridge Cleaver, and a novelist they knew, a name Esme had never heard.

"His sense of humor isn't what it ought to be," Don said.

"His latest book isn't what it ought to be," Abby said.

"I told you this story, didn't I?" Will said. "The time he got drunk at our house and made a pass at Beverly. It was more of a grope. A lunge, actually. He knocked over a candlestick with a lighted candle in it."

"Subtlety was never his strong suit," Don said.

"Or grace," Abby said. "Despite what he called his first book."

"What was that?"

"*A Time of Grace.*"

"What an awful title."

"Maybe it was called *A Time of Subtlety.*"

"It's not exactly the best time for it, is it?" Will said. "Subtlety, that is. You have to make a good bit of noise these days to compete. Even to be heard."

"It depends what effect you're after," Don said. "If all you want is to *record*, well, yes, you do have to shout, but presumably an artist has a higher—"

"But what about a journalist?" Will said. "Does he have an obligation to be subtle?"

"No one has an obligation to be subtle," Abby said. "That's just a matter of taste."

"But what's taste?" Will said. "Is it influenced more by personality or politics?"

"Culture," Don said.

"Culture," Will repeated and paused. "Then is culture what Matthew Arnold says it is—the study of perfection—or what Andy Warhol says it is—"

"Or what Diane Arbus says it is," Abby said. "The study of freaks. Girls, do you want something more to drink?"

"No, thanks," Esme said.

"Leah?"

Leah shook her head.

"Speaking of freaks," Will said, "did you see the new film about the psychiatric ward?"

"We thought it was marvelous," Don said.

"What's it called again?" Will said.

"*Titticut Follies.*"

"Brilliant," Don said.

"It is a fine movie," Will said. "I don't know if I'd—do you really think so?"

"Absolutely. The conceit. The camera work. More wine?"

"Sure."

"Abby?"

She nodded and held out her glass.

"What about Norman's movie?" Will said. "Have you seen that?"

"No, how is it?"

Will made his hand shimmy. "Just so-so. You know he's running for mayor."

"We heard that at a party the other night. We thought it was a joke."

"He can't be serious," Abby said.

"He is. He wants to form, quote, a hip coalition of the left and right, unquote."

"Sounds like him," Abby said. "Insane."

"Why insane?"

"He's not a politician. He's a journalist."

"He's a writer," Don said.

"Jesus, Don, let's not get into that again."

Don turned to Will. "Abby took his little display here last Christmas personally."

"I didn't take it personally. I just said I didn't want him in my house again. And I certainly wouldn't vote for him, even if he were running for dog catcher."

"Lighten up a little," Don said.

"Really, Mother, you should."

"You adored *Armies of the Night*," Don said.

"I most certainly did not. I ad*mired* it. As much of it as I could stand to read."

"He is more of a man's—" Don started to say.

"Oh, balls."

"All I meant was—"

"I know what you meant."

"How can you know—"

"Leah," Don said, "what do *you* think about Norman?"

"Mother's right about his manners." She turned to her father. "So I guess I'd say he's brilliant but insufferable."

"That's exactly what your mother thinks," Don said.

"It is not!" Abby said.

"Mother, you always get so excited about this," Leah said. "It's really not—"

"I'm sure Esme is used to a little healthy dissension at the dinner table," Don said. "Aren't you, Esme?"

She nodded.

"And what do *your* parents fight about over dinner?" Will said. "Surely Norman Mailer can't inspire every domestic altercation in New York. Although I'm sure he'd be thrilled to think that he did."

"They don't fight about anything," Esme said. "They're divorced. Which they've been for ages, since before it was chic."

"Is that what they're calling it these days?" Abby said.

"Well, some people, like my mother—" She had thought she was being so clever, repeating one of her mother's lines. From now on, she would just answer yes or no, and if she did not know which was right, she would fake it, nod or shake her head so faintly that it could mean either.

"That is an interesting way to characterize it," Will said. "Tell me, what else do you think is chic?"

"Me?"

He nodded.

She felt her throat constrict. "I guess I was just kidding."

"Come on. Let's hear."

She tried to look like she was thinking, putting her mind to it, but she was dizzy with nervousness. "I guess things that are chic would be—"

"What about drugs?" Will said. "Are they chic? Or maybe it depends which drug we're talking about."

"I guess so," Esme said.

"Chic doesn't mean popular," Leah said. "It means fashionable. Which is entirely different. Rollers are popular but not chic. Polyester is popular but not chic. But Esme was using chic ironically. Weren't you?"

Esme nodded.

"Maybe she wasn't being ironic," Will said. "I read in the *Times* the other day that one in four marriages ends in divorce. Isn't that incredible?"

"That it's so many or so few?" Abby said.

"My, my," Don said.

"My, my what?"

"You've started to speak so cryptically."

"Not really."

The phone rang in the alcove across the room.

"Leah, love, would you get that?" her father said. She got up and left the table.

"It's probably Beverly," Will said. He looked at his watch. "Jesus."

"What time is it?"

"Eleven."

"Would you like coffee or tea?"

"It's too late for me."

"Don?"

He shook his head.

When Leah returned to the table, Don said, "Who was it?"

"No one." She sat down and put her napkin back in her lap.

"What do you mean, no one?"

"Just no one."

"A wrong number?"

Will turned to her. "She must have a suitor. Maybe even a beau." Her cheeks reddened. "Goodness, I think I've hit the jackpot."

"Leave her alone," Abby said.

"She's not too young for a beau," Will said.

"No girl is ever too young for a beau," Abby said.

"Is that the advice you give your patients?" Don said.

"Only the ones old enough to handle it. If you're finished, would you pass your plate down here."

They have answers for everything, Esme thought. They speak as if their lines had been written for them, as if they had been taken from a play, from one of the foreign movies Leah took her to that she pretended to like.

"Esme, can I drop you off somewhere?" Will said. "As soon as I hear from my wife, I'll hop a cab."

"I can walk. It's not far."

"But it's so late."

"I usually walk. I just live a few blocks from here."

"More like ten," Don said.

"It's okay. Don't worry about it."

"You sure you don't want to stay over?"

She nodded.

"Is that yes or no?"

"No. No thank you."

"Well, the least Will can do is drop you—"

"Daddy, she doesn't want him to. She really doesn't. I know she doesn't."

"For the life of me, I don't understand why not."

"Just take it as a given," Leah said. "Along with the two hundred photographs and the magnificent women."

.   .   .

She adored the anonymity, the night, the tall street lights on Madison, her shadow on the curb, her reflection in the window of a dress shop for pregnant women. No more explaining to do, apologizing to them for who she was, who she was not. Here on the street she was safe, she was happy. Her heels clicked against the pavement. A scaffold had just gone up, they were digging a pit in the ground, a crane twenty stories high was parked on the street. Near the corner of Eighty-sixth Street, waiting to cross, was a man who looked like Warren Gold, except Warren lived in the Village.

"Hey, is that you?"

"What?" he said and turned to her.

"Warren, right?"

He nodded faintly. He did not know who she was.

"I'm Esme. I met you at a party at Sy's, you know, the decorator, a few years ago. I think two years ago." She knew exactly when they had met, because the following day, and in the days and weeks after that, she kept calling him and hanging up as soon as he answered the phone.

"Yeah. I remember now." He held out his hand. She shook it. He was her height, his curly hair was grown to a thick Afro and starting to thin in front.

"I wasn't sure it was you," she said. "It's been a long time."

"It certainly has. I don't think I'd have recognized you. You look different. Older, I guess." He dug his hands into the pockets of his aviator jacket.

"Which way you going?" she said.

"Eighty-fourth."

"I'm going to Seventy-ninth. You mind if I tag along?"

"Not at all."

She swung her book bag over her other shoulder as they crossed the avenue.

"This has been my day for running into people," Warren said. "A guy I went to college with on the subway this morning. Hadn't seen him in years. Thought he lived on the West Coast. And now you. What've you got in there?" He tapped her book bag. "Looks like a bag of bricks."

"Books. School books. I went to a friend's after school and stayed for dinner."

"That's nice."

She would have to tell him something more interesting than that to get his attention, to impress him, this man she used to dream about kissing with her mouth open. "It was Don Marks's house. Did you ever hear of him?"

"The photographer?"

"Yeah."

"Sure."

"His daughter's a really good friend of mine. Will Kluger was there too. He's a writer. Have you ever heard of him?"

"Don't think so."

"I think he wrote a book about modern art. He knows heaps of writers. He's really smart. I didn't think you lived around here." She knew exactly where he lived, because she had looked in the phone book for his number, and had memorized his address.

"I don't. I'm going to visit a friend. I usually take my bike but it needs a new clutch. You live around here, don't you?"

She nodded.

"A real Upper East Side girl, huh?" He smiled and touched her arm as they crossed the street. "Just like your mom."

"Thanks." She took a long step away from him.

"Hey, Esme, don't take it so serious."

She breathed deeply, she marshaled her courage. "I happen to think that the East Side is extremely bourgeois." She looked

ahead as she spoke, her book bag thumped against her back. "*I'd*
prefer to live on the West Side but my mother thinks it's too
dangerous." She turned to him. "Kids in my school carry switch-
blades, and *she* thinks it isn't safe to live on the West Side."

"Do they really?"

"Not a lot of them. But some."

"That's a good thing."

She was sure she had said the wrong thing, all of the wrong
things. She did exactly what her mother did, she talked too much,
embarrassed herself.

They walked in silence past the German delicatessens, the
Irish bars, O'Reilly's, O'Malley's, the typewriter store, a man
sleeping in a doorway.

"So. What grade are you in?"

She could not possibly tell him the truth, any more than
she could have told Will Kluger that her mother sold makeup
at Bonwit Teller, that her father had just moved to Las Vegas,
and when she had asked him what he did there, you know,
for work, all he had said was, "I wheel and deal and pray
like hell."

She turned to Warren and smiled. "You go first. What grade
are you in?"

"Twenty-ninth."

"Is that how old you are?"

"I'm thirty-four. How old are you?"

"Twenty-nine," she said.

"They say it's the perfect age."

"They're right." Esme looked at her feet as she walked.
"Where do you work?"

"How come you're so sure I do?"

"What?"

"I'm an actor. I hardly ever work. It just so happens I'm
working now. I'm in an off-Broadway play called *Cheetah, Baby,
I'm Yours.*"

"Are you kidding?"

"No. I play a kid who goes to see his guru in India and the

guru turns out to be a woman. She teaches him all about trans-
cendental fornication."

"Oh." She was not sure what that was.

"Come see it some night. It'll be on for the next two weeks.
I'll take you out for a drink afterward."

"When should I come?"

"Any time you want. It's at the Grand Theatre on Second
Avenue. Call me first."

"Where?"

"At home. I'm in the book. On West Third." He touched
her arm and tipped his head to the side. "This is my stop." A
well-kept brownstone. She saw the row of mailboxes and the
buzzers with nameplates in the entranceway just beyond the
door. "I'm really glad I ran into you."

"Yeah. Me too."

She walked away and turned back to watch him through the
glass door, to see which buzzer he pressed. Either the second or
the third from the top.

She bolted and ran, overjoyed, delirious, in love.

It was after midnight when she took out her diary, sat down on
the floor of her bedroom and began to write. *Dreaded coming
home tonight after fabulous, esoteric dinner at L's. But for once,
thank j. h. christ, G. already asleep & no damage except that she
didn't doublelock the door or clean up dinner. Usual love note
to me and entire universe on foyer table. She doesn't even realize
how fallacious she is. And she'll die when she finds out about
me and Warren. He probably thinks I'm 18 or at least 16. A cab
driver the other day thought I was 17 and Leah was 16. Why is
he visiting someone at 11:30? I'll find out who it is tomorrow
from the nameplate. Leah has the best parents, the best everything, even though she tells me what to do alot and makes me
feel like a moron, which its no secret to anyone that I am. I'm ½
way through Crime & Punishment and Leah says I should read
something called The Sun Also Rises next. Your vocabulary, she
told me the other day, your vocabulary is abysmle. Haven't you*

*ever opened a dictionary? Haven't you ever read a decent book?
So I'm trying.*

She sat back against her bed and let the notebook fall off her lap. Strange that you could start out at the top of the page writing one way, like your life is just beginning, like you are ready to take on the world, and by the bottom of the page you want to die. A mountain of flaws, failings, books you haven't read, words you don't know the meanings of. The man you want to kiss went to someone else's house tonight. Your best friend thinks you're an idiot.

She needed a cigarette.

She got up and went looking in the living room, the dining room—that's what her mother called it, the tiny alcove off the living room, enough space for a table and chairs, and you had to hold your breath if you got stuck sitting in the corner chair against the wall. Now the ashtrays were full, there were some dirty wine glasses, two or three tumblers, lipstick marks around the rim. Georgia had had company. No company like Will Kluger, that's for sure. Dirty dishes on the table, splotches of gravy and ashes, chicken bones, a *TV Guide*, a bowl of uneaten cauliflower. When Georgia drank, really drank, she forgot to eat. She left things in the oven, she smoked in bed. Esme was going to come home one day and the apartment would be on fire. Her mother dead. It would serve her right. No skin off Esme's back; she'd love to live by herself. Though they'd probably ship her off to Las Vegas. Maybe she could get Don and Abby Marks to get custody of her. She found a pack of cigarettes on the kitchen counter next to a stick of butter that had not been opened. One cigarette left. She bent down and lit it with the flame from a front burner on the stove. If she were their adopted daughter— it would take her years to catch up with them. All the books they'd read, the things they knew. Something stank. Cheese, spoiled meat. The mess was not always so awful; it must have been a bad night. Too much to drink. Georgia gets weepy and starts talking about her father. That's probably what happened. She only talks about him when she's loaded.

Esme's throat filled up with smoke, heat, the taste of menthol. She thought of escape, perfect lives, the beautiful photographs Don had taken, books that Will Kluger had written and read, books that could sit on your bookshelf and announce who you were. Someone who knew many things. Someone extraordinary.

She turned off all the lights and stared at the bright orange tip of her cigarette. It glowed brighter when she took a drag. She moved her arm in circles and made an orange lasso of light.

This was it. This was goodbye. She was going to forget about her mother. All she ever did was get drunk and cry, and what do you bet she'd never even heard of *zabaglione?* Forget about her father. Mr. Wheel, Deal, and Pray Like Hell. Esme needed the two of them, and this was no joke, she needed them like she needed a hole in the wall.

SHE WAS LIKE an adult, a boarder, the way she lived with Georgia now. Georgia, whose boyfriend Tommy Troy, the travel agent, had moved in with them a few months before. When Esme spoke to Leah, she called him "My mother's faggoty boyfriend." To Georgia she said one evening before he got home from work, "Are you sure he isn't queer, because he sure acts like it."

"Quite sure," Georgia answered.

"Well, Georgia, it's your life, not mine."

"Let me tell you something, young lady. The hardest thing in the world to find, the hardest thing to find in this goddam hard awful place, is love. Sometimes you have to settle for less."

"So he is queer."

"That's not what I mean. I mean just what I said. You have to settle for less than the knight in shining armor."

"You thought Billy Maxwell was the knight."

"Until I woke up I did."

"I'm not going to settle for less," Esme said.

"I never thought I would either."

"*I'm* not going to change my mind."

"Lots of luck, sweetheart."

In this way—in other ways, in every way—she severed her ties to her mother. Her life, my life: two entirely separate entities, like countries across the globe from one another, like two people who have never met. It was as simple as that.

The nights Esme was home at dinnertime she ate in her bedroom, read books Leah had told her to read, looked up words she did not know in the dictionary. She read *To the Lighthouse* and copied passages into her diary. "*It was a splendid mind. For if thought is like the keyboard of a piano, divided into so many notes, or like the alphabet is ranged in twenty-six letters all in order, then his splendid mind had no sort of difficulty in running over those letters one by one . . . until it had reached, say, the letter Q. He reached Q. Very few people in the whole of England ever reach Q. . . . Still, if he could reach R it would be something. . . . On, then, on to R."*

She adopted that last phrase as her inspiration and wrote it on a large sheet of poster board. She tacked it to her wall, in the place where the Jimi Hendrix poster used to be. "What does this mean?" Georgia asked. " 'On to R'?"

"It's from a book."

"But what does it mean?"

"It's my ambition."

" 'On to R' is your ambition?"

"Yes."

"Your ambition to what?"

"You wouldn't understand."

"I certainly won't if you don't explain it to me."

"It's not that important."

"What about this? What's this?"

Esme looked up. "I can't see what you're pointing to."

"This postcard. It says, 'What You Can See You Can Photograph.' "

"It's a reproduction of an advertisement from the nineteen-twenties. An ad for a camera."

"Where did you get it?"

"A card shop in the Village."

"Esme, close your book and talk to me."

"I don't have time. I have an assignment to finish."

"At eleven o'clock at night?"

"I said finish, not start."

She was writing a book report, for a composition class, on a biography of Brassaï she had found in Don Marks's bookcase. For five or six years in the 1920s, Brassaï slept during the day and roamed the streets and cafés of Paris at night. At the end of those years, when he was thirty, he picked up a camera for the first time. The pictures he took, published four years later as *Paris de*

Nuit, were of the night people, the sailors, lovers, freaks, the ones who could not sleep, the ones who had better things to do than sleep.

Esme relished anecdotes about Brassaï, and stories of other late bloomers, years of indolence that came to a propitious end, achievement no one would have predicted. That's what people would say about her, if she ever became a success, if there was ever a story to tell about her life.

. . .

"Your hat," he said. "You left it by Stravinsky."

There were so many crazies, so many weirdos, even here. She kept walking.

"Isn't this yours?" His voice was louder.

She touched her hand to her bare head and spun around.

He held it out to her, the black felt hat with the wide brim, the pheasant feather stuck in the band. "You left it on the Stravinsky shelf. I'm sorry it got crushed."

"That's all right." She took it and looked at him. "It was always kind of crushed." Tall, lanky, with long black hair, a scar on his upper lip, a boy about her age in a blue blazer, ratty jeans, a private-school outfit. Probably Horace Mann or Trinity. She put the hat on her head, pulled it down a little in front. "It's from the Polio Thrift Store."

"What's that?"

"It's not really called that. It's on Third Avenue. My best friend and I call it that. You know, like the Sloan-Kettering Cancer Thrift Store. Or the Thrift Shop for the Blind. If you were blind, you'd be home now. That's her expression. I guess you had to be there. Well, anyway, listen, thanks. I mean, for finding my hat."

She turned quickly, embarrassed by her breathiness, the unexpected speech, the stranger's attention. Under her arm the library's worn copies wrapped in brown, covered in plastic, *The Rite of Spring, The Four Seasons,* Mozart's earliest symphonies, the list of recordings Leah had written down for her. And Georgia muttering in the corner of her mind, as she had muttered when Esme brought home the *Moonlight Sonata*, Von Karajan conducting the *Eroica*, "What do you want to listen to those guys for?"

At the checkout counter she put her library card on top of the records. She pulled the brim of her hat down further, furtively turned a quarter turn, another, and scanned the sprawling, carpeted room for him. Airy modern space, a wall of framed posters of library exhibits. Italian composers on the three-hundredth anniversary of their birth, the plays and operas that had been performed in the buildings next door, at the Beaumont, the Met.

There he was, his profile, at the far end of the room, at the bank of card catalogs, flipping through a drawer. He coughed. He looked at her and looked away quickly.

The next time she looked for him, he was gone.

"Miss, don't forget your card." The man behind the counter held out two fingers, forefinger, middle finger, and the library card wedged between them, this item of recent, compelling value to her, already worn at the edges.

Nice shot, she thought, just like that, and clicked the imaginary shutter that Don Marks had told her photographers needed to cultivate before they ever learned how to use a camera. She would have to start with that, because she wasn't going to go around sticking her crummy Instamatic into people's faces, pretending she was a photographer. It would be different if she had a Leica or a Nikon, then at least she'd look like a pro. In the meantime, she'd do what Don said. Focus and shoot with her eye. The scrawny librarian, glasses as thick as goggles, a button on his collar that said SMILE IF YOU WANT SOME. Click, it went, click, click.

It was dusk as she left the building, the first month of 1970. This was all you needed, this life she had invented. The records, the books in her book bag found at Leah's house or on library shelves, discovered like the love letters from Billy's dead wife hidden in the closet, things you cannot imagine existed, and there they were. *Women in Love, Tropic of Cancer, Long Day's Journey into Night.*

The air was clear, dotted with the lights of Lincoln Center, Broadway. Dabs of orange across the sky, hot pink, the sun setting across the river. Endless possibilities in this city at this moment, this hour, the chance to become someone else, someone who knew many things. Such people were called polymaths.

She imagined that she was twenty-one, twenty-two, finished with college, about to start a life. A life in the Village, taking photographs, working in an art gallery. Her lover would have long, wild hair and a motorcycle. He would be a film maker, or maybe a writer. She would have dinner parties and serve gazpacho, take birth control pills and speak fluent French.

"I thought I would sort of wait for you." The voice came from up ahead on the plaza. He was leaning against the ledge of a planter in the shadow of a light beamed from the Philharmonic. She had to pass him in order to get by, there was no other way, unless she turned around. But she was not going to stop just because he was sort of waiting for her, the guy who had found her hat.

He took small steps. His legs were long, he was slightly pigeon-toed. He had a green book bag like hers, with a drawstring, smooth, full cheeks, the faint beginnings of a mustache. "Hi." When he smiled he looked shy.

"Hi."

"I like your coat. It goes well with the hat. I was going to tell you before."

"Thanks." She swallowed hard. "It only cost nine dollars."

"Where? The Polio Thrift Store?"

"A place on St. Mark's and Second where all they sell is fur coats. Used."

"What kind is yours?"

"Muskrat with sable trim."

"*Très elegant.*"

"Thanks."

"How come you came here?"

"Here? You mean—" She pointed to the place where she stood.

"No, I mean, the library."

"It's the best one in the city for music. I mean, records. Classical."

"I meant, what did you need them for?"

"Just myself."

"Not for school?"

She shook her head. "What about you?"

"I'm doing a project on Bartok. I had to look at some sheet music."

"What school?"

"Friends. What about you?"

"I don't go to private school. I go to Music and Art."

"Do you do music or art?"

"I do photography sometimes, but not at school. I hardly do anything there. The place is a real joke."

"That's what I've heard."

"I guess Friends isn't a joke."

"I'm just about to the end of the line, so I'm kind of—"

"What do you mean, the end of the line?"

"I'm a senior. It's over in a few months. Then I'm off to Harvard, with any luck. I find out in April."

"Oh. Yeah. Well, look—" Then what did he need with her, a dumb girl from Music and Art? She turned her head, dug her hands into her pockets. "Do you know what time it is? I'm kind of—"

"Do you have to be somewhere?"

"At six."

He looked at his watch. "It's quarter to five. You want to get something? There's a coffeeshop across the street."

She blurted out, almost an accusation, "I'm in tenth grade."

"What of it, mate?" He put on a thick British accent.

She bit the inside of her cheek. "I just thought you should know."

"Now I know. Should we get some coffee?"

"You still want to?"

"No, I changed my mind."

"Oh." She took a step back, almost tripped on her book bag.

"I'm kidding. Come on. What's your name?"

"Esme Singer."

They walked across the wide plaza toward Broadway.

"Esme," he repeated. "Like the girl in the story."

"That's who my parents named me after. My mother also liked that it sounded so French. She has her little cultural pretensions, if you know what I mean."

"I detest Salinger. Really loathe him."

"Oh." She had thought her lie would make her so interesting, so appealing to a boy who was going to Harvard. She could barely bring herself to ask. "How come?"

"Every jerky junior high school kid in America thinks *Catcher in the Rye* is the story of his own, personal, banal adolescent depression. Spare me another moment of it. Spare me another kid who thinks he knows all about jaded sophistication. Aesthetically speaking, that book's on a par with—" He stopped and turned to the front of the opera house, arched windows lighted up for the night. "Those." He pointed to each end of the wide building. "Bloody Chagalls." The mammoth paintings behind the glass, two stories high, filled with animal figures, people, musical instruments, the startling yellows and greens. "They want you to think his paintings are the height of culture, the height of civilization. It's just wallpaper. Chagall and his dumb rabbis who play the violin. Jesus. You know what I think they should do with them?"

She shook her head. She had no idea.

"Deport them to Israel." He turned and cocked his head toward Broadway. She followed. She had to walk fast to keep up with him, his long steps, his energy. He knew everything, had made up his mind about all of it. It wouldn't be long before he figured out who she was, who she really was. A fraud, a girl who kept lists of words so she could pretend that she had always known them, lists of books she had not read, that she would probably never read, they were so dreadfully long and boring.

"So I guess you're not Jewish," she said.

"I am. I'm just not a bleeding Zionist."

"I am too. I mean, Jewish. But just half. The top half." They walked down the steps to the sidewalk, dodged the people going the other way, the musicians, dancers with hair pinned up tightly, gaunt faces, Pan Am shoulder bags for their leotards, their pale pink ballet slippers. "Protestant on the bottom. Not religious at all. Who is these days, anyway?"

"Opiate of the masses, as Marx says."

"Absolutely."

He pointed across Broadway. "That's the place I was thinking of. It's really cheap. They don't bother you even if all you get is a Coke."

She turned to him, his profile in the dark, the curled ends of his hair a sort of scarf around the collar of his blazer. "Aren't you cold?"

"I like the cold."

She had once stood with Warren on the corner of Bleecker and West Fourth waiting for a bus and French kissing, so cold out that kissing that way was the only way to keep warm.

"I like it too," she said.

" 'When you wet the bed, first it is warm then it gets cold.' "

That was an odd thing for him to say. "Aren't you a little old for that?"

"It's from the opening of *Portrait*," he said. "*Portrait of the Artist as a Young Man*. James Joyce."

"I knew that," she lied. "I was just—you know, trying to make conversation." It would serve her right if he changed his mind right here on this island in the middle of Broadway. Right here, right now, went away before he found out all of the other things she didn't know.

He was taller than Warren but not nearly as handsome, as mature. Warren, who shaved every morning, who had taken her to a play in a loft with people actually fucking on stage. Who had taken her on his BMW for a ride in the middle of the night up the West Side Highway. This guy, this boy, he didn't come close to Warren.

"I just realized I don't know your name," she said.

"You only need to know it if I'm in a crowd and you want to call me."

"Supposing I did?"

"Gene Kauffman." As they reached the door to the coffee-shop, he took a long step forward and opened the door for her. "*Après vous, mademoiselle*." He bowed as she passed. "Welcome to Broadway's most ordinary dining emporium." He tossed his book bag onto the seat of a booth near the front door and slid in. "Take off your coat and hat. Stay awhile."

She put her book bag on the table and began to take off her coat. She wished this body was not her own, arms and legs so long and clumsy that they felt like extra appendages, or a suitcase, the way her knees and elbows knocked into everything, everyone.

"You know who you look like?" he said.

She slid across the seat and dug her hand into the back pocket of her jeans. She pulled out a pack of Marlboros. "Mama Cass."

He smiled. "Not quite."

"Want one?" She held open the pack for him.

"No. It's a disgusting habit."

"It helps me keep my weight down." She lit the cigarette and fanned away the smoke.

"And I suppose your hat helps you think." He reached his hand across the table, and as she saw the hand come toward her, she pulled back. "I was just going to touch your hat." She leaned forward again. "Like this." He scratched the brim gently. "To see if it has magical properties that help you think. Like the character in Beckett."

"Oh, yes. Beckett. The Irish playwright."

"Yeah. In *En Attendant Godot,* Pozzo says Lucky can't think without his hat."

"Me neither. Can't do a thing with my hair, either. That's the real reason I wear this."

"Let's see."

"I'm just kidding. Well, actually, I'm not. It's just . . . " She dragged on her cigarette, she tried to look pensive as she stared out the window.

"You want something besides coffee?"

"No. I guess just coffee."

A man passing by the window of the shop caught her attention. She was sure it was Warren. She saw him all over the city, on street corners, buses, subways, in bookstores and coffeeshops where he had never set foot. She had even seen him once in the Polio Thrift Store when she was shopping with Leah. "It's him," Esme had whispered, "I'm sure it's him this time. Over there by the bathrobes." "Oh, Esme," Leah answered, "if you had polio, you'd be home now. What do you think about this?" Leah had held up a peach-colored cashmere sweater that cost a dollar. "The color is revolting," Esme had said. "And much too close to yellow." They had vowed they would never wear anything yellow. It was too frivolous, nowhere near grim enough for intellectuals.

Gene asked a battery of questions. Where she lived, what school she went to before Music and Art, how long she had lived in New York, what her father did.

"He's dead." She stubbed out her cigarette. "What about yours?"

"He works at one of the Rockefeller foundations. He's in charge of giving out money to the groups that want to eliminate war, poverty, and injustice. He's got a terminal case of *noblesse oblige,* but the adopted variety, not the inherited one. First-generation Jew, first one in the family to get an education, all that emotional *Sturm und Drang.* Here's the coffee."

She fingered the heavy white institutional cup, the chipped saucer, the small stainless-steel cream pitcher. She got a whiff of the sour smell from the washcloth the table had been wiped with. If she got up and left right now, she would not have to make up more lies about who she was.

"What's this?" He touched the corner of a book sticking out of her book bag.

"A book I borrowed. Cartier-Bresson photographs." She loosened the drawstring and pulled out the small book that she kept in a plastic bag. She flipped through it. "I borrowed it from Don Marks. The photographer. Have you ever heard of him?"

"Who hasn't?"

"His daughter's my best friend."

"So you like old C.-B.?"

"I adore him. Do you know he never gets his photograph taken? Never. Do you know why? Because he doesn't want to be obtrusive. He doesn't want people to know what he looks like so he can take pictures anonymously. I read that somewhere. That's the kind of photographer I'd be. If I were ever a photographer. What do you think of this?"

She held up the book, a photograph of a child running up steps in Greece, stark white buildings like adobe, the surfaces, doors, and windows in the busy foreground, the child far in the back at the top of the stairs, tiny, hidden almost. "The kid," Esme said, "the kid is what draws your eye to the center, the kid is what makes this photograph."

"I've seen it a million times," he said. "A print of it's in the photography collection at MOMA. The far wall. Next to the Ansel Adams. Whom I also detest. All that natural, trendy Sierra Club ecology business. The posters with the odes to trees and rocks. They don't even rip off Wordsworth. They just make up their own flowery bullshit. It sounds like the Pledge of Allegiance."

Esme leaned her head down, hid beneath the brim of her hat, pretended to look at the photographs.

Nothing she said was right, nothing she liked was the right thing to like. And she had worked so hard. He had no idea how hard it had been for her to learn all of this.

"So," he said. "You take pictures?"

"Sometimes. I don't have a good camera right now. I just fool around and read a lot about photographers. But if I had a good camera, I'd—"

"What kind do you have?"

"This cheap one my mother bought me in a drugstore a few years ago."

"Thirty-five millimeter?"

"Not hardly."

"It really helps to have one."

"I know it."

"There's an exhibit of surrealist photographers at a gallery on Fifty-seventh Street," Gene said. "Would you like to go sometime?"

"Sure. Yeah. I guess so. Sometime."

"If you don't want to—"

"It's not that. It's just—"

"You have a boyfriend."

She shook her head. "Not really."

"Not really?"

She lit a cigarette. Not really, no. Unless you counted how much time she spent thinking about Warren. "There's this guy, but—" She shrugged. "It's finished, really." It had never really started, except in her head. Except for the play, the ride on the motorcycle. He had never kissed her, except once on the cheek. She had French kissed another boy waiting for a bus in the Village and had imagined it was Warren.

"You look like an actress," Gene said. "I can't think of her name."

"Shelley Winters."

"Jesus, no. What's-her-name Redgrave. Vanessa."

"More like Lynn. The fat one."

He shook his head. "You need glasses."

"So do you. The only thing Vanessa and I have in common is that we're as tall as giraffes."

"Are your parents tall?"

"My mother's as tall as I am. My father's about an inch shorter."

"I thought he was dead."

"Well, he's—" She stopped talking, shrugged.

"Not dead?"

She shook her head.

"Yes or no?"

"Not really."

"I don't get it."

"That's all right. Don't worry about it. You want some more coffee?"

"How can you not be sure if your father's dead? Is he in a coma?"

"Sort of."

"In a hospital?"

She inhaled deeply, tobacco almost down to the filter, and shook her head.

"An institution?"

"Look, forget it, okay?" Smoke caught in her throat and she began to cough.

"Is he in jail?"

"It's really not that important."

"So he is in jail."

She shook her head.

"But he's not dead?"

She shook her head.

"Then where is he?"

"Those aren't the only two places someone can be, not in jail and not dead."

"I know. That's why I'm asking."

"He's in Vegas."

"Las Vegas?"

"Is there any other Vegas? What time is it? I have to go." She grabbed her cigarettes, her book bag.

"How do you know you have to go if you don't know what

time it is?" He pushed the cuff of his blazer away from his wrist and read his watch. "Almost quarter to six."

It was as if he were not even there. She simply got up and got her things together, threw some change from her coat pocket onto the table. "I'm going to be late—" not looking at him, just hurrying—"I'm going to be so late they'll kill me."

He grabbed her hand. "Wait a second. Just wait."

She yanked her hand back and started for the door.

"Hey, come back. How can I find you?"

"You can't," she said under her breath.

"What?"

"I don't know," she called out and leaned into the heavy glass door to push it open.

She knew that she could catch a cab and borrow money from the doorman in her building to pay for it when she got there. Use the money she would make that night babysitting to pay back the doorman for the cab. Play parcheesi with the children. Put them to bed. Read the sex manuals on the top shelf of the parents' bookcase. Touch herself in the bathroom, eyes shut, eyes open. Watch it all in the full-length mirror on the back of the door. Click, it went, click, click.

She held up her hand and hailed a Checker.

The Water Lilies

THE DAY AFTER Esme met Gene Kauffman, she stood outside the Friends School in the cold for an hour, leaning against an abandoned car stripped of three of its doors. When she saw him, she would say, "I thought I would sort of wait for you."

When she saw him, she did not say anything, she just smiled, because he did not look displeased to see her. He did not grimace or flee. He just said, "Well, hi," and pulled on the brim of her hat, a playful, teasing tug. As simple as that.

He lived in a house on Washington Square Park. His mother was a doctor, a pediatrician, and had her office on the ground floor. They lived above it, you entered at the top of the stoop stairs. Another house like Leah's. High ceilings, books everywhere, lithographs hanging crooked inside the frames, bare wood floors, furniture that did not match, an ancient refrigerator, austerity. "Henry James used to live in the house next door," he told Esme, "a few years before we moved in."

He closed his bedroom door behind them. The high ceiling, the tall, narrow windows that looked into a courtyard, the backs of other townhouses. He took off her hat, began to unbutton her shirt. She put her hand to it, forefinger pressed on the third button from the top, and whispered, "Wait." Strewn on the floor were Harvard College catalogs, dictionaries of film and modern art, French paperbacks. He leaned toward her and pressed his lips against hers.

He wrapped his arms around her, walked her backward to the bed.

"My shoes," she said.

He bent his knee and pushed it between her legs. His mouth tasted sour, like cottage cheese. He moved on top of her, their winter clothes rubbed together, his tongue went deeper into her mouth. She did not even like him, she did not want to be here. Feign means to pretend, she said to herself, dissemble means to fake.

"Stop," she said quietly.

"What?" He opened his eyes, emerged as if from a deep sleep, raised himself up on his arms.

"Nothing." *I'm a woman, you're a man. Why waste the afternoon?* It meant to have sex with someone you weren't married to, but maybe it also meant to have sex with someone you didn't know very well, or care about. She pulled him to her, held him tightly.

"I thought you said stop."

"I felt weird for a minute."

"Still?"

"No." She did not know if it was a lie. The room had grown darker, he had not turned on a light. The venetian blinds made slatted shadows on the wall, the bare wood floor. The sun is going down, the lovers need each other to survive the cold, lonely night. It could be the photograph of the start of a love affair, a picture of the slatted shadows and the lovers' feet entwined at the end of the bed.

She let him kiss her. She would grow to like him. There were some people you thought were handsome right away, and some you had to take your time with. She let him unbutton her shirt and touch her breasts. She tried not to feel anything but it did not work. A sound started in the back of her throat and escaped from her mouth. He moved his hand to her zipper, his mouth to her bare nipple. The noise of the metal, the noise of his sucking, the hard lump against her thigh beneath the corduroy, rubbing and pressing.

His fingers were cold inside her, then warm. She heard herself moan, she heard the awful sloshing sound her body made, down there, and closed her legs, clamping his hand between them. He moved it faster, deeper, his mouth tighter over her breast. She gripped his shoulders, let the sounds come out of her mouth. I love you, she thought, I love you, Warren, I really do.

. . .

"I can't believe how smart he is," she said to Leah a week later. "I just can't believe it. I mean, applying to Harvard. And Amherst."

"You told me three times, Esme. At least three times."

"All right, we're here." They had just reached the corner of Forty-fourth Street and Ninth Avenue. "Which place will it be?"

"This was your idea."

"You're the one who said you were broke," Esme said. "I'm just trying to help out. Pick one."

"Which is the best?"

"How should I know?"

"You said you've done this before."

"It wasn't a pawnshop," Esme said. "It was a diamond merchant on Forty-seventh Street. And it was years ago."

They stood in the winter-afternoon cold, on a block filled with dingy old pawnshops.

"Let's try this one," Leah said and tipped her chin to the one before them, 9TH AVENUE BUY & TRADE, a window crammed with watches, old typewriters, radios, bracelets. Painted in cracked gold lettering in the corner: SINCE 1925.

"You have all the stuff?" Esme asked.

"I have mine. You have yours?"

Esme reached again into the pocket of her muskrat coat and felt the two gold rings she had gotten as a child, and a watch her aunt in New Haven had given her three years ago. She nodded.

"Tell me what you say again," Leah said.

"You say—"

"Me? I thought you were—"

"It was the royal 'you,' Leah. I'll say, 'We have some items to show you.' Then the guy says, 'Let's have a look.' Then I take

the stuff and show it to him. You take your stuff out too. Then
he'll say, 'How much do you want for it?' Then I'll say, 'Make
me an offer.' "

"Are you sure this is the way to do it?"

"It's the way I did it with the diamond merchant."

"You did it? I thought your mother did it."

"It was her ring. But I told her she should sell it. And I told
her what to say to the guy." Esme cleared her throat and stood
up straighter. "You ready?"

Leah nodded.

The door creaked when they opened it. The room was
musky, the ceiling was high, it smelled pungent, stale, like the
old-age home where Esme had met her great-grandmother when
she was eight. There were long glass counters with dark wood
trim, trays of fountain pens, half a wall of stereos, can openers,
typewriters, an accordion, a shelf of trumpets, a glass cabinet of
cameras. "Can I help you young ladies with something?" The
man spoke from the back of the store, from behind a counter.
He was old and wore a yarmulke.

"We're just looking," Esme blurted out.

Leah turned to her.

"For now. Later we might—"

"I'll be right here," the man said and tapped the counter
top. "Been here since 1925."

"We know," Esme said.

"How do you know?"

"We saw the sign in the window," Leah said.

"Smart girls."

"Actually, we do have some items to show you," Esme said
and led the way to the back, the cluttered counter where he
stood. "We were wondering—"

"Let's have a look-see."

They reached into their coat pockets and held out their
hands.

"You first, " the man said to Leah. She handed him a ring, a
charm bracelet and a sterling silver key ring.

"For this—" he held up the ring to his eye, a thin silver and turquoise band—"nothing." He put it down and picked up the charm bracelet. He shook it two or three times and looked at Leah. "It's heavy."

"It's from Italy. Florence."

He looked at it closely for five seconds, ten seconds. "Two dollars."

"Two dollars?"

"It's plate. It's not gold."

"What about this?" She held out the key ring.

"Three dollars."

"But it's from Tiffany's."

"Darling, I don't care if it's from the *Titanic*. Three dollars. Take it or leave it."

Leah looked at Esme. Esme shrugged.

"Let's see what you've got," the man said to Esme.

"Oh, just—" She emptied her pockets onto the counter top. "Not very much."

He went through her things the way he had gone through Leah's. Two dollars. Nothing. Two-fifty.

"We thought it would be more," Esme said.

"Bring me a good TV. Twenty-five. A good violin. Fifty. A camera. It depends."

"We thought jewelry would—"

"If it's gold, if it's diamonds, sapphires, emeralds. But not plate, not pieces of glass."

"What about the watch I just showed you?" Esme said.

"Who's going to buy this watch from me for thirty dollars when they can get a new one at Walgreen's for fifteen? I didn't make you such a bad offer. Four-fifty for you. Five for you. Almost ten altogether. You could do worse."

"I'm *sure* we can do better," Esme said, "down the street."

"Be my guest."

"We'll think about your offer," Leah said. "We'll look around the store and we'll consider it." Leah pushed Esme's pile of jewelry toward her.

"Take your time," the man said.

Leah grabbed Esme's elbow and guided her to the front of the shop, whispered into the shoulder of her coat. "You were so obnoxious to him."

"Me?" Esme whispered back.

" 'I'm *sure* we can do better down the street,' " Leah imitated in a whisper.

"We probably can." Esme stopped at a tall glass cabinet and stared into it. "He offered us practically nothing," she whispered.

"Don't talk so loud."

"Jesus, Leah."

"Look at that camera. My father has one just like it. It's an old Rollei."

"Which one are you looking at?"

"The third shelf. Second one in."

"I wish I had a good camera."

"You always say that, Esme."

"Because it's true."

"Buy one."

"I don't have the money."

"Ask your parents for one."

"Are you kidding? Since when do my parents do anything for me?"

"Tell them to chip in."

"Right. Maybe my mother can hock her old lipsticks and my father can send me some gambling chips. Even if I got a camera, I'd never have the money to buy film and develop it. It would cost a fortune to set up a darkroom in my bathroom."

"If you're not going to do anything to get a camera, quit talking about it. It's really tiresome."

"Pardon me, Leah, pardon me for breathing."

"Do you think we should take the money the guy offered us?" Leah whispered.

"Hell no."

"How much did your mother get for her diamond?"

"They only offered her two hundred, but it cost two thousand. So she didn't sell it."

"Let's get out of here. Let's get some cigarettes."

The door creaked again when they opened it. They did not turn back, they stood on Ninth Avenue in their used fur coats, their high suede boots. It had grown darker, the temperature had dropped. They could see their breath. "This way," Esme said and touched Leah's arm. "I saw a deli down here."

"How much money do you have?"

"I don't know. Seventy-five cents. How much do you have?"

"The same."

"It's not enough to buy cigarettes and get home."

"Let's just buy the cigarettes," Leah said, "and walk home."

"It's forty-five blocks to my house. We should have sold him one of those rings."

"For a dollar, a frigging dollar?"

"We can go back in there and get nine-fifty if we want."

"But we don't want to, remember?"

"Yeah, I guess." Esme was thinking about the cabinet of cameras, how much a good camera would cost and who might buy it for her.

"Now that it's over," Leah began, in the manner of a proclamation, "I have to say that I thought it was a humiliating experience."

"Humiliating? Which part?"

"Not for us, for him. Here we are, middle-class girls from the Upper East Side trying to chisel this poor Jewish man out of a few dollars. Think of how he must have felt. Bargaining with high school girls."

"First of all, he didn't do any bargaining. It was strictly take it or leave it."

"I guess you're right about that."

"Second of all, he isn't poor. Third of all, you're middle-class. I'm lower-middle. Maybe even lower than that. Let's go in here." Esme led her to the door of a deli. "What kind should we get?"

"The usual."

"Have you noticed I haven't mentioned Gene in more than half an hour?"

"I noticed."

"I can't believe I'm really going out with someone who applied to Harvard."

"Anybody can apply, Esme."

They lit their cigarettes and started up Ninth Avenue. Crowded rush-hour sidewalks, exhaust fumes from buses and trucks, dirty movie houses, pizza by the slice, the world's best cup of coffee. Faces that broke your heart, lonely, decrepit, disfigured. She had her Instamatic in her book bag, but she knew Leah would make fun of her if she took it out and started taking pictures. She'd say what she had said last time, that it was too dark to take pictures and that Esme would never get a good picture from *that* camera anyway.

"The question is," Leah said, "does he want to sleep with you."

"I've only seen him a few times."

"Do you think he will?"

"We agreed we wouldn't do it until we were really in love."

"You and Gene agreed that?"

"You and I. Don't you remember?"

"Of course. I just wanted to see if you changed your mind. Let's go east on Fifty-ninth."

"Okay."

"So I guess you're not in love with him," Leah said.

"It doesn't happen overnight. It might happen soon."

"Maybe it'll happen when he gets into Harvard."

"What do you mean?"

"It sounds like that's the thing you like best about him. The Harvard Factor."

"He's no Warren Gold. I mean, he's smart, but he's definitely a *boy*. He's not suave."

"Of course he isn't suave, Esme. He's seventeen. Warren is The Older Man. Warren assumes mythic proportions in your schoolgirl mind."

"Warren also has another girlfriend. I told you he told me that when I called him last month, didn't I?"

"Of course you did, Esme. That just enhances his appeal. The Unavailability Factor."

"But I told him I had a boyfriend too. To enhance *my* appeal."

"You do."

"This was before I had one."

"He probably doesn't care that much."

"What's that supposed to mean?"

"Esme, he's twice your age. He's not pining away for you, that's for sure."

This is what it feels like to be punched in the stomach. When you suddenly lose your breath, when the room starts to spin. But it is not the room, it is Seventh Avenue and Fifty-ninth Street, and the only thing to do is to keep walking, ignore everything that Leah has said, because even if she is right, she does not have to be so uppity, so disgustingly sure of herself, so fucking rude.

"For Christ's sake, Esme, don't pout," Leah said.

"I'm not pouting." She could barely speak, barely project her voice. "I'm ruminating. Not everyone can walk, smoke a cigarette, and talk at the same time."

Leah smiled.

She knew that Leah was right. About the Harvard Factor, the Unavailability Factor. About Warren.

"I think you ought to forget about this guy," Leah said, "this Warren."

"I know. But I don't know how."

"Try. You really have to try."

.   .   .

On their third date, Esme and Gene sat on a bench in front of "Dance" by Matisse, a huge canvas of naked women in a circle holding hands, the rich blue of the background and the kelly green of the ground meeting halfway; no other colors in the vast landscape.

"What do you see on the other side of that?" Gene said.

"What?"

"André Breton says that a picture is a window on the other side of which you may see something."

"I'm not quite sure." She was not sure at all, not sure of anything with this boy.

"I can never decide whether Matisse is a simpleton or a revolutionary. When you look at what people like Tzara and Duchamp were doing at the same time, raising holy hell, issuing manifestos, taking on the art authorities. Then you look at that—" He pointed across the room to "Red Studio," a large painting of the artist's studio, the bright red walls covered with beautiful miniature Matisses, paintings within the painting. "What do you think?"

"I guess I like them. I mean, for what they are." But even that might not be the right thing to say.

"I like them too. I just wonder where Matisse fits in." He stood up. "How history will assess him."

She followed him to the next room.

"I suppose you hate 'The Water Lilies,' " she said.

"Don't you?"

She nodded. Yes, of course.

"Give me a third-rate Surrealist over Monet any day. Manet, too. Surrealism is the most valid—the most truthful—expression of reality. It brings the unconscious into the open, up to the surface. Everything else is artifice. Everything else is decoration."

The room with the sculpture, the attenuated Giacomettis, the slender bronze Brancusis, the chiseled stone called "The Kiss." Gene reached for her hand as they read the cards on the wall, the names and dates of the works, when they had been acquired.

"My parents used to bring me here when I was a kid. I must have been three when they started. My mother tells a story that when I was about five I pointed to that—" he pointed to Brancusi's "The Negress"—"and said why does that lady have such big lips. My father went into an elaborate euphemistic historical-physiological explanation, which he later told me he had invented on the spot." If she listened to Gene carefully enough, she might begin to acquire some of the words he used, the complicated phrases that rolled off his tongue. "My father is so persuasive when he talks," Gene said. "He makes up things all the time, but they sound encyclopedic. He sounds like he's reciting original sources. Invariably it turns out he isn't. He's improvising. He's absolutely—"

Esme let go of his hand and turned away.

"What's wrong?"

"Nothing."

"Something's wrong."

"Nothing's wrong," she lied. But she did not know what it was. She started to walk into the next room.

"What did I say?" He caught up to her, put his hand on her shoulder. "What happened?"

He followed her through room after room, the Fauves, the Cubists, "The Three Musicians." "Esme. For god's sake. Talk to me."

She stepped through the next wide doorway and saw, to her surprise, "The Water Lilies." Three huge canvases set out side to side, almost a half-circle around the room, a sea of light purples, deep pinks, strands of green, the surfaces thick, pasty, out of focus.

"No one in my family—no one knows about art or culture or—" She turned to him to say this, and then turned away again, because the failings of her family were not the reason she had fled from him a minute ago. She had fled, she realized now, be-

cause she knew that she was not in love with him and would
never be in love with him.

She turned back and touched his arm, his blue blazer with
the frayed elbows. She would stay with him. Because she needed
to forget Warren. Because she needed to learn all the things Gene
knew. Because maybe she was wrong about love. Maybe love
crept up on you, came in quietly through the back door and was
well into the house before you noticed it was there.

"My mother is so stupid that for Christmas when I was
eleven," Esme said, "she bought me a copy of Sammy Davis,
Jr.'s autobiography. You know why? Because he's Jewish. She
had some idea it would make me proud of my heritage."

"Or revolted by it," Gene laughed.

"The point is that she didn't know of any other famous
Jewish people. Except for Barry Goldwater. If he'd written an
autobiography that year, she would have given it to me. That's
how stupid she is."

"That's what upset you just now?"

Esme shook her head and then nodded. She was lying, she
was telling the truth, she was saying whatever came to mind.
"What upset me was thinking about my parents. How I can't
stand them. How different they are than yours."

"From yours."

"From mine?"

" 'Different *from*' is correct. 'Different than' is not."

"Didn't I say that?" Now she did not know what she had
said.

"You said 'different than.' "

"Well, I meant—" She lost her breath for a moment, her
voice. It would be better if she did not speak. If she listened to
him, listened to every word, and only talked the way he talked.
"You know the part in *To the Lighthouse* about the letters of
the alphabet?" She knew she had this right. She knew she was
not going to make a mistake. "The part where Mr. Ramsay is
trying to go through all the letters, and how hard it is, and he's

gotten to Q, but he wants to reach R? You know that part?" Gene nodded. "That's what I'm trying to do. I try to do everything different than—I mean, different *from* my parents. The exact opposite." She looked away and everywhere she looked were "The Water Lilies." "But sometimes I feel like my head is being crushed."

He stepped closer to her, raised his hands to the sides of her head and held them there, at her temples. "Poor you."

She nodded, lowered her eyes from his gaze.

"Poor thing."

It was not wrong to kiss someone you did not love. It was not wrong to have a boyfriend you did not love. The truth didn't show, like acne, like a broken leg. No one had to know what you were doing. As long as you were just a teenager, as long as you held out for love when you were an adult, when it really mattered. "Would you kiss me?" she whispered and looked into his eyes, so she would not have to look at "The Water Lilies." It's no crime to want a little company, no crime to need a guy the way she was sure she needed this one.

Staying Afloat

THREE MONTHS OF teenage sex, anguish. After school, their eyes closed, his younger brothers and sisters barging into the room. Titters, confessions, terrible quarrels. Bare skin. Pleas for more, for restraint, the discovery of new languages, one for pleasure, one for denial. She would do everything but that. And that.

"How can you be so prim and proper?" Gene said. "You, of all people." They lay on her bed one afternoon with their shirts off, their legs entwined. "Your mother's living with Tommy Troy, and every time you call your father a different woman answers the phone. Do you think they're playing chess? The thing is—" He cupped her bare breast. "The thing is that you like it so much, I just don't know." He fondled her breast, stroked it, held the hard nipple between his thumb and forefinger. "Twelve-year-olds are screwing in Central Park, Leah's parents have a dinner-time discussion about the blow job in *Portnoy's Complaint,* and you've decided to be a virgin forever."

"Not forever, just until—"

"I know, you're trying to be different from your parents."

"Not just that. Leah and I—"

"Oh, yes, your famous pact with Leah."

"It's not a pact, it's just that we're not going to sleep around. We're going to be different. We've already decided."

"Sleeping with me isn't exactly sleeping around."

"According to Leah—"

"I'm sick of hearing about Leah. How bloody smart she is, how dumb you are. If even half of it were true—"

"It is true!"

He shook his head. "Why do we go through this all the time? I can't spend an hour with you and not hear something about your fabulous Leah. If you want to know the truth, I don't think she's any great shakes."

"You don't think she's pretty?"

"Not as pretty as you are. I wouldn't have started talking to her in the library. I would have just—"

"You don't think she's smart?"

"Yeah, she's smart. But so are you."

Esme turned over, gave him her bare back. "When you first saw me—" this was her coy voice, this was his cue—"what did you think?"

"That you lost your hat." She loved to hear the different answers he gave her. He moved next to her, nuzzled up to her back, reached his hand around to her breasts.

"What else?" she said.

"Let's see." He kissed her back, pressed harder against her, against the pants she let him rub with his hand, let him rub against with his body. "That you liked Stravinsky. That you'd think I was a jerk for waiting for you outside."

"And all for this." She turned over to face him. "This sorry sight."

"Poor you, poor you," he said and wrapped his leg around hers. He repeated the words like an endearment, his special name for her.

"Poor me," she said softly, "poor me." She nodded her head rhythmically against the pillow and took his tongue into her mouth like nourishment, like love.

She cried a month later when he told her that Harvard had accepted him. "You can always visit." They were in his bedroom; he handed her a box of Kleenex.

She shook her head.

"Why not?"

"Because it won't be the same."

There was a pause. "Thank god."

She stared at him.

"All I meant was—"

"I know what you meant," she said. "I'm not stupid."

"I never thought you were. You're the one who thinks that.

It's all you ever talk about. Except for how awful your mother is.
And how awful your father is."

"Then what ever made you think I had any brains?"

"Stop it, all right? Just quit it."

"You can't even answer me."

He waited. "I choose not to."

She picked up her book bag from the floor, her muskrat
coat from the bed, the coat she wore even now that it was spring.

"That's how you deal with everything," he said. "You walk
away. Just like the day I met you."

"That's what you want, isn't it?" She heaved her coat up
over her shoulder.

"It's not what I want, it's just—" He stopped.

"What?"

"I'm tired."

"Of what?'

"Of telling you things you don't believe. I say you're beautiful, you say you're ugly, I say, oh, I don't know, something about
an artist, a writer, and before I even finish my sentence—"

"I know, I know."

"Let me finish."

"I know. Poor me, poor me, that's all I ever say."

"That is all you ever say. You think you're the only one in
the world who got a crummy deal. Who has a fucked-up family."

"I am!" She dropped her book bag, pressed the coat against
her face and cried into it.

He walked over to her and put his arms around her, nuzzled
the coat away from her face. It fell to the floor between them.

"I'll do it now," she sputtered, and wiped her eyes with the
back of her hand.

"What?" He had not heard her.

"I'll do it now," she said more clearly.

"Do what?"

"You know." Her voice was hoarse, thick from crying.

He held her tighter. Her face was wet, her forehead was
sweaty. "Not now."

"Why not?"

"Shhhh." He shook his head in a rocking motion.

"Gene?"

"What?"

"Do you still want to?"

"Of course. But not now."

"Sometime?"

"Yeah."

"Soon?"

"Yeah."

She turned her head and kissed him, felt him flinch, kissed him harder, deeper. He shook his head, tried gently to twist it away from her mouth. "I thought you liked that," she murmured.

"I do."

She reached for his pants, his belt.

"Esme."

She licked his lips. "What."

"Don't."

"But you're so hard. Look." She unzipped his pants, she looked down, stroked him the way he liked, the way that made him breathe hard.

He looked down too and began to thrust gently. "Tighter," he said.

"Step back."

He stepped back, fell against the narrow bed. "The door's not locked."

"No one's home, are they?"

"Lock it."

She was afraid to move, afraid to stop touching him. If she let go for a minute he would change his mind, send her away. She bent over and opened her mouth, held the head of his penis between her lips. He had always wanted her to do this and she never would. She moved her tongue, tightened her cheeks around it. It was not as strange as she thought it would be, having this in her mouth. The worst part was that she would have to look at him afterward, knowing what she had done. He touched her hair, pushed deeper into her mouth.

"The door," he moaned. "I hear someone, oh, god, oh, Jesus, oh, god." He gripped a handful of her hair. "That's so good."

She rose, locked the door and began to undress.

"Come here," he said. He was on his back, he was pulling off his clothes.

She dropped her skirt on the floor and went to him. "I'm freezing."

He pulled at the elastic waist of her underpants. She took them off and stood before him, arms crossed over her breasts, completely naked for the first time. "Let me see," he said.

"I'm cold."

"Come here."

"I'm scared."

"Squeeze me."

She lay down next to him and opened her mouth, gave him her tongue. She felt so warm underneath him, her legs opened wide. She did not know if it had started yet, if it was really there. "Put me in." She shook her head. He reached down between them. It was his fingers she felt now, in and out. Or maybe this was it. It did not hurt like it was supposed to. It did not feel like anything, but it did not feel like anything else. Then she began to cry out. He covered her mouth with his. She knew it would hurt the first time, but not like this.

Afterward, she asked, "Was it all right, was it good?"

"Yeah."

He was silent for a few minutes, he held her. "You should go to a doctor," he said. "For pills."

"Who?" She laughed. "Your mother?"

"I'll get a name for you. Girls at school are always talking about this hip gynecologist who gives discounts to minors."

"Really?"

"Yeah. And I'll give you some money."

She turned to kiss his neck.

The smell of skin, sweat, sex. She closed her eyes and tried to separate it from the others. Yes, that was it. There and gone and then back again, like warm spots in a cold swimming pool.

"Look, we can't keep doing this," he said and took his arm from her.

"You just said you would help me pay—"

"I know. But I shouldn't. I can't. It wouldn't be right."

"Why not?"

"It's not what I want."

"Maybe you'll change your mind. You changed it just now."

"I won't. I've already decided."

"Let's not talk about it now," she said. She knew he would change his mind, now that she had done it with him.

"Okay. Not now." He closed his eyes. She looked at him and tried to imagine his life at Harvard. Winthrop House, Dunster House, the Harvard Commons, the Harvard Coop, all the wonderful places he had told her about. She would call the train station later to find out how much a round-trip ticket cost.

He turned over, turned his narrow, freckled back to her. She touched his waist. He did not move. She touched it again. He did not move. She lay near him, staring at his back. She held her breath for as long as she could. He might notice if she stopped breathing. But she could not hold it long enough, and he did not care. There was a foot between them, they were as silent and stiff as mannequins, dead bodies. She knew suddenly—the emptiness in her stomach said she was right—that they would never be close again. It was over. She had made a mistake, made a hundred mistakes, had never done anything right. She was not going to cry, not now, not in front of him. Or behind him. She allowed herself a smile.

The beginning of her next thought surprised her. It was even more frightening than the others, than even the ending, *this* ending, of their romance. The thought that she could go to Harvard herself.

. . .

"Esme, is that you?"

"Yes."

"Sweetheart, come in here, I'm in the kitchen, I have something for you. My god, you look awful. What happened?" Georgia wiped her hands on her apron and reached to touch Esme's cheeks. "What happened? Are you sick? Where were you?"

"Gene's." Her voice was thick, her eyes were puffy. He had given her money for a cab and she had cried all the way uptown. "He got into Harvard."

"That's not a very good reason to cry your eyes out. Let me get you something to drink. Some juice. Take off your coat, put your book bag down, for heaven's sake." Georgia turned away from her and opened the refrigerator.

"We broke up."

Georgia spun around. "Sweetheart, why didn't you say so?" She threw her arms around Esme. Esme could hardly feel her, through her muskrat coat. But she let her head rest on Georgia's shoulder.

"He wanted to," she said. "Not me."

"Poor darling, poor thing."

"Don't call me that."

"Sweetheart, I'm just trying to—" Georgia stepped back and scanned the counters for something.

"Your drink is right here." Esme pointed to a glass.

"I was looking for this." Georgia picked up a letter and handed it to her. "Special delivery. From your father."

"Him and his special delivery."

"Aren't you going to open it?"

"Maybe later." Esme tossed it back on the counter.

"Open it now."

"Why?"

"Because you'll be pleased with what it is."

"How do you know? Did you look?" Esme picked it up and slid her finger under the back flap, looking at her mother. "Did you?"

"I held it up to the light. For a second. To see if it might be good news."

"So what does it say?"

"Esme, I didn't *read* it, I just—"

Esme pulled out a small sheet of paper wrapped around a check, for two hundred dollars. Drawn on a Las Vegas bank. The note said:

> Magoo,
> *If you play your cards right there will be more where this came from pronto or thereabouts.*
>
> *Love, Stu*

"Not bad," Esme said.

"What do you mean, not bad?"

"Just what I said." She put the envelope in her book bag. "Not bad."

"How much is it for?"

"Two hundred."

"I think it's better than 'not bad.' When's the last time he sent a dime?"

"He sends some money and all of a sudden you think he's a prince, you think he's Walter Cronkite." Esme stormed out of the room and heard her mother crack open an ice tray and dump the ice cubes in the sink.

She slammed her bedroom door shut and threw her coat and book bag on her bed. The envelope from her father slid out with a few books. If today had not happened the way it did, she could use the money to visit Gene next year in Cambridge. She could use it to go to a gynecologist to get birth-control pills.

She sat cross-legged on the floor, picked up the phone and dialed information. She asked for Warren Gold, at his address in the Village. She lit a cigarette. The number they gave her was the same one, the one he'd had for years. She wanted to tell him everything, tell him how much it hurt when she did it, and how much it had hurt before and after, not the sex—that didn't hurt half as much as the other things. She wanted to tell him about hearing ice trays being broken in the sink in the next room, about all the men who had tried to rescue her mother and ended up almost drowning themselves, how hard she worked, she, Esme, this person right here, to stay afloat, to make sure they did not pull her down with them, and the reason she cried so much when Gene broke up with her was not because she was in love with him but because she was counting on him to keep her from sinking, and the reason she cried so much in the cab coming home was not because she had lost her virginity but because she had lost it with someone she did not love.

She dialed Warren's number and took a deep breath.

It was extraordinary. He answered on the second ring. It was his voice, his actual voice. "Hello," he said. He waited a moment. "Hello." Another few seconds. "Hello? Hello?"

Esme put the receiver in its cradle as quietly as she could. Not that it mattered how you hung up on someone. Wasn't like they knew it was you and you had to make a good impression. She wanted to make a good impression. She wanted Warren to take care of her. Wanted him to come by with his motorcycle and take her to an off-Broadway play, tell her that she was fabulous, that she deserved a real man, not this kid Gene, even if he was going to Harvard. But she was afraid to talk to Warren now, even though she had called him and actually talked to him a few times, but not in five months, not since before she'd met Gene.

She crushed out her cigarette and looked at the check her father had sent her. Esme Singer. Two hundred and oo cents. The Bank of Nevada. April 12.

"Sweetheart, are you in there?" Her mother knocked on her door. "Can I come in? You left your juice in the kitchen." She opened the door. "Are you better?"

"Sort of."

"Will you have dinner with Tommy and me tonight? Here, sweetheart, take this, drink this down. You'll feel much better."

Esme took the glass and looked back at the check. That was when it hit her.

"What about dinner? We'd love it if you—"

Esme cut her off. "I have to make a phone call. I'll talk to you later. I'll be right out." She reached for the phone and dialed Leah's number. Leah answered the phone on the first ring.

"I was wondering if you could do me a big favor," Esme said.

"What's that?"

"Ask your father what kind of camera I should buy. Tell him I have two hundred dollars. My father just sent it to me."

"That's great. Maybe he isn't such a creep after all."

"He's not a creep."

"You always say he is. And when does he ever send you any money?"

"He's sent me plenty of money, Leah."

"That's not what you usually say."

"Ask your father about the camera, all right? And write down the kind he says I should get, so you don't forget."

"I'm not going to forget, Esme."

"Guess what."

"What."

"Gene and I did it," she whispered.

"Did what?"

"It."

"Are you serious?"

"Yes."

"What happened? What was it like?"

She could not possibly tell Leah the truth, the fight they had had about Harvard, that she had begged him to do it with her, that she had hoped it would make him change his mind. "It was weird."

"Fun?"

"It's not supposed to be, the first time."

"I know that. Everyone knows that. Did you use any, you know, birth control?"

"No."

"I hope you don't get pregnant. That would be awful."

"Thanks for reminding me. The other thing I was going to

tell you is that we also—" She did not want to say it, but she had to. "We broke up."

"You what?"

"And he got into Harvard. So I guess it doesn't really matter. Because he's going away soon anyway."

"Did you break up before or after you did it? I guess it would have to be after, wouldn't it?"

"It's kind of hard to explain. I really have to go now. I'm exhausted. I'm kind of upset too. Could you call me after you talk to your father."

"Yeah."

"I'll tell you what happened then, okay? All the details."

"I can't wait to hear them."

She put the receiver back. She was going to get a good camera. A real camera. Something Leah could not make fun of. Tonight at eleven, at a few minutes after eleven, she was going to call her father and thank him for the money and tell him that she was going to go to Harvard, and could he start saving money immediately, now that the money was starting to come in. Now that he had this reputation, Walter Cronkite's reputation, to live up to.

What You Can See
You Can Photograph

"SMILE," ESME SAID as Georgia walked in the front door. "Pretend you're modeling the coat."

"Let me put my things down. Let me get a drink before you start with the camera again."

Esme had bought a Pentax Spotmatic three days before, on sale at Willoughby Peerless. "Look this way," she said and focused. She pressed the shutter. "For Christ's sake! You closed your eyes."

"For Christ's sake, Esme, give me a minute." Georgia tossed her coat onto the couch and headed for the kitchen.

Esme followed her, holding the camera that hung on a strap around her neck. "When's Tommy coming home?"

"I don't know. Whenever he gets here." Georgia took an ice tray from the freezer, a bottle of scotch from the liquor cabinet.

"Maybe you could model for me before he comes. Put on a long dress. Do you have a long black dress?"

"Why black?"

"Because it's black-and-white film. I want you to stand against the wall in the living room in a black dress, so it'll be black against white. It's an experiment. If we still had black walls, you'd have to wear a white dress." She looked down again for the thousandth time at all the buttons and levers. The ASA knob, the shutter speeds, the little infinity sign on the rim around the lens. "After school I bought a roll of very fast film. So I can take pictures inside. But we still need to have all the lights on. I'll bring the lamps from all over the house into the living room."

"Is that really necessary?"

"If I had a flash attachment, it wouldn't be, but Leah's father said I didn't need one in the beginning. Do you have a black dress or not?"

"Not a long one."

"What color long dresses do you have?"

"It's been such a long time since I've—"

"You go look—" Esme started back to the called out— "and I'll get the lamps and arrange up before it gets too dark."

"The darker the better, at my age."

Esme brought three table lamps into the living room ,.ugged them in and took off the lampshades. She pushed aside an armchair and an end table, and removed a painting from the wall.

"Stand over there, where the painting was. Yeah. Like that."

"Are you sure there's enough light?" Georgia was wearing a long flowered muu-muu and a beige hat with a wide brim.

Esme looked through the viewfinder. "There's a little red light inside here. It's on now. I think that means there's enough."

"What do you want me to do?"

"Just model. Like you were in a commercial. That's good." Click. "Look over there, to the window." Georgia smiled and showed her left profile—click—her right profile, she did things with her arms—click, click—she put her hands on her hips—click, click. "That's great." Click. "That's really good."

"How many have you taken? It sounds like a hundred."

"About fifteen." She loved the click sound the shutter made when she pressed it.

"Why don't you check, sweetheart. You don't want to waste the whole roll on me and this ridiculous dress."

"I have plenty." Esme pressed it again and again. "Step back. Like that. A little to the right. Smile. Really smile. Not like that." Click. "Good. Yeah. Oh, shit."

"What is it?"

She looked at some of the numbers on top of the camera. "That's it for this roll. They'll be out next month in *Vogue*."

"Good. I've got to get started on dinner."

"Wait a minute." Esme looked up suddenly. "Just a minute, okay?"

eorgia reached down to the coffee table for her cigarettes, ith her back to Esme.

"I wanted to tell you something," Esme began, and Georgia turned to face her as she lit the cigarette. "I'm going to college."

"Of course you are, sweetheart." She dropped her match into the ashtray.

"You don't understand, I'm *going* to college."

"I always hoped you would. Lord knows, no one else in the family has gone yet."

"Could you sit down? We have to talk about it."

"This minute?"

"Yes."

"It can't wait until after dinner?"

"No."

"Why is that, if you don't mind my asking?"

"Because—" Esme tried to think of a lie. This was not the time to let Georgia have it with the truth—that she was usually half in the bag by the time she put dinner on the table, and good for nothing by the time it was over. "Because I don't want to talk about it in front of Tommy."

"Why's that?"

"Because it's private. Sit down, please."

"What kind of college do you have to go to that's so private?"

"I'll help you clean up if you talk about it now. Mom, please."

"I don't understand what the rush is about. You're only in tenth grade."

"Tenth grade ends in five weeks."

"All right, all right." Georgia sat down on the couch, took off the beige hat, and laid it down next to her.

Esme set down her camera and reached into the pocket of her jeans for the page of questions she had prepared. "There're some things I have to ask you." She sat across from Georgia and read from the paper. " 'How much money have you saved for my college education?' "

"Saved? You know that I can barely get along with—"

"Nothing. Is that the answer?"

"You make it sound like I deliberately—"

"I'm just trying to get some information. So I'll know how to proceed. Am I right, no savings?"

"Yes," Georgia said softly.

"Okay. Next question. 'Do you think you can save a small amount of money over the next two years that could be applied to—' "

"You make it sound like I'm going out of my way to deprive you of—"

"I didn't say that. But if you won't be able to save anything, say so."

"Esme, I think you have some idea that I can decide what should happen in my life and it will happen that way. Just because I want it to. Let me tell you something. Life doesn't work that way. Half the time, three-quarters of the time—"

"I'll put you down for zero Savings and zero Anticipated Savings." She read the next question. " 'Would you be willing to co-sign a student loan for me?' "

"What do you know about co-signing loans?"

"I called the bank. I asked them what I'd have to do to get one. Yes or no."

"Of course I would. Of course."

" 'What kind of collateral do you have?' "

"This is insane. You've got two years left to worry about this and I frankly don't see—"

"I figure the diamond ring Billy Maxwell gave you is good for a start. I can't think of anything else you could put up. Can you?"

"If you give me a few minutes, I might—"

"Those are all the questions I have right now." She folded the piece of paper and stood up.

"Would you please tell me what is going on here?"

"I'm collecting data."

"Who else are you collecting it from?"

"My father, for one. He'll pay for me to go to college."

"Then why did you just grill me?"

"Because—" she said the first thing that came to mind— "it's not fair that he should pay it all. Considering how much it is."

"How much is it?"

"Four thousand a year."

"Four thousand! What college are you going to?"

"I'm thinking of Harvard. Until this year, girls went to Radcliffe. Now it's all coed. Gene told me."

"Is that why you want to go there, to be near him?"

"Mother, we broke up *weeks* ago."

"That doesn't mean you wouldn't go off and do something crazy to remind him of your existence."

"Why is going to Harvard crazy?"

"Your grades aren't exactly—"

"Not everyone who goes there has straight A's. They look for people who have interesting extracurricular activities."

"What are yours?"

"I take photographs for the school newspaper and the yearbook. I signed up yesterday."

"It might do you more good to study math than photography."

"Since when do you care so much about my education? Since I asked you to pay for it, right?"

"No." Georgia crushed her cigarette and lit another. "Since you told me you expected your father to."

"He will."

"When did he say that?"

"Two nights ago. I called him to tell him I bought a camera with the money he sent me. He told me he just started a new business."

"I've heard that before."

"I believe it's going to be very successful. It's an idea whose time has come."

"He has a suitcaseful of ideas whose time has come. And gone."

"The new company is different. It isn't like the others."

"Haven't you learned? Haven't you been through this enough times to know that what he says isn't—" Georgia shook her head. "I need another drink if I'm going to hear any more of this." She got up and went through the wide doorway into the kitchen.

"It's a company that's going to sell light bulbs," Esme called out.

"Great. Terrific. That's what the world needs. More light bulbs."

"They're special light bulbs." Esme crossed the room and took a seat at the table in the room Georgia called the dining room. She had a long view of her mother in the kitchen. "They found out that regular fluorescent light bulbs—"

"Who found out?"

"Meyer has a team, a company. There's him, there's a scientist, and a marketing guy." Esme watched as Georgia poured a double shot of scotch into her glass. Then she slipped an apron on over her muu-muu. "They found out that fluorescent lights are harmful but the government has been repressing information about it." Georgia took a head of cauliflower and chicken wrapped in plastic from the refrigerator.

"The new company has developed a very powerful light bulb that isn't harmful." Esme picked up two forks from the table and held them back to back, then front to front, like interlocking fingers, like lovers' legs entwined, the way her legs had been with Gene's that day three weeks ago. "They're going to take on General Electric." Georgia unwrapped the chicken and ran each piece, the wings, the breasts, the drumsticks, under water. "Fight them tooth and nail. They're going to raise a million dollars from investors and then start producing the light bulbs and then advertise all over the place, TV, radio, *The New York Times*, the *Wall Street Journal*, and then—"

Georgia spun around, a raw drumstick in her hand, and glared at Esme. "Then what the fuck do you need me for?"

Esme dropped the forks.

"Georgia!" Tommy called out. The front door swung open. "You home yet?"

It was a moment before she spoke. "I'm in here." She turned back to the sink and ran chicken parts she had already washed under water.

"What the hell happened in the living room?" Tommy said as he walked into the kitchen. Esme watched his entrance, watched the scene, play by play. Tommy holding out a brown paper bag to Georgia, pulling apart his tie, tweaking Georgia's behind. "What are you doing in that get-up?"

"Esme was taking pictures of me with her new camera. She rearranged the living room. I was modeling."

"Do I have a story for you," he said and took a glass from the dishwasher. "You're not going to *believe* this one." He happened to look in Esme's direction. He held up his hand to her. "Hiya, kiddo."

"In case you forgot, my name is Esme."

"Don't start," Georgia said. "I've had enough already tonight."

"What's the matter?" Tommy said. "You broads fighting again? Wait'll you hear this story. You'll scream." He was tall, lanky; he had a face that was badly pockmarked. Her mother's faggoty boyfriend. He didn't swish, he was just narrow and frail-looking. He fixed his drink at the kitchen counter as he began to speak. "So the story's this, this old fart—"

"Esme, set the table," Georgia said and pointed to it. "The silverware's already out."

"Are you going to listen, or are you going to talk to her?" Tommy said.

"I'm telling her what to do."

Tommy dropped a few ice cubes into his drink, he coughed into his fist. A smoker's cough, a gravelly voice. "This old fart—"

he coughed again. "I mean *old*, eighty-something, could be pushing ninety. He books a trip to the Caribbean with us. Shirley's the one who did all the paperwork. A scuba-diving gig to Aruba." He drank down about a quarter of his drink. "He goes with this broad. She's nineteen, maybe twenty, a few years shy of jailbait. And guess what happens?"

"He has a heart attack and croaks," Georgia said.

"How did you know?"

"Woman's intuition."

"Come on."

"It had to be something like that, from the way you started."

"But not only does he croak," Tommy said, leaning back against the counter, taking another long swig, "he croaks *while in the act*. Under water, if you can believe that one. It happened two or three days ago, but the hotel people didn't get ahold of Shirley until this afternoon, it was about quarter to four. I tell you, we laughed till it hurt. Is that a story or is that a story?"

"That's really a story," Esme said under her breath.

"It's a riot," Georgia said. Tommy began to laugh. His laughter softened her, made her smile, made her look at him over the rim of her tumbler, and he looked back at her, the way people do when they're in love, a look of conspiracy and lust, the only two members of their private club. But with them it wasn't really love, Esme knew, except when they were on their way to being drunk.

"What a way to go." Tommy burst out laughing. "I hope to Christ I go like that."

"Listen to this, sweetheart."

"I'm all ears."

"Esme's going to Harvard."

"I thought you had to be rich to go to Harvard."

"Esme has a rich father."

"That's news to me," Tommy said.

"It's news to him too."

"I never said—" Esme began.

"Sweetheart, we're just having a little fun with you. Aren't we, Tommy?"

"Of course we are. We love to have fun." He picked up the bottle of scotch and poured another shot into his glass, into Georgia's glass. "It's happy hour, baby," he said. "Two for the price of one."

Esme got up and stood for a moment at the table, ten or twelve feet from them. She watched them touch and flirt and look into each other's bloodshot eyes. Diane Arbus took pictures of families of freaks. Midgets in their living rooms or giants or people covered from head to foot with tattoos. Easy to see what was wrong with them. *What You Can See You Can Photograph.* Esme did not know how to take pictures of her family— if you call a family Georgia and this creep she lives with—and show what was wrong with them. That they went through a fifth of scotch every other night, that they started out at six all lovey-dovey and ended up, around midnight, hurling plates and plants. Got up the next morning like nothing had happened and went off to work. No way to convey that in a photograph. Even if you could, you wouldn't want to. Wouldn't want anyone to know.

From now on, she was going to take pictures of strangers.

Smarter than Usual

"ESME'S BEEN TAKING pictures," Leah announced at dinner. "She showed them to me upstairs." It was the middle of April, the end of their junior year in high school. They went to separate schools now, and only saw each other once or twice a month.

Don turned to Esme. "Pictures of what?"

She thought for a moment. She had wanted to be asked such a question, but in her wanting she had forgotten to prepare an answer worthy of Don Marks, of this dinner at his house. "Things I see."

"I should hope so." Don smiled. His jowls sagged, his voice was deep and gentle, but still she was afraid of him, of all he had achieved, all that he assumed. "What do you see?"

"I don't think I have a style yet. I'm still looking for one."

"Isn't style how you see, rather than what you see? Or maybe you think that style is something you find after a long search, like a house or a new car."

She had no idea what to say but he seemed to be waiting. "Well. I've been reading a lot of books about photographers and they all say that it takes years to manifest your talent, to develop your true style, your own distinct . . . "

"The evidence is all on the other side—" Don poured wine into his glass with a flourish, a twist of his wrist— "from Huysmans to, say, Susan Sontag. Style is not decoration, it's character. Character dictates style. Do you know what Cocteau said about this?" Esme shook her head. " 'Style is the soul, and unfortunately with us the soul assumes the form of the body.' But it also works the other way around. The body assumes the form of the soul." Esme nodded. "You won't *find* a style, any more than you'll *find* a personality. Did you think it was otherwise?"

"No, I was just—"

"Esme," Leah's mother Abby said from the other end of the

table. Esme turned to her. She was certain to have another round of questions, another interrogation. "Would you like some more veal?"

"Yes. Please. It's very good."

"What kind of camera have you got?" Don said.

"The Pentax you told me to buy last year."

"I told you?"

"I asked you—" Leah said, looking at her father— "what kind of camera Esme should get and that's the kind you said. Then I told her. She'd just gotten a heap of money from her father."

"I'd forgotten. You're not around as much as you used to be, now that you and Leah are in separate schools."

"And your memory isn't what it used to be, is it, dear?" Abby said. She had bangs, long auburn hair pulled back in a pony tail, a heavy silver bracelet with inlaid bands of lapus lazuli and malachite; Esme had asked her once what the stones were called.

"It just needs jogging now and then," Don said. "Like an old horse. I do remember now, talking to Leah about the camera. What kind of lens did I tell you to get?"

"The standard one that comes with it," Esme said. "The fifty millimeter."

"What else have you got? A zoom, a wide angle?"

"I can't afford anything else, I can barely afford—"

"You don't need them, really. It's a lot of advertising they foist on you. If you can't take a good picture with a fifty millimeter, you won't be able to take a good one with a wide angle. Or any other lens."

She felt the need to set the record straight. "I'm not just working on my style. I'm on the yearbook staff at my school. It's very different from shooting your own pictures. With the yearbook, subjects come to you, or you go to them. It's extremely blatant. Here, take a picture of the debating team. Here, the French Club, the music faculty. It's very orderly, very—"

"Dull," Don said.

"Yes, dull, but what I was thinking is that it's the opposite

of your own work. With your own work, you go out there and try
to catch people off guard. You sit along the sidelines, you pretend
you're not there, and then take a picture. With the yearbook,
there isn't the same adventure. The same challenge." She stopped
for a moment. "I guess that is what makes it dull."

"I think that's exactly what makes it dull. But it'll help you
get into college, won't it, all that extracurricular hoo-ha."

"I guess so. I mean, I hope so."

"Where are you thinking of going?" Leah's mother asked.

"I haven't decided." She had not told Leah her aspiration
to go to Harvard, what she called in her diary "T.H.C.," which
stood for The Harvard Campaign.

"We tried to convince Leah to think about Barnard," Abby
said. "Her brother went to Columbia and adored it—but she
won't hear of it. She's determined to leave New York."

"So am I," Esme said. "Extremely determined."

"Keep taking those dull pictures," Don said. "Take a million of them. It'll look great on your application. Wherever you
apply. Jesus, I've taken at least two million dull photographs in
my life."

"You? Really?"

"I spent five years in advertising before I went out on my
own. I took pictures of Jell-O, toothpaste, radial tires. When I
was twenty, I thought I'd be able to make it as an 'art' photographer. I went to Paris, naturally—that's where all aspiring artists
went in those days—and ran out of money in very short order. I
had a roomful of books and a camera and about thirty dollars to
my name. I vowed I'd sell my books before I'd sell my camera,
and I did. I carted away every last book and got enough money to
support myself until I sold my first photograph. To Magnum. It
was a picture of twin girls sitting in a café with a very stern-
looking nanny. I didn't sell my next one for six months." He
laughed. "By which time I'd already come back here and started
looking for a job on Madison Avenue. Most people can't leave it
once they get there." The phone rang. Leah jumped up to answer
it. "Advertising, that is. Can't leave the money. Can't leave the

security, if they have any. And their art has turned to porridge by the time they've spent five years taking pictures of lawnmowers and disposable diapers."

"Daddy, it's for you," Leah said. "It's that guy Rory Dean."

"Oh, yes." He left the table.

"Who's Rory Dean?" Abby asked.

"He was here the other night," Leah said, "dropping off a package. The night you came in late. The one who looks like Jean-Paul Belmondo."

"I should have paid closer attention," Abby said. "Esme, would you like some more?" She held out a bowl of noodles.

"No, thank you."

"I must say, you've lost weight since we first met you."

"I guess I have."

"Quite a lot. That's marvelous. I wish I had half that much willpower. Or maybe it was just baby fat—you know, bound to come off."

"Mother, really."

"What's wrong with baby fat?"

"Nothing's *wrong* with it, but maybe Esme doesn't want to talk about it."

"She's not required to say a word. I just wanted to tell her how super she's looking these days. The two of you, actually. Some Rory Dean somewhere will sweep you both off your feet. With any luck—" Abby smiled—"there'll be one for each of you. At least one."

"I'll take Rory," Leah said.

"I think he's a little old for you, my love."

"He's not more than twenty-five."

"And you're sixteen."

"Seventeen in a month."

"Don't I know it." Abby got up and began to clear the table. "Stay tuned for the next course." She carried their plates into the kitchen.

"My father says he's a first-rate photographer," Leah said.

"Who?" Esme said.

"Rory."

"Leah, it's terribly Freudian to go out with someone who does what your father does."

"I'm not going out with him. But I'd certainly like to. You would too—" she lowered her voice as her father approached—"if you knew him."

"Smart kid," Don said to himself, as he sat down.

"What did he want?" Leah asked.

Abby returned with a bowl of strawberries, a small pitcher of cream. "Esme, you'll have strawberries, won't you? They have almost no calories."

This was almost as bad as being fat, being reminded that you used to be. "Yes, please."

"He wanted to talk some more about promoting his book, the one I wrote the introduction for. He dropped off a copy the other night. Photographs of nude women."

"I didn't know you knew anything about that," Abby said.

"Just what I've read."

"Nude women?" Leah said.

"Anyone we know?" Esme said brightly.

"I should hope not. They're all drug addicts."

"What a macabre idea for a book," Abby said. "Who'd want to look at—"

"It is a ghoulish idea, and I had my hesitations before I saw them. But he's done remarkable things. Turned the notion of the beautiful photographer's model on its ear—but without falling into the trap of making it a freak show. There's something very dignified about the women."

"How did he get them to disrobe?" Abby said. "Where did he find an entire bookful of naked female drug addicts?"

"San Francisco." Don smiled and ate a strawberry. "Where else?"

"Have some cream with those," Abby said and held out the pitcher.

"I don't want to ruin the taste. I can't stop eating them. I wish we could have them all year long."

"We can. Five dollars a pound. Imported from New Zealand."

"But they don't taste the same. I met someone once who didn't like strawberries. Can you imagine?" He turned to Esme. "You'll have to bring your photographs around sometime."

"And you'll write the introduction?" Esme said.

"Absolutely. I'll write it now, sight unseen."

"They're upstairs," Leah said.

"What's upstairs?" Abby said.

"Esme's photographs."

"Bring them down, why don't you?" Don turned to Leah. "You started to tell me something before dinner about what you wanted to do when we're in Paris this summer. What was it?"

Esme did not move. She had nothing so compelling as pictures of naked drug addicts. She did not have a style. She did not know if she would ever have one, or how she could turn her personality into one, if that's what he had been talking about before. He wouldn't like her photographs anyway, a bag lady on Madison Avenue, a hippie in Central Park, a kid holding a helium balloon by a string on the steps of the Metropolitan Museum.

" . . . so instead of my staying in Paris with you for all of August," Leah was explaining to her parents, "I'd spend half of the month in the Dordogne. Jenny Saunders's parents have a house there. She invited me. I'd meet you in Paris afterward."

"She's the girl we met the other night, isn't she?" Abby said. "The one from your school."

Leah nodded.

"I thought you were talking about plans for all of us," Don said.

"No. Just me."

"That's all right with you, isn't it, Abby?"

"Who are her parents?"

"Her father's Frank Saunders. I told you before."

"The artist?"

"Of *course*, the artist. I told you that ages ago."

"I don't remember," Abby said. "Do you remember, Don?"

"I don't either, but don't forget, my memory isn't what it used to be. Actually, it's never been what it used to be."

Esme started to laugh and stopped when she saw that she was the only one laughing.

"Well, Leah," Abby said, "aren't you glad that you go to a school where you can meet such interesting people?"

"The parents may be interesting," Don said. "The kids have a ways to go before—"

"Go off with Jenny to the Dordogne, that sounds fine to me," Abby said. "Just don't let her father do a sculpture of you. I hear you have to sit in plaster for hours."

"Did you see his show last year at the Modern?" Don said.

"I did," Leah said.

"I did too," Esme said.

"We went to that together, didn't we, Abby? Did Leah come with us? I don't remember, but that's nothing new."

"I think we went together, but I'm . . . "

Esme stopped listening carefully. She knew all about Frank Saunders. She had been to the exhibit; she had read the catalog. But Leah had not told her about this new friend from her school, the private school where everyone's parents were famous and fascinating.

"What do you think of Saunders's work?" Don said.

"Me?" Esme said.

He nodded.

She thought a moment. She visualized the life-size plaster figures staring off into space, looking past one another, even when there was a roomful of them. "I think it's about loneliness."

"That's what struck me too," Don said. "I suspect most art springs from that."

"From loneliness?" Abby said.

"Or torment. Look at Edvard Munch."

"Photographers don't seem like a very tormented crowd to me," Abby said.

"That's just because you know the successful ones," Don said and laughed.

"I don't think a tormented personality is a matter of circumstance," Abby said. "If it were, all successful people would be happy."

"That assumes that success is a positive rather than a negative circumstance."

"Since when have you thought otherwise?" Abby said. "Since you gave up taking photographs of radial tires for a living?"

"And what about Esme?" Don said. "Does she want to be a photographer because she's tormented or because she isn't?"

"I haven't heard Esme say she's set on being a photographer," Abby said. "It's not fair to lump her in with all of them until she's actually declared herself, don't you think?"

"I suppose so," Don said and finished the wine in his glass. "You girls must have homework to do."

They're talking about me as if I'm not here, Esme thought.

"Yes," Leah said.

"Yes," Esme repeated.

"Well, then. Why don't you take your dessert plates into the kitchen." He reached into his shirt pocket for his cigarettes.

She had expected something more to happen, something deeper and richer to be exchanged between them, among them. Something she could cherish, dream about, recall word for word and write down in her diary when she got home. To the dungeon where she lived.

Leah led the way up the stairs in the dark. "I've got a lot of reading left to do tonight," she said.

"Me too," Esme lied.

"I have to finish *Ten Days That Shook the World*. You can get your things together up in my room and then head home."

"I was planning to."

"You did good tonight," Leah said.

"What do you mean?"

Leah stopped on the third-floor landing and switched on an

overhead light. "You were smarter than you usually are in front of them."

Esme called Leah as soon as she got home. "I was wondering if your father is going to be home tomorrow night."

"You saw him ten minutes ago."

"But I wanted to show him my photographs."

"He asked to see them. You could have just gone upstairs and—"

"I was . . . I don't know, embarrassed."

"You really shouldn't be so mousy, Esme. You'll never do anything well if you—"

"Is he going to be home or not?"

"How am I supposed to know? What's tomorrow? Friday. They usually go to the country around eight. He's here until then. Most of the time."

"Are you going to be there?"

"They're putting on a play at my school. I'll be leaving here at seven-thirty."

"Would you mind telling your father—would you mind asking him—"

"If he'll look at your photographs? He already told you he would."

"Then tell him I'm coming, all right? Tell him it'll just take him a few minutes."

Leah did not respond.

"Well? All right?"

Leah mumbled something.

"What?"

"I said, I'll do it."

"Thanks."

"You should have spoken up before."

"I *know*, Leah. Christ, I *know*. But things don't happen just because you want them to happen that way. Half the time, most of the time—" She stopped the second she heard. Her mother, *that* was her mother talking.

"Esme. I have to get off now. I was in the middle of—"

"I do too. I'll talk to you soon. Bye."

It was like dieting, what she was doing. You had to change your habits, stay on course, slap your hand whenever you started to stray, whenever you heard yourself say something that could have come straight out of Georgia's mouth.

· · ·

"Leah's upstairs," Don said. "Go on up."

"Didn't she tell you?" It was a warm evening. Esme did not move from the doorway. She held the manila envelope of photographs under her arm.

"Tell me what?"

"That I was going to come by."

"She didn't mention it."

"Oh."

"Come on in. Are you going to the school play with her?"

"No."

"I think she's about to leave."

"I was just wondering—" She was still standing in the doorway. "You said you might take a look at some of them."

"Some of what?"

"These." She held out the envelope. "My pictures."

"Sure. Hand them over. But come in, for god's sakes. I can't see a thing in this light. I don't have long. We're about to leave for the country." He led her into the sitting room on the first floor, the heavy old furniture, the high wall of books, a Persian rug so thin in spots you could see the wooden floor. "Leah and I have just been talking about your favorite subject. Take a seat."

"What's that?"

"What college you should go to."

"What college I should go to?"

"You, Leah, the rest of the upper-middle-class kids in eleventh grade in America in the nineteen-seventies. Such a complicated business. In this country, anyway." He sat down on the love seat across from her and undid the clasp on the envelope. "Tell me again where you want to go."

"I was thinking of—" she took a deep breath— "maybe Harvard."

"So's Leah. As I'm sure you know." He gently reached his fingers into the envelope, he seemed to want to remove the photographs without touching them.

"They're not very good."

He looked up at her. "Never say that to anyone before he looks at your work."

"How come?"

"Because if you're showing your pictures, it means you think enough of them to show them. If not, you wouldn't be showing them, would you?"

"I guess not."

They were eight-by-ten black-and-whites. He went through them slowly, he bit the inside of his cheek as he examined them. He smiled now and then, he licked his upper lip. "Why on earth do you want to go to Harvard?"

This was worse than she had expected. She should not have told him. "Well." She could barely bring herself to speak. "I don't *really* want to go there."

"It would be a dreadful place for you." He stared at the photograph in his hand. "Perfectly awful."

She had worked so hard. She could not believe he was saying this to her. "Are you serious?"

"The question is—" he looked at her—"whether you're serious."

"What?"

"Because if this is just a hobby—"

"Well, right now—"

"—it shouldn't be."

"I know, but—" She did not say anything for a few seconds. "What did you say?"

"You ought to think about going to art school. These are

very good. Contrary to what you think, you do have a style." He looked at the picture in his lap as he spoke.

"Really?"

"At least the beginnings of one." He put that one aside and looked at one beneath it. "There's a certain directness and austerity here that's— Every one of these people looks you straight in the eye. And they all have a sort of mournful quality that I like."

"Well . . . " She felt light-headed, almost giddy. "I'd been hoping—"

When he looked at her she stopped talking. "But that's not enough."

"What?"

"There's style and there's mastery of craft. You won't be any good if you have one without the other."

"I know."

"Of course you know. Every artist knows that. Or pretends he does."

Before she had a chance to respond, Leah came in. "I was just looking at Esme's photographs," Don said. "They're wonderful. I've convinced her to forget about going to Harvard and to—"

"You want to go to Harvard?" Leah said.

Don made a pile of the photographs and put them on the end table.

"I didn't say I wanted to, I said I was thinking about—"

"Esme, dear." Don stood up. "Abby and I are trying to finish packing upstairs. I've got to run. I'll catch you on my way out. If you're still here."

"Okay."

"We can talk some more about this. Whenever you'd like."

"Great."

Leah stood by her father's seat when he left. "You never told me you were applying to Harvard."

"I haven't decided. I'm considering it."

"It's really hard to get into."

"I didn't know that, Leah. Thanks for telling me."

"How could you not know?"

"How could you not know I know?"

"Oh."

"Jesus."

"What?"

Esme stood up. "I've got to go." She snapped up the photographs. "I just came by to show these to your father." She tried to slide them into the envelope but she did it too fast, she was starting to tremble. The corners jammed into the sides of the envelope.

"Let me help you."

"I can do it myself." She started over, made a neat stack of the photographs and eased them in. She headed for the hall, she did not look back. The envelope was under her arm. The front door was twenty feet ahead of her.

"Esme, come on, don't be so thin-skinned."

"I'm not thin-skinned. I'm just trying to get out of your way." She turned around suddenly. "Say goodbye to your father, all right?"

"Yeah."

"Tell him thanks, okay?"

"Thanks for what?"

"He'll know." She took a few steps toward the door and stopped again. She was afraid she would start to cry if she spoke, she was that close to tears, so she kept her back to Leah. "Have fun in France," she said.

"I'm not leaving for months. Not until August."

It was strange talking to her this way, without seeing her face. "I know."

"Then why are you—"

"Because it's time." She felt her knees almost give way as she pulled open and pulled shut the heavy front door. She walked three blocks before she realized that she was going the wrong way, and that now, now she was on her own. Except for the pictures under her arm, and what Don Marks had said about them.

.   .   .

On Monday afternoon she went to the guidance office at Music and Art to look through art-school catalogs. There was good news for her father—art school was cheaper than Harvard. About twenty-five cents on the dollar.

That night, at two minutes after eleven, when the cheapest rates were in effect, she sat down on the floor of her bedroom with the telephone and a piece of loose-leaf paper on which she had written the information about art-school fees. She was going to call her father in Las Vegas to tell him the good news. Hi, Stu, she was going to say, this is me, this is Esme, and have I got a deal for you.

She lit a cigarette and dialed. She heard Georgia and Tommy fighting. The yelling was muted. They were probably in their bedroom, across the apartment from Esme's room, as far away as they could be from her. A recording came on after the second ring: *"The number you have dialed has been disconnected."* She tried the number again. *"The number you have dialed has been disconnected."*

She called information in Las Vegas. Got the same number she had just called.

She put the phone down and looked at the clock. Too late to call her grandparents, to find if they had another number for him, if they knew what had happened to his phone, to him. But all of this might be news to them. He usually lay low when he was in trouble. No news, with him, was bad news.

"Esme!" Georgia called. "Are you in there?"

"Where else would I be?" she said to herself.

Georgia burst into the bedroom.

"What happened?"

"He locked himself in the bathroom." Georgia hobbled barefoot across the room, sat down on Esme's bed, and picked up her right foot, rested it on her left thigh. She shook her head and began to knead her toes. "He wouldn't answer me, so I kicked the door. I kicked a hole in it. I think I broke my toe. That bastard. Sweetheart, would you get my drink, I think it's in the living room. Thank you, sweetheart. Thank you, thank you, thank you. I don't know what I'd do without you."

. . .

Her grandparents called—they hardly ever called—two months later, the evening of her seventeenth birthday. "Happy birthday," her grandfather said. "Hole the wire. Dot," he called, his mouth away from the mouthpiece, "pick up the phone. She's on." He spoke into the mouthpiece. "She'll be right here. How are you, dear?"

"Fine. How are you?"

"Fine. Everything's good."

"Esme?"

"Yes, Grandma?"

"We're calling to say happy birthday. Did you get the card and the check? I mailed them the day before yesterday."

"Not yet. I'm sure they'll be here tomorrow."

"Then it's a good thing we called. Tell me, what do you hear from your father?"

"He called me this morning," she lied, "to wish me a happy birthday."

"That was thoughtful of him," Dot said. "How'd he sound?"

"He sounded fine. His business is doing well."

"I don't know what type of individual lives in Las Vegas, but if he's making a living and he's happy . . . "

"Have you heard from him?"

"It's been a while," Dot said, "quite a while."

"Last month," Goody said. "He called the house."

"It was more than a month ago," Dot said.

"I'm telling you," Goody said, "it was a month ago. He called about ha' past seven. Herb and Janice were over t' the house. They got on the wire. They hadn't talked to him since years before. How's your mother?"

"She's on her way home from work right now. We're going out for dinner, for my birthday. To this Italian place up the street."

"How's her job? Is she still at that Vidal outfit?"

"Yeah. Last week Barbra Streisand came in and got her legs waxed. My mother was the one who booked her appointment."

"Isn't that something. People like that have more money than they know what to do with. And very often they're ill-mannered."

"My mother didn't say anything about that."

"Naturally. Your mother is very polite. Extremely polite. We were going to ask the two of you to come up for Thanksgiving. You and your mother. Your father probably won't have time to come back for that, with his busy schedule."

"Thanksgiving? That's five months from now."

"We like to plan ahead. It's been so many years since the whole family got together. Now that you're older, you should meet all of your relations. And quite frankly, I don't remember the last time I saw your mother."

"I'll be there," Esme said. "I'd love to come. Maybe we can go to Shoe Town."

"You need shoes?" Goody said.

"I might." She smiled. "In five months, I might."

"Good," her grandfather said.

"Tell your mother we'd like her to come too," Dot said.

"I'll tell her. But I never know what her plans are."

"Dot," Goody said. "It's enough already. Let her get off the phone."

"I'm not keeping her on the phone."

"Esme?" Goody asked. "Are you all right?"

"I'm fine."

"You know what I always say?"

"He's got something to say about everything," Dot said.

" 'You should never be in want,' " Goody said. " 'If you need money, holler.' Remember that. Don't forget it."

"Speaking of money," Esme said, "I forgot to tell you. I just got a job. It starts next week and goes through the summer. Part time now. Full time in the summer. I'm going to scoop ice cream at a place that opened two weeks ago. It's a few blocks from here."

"Good. Good to hear."

"Let us know what it's like," Dot said. "Have a happy birthday, sweetie. Give my regards to your mother."

"Go eat your dinner," Goody said.

"I will. I'll look for the card. Thanks for calling. Thanks a lot for calling."

"It's the least we can do," her grandmother said. "The very least."

She hung up the phone. She did not know why she had said her father had called that morning when he had not. She had not told them, or her mother, that his phone had been disconnected. No news was bad news. Even worse, she had sent him a letter a month ago and it had been returned last week, NO FORWARDING ADDRESS. In the meantime, you had to put the best face on things. She had lied to her grandparents for the sake of appearances. For the sake of the children. Maybe her grandparents had lied to her too, lied that they had talked to him last month, or the month before. Maybe they knew his phone had been disconnected and that he had left no forwarding address. Maybe that was why they had invited Georgia for Thanksgiving, because they couldn't find Meyer, and figured he'd never come for Thanksgiving anyway. Esme was not going to tell her mother about their invitation to her. Because where her mother went Tommy went. Where Tommy and Georgia went, as long as there was a bottle of booze, as long as there was a liquor store within a hundred miles—it was no place for the uninitiated. Jesus. Hordes of relatives Esme had never met. All they needed was to see Georgia careening around the living room after eight or nine drinks. Georgia and Tommy slugging it out. What a charming mother you have, they would say. What other tricks does she do?

"Esme?" Georgia called out. "Are you in there? Are you there?"

"Yes, Mom."

"Sweetheart." Georgia must be yelling from the kitchen or from her bedroom. "Tommy and I just got home. Are you ready to go to dinner?"

Her mother was the only one who called it the way it was when it came to Meyer. *Your father consults* Ripley's Believe It or Not *when he's trying to figure out what to do with his life.* It was not possible that her drunken, dithering, dimwitted mother could be right about anything so important. It was not possible, but there it was, the truth.

"Yes," Esme called back. "I'm ready."

"Happy birthday, sweetheart." Georgia appeared at her door, holding a small box at her side, smaller than her hand. "It's too bad you can't take a picture of yourself right now. You look beautiful. Simply beautiful. Here." She held out the box, wrapped in silver paper, topped with an ornate white bow twice as high as the box. "Here, my love. This is for you. Because the day you were born was the happiest day of my life."

Knee-Deep

SATURDAY MORNING, ALMOST ten, sitting up in her bed, the covers were up to her waist. Books in the folds of the sheets, under the pillow. Catalogs from art schools, colleges; books of photographs she had bought at used-book stores in the Village, on the Upper West Side. The autumn of her last year in high school, days that were unexpectedly warm, Central Park thick with leaves the color of daffodils, the color of Georgia's bright red lipstick. Esme loathed color pictures, the pictures Sunday photographers take of the leaves. They are too easy, too likable. They do not lend themselves to melancholy, to true depth.

This was heaven, heavenly, this solitude, surrounded by possibilities—the art-school catalogs—and achievement—the books. This book in particular: *Junked Up* by Rory Dean, With an Introduction by Don Marks. She had found it last night at a used-book store, half price. She would write in her diary later, not now, *I was meant to be a kept woman, meant to live without a care in the world but art, my art. All other endeavors, except love, are utterly fatuous. But where is love? Love might be right here in this very bed with me right now. Or I might have to go to Washington to find it. Maybe hitch a ride there next weekend with Jon P., who invited me last week. No need to tell him exactly why.*

She turned to the back cover of *Junked Up*, the two-by-three photograph of Rory, his ten-line biography. He did look like Belmondo in *Breathless*, a look Leah once described as *enfant maudit*. On his way to a car theft, the collar of his leather jacket turned up, he deigns to be photographed. He was divine. He grew up in Pittsburgh and has lived in London, Paris, San Francisco, and New York. He was awarded the prestigious Young Photographer's Prize in 1970. He teaches photography at the Corcoran School of Art in Washington, D.C. *Junked Up* is his first book. She looked closely at his photograph, the credit in tiny letters beneath it. Sam Browning. A good sign. A woman had not taken the picture. If there was a woman in his life, Rory would have gotten her to take the picture.

Then she turned to Don's introduction and read the opening over and over: "*Rory Dean came to photography relatively late in his life. He was twenty-one when he picked up a camera for the first time. When he did, it was with a vengeance. I happened to meet him four years later. Actually, he tracked me down. He told me later that he went to considerable effort to get my home address, to which he sent a batch of photographs. He didn't want the photographs to get lost in the mass of unsolicited photographs he assumed I receive at my office. He needn't have gone to all that trouble. His photographs would have caught my attention if I'd seen them in a stack of a thousand. The truth is that talent stands out, rises, like cream, to the top.*"

There was a knock on her door, and then it opened. "You got some mail," Georgia said and crossed the room looking down at the postcard in her hand. "Sounds like a super place to live. Post Office Box three-twelve, El Paso, Texas. The armpit of the nation."

"Who lives there?"

"Guess." Georgia handed it over, the change-of-address card, Post Office issue, from Meyer.

"No one asked for your opinion," Esme said as she took it.

"No one ever asks, sweetheart. That's why I have to volunteer it. Did you know?"

"Know what?"

"That he'd moved to El Paso?"

"No."

"When's the last time you talked to him?"

"I don't know. A few months ago." Actually, many months ago. The last time she had talked to him, he'd told her that he was starting the light bulb company and that he would pay—no problem, Magoo, no problem whatsoever—for her to go to Harvard. She began to clean her fingernails with the corners of the card, waiting for her mother to leave.

"I suppose anyplace is better than Las Vegas."

"Unless you're a gambler," Esme said, digging under her nails with the care of a model, a contestant in a beauty pageant. "Or a stripper. Or the guy who owns Caesar's Palace." The pinkie of her left hand, ring finger, middle finger. "I don't suppose his name is really Caesar."

"What time do you have to be at work today?"

"Eleven," Esme said. "Till five."

"And you have a date tonight, don't you?"

"I don't date, Mother."

"What do you call it when you go out with someone of the opposite sex?"

"Going out."

"I was going to ask you and your date, or whatever you call him, if you want to have dinner with Tommy and me and then head out."

"His name is Jon. Without the H. But we can't. We're going to a movie."

"Which one is Jon?"

"I met him at a lecture a few weeks ago at N.Y.U. He's a sophomore there. He's got a car." Her best singsong voice, cleaning her nails while she spoke. "He's two inches taller than me. His father's a brain surgeon. He has a sister who's a senior at Georgetown. She was Phi Beta Kappa in her junior year and has a mild case of anorexia and no boyfriend at the moment. He invited me to drive down there next weekend to visit her. Anything else you want to know?"

"Is this serious?"

"Going to Washington?"

"No. Him."

"Is him serious? No, him isn't. But going to Washington might be. There are some art shows I want to see down there. And I want to check out the art school down there."

"I think it might be nice," Georgia said, "if you *went out* with someone who showed their face around here once in a while. Particularly if you're going away with him next weekend."

"Speaking of going away, could you excuse me, please, I have to make a phone call." She reached for the phone on her night table, gripped the receiver without picking it up.

"You're not calling your father, are you?"

Esme looked up. "It's not allowed?"

"Of course it's allowed. I was just surprised. When's the last time you called him?"

"First of all, I didn't say I was going to. Second of all, I called him a few months ago. Third of all—" she held up the back of the card for her mother to see— "there's no phone number."

As Georgia peered down to look at it, the phone rang.

Esme lifted the receiver. "Hello."

"Hello there. This is Grandpa."

"This is Esme. What a surprise."

"How are you today?"

"Fine. How are you? Are you all right?" Something had to be wrong for them to call. The second time in four months.

"Everyone's fine. Hole the wire. Your grandmother wants to talk to you. Dot!"

"Esme, are you there?"

"Hi, Grandma."

"We're calling about Thanksgiving. It's a month from last Thursday."

Esme looked up at her mother. She had forgotten completely about their invitation. She waved her hand toward the door. Georgia turned and crossed the room. Such an obedient mother. "I'll be there," Esme said into the mouthpiece when Georgia left the room.

"Good," Dot said. "Just like we thought, we never did get ahold of your father. Have you talked to your mother? Is she going to be coming with you? We'd love to have her."

"I'll try to pin her down," Esme said. "But I have a feeling she's got plans. She and her boyfriend usually—"

"You just let us know if we should set a place for her."

"I will."

"What else is new with you?" Dot said.

"I'm working on the yearbook in my school. And I'm about to leave for work, in twenty minutes."

"Still scooping the ice cream?"

"Yeah. And I'm looking at art schools, trying to figure out which ones I'd like to go to. I'm probably going to Washington next weekend to look at a school called the Corcoran. I sort of know someone—" she looked over at the back cover of *Junked Up*— "I sort of know someone who teaches there."

"They say it's not what you know," Dot said, "it's who you know. I don't suppose you've given any thought to staying in New York."

"Not really."

"Since you're set on this photography business, there must be art schools right in your backyard. You could live with your mother and it wouldn't cost you nearly—"

"I have to leave New York. For a change of scene. Photographers have to see things with fresh eyes, or else their work gets stale. All the top photographers say that."

"Of course, you know best," Dot said. "We'll let you go now, sweetie. Call us soon about Thanksgiving."

"I will. Grandpa, are you still there?"

"Yup."

"I'll call you soon."

"Good."

"Are you really all right?"

"Fine," Goody said and paused. "Everything's fine."

Esme hung up. Within seconds, Georgia was back in the bedroom. "What did they want?"

"What do *you* want?" Esme reached for her cigarettes.

"Esme, all I did was ask a simple question."

"They wanted to know if I got my father's change-of-address card."

"That's all?"

"And if so, whether mine had a phone number on it—" Esme stopped to light a cigarette—"because theirs didn't, and they didn't know if that was an oversight or—"

"Or that he doesn't have a goddam phone."

"Yes. That's exactly the way they put it."

"I'm going grocery shopping. Is there anything you need?"

"Yogurt. Plain yogurt."

"I don't know how you can stand eating that."

"It's good for me. Could you close the door on your way out? Thanks."

"Close your own damn door," Georgia muttered as she left.

Esme picked up the phone. She was going to call Jon, her "date" for tonight. He had kissed her the night before last, and had put his hand on her breast. She had let him kiss her but had removed his hand. He kept it off. Some of them, when you pushed their hand away, they put it right back on, like they couldn't help themselves. Like your boob was a quarter sitting on the curb and it belonged to whoever got there first. But not this guy. He was okay. He would not expect her to put out, he would not get mad if she didn't.

She dialed his number. "Hi," she said when he answered, "this is Esme."

"I was just thinking about you."

She wished he hadn't been.

"Remember when you were talking last week about driving to Washington next weekend to visit your sister and you asked me if I wanted to go. And I said I wasn't sure. Well, I've decided."

"In which direction?" he laughed.

"I'd like to go. To take a look at the Corcoran Art School. I told you, I'm thinking of applying there."

"You mentioned that."

"I'm about to leave for work, and if I want to take next weekend off, I have to tell them today. So they can get a replacement."

"Am I still going to see you tonight?"

"Of course. I was just calling to see—to see if the offer was still good. About Washington."

"All my offers are good."

"I didn't want to presume."

"Presume all you want. Your wish is my command. By the way, what made up your mind about Washington?"

She looked over to the photograph of Rory Dean. "I've been hearing good things lately about that art school. I want to take a look for myself. I have to go to work now. But I'll meet you at quarter to seven, like we said."

"Great. See you then."

She got out of bed and began to dress. A denim miniskirt, a turquoise cotton T-shirt. She was knee-deep in lies. She put on her sandals, the silver Mexican hoop earrings her mother had bought for her birthday, and the embroidered Mexican belt. Knee-deep. Or about to be. She was not going to say a word about her grandparents' invitation to her mother. If Georgia found out, Esme would tell it to her straight: You're entitled to ruin your own Thanksgiving, but not mine.

If her grandparents found out she had not invited Georgia —that would be tough for her to get out of, unless she told them the truth about Georgia, the whole truth, nothing but the—

And this business with Jon. It was not a lie, going with him to Washington. She was not misrepresenting herself. She had kissed him the other night. But that didn't mean that she had to go all the way, just because he was giving her a ride. A place to stay in Washington. A chance to check out the Corcoran. A chance to check out Rory Dean. Whom she had never laid eyes on, except for the photograph on the back of his book. She would introduce herself to him. You don't know me, she would say, but we have a mutual friend. A mutual mentor. She had impeccable credentials. Not everyone could throw Don Marks's name around the way she could. She would tell Rory how much she admired his book. She would tell him that she had driven down there with a friend and let him know that the friend was a man. So he would not think that she was a desperate, lonely girl looking

for someone to fall in love with. Someone like him. Not someone like Jon, even though he was tall and had a car and said, I've
just been thinking about you, when she called him up.

She pinned her hair up in a bun, hair that came down to the
small of her back, and wrapped a hairnet around the bun, ice-
cream-parlor regulations. She picked up her regulation shoes
from under her dresser and tossed them into a shopping bag.
She would change into them when she got there. White clunkers.
Nurse's shoes. Then she'd have a cup of vanilla ice cream before
her shift started. A girl at Music and Art had told her about this
ice-cream diet. You could eat six scoops of ice cream a day, as
long as there were no nuts, chips, or chocolate swirls in the ice
cream, and as long as that's all you ate that day. Believe it or not,
you could lose four pounds in three days. She threw her cigarettes
into the shopping bag and left her bedroom. She was allowed to
smoke during her break. Thank god for these—she lit one as she
waited for the elevator—these cancer sticks, these life shorteners,
knock two hours off your life for every cigarette you smoke, a
small price to pay, thank god for them, she thought, thank god
there was something that kept you from eating.

Not Dead Only Sleeping

" 'A BOOK OUGHT to be an icepick to break up the frozen sea within us,' " Rory Dean said and paused. "Kafka." He took two steps back from the lectern and lowered his eyes. She sat in the back of the classroom, as she had last week, for the first class, and wrote down the dazzling pronouncements that came out of his mouth. "For the word 'book' in that sentence, substitute 'photograph.' That—" he scanned the room, she was sure it was in order to get a look at her—"that is what we are after." He sounded solemn. He sounded like a preacher, a doctor about to deliver a disturbing prognosis. "That is why we are here." He smiled, almost began to laugh. "We're certainly not in it for the money. For next week—" he drew in again, looked down at his papers on the lectern— "I'd like you to read the first five chapters of the Newhall history, and to begin work on your projects."

She raised her hand, fanned her fingers. "Will you be in your office later today, if we want to discuss our projects?"

"From three to four."

"Or our prospects," she said to herself as the class dispersed, as she picked up her notebook, camera, small knapsack. Prospects for love and fortune, love and fame. Love. Love itself. It was five minutes to three.

She headed downstairs to the student lounge for a pack of peanut-butter crackers. A basement room with no windows, a wall of vending machines. Not much in the way of aesthetics, for an art school, except the wall of posters and announcements. Monet at the National Gallery. Walker Evans at the Library of Congress. Robert Frank in a gallery on P Street. Chinese drawings at the Freer. "Landscapes of the Mind: A Group Show of Young Photographers." She lit a cigarette. She fished in her pocket for change. Two minutes to three.

You'd think this was a huge state university, the way people ignored you, like the two guys who just walked into the lounge. Esme dropped a quarter into the vending machine, pressed the button for the crackers at the end of the row. There'd been days since she got here that she had eaten yogurt for breakfast, peanut-butter crackers for lunch, and two slices of pizza for dinner. Total: two dollars and fifty cents. She was svelte. Positively svelte. She was broke. Positively broke. Wouldn't get paid until the day after tomorrow, for her three days of work last week. If all she ate was yogurt for breakfast on the days she worked, she'd pass out by eleven. Those days, she had to fill up on carbs. Drink gallons of water. She did not know how long she would last in that line of work. It was three on the dot.

"Got an extra cigarette?"

Esme turned. It was one of the guys who had just walked in. "I guess so. Sure."

"Fuckin' things." He came forward, held out his hand as she held out her pack. "I don't buy 'em anymore, I bum 'em. Cuts down my consumption."

"Mine too. Because I give them to people like you."

He froze, with his hand outstretched. "Sorry I asked." He started to walk away.

"Hey, I was kidding," she said. "Here. Take it. Come on."

He plucked one from her pack, mumbled "Thanks" and shuffled away.

She opened her mouth, she wanted to summon him back, apologize. But for what? She walked out of the lounge. She should not have come here. To the lounge. To the Corcoran. To Washington. Apologize for her sense of humor. *Mine too. Because I give them to people like you.* It's all in the delivery. She should have smiled. Should have said, *Sure, of course, take two, they're small. Stick around. Just between you and me and the vending machine, I haven't talked to anyone in days.*

Except Rory. In her head. Looking forward all week to this conversation that was about to take place at the top of the stairs, in his tiny office. She would tell him about the project she had just decided on, a photographic record of Washington. She rehearsed her speech as she loped up the stairs. Not the monuments, god no, not the monuments, who'd be stupid enough to waste film on the White House? No, she was after a photographic record of The Other Washington. The Slums. The Ghetto. The Poor and the Disadvantaged. She'd read an article in the paper that morning about racial tension in a neighborhood called Anacostia. She would do for Washington's ghetto what Bruce Davidson had done for Harlem, for East 100th Street. She had gone to see his show at the Museum of Modern Art two years ago. She had seen the poster from the show in Rory's office last week. A virtuoso performance. Not social history. Not documentary photography. No relation to photo-journalism, not even distant kin. This is Art we're talking about, High Art. The worn leather soles of her sandals slapped the marble stairs as she imagined her own show at the Museum of Modern Art. Rory would escort her to the opening. Rory would write the introduction to the book.

She poised herself, head up, hand out, to knock on his door. She hesitated three or four seconds. The door swung open. "Oh. Hi," he said. "I was just—"

"Leaving?" Her heart sank. She had come too late.

"Temporarily." He pointed across the hall. "The john. Come in. Sit down. I'll be right back."

His office was the size of a closet, sparely furnished. Barely furnished. A gray metal desk, two hard-backed chairs, a small bookcase, a single poster, from the Bruce Davidson show: a child on a fire escape, probably a girl, baggy underpants, long, curly hair, thin as a stick, a girl, but it could have been a boy. Esme was breathless, sitting in this sanctum. At the edge of her seat. Literally. She noticed some three-by-five cards taped up above his desk. She leaned forward and squinted to read the one closest to her. *I am after the one unique picture whose composition possesses such vigor and richness, and whose content so radiates outwards from it, that this single picture is a whole story in itself. H. Cartier-Bresson.*

It made her shiver. Something to believe in, something grand, almost unattainable. She took out her notebook and began to copy it down on the inside cover. If Rory walked back in before she was finished, he'd know what a good student she was, how eager she was to learn. Her back was to the door as she wrote, her shoulders almost bare. The middle of September in Washington, it was still hot, unbearably humid. She wore a ribbed cotton tank top, her shoulders were broad, square. She moved a little to the right, so he would have a better view of her back as he entered the room. Maybe he would think of Vanessa Redgrave in *Blow-Up*, when she takes off her shirt and there is her bare back, her magnificent back, a back for all times. And when Rory came around to the front, her legs, loose-fitting shorts to the middle of her thighs, her legs shaved smooth as baby skin.

"So . . ." She heard his voice before she saw him. "What can I do for you this afternoon?" She slammed her notebook shut. He sat down in the chair to the side of his desk. He wore jeans, a white undershirt with short sleeves. He was tall and wiry. Not the *enfant maudit* at all, not in real life. Maybe he had been posing in the photograph on the back of his book, trying to look tough. But here he was in the flesh, this skinny guy in beat-up white sneakers, no socks.

"First of all, I wanted to thank you again for letting me take your class. Without having taken Basic One."

"You're taking that too now, aren't you?"

"Yes. Absolutely. It started last week."

"You know what they say about rules."

"What?"

"They're made to be broken. Especially for friends of Don Marks. Have you found a good place to live yet? Last time you came by, you said you were waiting to hear from some people and you weren't—"

"I found something near Massachusetts and Rhode Island. Let me tell you, it's a helluva commute."

"Do you walk?"

"It was a joke. You know. Rhode Island Avenue. But also the state of Rhode Island. A newcomer's joke."

He smiled. "Are you in a group house?"

"A rooming house. I have a room, with a hotplate and a fridge down the hall. These people rent out the top floor of their house. Me and three nursing students from G.W. Separate rooms. Thank god for small favors."

"That doesn't sound very inviting, I mean—"

"Sixty-five a month. That's inviting."

"What about the rest of your life? Are you enjoying Washington?"

"Oh, sure." Oh, sure. "It's really different from New York."

"It certainly is."

"Not as dirty. Nowhere near the amount of sheer filth, garbage in the streets, noise, soot. In fact, it's pretty bland here. More like a garden than a jungle. Of course I knew it would be. Because I'd been here before." He nodded but did not speak. "Well, I was just— The reason I stopped by was to talk to you about my project. I've been reading about Atget. Eugène Atget. And how he set out to make a photographic record of Paris. What I was thinking of was—it just came to me today—I don't know whether I told you this, but I'm a bicycle messenger three days a week. I just started last week. It's *nothing* like being a messenger in New York. The guys there really ride to kill. The place I work, it's very low key. They hire a lot of students because they'll work so cheap. The point is that I get around town, and I was thinking of making a record of Washington for my project." She held up her hand, palm out. "Not the monuments. I'd never do that. You really have to be a moron to spend your time—" He just sat there listening, in all his splendor, the black curly hair, the dimpled chin. A man with a dimpled chin. Cary Grant. Or were his dimples in his cheeks? "A record of the ghetto. Fourteenth Street. Maybe Anacostia. Like Bruce Davidson did in East Harlem."

He said nothing. He crossed one leg over the other. He kept looking at her. Solemn. The way he looked in class.

"It's just an idea," she said. "I guess not a very good one."

"It's not *bad*. Are you planning to go into people's houses, the way Davidson did?"

"Not at the beginning, I mean, it would take some time to—"

"To get to know them?"

She nodded.

"Have you ever done anything like this before?"

She shook her head.

"You won't last long in Anacostia in that outfit you've got on." It was about time he noticed. Her thighs. Her legs. Shoulders that were almost bare.

"I wouldn't dress like this. I'd wear—" she looked down at herself—"I guess I'd wear fatigues."

"I don't know if that would help. If it would be enough, shall we say, to neutralize your presence." Neutralize her presence? Maybe he meant something else, maybe that was a euphemism or— "There's another issue, which may be more important. I don't know you very well. What is this, the second or third time we've talked?" How could he not know that this was the *fourth* time? "In any event, I wouldn't presume to know you when I don't. But I have the feeling that Anacostia isn't you. Fourteenth Street isn't you."

"Of course it's not me. Isn't that the point of photography, that you get to—" she searched for the right word— "*explore* things that aren't you? Bruce Davidson didn't *live* on East 100th Street. He went home every night. It wasn't to East 101st Street, either. I'd put money on that."

He began to laugh. "You're right, of course. But—" He put his palms flat together, as if he were about to pray. He seemed to be biting the inside of his lips. "If you brought me a photograph of a tree, you know what I'd tell you?"

" 'You seen one, you seen 'em all'?"

He smiled and shook his head. "I'd tell you that I'd much rather look at a tree than a photograph of a tree. I'd tell you that if you're going to take pictures of trees, the pictures have got to be infused with *you*. The most interesting thing about a photograph is the person who took it. You look a little confused."

"Well. I'm not sure what the connection is, between trees and the ghetto."

"Let me tell you straight, Esme. You're the third person in the class who wants to photograph the ghetto for their project. This verges on tourism. The ghetto is this year's monument, this year's—"

"All right," she interrupted, "I understand." She was not going to sit here and let him berate her.

"Hey, it's not the end of the world. It is by *no* means the end of the world. It may be the start of a beautiful relationship."

"Between who?"

"You and your camera. You have any brothers or sisters?" She shook her head. "Then take pictures of your mother. Your grandmother. Go see them for a week, or for a string of weekends. Take a few hundred pictures. Find out who they are and where you come from, before you go tripping off to the ghetto with an expensive camera." He leaned forward. Maybe he was going to touch her. "Jesus, don't look so down-hearted. I didn't tell you to do away with yourself. All I told you—"

"I decided a long time ago I wasn't going to take pictures of my mother."

"What about your father?"

"I'd have to be a magician."

"What?"

"I don't see him often. Like hardly ever. Like never, if you know what I mean."

"Where does he live?"

"Texas."

"Texas is a big place."

"Houston. He moved there a few months ago."

"What does he do there?"

She shrugged. "I think he's trying to find himself."

"What about your mother? Is she still in New York?"

"Yeah. My parents are crazy. Really crazy. Both of them. In their own unique way."

He put his palms together again, held them up to his lips. "It seems to me that you can use your crazy parents for your own purposes as a photographer. That is, if you want to."

"They're not freaks. Their problems don't *show*."

"That reminds me—this is in the nature of a footnote, not serious pedagogical advice." He smiled as he spoke. "Do you know that the Red Cross buys unsolicited photographs? You'll never guess what they're looking for."

"Pictures of blood?"

He shook his head.

"Pictures of blood donors?"

"Close. Pictures of disasters. The ravages of earthquakes, tidal waves, god knows what. I had a friend in New York who sent them pictures every now and then. *There* was a guy who loved a good disaster."

"I'm not sure that's my kind of thing. I tend to avert my eyes from violence. Having grown up with so much of it."

"Was it really that bad?"

"It might not win prizes at the Red Cross but—" She shrugged. She had his undivided attention, but she did not know what to do with it. "My mother spends her time waiting for a knight in shining armor and living with an incredible creep. My father consults *Ripley's Believe It or Not* whenever he's trying to figure out what to do with his life."

"How come you want to take pictures?"

"I *do* take pictures."

"Why?"

"Because it seems like there are moments in the world, split seconds actually, of great beauty or great sadness, and they need to be recorded." She had read something like that recently, an obscure photographer's explanation for what he was trying to achieve. But these words were her own, unrehearsed, and they surprised her.

"The decisive moment?"

She nodded. "Even things that aren't inherently sad, they become sad, because they're evanescent—" it was sounding better all the time— "because the moment is evanescent. And maybe there's less sadness if you have a picture of those moments. A permanent record. So people will know that they happened."

He kept looking at her, he did not say anything.

"I guess that's why." She changed gears. She slipped into deadpan. "I'm certainly not in it for the money."

"Why did you come here?"

"Here?" She pointed to the floor.

"The Corcoran."

"Because it's cheap. Because I can just take a class or two. Leave whenever I have to." And because she had thought that Rory would take care of her, the newcomer, Don Marks's young friend, take care of her until she learned her way around, take care of her, maybe fall in love with her, or introduce her to someone who would.

"Leave whenever you have to?" he said.

She rubbed the tips of her fingers of one hand together. "To make money. I thought about going to RISD. But it's really expensive, and you have to sign up for four years in a row. All I could see was years of student loans, debts up to here." Her hand to her nose. "And graduating without having learned to do anything but take pictures. You can hardly make a living taking pictures, right? Make a living *plus* pay back ten thousand dollars. Unless you're Don Marks."

"Don't forget, Don has paid his dues. He's been taking pictures for thirty years. When you've got thirty years behind you—"

"I guess you're saying that I should forget the ghetto."

"The reason Bruce Davidson's photographs about Harlem are brilliant isn't because they're about 'the slums,' it's because he *lived* there. I don't mean that he moved in. I mean that he was there every day for two years. He *knew* those people. He wasn't just sneaking up to the edge of the ghetto with a powerful zoom lens. If you're prepared to do that, if you *can* do that, then by all means—"

"I won't do it if you think it's a bad idea."

"Esme, it's not that it's a bad idea. Jesus, it may be a great thing for you to do. I'm not the one doing the project. But I—"

"What about if I hung out at a day-care center? For black kids. Every day for weeks. Weeks on end."

He inhaled deeply, did that with his hands again, like he was about to pray, which maybe he was, pray that she would go away.

"I guess that's a dumb idea too."

He shook his head. "You want to hear a Bruce Davidson story?" She nodded. "He went to Paris in the mid-fifties, he was posted there in the Army. He met an old lady who happened to be the widow of a painter, a minor Impressionist painter. He spent his weekends taking pictures of her. This old lady in Paris. That's all. Nothing fancy. Nothing 'relevant.' He got to know her and he photographed what he saw, what he knew. The pictures are magnificent. But it wasn't what you'd call an ambitious project. It was one woman."

"Anyone can take good pictures in Paris. I mean, Paris. There it is. Just focus and shoot." She stood up.

"Wait a second."

She remained standing but did not move from her place. She looked straight ahead, straight into the sad eyes of the scrawny little girl, or maybe it was a boy, on the fire escape on East 100th Street.

"Let's finish talking about your project. Sit down. Please."

She plopped down on the seat and looked off into the corner of the room. "What am I supposed to do? Go find some old person and hope they used to be married to an Impressionist painter?"

"Of course not."

"That's slumming it too, you know, that's almost the same as hanging out in the ghetto. If you ask me."

"I can't tell you what to do for your project. But I can say that I think you'd do better to start with something small and learn as much as you can about it. Instead of something immense—"

"Immense like the ghetto."

"Yeah."

"I do have grandparents," she said, "who might be good subjects. But they live in New Haven. It's seven or eight hours on the train."

"I may be able to help you. The woman I live with—" The woman he lived with? "—teaches art in a nursing home in Bethesda. Part-time. She might introduce you to the people in her class. There's one guy she talks a lot about—"

"I'll think about it." She stood again, picked up her camera from the corner of his desk, slung the strap over her shoulder.

He stood up too, he was as tall as she was, he looked into her eyes. "Let me know what you decide." *A book ought to be an icepick to break up the frozen sea within us.* Who did he think he was, issuing proclamations like that, looking into her eyes, living with another woman?

There was a knock at his door.

"Will you let me know?"

She nodded and reached for the door, twisted the knob. A woman waited on the other side, petite, blonde. "Is this Rory Dean's office?"

Esme nodded and brushed past her. She wanted a cigarette. She wanted to die.

The hell with old people, she said to herself and raced down the hall, the hell with taking pictures of her grandfather, or anyone else's. She yanked open the exit door to New York Avenue. New York the Avenue and New York the City. A little joke. What was she doing here? In this heat. This humidity. She unlocked her bicycle and got ready to ride, dropped her camera and notebook into the backpack. This dreary place, this sterile slum. Ridiculous monuments. Hideous new buildings. She was going to go to an old cemetery she had discovered last week in Georgetown. She started up Seventeenth Street. Droves of men in suits, men with tortoise-shell glasses frames, men who worked in the White House. This was no city for an artist. No place for a photographer. She could never live here.

She crossed Pennsylvania Avenue against the light and pedaled hard, riding right alongside the cars. They honked at her. She gave one guy the finger. He honked again. She shot ahead, she didn't need that kind of abuse. It was true, what she had told Rory, that she got around town. But never to Anacostia, never to the burned-out blocks of Fourteenth Street. No one sent messengers there. What message could the Ambassador from Canada possibly have for the welfare mothers she had read about in the paper this morning? The cemetery was up here, at the top of this hill, an oasis, a sanctuary. Last week, when she found it, she had been making deliveries all over Georgetown and had not had the time to go in.

Now she locked up her bike and headed in. The cemetery was set on a steep hill. The top of the hill was the street, you walked down and down. The markers and mausoleums were ancient, they were grand. There were many winding dirt paths; from high up on the hill, they made circular patterns on the ground. Below, at the foot of the cemetery, was a sharp drop, perhaps fifty feet, to a busy road, a park, a winding creek that was almost dry. She took her camera out of her backpack and began to take pictures of headstones from 1767, 1864, 1817. *Thomas Thatcher. Martha Ruggles. Vivian Spencer. Anna Hart Philips. Morris Philips.* A picture of a statue of an angel with this engraved on the base: *Sarah Watts Matthews of Westbury Wills, 1867–1875, Not Dead Only Sleeping.* She took pictures of statues of women who looked like Rossetti's Ophelia, diaphanous robes made of stone, the worn tombstones of boys who had lived for six years, eight years, two months and three days. Pictures of the landscape, the winding paths, the headstone of *William Crofton. A native of Derbyshire, England, but for the last 44 years a resident of Washington D.C. Resting Peacefully in the Sight of His Maker.* She thought she should be afraid, deep in the deserted cemetery, here with the dead. But she was not. She walked farther and farther down the hill, away from the street, and sat cross-legged on the grass, next to a headstone that said: *There is no Death. What seems so is transition.* She looked down to the dry creek. It cut through the lush park, thick, green, wooded, wilder than any park she had ever seen. She took a photograph but knew she could not do justice to the view. She needed a wide-angle lens. She needed to take two hundred pictures to get one good one. She needed an icepick to break up the frozen sea within her. It was astonishing, the lies people told themselves. The lies they engraved in stone. Not dead, just checking out the view.

It was rush hour when she rode back through Georgetown to the Corcoran to print the pictures she had taken. She passed blocks of tiny rowhouses painted pastel colors, mansions set back from the street, circular driveways, manicured gardens, canopied verandahs, men in pinstripe suits coming home from work. Warm air against her legs, two rolls of thirty-six exposures in her backpack. One of them, maybe one of them would be good.

She pedaled up Pennsylvania Avenue, her heart pounded, it thundered inside of her chest. She was going to stop smoking. She had to. She had read an article in the paper the other day about a nineteen-year-old girl who'd played tennis in the afternoon and came home that night and dropped dead. Heart failure. She stopped for a red light on Twenty-second and Pennsylvania and straddled the bar of her bicycle, breathing for her life, heart pounding like a drum. Rory had hit it on the mark: she would be one of those odious photographers who sneaked up to the edge of the ghetto to take their photographs—but she didn't even have a zoom lens, because she couldn't afford one. Let's face it. She was no Bruce Davidson. She would not get to know those people, the people who live in condemned buildings on Fourteenth Street, the woman she had read about, whose son the police had killed last week. She could barely speak to the other students at the Corcoran. How did she expect to talk to strangers in Anacostia? The nerve he had, the nerve Rory Dean had, living with a woman, the nerve.

Her Wildest Dream

SHE WANTED TO take pictures that moved, that sang, that made your heart stop. She believed what Cartier-Bresson believed, the words copied from a book, committed to memory, taped to her wall next to the quotation she'd copied from Rory's office: *Only the picture that springs to life is of interest to me.* But in the weeks after she discovered the cemetery in Georgetown, she went to cemeteries all over Washington. She took hundreds of pictures of graveyards, tombstones, shrines to the dead. Close-ups, long shots, landscapes.

In the meantime, she continued to sit in the back of the class during Rory's lectures, and to write down in the margins of her notebook the marvelous things that he said, stories about photographers, artists, writers, the well-known, the sought-after, the life she would like to lead. He knew Diane Arbus, he had interviewed Walker Evans for *Art in America*, he had talked just the other day to Don Marks about the dangers of formalistic photography for beginning photographers. When he said that about Don in class, Esme was sure that he was talking to her.

Now, this afternoon in the middle of October, she had something to show him, eleven good work prints from the hundreds of cemetery pictures. Her excuse to go to his office and talk to him, here in her hand. "I won't take up much of your time."

"Don't be silly. Have a seat."

"I have these—" she held out the manila envelope, she did not sit down— "these photographs. I was wondering if you could look at them."

"Sure."

"They're not very—" She caught herself and sat down. She heard Don Marks in her head. "Well, you can see for yourself." She sat back in her seat, he opened the envelope. "Do you mind if I smoke?"

He handed her an ashtray.

She was wearing a denim skirt, a tie-dyed T-shirt with long sleeves. He would take one look at the pictures and say, It looks like you're in a rut. It looks like you're being pursued by death, which was not true. She lit her cigarette.

"That's not a joint, is it?"

"No. Tobacco. I roll them myself."

"How come?"

"It's cheaper."

"Have you always? I don't remember you—"

"Just lately."

He looked from her cigarette to her eyes and held her gaze, not afraid to hold the gaze. That's when she noticed: his eyes were green, tinted blue. Amazing. Like he'd mixed the colors himself. His lips parted slightly. They were dry, they were full. A staring contest. She counted to four—she did not know why, why four, why she counted at all—and looked away. He looked back down at her photographs. "I like the texture of these. I like how grainy they are. You know, they're haunted. Especially this one. You can feel how rough the stone is, you can feel—"

"What's wrong with them?" she interrupted.

He looked up. "What do *you* think is wrong?"

These were the best she had taken, of the hundreds, but she knew there was something off about them. "They're flat. They're static." She knew now, this second, exactly what it was. "They're dead."

"In a way they are, but—"

"I don't mean the subject matter."

"I know you don't. I don't, either. Although, of course—" He looked down at the photograph in his lap, an eighteenth-century headstone. "The texture is superb. The composition is good, the light, the shadows are wonderful. They're still-lifes."

"But I don't want to do still-lifes."

"I know."

"How do you know?"

"Because of what you told me the first time you came in here."

"The first time?"

"When you told me you wanted to photograph the ghetto."

The third time, Rory, that was the third time, not counting the first time I came to Washington with that guy from New York. "Yeah, that time," she said.

"They're great still-lifes—"

"They're not great, they're—"

"They're okay, they're better than okay. In my book, that's high praise. Most of the people in the class—certainly the first-year students—aren't doing half this much work. And then they think that every damn negative they print should hang in the Museum of Modern Art. The problem with these—" he slapped the pile against his knee, as you might a rolled-up newspaper—"is that they're not what you want to be doing—but you don't know what else to do."

"How did you know that?"

"Because I've been there."

"Really?"

"Of course."

"When was the last time?"

"The last time?" He laughed. "I'm at loose ends whenever I'm not in the middle of a project. When I'm at the beginning, I'm sure it won't work. When I'm at the end, I'm convinced I haven't achieved half of what I set out to do. It's never easy, it's never—"

"What were you doing when you were eighteen?"

"When I was eighteen? Don't remind me. I was about to flunk out of my first semester at Dartmouth, which fortunately I did. Then I—" He stopped talking and looked over at her. A different sort of look, no lust, no intrigue, no curiosity. "I just had an idea. Do you like fish?"

"To photograph?"

"To eat."

"Yeah. I guess so. Certain kinds."

"Are you doing anything for dinner tonight?"

"I don't think—" she put her fingers to her lips, she might have heard him wrong. "Dinner? Tonight?"

"Yeah."

"I'm pretty sure I'm free."

"Good. And you like fish." She nodded. "Do you mind eating early?" She shook her head. This was probably a dream. In a minute, she would find herself alone, in bed, and it would be time for breakfast, not dinner. "What if I pick you up at five-thirty? There should be enough light if we—"

"Where are we going?"

"It's a surprise. Bring your camera."

"To dinner?"

"Yes. What's your address?"

"I'm not going home now. I was going downstairs to the darkroom to develop some film. We could meet here. If it's all right—"

"It's a date," he said. "I'll go downstairs and find you at five-thirty."

She stood and held out her hand for the photographs.

"I'd like to look through them again," he said, "if you don't mind."

"You don't have to."

"I know I don't."

"I kind of need them right now, to figure which ones I've got, so I can figure out which negatives to print, it's—"

"Say no more." He held out the photographs. He met her eyes again. Again. She counted to five, six—it was like staring at the sun: you know you shouldn't, you know you'll pay for it later—eight, nine. "I'll see you at five-thirty," he said finally.

She nodded and left his office in a daze, clutching her photographs like a life preserver. They were the only things that were real right this minute. Recognizable images with physical properties, height, width, depth. They could not be mistaken for anything else. But the way he had looked at her just now, the way his eyes had met hers and would not let go—

what did it mean? Love. No, not love. The beginning of love. Maybe. It had to mean something, it had to define a sentiment, represent a feeling deep within him. Or maybe it had not even happened the way she thought it had. Time might have been distorted, it might have been two seconds, not fifteen or twenty. Yes, that was it. There had been no long gaze, no communion of eyes. She gripped the bannister as she went down the stairs. It had not happened that way at all. She had counted wrong, he had not meant it when he had looked at her that way. That way. Now she was sure of it. The best things that had ever happened to her—surely that look was high up on the list—she had imagined at least half of them.

But this was real, sitting with Rory in his old yellow Volkswagen, with the Beatles on the radio singing "Back in the U.S.S.R." This was magic.

They traveled over a narrow highway at the edge of the city. On their right was an immense pond, the Jefferson Memorial on the other side of it, a deep-blue sky, airplanes flying very low. "National's over there." He pointed. "Maybe half a mile from here, as the crow flies. There's a park at the foot of the airport. The planes fly right over your head, about fifty feet up. In good weather, people stand around and watch them land. If you're ever in the mood for a thrill—though it doesn't quite match walking through Times Square. Do you miss New York a lot? Most of my students from up there have a hard time adjusting to our sleepy Southern ways."

"I was desperate to get out."

"Of the city?"

"Of my mother's house."

"Oh, yes, I remember now. Your crazy mother. How's she handling your absence?"

"When she's sober, she handles it fine. When she's drunk, she cries about it. Since I've been here, I've gotten two sober calls and two drunk ones."

"That's too bad."

"She doesn't have it so bad. She lives with someone. I mean, she's got someone to keep her company." What she meant, what she had started to say was, She's got someone to keep her company—if you call Tommy Troy company—and I don't.

"I meant it was too bad for you."

She shrugged. "I've had some good days since I've been here." Like today. Today was the first good day she had had.

"It's always difficult, starting someplace new."

"I'll survive." She laughed. "Maybe."

"I'm sure you'll survive. Well. We're almost there."

There was a fork in the highway. Rory took the right-hand turn. The road narrowed, on one side was a parking lot, a cluster of small buildings that looked abandoned. Just beyond them was a sloppy hand-painted sign that said FISH MARKET with an arrow pointing to the right.

Rory parked in a gravel lot between JOE'S FISH CLAMS CRABS and CAPTAIN'S CATCH SINCE 1962. There were five or six other stalls. It looked like a carnival, a state fair, another country, the Third World. No monuments, no manicured lawns, no men in pinstripe suits. The smell of fish, a fat woman selling clams, men in long plastic aprons, wool skullcaps, short-sleeve T-shirts, tan marks where the shirt inched up a tattooed, muscular forearm. "This is wonderful," she said.

"I thought you might like it."

"Do they mind if you take pictures?"

"The fish? They love it. Especially when the photographer is a beautiful woman."

She could not acknowledge that, she could not believe he had said it, that he had meant her. She took the lens cap off of her camera. She held it up to her face and began to focus on a sign, FRESH FISH DAILY, at the end of the walkway, about forty feet away. She thought of Walker Evans's photographs of signs, storefronts, billboards. There was just enough light for this shot. A terrible shot. Postcard stuff. Tourist stuff. She was no Walker Evans. No Bruce Davidson. Not yet. She took the camera from her face and turned to Rory.

"Go." He touched her elbow. "Look around. Just don't jump overboard. The Potomac's right behind that building. We're standing on a wharf."

"Why aren't we wobbling?"

"Aren't you wobbling? I am." He smiled. "It's made of cement, not wood. Go. Take pictures. I'll see you later."

"Where will I meet you?"

"I'll find you."

She watched an old man hose down a raft of red snapper. Watched and watched. Handmade signs held up with clothespins hung on a line above the rows of fish. WHY PAY MORE! pan trout! WHY PAY MORE! porgies! WHY PAY MORE! croakers!

"Do you mind if I take a picture?" she said softly.

"What?"

"Do you mind if I take a picture?"

"Nope." He looked at her. His lips curled up. There was not enough light. She had slow film in the camera, she had been shooting in bright sunlight the day before. She took the picture anyway. "Where you from?" he said. He pointed the nozzle of the hose at the fish, squeezed it hard, let the water run over them. WHY PAY MORE! seabass!

"New York."

"Vacation?" He rearranged four or five fish.

"I go to school here."

"Lotta people do." He turned on the hose again.

"Can I take some more pictures?" Practice, not at taking pictures—it was too dark for that—but at asking permission.

"Sure." He held the hose down at his side. He looked like a man who felt he was being taken seriously, posing for a state portrait.

She took four more shots and crossed the wharf to another stall. Three men in white cloth aprons and baseball caps. If she could get them all together . . . If the sun was out . . . She had five exposures left. Practice asking. Practice the easy stuff. She was scared. She focused on a row of shiny, slithery turbot, 99¢

a pound. But she was not going to take pictures of fish. She stepped back a few feet and brought the camera to her eye. Bushel baskets of jittery crabs, tiny legs kicking rhythmically, in and out, in and out. She walked backward four or five steps, camera still at her eye. She focused on the back of a man standing by the crabs. It was Rory. She took the picture. She would have to get a zoom lens. Then she could follow him around Washington and take pictures of him and he would never know. A zoom lens with a silencer, her own invention. But she would never be able to show him the photographs. And if she only took pictures of him, she would have nothing to show him. No excuse to see him at all. She pressed the shutter again. She would enlarge the best one. Poster-size. Maybe life-size.

"You were right," she called out and sauntered up to him.

"About what?"

"That you'd find me."

"Or you'd find me. You like soft-shelled crabs? With butter and garlic?"

"I think so. I'm not sure."

"No sand," the man behind the counter said. "Guaranteed. No sand."

Rory sidled up to her and spoke softly. "There's a restaurant up the street that gets their crabs from this guy. How 'bout it?"

"Now?"

"Whenever you're ready."

"I'm ready."

He smiled, a broad, enthusiastic smile, a kid on his way to a baseball game. Something she had never noticed—his left front tooth was crooked. His first imperfection. She was deeply moved, as if he had told her a secret about himself.

"What's wrong?" he said.

"Nothing."

"You look like you just—" another broad smile; he tipped his head toward the car. He was deep in thought, contemplating the end of his sentence as they crossed the wharf—"like you just smelled a fish."

"I did," she laughed. "It stank."

The sky had grown dark, there were a handful of stars. Rory leaned over and unlocked her door. Suddenly there were possibilities, a reason to have come to Washington, a reason to live. He pulled out of the parking space and turned on the radio. *She's as sweet as tupelo honey*, someone sang, and sang.

This was real, this moment, this was magic.

"You've barely touched your food," he said.

"I've eaten half the fish and one of your crabs."

"Eat, eat," he joked and finished the beer in his glass. "I'm sitting in for your Jewish mother."

"It's my father who's Jewish. My mother's—a hybrid. A generic Christian. The most organized thing about her religion is that she subscribes to a little magazine called the *Daily Word*. A lot of 'God loves you and God loves me and God gives me the strength to love you and the doorman and the bus driver.' I'm really babbling away, aren't I? I haven't talked so much since—"

"Do you want a refill?" He pointed to her empty glass of wine.

"If I have more, I won't shut up for two days."

"You've only had one."

"One more than I usually have."

"Come on. Live it up." He motioned for the waiter. "Finish your fish." He laughed. "But leave room for dessert."

"Did I tell you this? My mother's other religious tic is lighting candles in St. Patrick's Cathedral." She obeyed him, she continued eating. "She used to take me when I was a kid and give me money to light candles." She remembered her mother's words but did not, could not, repeat them to Rory. *Make a wish, say a prayer, remember someone you love.* "That's her idea of how to get what she wants."

"What does she want?"

"God knows what she wants now. She used to want a knight in shining armor. It was something of a guiding principle for her. The knight at the end of the tunnel." Esme smiled at her cleverness. Rory smiled back. "My father's guiding principle is the greenback at the end of the tunnel. And *Ripley's Believe It or Not*. He called me when I moved to Washington. He thinks everyone who lives here gets invited to dinner at the White House. I think he was calling to find out if I'd gotten my invitation yet."

"What's your guiding principle?"

"I thought you would never ask." She smiled. "I make mine up as I go along."

"That's not a very good answer."

"Why not?"

"It doesn't have, as they say, the ring of truth. I might buy it from someone else, but it doesn't suit you at all."

"How's this? Reverse psychology. Whatever my parents did, I'll do the opposite."

"I'll buy that."

"What about you, what's yours?"

"Mine?" he laughed. "I *do* make mine up as I go along."

She had expected him to say something noble about the pursuit of art, the value of culture, the virtue of hard work. Or even something about his childhood, the things he was most afraid of, what his true feelings were for her. So she decided to guide him in the direction of the personal. "Why did you take me to the fish market?"

"It seemed like a good idea at the time." The waiter appeared. Rory ordered another beer for himself, a glass of wine for Esme. "I wanted to show you someplace in Washington funkier than Foggy Bottom. A place with its own culture, its own texture. Halfway between the ghetto and the graveyard."

"The fish are dead but the fishermen aren't, is that what you mean?"

He smiled. "Something like that."

"I'm glad you did. I've been kind of down-hearted about my photography lately. I went through a period in New York, the year before last, when I was fearless. When I could just go up to people and shoot. The pictures from around then—Don really liked them. Those were the first ones I ever showed him. I feel much more intimidated now. Like I shouldn't intrude into people's lives. Like I have to keep my distance."

"It happens."

"What do you do when it does?"

"Try to force yourself out of it. Do the thing you're most afraid of, which is the Norman Mailer approach to fear."

"And if you're not Mailer?"

"The James Boswell approach. Exploit your weakness. Turn it to your advantage. Do you know Macaulay's essay on him?" Esme shook her head. She would have to look it up first thing in the morning. "What he says is that Boswell was a great writer because of his foolishness and weakness, not in spite of it. He had absolutely no shame, no discretion, didn't give a damn that he was being insulted and ridiculed. He badgered his way through life without hesitation or self-consciousness—and wrote a remarkable book as a result of it. Isn't that superb?"

"I'm not sure I could put up with insult and ridicule, as a regular-type thing."

"My point is that you can take your weakness, or what you think is your weakness, which may be this fear you're talking about, which—" The waiter came back, served Esme the bottle of beer and Rory the glass of wine. When he left, Rory switched their drinks, and Esme thought that there was a kind of grace with which he made the switch, and that when he kissed her, if he ever kissed her, he would know exactly what to do, which is what you wanted in a man, a man was supposed to know what to do at all times. "If you're afraid of taking pictures of people right now, don't take them. It's as simple as that. But don't be half-hearted about the pictures you do take. Don't feel like they're second-rate, just because they're not what you want to be doing." He stopped for a moment. "Why am I lecturing you? This is a terrible habit I've developed."

"No, it's not. It's very useful. I need all the help I can get."

"You'll do fine. You've got plenty of spunk. Plenty of resilience."

"But hardly any money."

"You should go live in Mexico. You can live there for a year on what you spend here in three months."

"You've been there?"

"Three or four times. I'm going back in December."

"For Christmas break?"

"I'll be there for a year."

Esme reached for her glass of wine and pushed it to her mouth.

"You look surprised."

"No," she protested. "Well." She put her glass down. "I guess I am, a little."

"I feel like I talk about it all the time, but it looks like I don't. Franca is sick to death of my Mexico talk."

"Franca?"

"The woman I live with."

"What are you going to do down there?"

"Teach a few classes at an art school in San Miguel de Allende and work on a book for *National Geographic*. It's not quite what Ansel Adams calls 'an assignment from within,' but the pay is phenomenal, and the job is to take pictures of Mexico for a year. How bad could it be?"

"What's—" she hesitated before uttering the name, such an exotic name—"Franca going to do down there?"

"She's not going."

"Because of her job?"

"Not really. We're going to separate when I leave. See if the flame keeps burning." He looked down, seeming to focus on his butter plate, and thrummed his fingers against the table. "I think half of being in love must be surviving the disappointment of it."

"What disappointment?"

"That the magic you feel at the beginning never lasts."

Esme nodded, signaling assent, understanding. As if she knew something about love, something about the lives of adults. Not adults like her parents; she knew all she wanted to know about their lives. *I'm a woman, you're a man. Why waste the afternoon?* That's what her mother had taught her about love, that it was all right to do it with people you can't stand, like Quinn Laughlin and Tommy Troy.

"So you've never been to Mexico?" Rory said.

"No."

"San Miguel is paradise. You really have to see it."

"Maybe I will. I love to travel. Even though I've hardly been anywhere. I got a lot of vicarious thrills from Leah when I lived in New York. She's been everywhere you can imagine."

"Who's Leah?"

"Leah Marks. Don's daughter."

"Oh, yes. I met her once or twice. Is she a photographer too?" Rory motioned to the waiter, drew a scribble in the air to get the check.

"No. She's just smart. Brainy."

Rory smiled. "That's a good thing to be. Especially if you're not a photographer."

"Are you making fun of me?"

"Not at all."

"Did you ever have dinner at their house?"

"At Don's? Once. No, twice. It was a few years back. Why do you ask?"

She shrugged. "They were the first people I ever met who were like that. You know, really smart. People who read books, knew a lot of things. I always felt like I was taking a final exam when I sat down to dinner there. I always failed miserably."

"I bet you didn't."

"I did. I used to be different. I used to be—very mousy. Like they'd say, What's your name, and I'd just sit there, because I was sure I had the wrong answer. I don't know how I'd handle it now. I'd probably still be a mouse."

"No, you wouldn't. You'd see through it."

"See through what?"

"Don is a wonderful photographer and a generous soul. But dinner at his house is a bit much, now that you mention it. It *is* kind of like a seminar. I'd never thought of it that way before. If you quit paying attention for five seconds, you can never catch up. And if you haven't read so-and-so's latest book, you're a pariah."

"I always think I should have read it."

"You'll drive yourself crazy with all of their 'should-haves.' " He took a long drink of beer. "You don't look convinced."

"I used to think that if I was going to be a smart person, I *had* to go to Harvard. Don was the person who told me to forget Harvard and go to art school."

"And you're going to resent him forever." Rory smiled. "Because you're missing out on all that fun."

"Leah goes to Harvard."

"How does she like it?"

"We haven't talked to each other since last summer. But I'm sure she likes it there. It's definitely her kind of place."

"What's your kind of place?" He took another long drink as he waited for her to answer. The waiter put the check next to his plate.

She shrugged.

"The Corcoran?"

She shook her head.

"I thought not. Listen, do you want to get out of here?"

"Washington?"

"The restaurant."

"Sure. If you do."

He drove her home the same way they had come, over the highway by the pond, the Jefferson Memorial and the airport in the distance, the lights of an occasional plane, the buzzing sound Rory's car made. Silence, there was an awful, unbearable silence between them. "It sounds like your car is about to fall apart," she said. It was the only thing she could think of to say.

"That's just the engine."

"It's kind of loud."

"It's a Volkswagen."

"Oh."

He drove block after block as if she were not there. Of course it was her fault that he had nothing to say to her. Why waste his time with this kid, this girl who got giddy with one drink and babbled on about her silly fears, her high school dilemmas, her fucked-up family. If only she could think of the right question to ask him. The question that would penetrate to his heart, that would unravel the mystery of who he was, that would let him know how perfectly suited they were for each other.

"Where on Rhode Island do you live? What's the cross street?"

"Sixteenth, right above where Massachusetts and Rhode Island meet."

"I didn't know they met."

"Of course they meet. At Sixteenth Street."

"How do you like that, I've lived here for two years, and I always thought Rhode Island intersects with Vermont."

"It does. It also intersects with Massachusetts."

"You certainly know your way around well, for someone who's new in town."

"It comes with the territory."

"What territory?"

"I'm a messenger."

"That's right."

"Take a left up here. Then take your first right."

"Yes, ma'am. Coming right up."

Maybe her geographic skills would strengthen her portfolio. Maybe they would make him feel like he could depend on her, like if he stuck with her, the two of them would never get lost.

"It's the second house after the turn. That house on the right, in front of the red car."

He stopped and put the car in neutral, yanked up the emergency brake on the floor between them, did not turn off the ignition. He leaned toward her to see out her window, brushed his cheek against her shoulder. "That?" She nodded. "It looks like an embassy." He sat back in his seat, turning slightly toward her. His face was in shadows, all she could see were the outlines of his eyes.

"Downstairs it does. Upstairs, where me and the nurses live, it looks like a dormitory. Well, listen. Thanks. Thanks a lot for everything. The fish and all."

She held out her hand for him to shake. He took it and held it for a moment. She kept expecting him to let go, to nod and put his hand back on the steering wheel, back on the stick shift, and drive away. He did not let go, he turned to her more fully and rubbed his thumb over the top of her hand as he held it. He said, "C'mere a minute," and wrapped his free arm around her back, let go her hand and drew his other arm around her too. "Relax," he whispered and held her tighter, this stranger, this man full of surprises. She was sure he could feel her heart pound, feel her tremble. Or maybe she was trembling inside, not outside. Maybe this was a dream, maybe the whole day, the fish and all, had been a dream. "Relax, kiddo," he said. "You've got to learn to relax about things."

"Do you mean *this*?"

"I mean your life, your whole, complicated young life." She let her head rest on his shoulder. He touched her hair, he stroked the side of her head. This was friendly, this was nice, this was because she was Don Marks's friend and she was alone in Washington, and it was no big deal to buy her dinner and give her a goodnight hug in his car and tell her to relax, with the emergency brake between them and the ignition running, no big deal, you had to remember that this was no big deal. Except that he seemed to be moving closer, and now his lips, his lips, were on her neck, kissing her neck, kissing it softly and then harder than he had kissed it a few seconds ago, and she was thinking, maybe this was what adults did, this was just a friendly hug the way adults do things, not the way kids do them, and it was not until he touched his tongue to her neck and whispered, "You smell so good," that she realized it was not just a friendly hug, it was something else, something more wonderful, beyond her wildest dreams, or not beyond them, this was, yes, this was her wildest dream, and so she drew her arms around his waist, pressed her face into his neck, let her lips touch his skin.

"I really have to go now," he said and drew back a little and kissed her cheek. Leaned forward and kissed her lips, kissed them with his lips, then with his tongue, soft, short strokes against her lips. "But I wish I didn't have to. Jesus, do I wish I didn't have to."

"Maybe you don't."

"But I do." He touched her lips with his tongue, he pressed his mouth to hers and kissed her finally, fully, her wildest dream, this kiss, this man in her arms, she would never let go. "I really do," he said and kissed her, cupped his hands around her face, kissed her again.

"No one ever kissed me in a car."

"Really?"

She nodded. "Or anything else," she said and leaned forward and rubbed her lips against his, "in a car."

"Poor thing." He did not pull away, he did not really have to go, she could entice him to stay, she did not have far to go. This was what adults did, they took things into their own hands. She licked his lips, she held his cheeks, rubbed the tips of her thumbs over his mouth. "You feel so good," he said. "I had no idea." A long, lingering kiss.

"Maybe you should turn off the ignition," she whispered.

He shook his head. "I have to go."

"You don't sound convinced."

"I'm not. But I am."

"Maybe you can come back."

"Yes. Maybe I can." Another kiss, his cheeks were as smooth as suede, his tongue was warm. "What if I call you tomorrow?" She nodded. "Do I have your number?" She shook her head. "Write it down for me." He kissed her lips and reached a hand into his back pocket. "Here." He held out a ballpoint pen and pocket-size notebook. "Try the last page."

"The phone is right outside my room." She wrote down her

name and number. "We all share it. Me and the nurses. What time do you think you'll call? Probably early would be better, because I have to go to work and—"

"Fine. That's fine."

She handed back his notebook. "But if someone's on the phone—"

"I'll call back."

"Right. Of course."

"Good night."

"Good night."

He watched her until she got inside the house.

The best things that had ever happened to her—she had not imagined all of them.

In the dark of her room on the top floor of the house that Rory said looks like an embassy, she sits up in bed and lights a cigarette. She listens for sounds from down the hall, from downstairs. There is someone going down the stairs, or up the stairs. One of the nurses, or the guy who owns the house, who often comes home late from his job on the Hill. Or Rory, maybe it is Rory. She leans back against the wall, she listens for footsteps on the stairs. Someone has let him in and he is going to sneak up and surprise her. He will come to her door, knock gently, to let her know that he is here, then open it, enter without speaking, enter as if he had been invited to arrive at this very moment. He will sit down at the foot of her bed and poke the covers to find her feet and tug on them, play with them, and they will laugh and move close to each other and kiss, oblivious to everything but their desire.

Not dead, she thinks, only sleeping. She draws on the cigarette glowing in the dark and speaks to him. This is what has been missing, she tells him. I have been asleep, I have felt like I was dying, but now, now I am waking up.

"Esme."

"Yes. Hi."

"I thought it might be one of the nurses."

"No. It's me."

"I didn't wake you, did I?"

"No, not at all. I've been up since—"

"I don't know how to say this gracefully," he interrupted. His voice sounded so deep, so commanding, on the phone. "What happened last night—it wasn't what I had planned, it wasn't—"

"Me neither." She laughed.

"No. Of course not." He did not laugh. "I wouldn't have expected— Look, what I'm trying to say is that I feel badly about what I did. I was trying to be your friend, I *want* to be your friend. But I got carried away. I hadn't expected— You're very special. But we can't go on like that." He said nothing for a moment. "Are you still there?"

"Yes," she whispered.

"What?"

"Yes," she said louder.

"I know this is no excuse, but I've been having a difficult time myself lately. Turmoil with Franca, turmoil about going to Mexico in December. I've been preoccupied, I've been—"

"I understand," she said.

"I hope we can still be friends."

"Sure," she mumbled.

"Good. Well, I'll see you in class next week, if I don't see you before then."

"Okay."

"What?"

"I said okay."

"Good. Well, listen, take care. All right?"

"Yeah." She dropped the phone into its cradle and stood in the hallway in her pink floor-length chenille bathrobe, two dollars at the Salvation Army Thrift Store. A picture of a woman who is going to be alone for the rest of her life, some woman in a Tennessee Williams play. She lives in a rooming house, has a cigarette before she gets out of bed. Men call first thing in the morning to tell her that they didn't mean it about last night.

She looks down at her bare feet. The phone is silent. She does not know who he will be or where she will find him or when he will appear, but the next man will not get away. The next man will not be allowed to walk out on her.

The Picture That Springs to Life

THAT SPRING, SHE wanted everything. The banal and the grand, new shoes, a wide-angle lens, money for her share of the rent, the patience to wait for the good picture among the two hundred mediocre pictures.

To be, someday, sought after.

To be loved the way she was sure Rory Dean loved the women he loved. Soaring passions, remarkable women, even their names. Maybe an Elena or a Pilar by now, now that he had been in Mexico for six months. He had sent her a postcard from Mexico City and two letters from San Miguel—and had signed the last one, "Take care for now. Love, Rory."

His love, if she could have it, would keep her from nightmares, from unhappiness as acute as her longing for him. His love would be the assurance of her worthiness to exist.

The love she had with Michael was a disappointment, despite appearances, despite all of the amenities. His airy first-floor flat with a backyard on S Street—she had moved in in February, two months after they met. The car he taught her to drive and that he now called "our car." His parents' summer house in Maine, where Esme and Michael were going to spend the month of August. Material comfort, aesthetic pleasures, down pillows, Marimekko sheets, framed posters from shows at the Galerie Maeght. Every girl's dream, to be taken care of this way. By a shrink no less, at least a shrink-in-the-making. A third-year graduate student in clinical psychology at Georgetown.

She wanted to tell Rory that he was right, that love equals disappointment, that the magic you feel at the beginning never lasts. But she hadn't even felt the magic with Michael, except for the first day, when they met across the counter at the camera store where she had just started to work, and the second day, when he came back to the store at closing time and took her out to dinner at a Cuban restaurant. Love is such a disappointment, she wanted to tell Rory. Even when sex isn't.

In the stillness, the intoxication of those few minutes just after —it was the beginning of May, early morning, sheets twisted around their feet—the telephone rang.

"Leave it," Michael said. It was on her side of the bed.

It rang six times, eight times. She reached for it, picked it up. He touched her breast, covered it with his hand, began to knead it. "Hello," she said.

"Hi, sweetheart, I didn't wake you, did I?"

She pushed Michael's hand away and sat up. "No."

"I wanted to reach you before your day started," Georgia said. "How are you?"

"Fine."

"You sound a little—"

"I'm fine, all right?"

"Yes. Yes. Well, guess what?"

"I can't guess."

"There's a new hotel opening in Washington and they're having a free promotional weekend for travel agents, next weekend. Tommy and I are going to come down."

"Oh."

"All expenses paid, including air fare. I'll finally get to see where you live and meet your new boyfriend and *see* you. I was thinking the other day how long it's been. Do you know how long it's been?"

"Christmas break. The week before Christmas."

"I don't even count that. Half a day and then you were off to see your grandparents. That's hardly a visit."

"I wanted to see them, I hadn't seen them since—"

"Of course you wanted to see them. I would never begrudge you time with your grandparents, bless their hearts, all the grief your father has caused them, they're fortunate they have you, I would never—"

"When are you going to get here?"

"Saturday, the twelfth. Our plane gets in at two in the afternoon. I think it's two. They're going to put us all in a limo and take us to the hotel, so you don't have to worry about—"

"What hotel?"

"Something with Vista in it. Or Plaza. I can't remember. Tommy knows all the details. But—"

"Why don't you call me when you get to the hotel and we can arrange when to meet."

"I hope we can spend some time together. I'd love to take you shopping. I hear they have beautiful things at Garfinkel's."

"It's very expensive."

"It couldn't be that expensive. Let's make it a date for Saturday afternoon. Then we can have dinner together, the four of us. I can't wait to see you."

"Me too. I'll wait to hear from you next Saturday."

"Bye, bye, sweetheart. Give my love to your boyfriend. Tommy sends his too."

"Okay."

She waited until she heard the click at the other end, her mother hanging up. She looked at Michael. "She's coming."

"So I heard." He touched her leg, he ran his hand over her knee. "Who knows, maybe it'll be fun."

"Don't bet on it."

"You hate to have fun, don't you?"

"I just don't like to plan on it." She smiled, allowed herself that pleasure. "Especially when my mother is involved. Where are my cigarettes?"

He pointed. "On your dresser."

She got up and crossed the room.

"I love your rear end," he said. Her back was to him. She did not answer. "The way it moves when you walk. You'll never know what that looks like, will you? Because you'll never see yourself walking across a room from behind." She stood at the dresser and lit a cigarette. "Come and sit next to me."

"Should I walk backward?" she said.

He smiled and nodded. "C'mere. I want to hold you." She went to him but not walking backward. She kept her eyes down, cigarette between her lips. He couldn't kiss her, couldn't get too close, when she had a cigarette in her mouth. She sat at the edge of the bed with her back to him. "I was just thinking," he said and touched her back, "these rites of passage are always more difficult in the imagination than in fact."

"Since when is a mother coming to visit her kid a rite of passage?" She turned to him.

"When it's the first time for both of them as adults. When it's no longer a mother going to see a kid at summer camp."

She turned away now, away from Michael and his theories, a theory for every occasion, a label for every impulse. "She can't wait to meet you."

"Same here," Michael said.

Esme stared at a picture she had taken of a fisherman down at the wharf.

"Hey, she can't be all bad," he said.

"She isn't all bad." She moved onto the bed, closer to him. She crossed her legs and pulled the sheet over her, like the doctors do to you. "Her pinkies are benign."

"What?"

Esme held up the pinkie of her right hand and wiggled it. Michael grabbed it and pushed her hand down to the bed.

"Want to arm wrestle?" he said.

She shook her head and crushed out her cigarette in the ashtray on the night table.

"Even if I let you win?"

"You'd do that, wouldn't you?" she said. "Let me win to make me feel better. You'll be a great shrink."

"It was a joke."

"You know what Freud says about jokes."

"I can see you're upset."

"That's very astute, Michael. Any other observations you care to make about my emotional state?"

"You might be overwrought."

"Give me a little time. I might work up to it."

"I could understand if you did. In light of what you just learned. That your mother's coming to visit. Given how estranged the two of you are, given your hostility to her."

"My hostility! My hostility, as you call it, is the only rational way to deal with her. When you use that word, you're saying it's an inappropriate response."

"I am not."

"If you listened more carefully to what you said, instead of holding forth on everyone else's neurotic behavior, you might—"

"Esme, wait, please."

"Wait for what?" She swung her legs off the bed and stood up as Michael grabbed her hand. She let him see her bare back, kept her back to him. He held tightly to her hand. "Let go of me."

"No." He held it harder. She could flail her other arm, she could kick him, she could press off with her foot against the bed and probably pull the two of them apart. But she did none of those. She gave up. She let her arm go limp, and he released her hand. "I love your rear end," he murmured and kissed it.

"Fuck off," she said and stalked away, down the hall into the bathroom. She slammed and locked the door behind her. Her cigarettes—she almost kicked her bare foot against the bathtub, she almost pounded her fists against the back of the door—her cigarettes were in the other room.

When she came out five minutes later, ten minutes later, he was sitting on the edge of the bed, on his side. He was dressed, he was putting on his socks.

"I'm sorry," she said and picked up her cigarettes, a pack of matches.

"I wish you wouldn't smoke."

"So do I." She flicked the match into the ashtray and sat on the edge of the bed, on her side. They sat back to back, with most of the unmade bed between them.

"You said you were going to stop last month."

"I know I did."

"When's it going to be, Esme?"

"I thought one of the basic tenets of shrinking is that people change in their own time, and not a moment before."

"As I've told you before, I think you ought to get some therapy. Among other things, it might help get you in the right frame of mind to quit smoking."

"As I've told you before, Michael, I'd rather use what little money I have to buy film. And if I had more money than I have, I'd spend it on a wide-angle lens, not a shrink."

"If you really wanted to, you could—"

"You know what I really want to do right now?" She crushed out her cigarette, stood up, and walked around to his side of the bed. She was naked, she sashayed up to him, touched her knee to his. "What do you have to do now?"

"Go to the library to finish the paper I'm working on. What about you?"

"I've got to be at work at eleven." She still worked part-time at the camera store where they had met. "I thought maybe we could—" she slid her leg in between his— "make up. Or something."

He touched her thigh. He leaned forward and kissed her stomach.

She closed her eyes and tried to pretend that this was love.

She wondered how much more she could stand. Whether she would last until August, until their month in Maine with his parents.

He wrapped his arms around her waist, pulled her toward him. "With your clothes on?" she said.

"Help me take them off."

She began to unbutton his shirt. "It's a good thing you're not the kind of guy who wears ties."

"Why?"

"It would take too long to undress you." She leaned down and kissed his neck, his bare shoulders.

"But think of how much fun it would be. The anticipation."

"I prefer the real thing." She laughed and pushed him down on the bed.

"You've got a point." He kissed her breasts, he drew circles with his tongue on her stomach. "You're so beautiful," he said.

"No, I'm not."

"That's right, I forgot. It was another girl I was thinking of."

She took to it, always, like an addict, a woman starved. Getting her fill, her fix, her due. She enjoyed it, she had decided once, in inverse proportion to the feeling of emptiness that had preceded it, that returned almost before she could catch her breath again.

And in direct proportion to the clarity of the image of Rory Dean that hovered over the bed, taking pictures of what he saw. The picture that springs to life. This minute, this second, sweet second, over almost as soon as it begins.

A Brand-New Pair of Roller Skates

"EVER HEAR OF a travel agent who hates to travel?" Georgia said. "That's Tommy."

"A little louder, Mom, the people at that table in the corner can't hear you." Michael drew his arm around Esme's shoulder as they sat around the small cocktail table in the lounge of the restaurant, waiting to be called to their dinner table. Michael's gesture was not one of affection, it was his way of telling her to keep her mouth shut. She stiffened and thought, So this is what it is to give someone the cold shoulder.

"Can you blame me?" Tommy said. "In this weather? Two hours on the goddam runway at La Guardia, rain like you wouldn't *believe*. An hour in the air—we might as well have been in a cardboard box." He held his cigarette deep in the V that his forefinger and middle finger made. "They don't serve a goddam thing on the Shuttle. You can't get a cup of coffee, much less a shooter. I get off the plane—three hours late, in case anyone's keeping score—and by this time it's stopped raining, but the humidity hits you—bam!—the second you're out of the terminal. The limo driver can't speak English to save his grandmother's life. What do you bet someone's going to steal our luggage from the coatroom before dinner's over. I said to the maître d', I said—"

"Sweetheart," Georgia interrupted, "next time we'll take Greyhound and leave the driving to them. Are you kids hungry?" She cocked her ear toward the ceiling. "Are they calling our name? That's our table. It's ready."

"There won't be a next time," Tommy said.

"He said that after the last trip," Georgia said and gathered up her cigarettes, her purse. "Did I tell you about our free trip to Miami a few months ago? We showed up at the hotel and they stuck us in a closet near the furnace, it was about as much fun as going to the Bronx." She looked over to the main entrance of the restaurant. "There she is, the gal who's doing the seating. Come on, gang. I love it here already. I don't think I've ever seen so many Tiffany chandeliers in one place. It looks like— what does it look like, Tommy?"

"It looks like a restaurant."

The walls were covered with framed news clippings, old sheet music, color-tinted drawings of all the Presidents, photographs of men in ten-gallon hats and top hats, signed pictures of J. Edgar Hoover, George Hamilton, Bobby Darin, John Kennedy.

"What do you recommend here?" Georgia said, when they sat down.

"Georgia," Tommy said, "I told you four times this is *the* place for beef in Washington. It's at the top of every list, every guidebook ever written on this town, every—"

"I know that, sweetheart. Every time I turn around, I see a picture of a cow. But maybe people who actually *live* here know the inside scoop."

"We've never been here," Esme said. "It's for tourists, and it's out of our price range. Among other things."

Tommy looked at her. "You're not going to tell me you turned into a vegetarian, are you?"

"No."

"Thank Christ for that. This country is going to hell in a hand basket, with all the vegetarians and health nuts. Everyone's got to be anti-this or anti-that. Everybody's got to be such a goddam individualist these days."

"I was here with my parents once," Michael said.

"It's the kind of place people go with their parents," Esme said.

"At least you do something with your parents," Tommy said, "besides fight with them."

"Michael, dear, what do your parents do?" Georgia said.

"My father's a judge," Michael said. "My mother's a librarian at Bryn Mawr."

"Isn't that interesting."

"You ready for another shooter?" Tommy said to Georgia.

"I'd like to order something first. Something to start with." Georgia began to squint as she read the menu. "Is it the light in here, or is it my eyes? Maybe I'll have the shrimp cocktail."

"It's dark in here," Esme said. "It's supposed to look like New Orleans. New Orleans at night."

"How do you know?" Georgia said.

"Because this room is called the New Orleans Room. There's a sign at the entrance."

"She notices everything," Georgia said. "That's why she's a photographer."

"It doesn't take a genius to—"

"I remember having the shrimp cocktail when I was here," Michael interrupted. "It's very good."

"Georgia, think beef," Tommy said. "That's why we came here."

"I'll think beef for the main course," she said. "For the appetizer, I'll think shrimp."

"I'm going to try the caesar salad," Michael said.

Tommy looked at him. "Are *you* a vegetarian?"

"I meant caesar salad for my—my salad, not my main course. Yes sir, I think I'm going to have some of that juicy prime rib for my entrée. I just saw a plate of it go by. It looked mighty tempting."

Esme could not believe Michael's tribute to beef, his phony play to get on Tommy's good side, on the off chance that Tommy had a good side.

"I wonder how the rib roast is," Georgia said. "Did you have that when you were here, Michael?"

"I think my mother did. You probably can't go wrong with it."

"Esme, darling, what are you going to get?"

"I was thinking of a hamburger."

"Hamburger?" Tommy said. "We did not come to this place, to pay these prices—"

"It's not hamburger," Esme said, "it's ground steak. It says so on the menu."

"We're going to have a nice time tonight, aren't we?" Georgia said. "We were a little late. We didn't have a chance to go shopping, but we're going to enjoy ourselves, and we are not going to fight. Is that clear?"

"That's fine with me," Tommy said and looked down at his menu.

The waiter appeared. "How are you folks doing tonight? Enjoying yourselves?"

"Yeah," Esme said. "We're having a blast."

"I'll have another one of these," Tommy said and touched the rim of his glass.

"Me too," Georgia said.

Esme excused herself and went to the bathroom. She had quit smoking the day before, but this afternoon she had bought a pack and stuck it in the bottom of her purse, just in case. In case she needed one. Like she needed it now.

"This is a *divine* piece of meat," Georgia said. "Simply marvelous."

"You've had three bites," Esme said.

"I'm stuffed. The shrimp cocktail filled me up."

"Shrimp cocktail doesn't make anyone full. It's the other cocktails that—"

"Do you know," Georgia interrupted, "I just realized, you haven't had a cigarette all night."

"I quit," Esme said.

"When?"

"Yesterday."

"You know what that reminds me of?" Georgia took a long drink of wine, finished what was in her glass. "When you were a little girl, a plump little thing, you'd tell me you'd gone on a diet and I'd say, when, and you'd say, just now." Georgia blew a stream of smoke at Michael. "Can you imagine, seven years old and she's talking about dieting? Only Esme, only my little sweetheart. Do you know that this girl was born mature? Did you know that?"

"I did not talk about dieting when I was seven," Esme said.

"It must have been some other plump little girl who said that to me."

"It must have been your idea. How would I have known about dieting?"

Georgia looked at Michael and reached for the wine bottle in the center of the table. "She knows about things I don't even know about. She always has. I always thought it was kind of spooky. Were you that way when you were little?"

"No," Michael said. "I was very ordinary. I liked to collect baseball cards and play stickball."

"Then why on earth are you going to be a psychiatrist and surround yourself with *kooks* all day long?" Georgia filled her glass with wine and looked hard at the bottle in her hand. "Empty, for a change," she mumbled and put it down.

"I'm not going to be a psychiatrist, I—"

"Esme said you were going to be a psychiatrist, didn't you, sweetheart?"

"A psychologist," Michael said. "Kind of like a psychiatrist but we can't prescribe medication."

"Voodoo," Tommy said. "My first wife went to one of them. She was crazy as a goddam loon. And you know what?"

"What?" Michael said.

"She was even crazier when she got finished with him. I said to her, Martha, you've got to take charge of your own life, you can't let some schmuck doctor tell you—"

"Here, Esme," Georgia interrupted. "I have something for you, sweetheart." Georgia put her purse on the table and riffled through it. She held out an envelope for Esme.

"What's this?"

"A teensy-weensy birthday present."

"My birthday isn't for a month."

"Make believe it's early this year."

"Mom, you didn't have to."

"Don't look a gift horse in the mouth."

In the envelope was a card with a picture of two cats in an

air balloon, and printed across the sky: WE NEVER TAKE YOUR BIRTHDAY LIGHTLY. Inside the card were five ten-dollar bills and a check for one hundred dollars. "Thank you. But why so much?"

"We were going to spend the fifty today at Garfinkel's. The hundred is mad money. All of it is mad money."

"Now you can buy a wide-angle lens," Michael said.

"Thanks very much." She was terrible at this, showing her mother appreciation, admitting that there was a reason to show it, especially when Georgia was sloshed. She leaned over and kissed Georgia's cheek. It was soft, she smelled her perfume. "But where'd you get it all?"

"She robbed a bank," Tommy said.

"Let's order another bottle of wine," Georgia said. "To celebrate. Sweetheart—" She puckered her lips at Tommy. It was that time of night, Georgia's words were starting to slur. "You order the wine, I'm going to tinkle." She turned to Esme and reached for her purse. "Which way's the—oops. Oh, dear, me." She had knocked over a water glass.

"I'll take you," Esme said and pressed her napkin against the table, trying to sop up the water.

"Sweetheart, you don't have to do that for your old mommy."

"Yes, I do."

Georgia turned to Michael. "Isn't she the nicest, sweetest little girl you ever knew? Even if she is taller than me now."

Michael nodded.

Esme stood up and held out her arm. Georgia took her hand, then wrapped her arm around Esme's shoulder. Esme led her across the floor, down the hall. "I have to tinkle like crazy," Georgia whispered. She rested her head on Esme's shoulder. "I *love* this restaurant."

"Me too."

"And you know what, sweetheart?"

"What?"

"I love you."

"Yeah. I know."

"You know what else? Your boyfriend is very nice."

"It's extraordinary, isn't it?" Esme said.

"What?"

"That I had the instinct to pick someone nice."

"Yes. You're right. It's very nice. He's a lovely young man."

Georgia was too smashed to have heard the insult. "Here," Esme said and pushed open the ladies' room door. "I don't have to go. I'll wait out here for you."

"Oh, sweetie pie." Georgia turned and threw her arms around Esme's neck. "Sweetie pie, sweetie pie." She held on to Esme like a marathon dancer, like she'd just been dragged out of the water, all of her weight around Esme's neck.

"Stand up," Esme said. She kept her arms at her sides, then she lifted them and tried to push Georgia gently against the half-open door, to push it all the way open, to get her into the bathroom.

Georgia would not let go. Her head fell on Esme's shoulder. "I have to tinkle, tinkle, tinkle." Suddenly Georgia loosened her grip and took a step back, draping her arms over Esme's shoulders. "Which way's the john?"

"You're in it."

Georgia turned. They were in a tiny room with two stalls. "I'll wait outside," Esme said.

"Okay, sweetheart." Georgia was groggy but she could stand up fine. Stand up and take six steps across the floor. "I'll be right out," she called from behind the stall door.

"Great," Esme said under her breath and left the bathroom. She wanted to keep going, down the hall and out the door, let them wonder for the rest of their lives where she had disappeared to. She fell against the wall just outside the door and took a deep breath. She should go back in there, to make sure Georgia didn't slip and break her neck, but she did not move. She looked over at the wall across from her, covered with old menus and photographs and buttons from presidential elections.

"Surprise," Michael said and appeared at her side.

Esme said nothing.

"Where's your mother?"

Esme pointed.

"Baby, what's wrong?"

"Nothing's wrong. I'm having a great time. What about you?"

"It's rough, isn't it? I'm sorry."

"Me too."

"Is it all right if I offer to drive them back to their hotel, so they don't have to take a cab?"

"Do whatever you want."

"Esme, I wish—"

"I told you, do whatever you want."

"Is your mother all right?"

"I have no idea."

"If you need me, I'm—"

"Fine."

She knew suddenly—staring at an old photograph of a fat man and someone who looked like Jimmy Durante, who was very probably Jimmy Durante—she knew what she was going to do with the hundred and fifty dollars her mother had given her. No wide-angle lens. No shrink. No dinners at dumps like this.

She was going to go to Mexico, to see Rory.

.   .   .

Sheets of rain crashed against the windshield faster than the wipers could keep it clear, as they drove back from Georgia and Tommy's hotel.

"Is the defroster on?"

"Yes, Michael."

"High beams?"

"Yes, Michael."

"Do you want me to drive?"

"You asked me if I wanted to drive. I said yes."

"That was before the storm started."

"If you can see through rain better than I can, then perhaps you should. Maybe you could even market your talent. Chauffeuring in difficult weather. Seeing for the blind."

"I didn't mean that you were incapable," he said, "or that I had any special skill. I was trying to be helpful."

On the radio, through the static, over the sound of rain hitting the roof as hard as pebbles, Melanie sang, "*I got a brand-new pair of roller skates, you got a brand-new key.*" Esme was struck by the absurdity of the lyric, and the appeal of it, this love song for eight-year-olds.

"Look, I know you're upset. I know it was awful for you."

"Awful? What could be awful? It's the longest-running show off Broadway. And I'm lucky enough to have a year-round subscription. Third row, center, come as you are, bring a friend, bring a—"

"You do have a right to be angry."

"Thank you very much, Dr. Freud. Thank you for pointing that out."

"Dr. Freud?"

"Don't you ever think about yourself? Or is it easier to think about me, try out your little theories, make me your Anna O., your Fräulein von P., your live-in hysteric."

"You're not a hysteric."

"None of them were either. They were just unhappy bourgeois ladies in Vienna married to guys who didn't know how to get them off. Isn't that the latest word on him?"

"I thought you were above that. Parroting all that feminist crap about what a sexist Freud was. The fact of the matter is he was a brilliant pioneer who just happened to—"

"You can analyze everyone but yourself, can't you? Me, Freud, my mother—"

"I didn't say a word about your mother."

"That's fitting." She was not about to let the truth get in the way of her argument. "Because she doesn't deserve a word."

They drove in silence down Connecticut Avenue. The only sounds were the rain against the windshield and the roof and

the lyrics to more songs that made no sense. Joe Cocker sang
"She Came in Through the Bathroom Window."

"Your mother needs help."

"Then go help her. Because I'm not going to."

"She isn't as bad as you say she is."

"Because she didn't throw up on the waiter? Because she
didn't take off her dress and dance on the table? I had to drag
her out of the fucking restaurant. I ought to get a Junior Life-
Saving card for that."

"She came to see you, Esme. She gave you a hundred and
fifty dollars. I think it was pretty big-hearted, all things considered."

"All things considered, I think her big-heartedness can-
celed itself out after the sixth or seventh drink."

"There are places she can go, to dry out."

"She doesn't want to dry out. She wants to drink. She likes
her oblivion."

"What about you?"

"What about me?"

"I guess I wonder how much you like yours."

"Mine!"

"Yes, yours."

"My mother and I wear the same-size shoes. That's where
the resemblance ends."

He said nothing.

"What's that supposed to mean?" she said.

"I didn't say anything."

"I know you didn't."

"I think you ought to see someone."

"Michael, we've been through this ten times. I can't afford
it. Whatever it is."

"Why don't you start with the money your mother just gave
you?"

"A hundred and fifty dollars? What do I do after my four
visits?"

"As you know, you can go to the clinic at Georgetown and see someone in training for ten dollars a session."

"Great. A graduate student. I can talk to one of those at home, for free."

"Ask your grandfather to help you. What is it you always tell me he says, every time you see him? About needing money? If he was willing to pay for your courses this semester—"

"I told him that money was a loan."

"Maybe it's time to ask him for another one."

"How am I going to pay back that kind of money taking pictures for a living?"

"Take pictures of something that pays. Portraits. And I don't mean welfare mothers in line at the *bodega*. I mean portraits that people pay you to take."

"Graduation portraits? Chintzy weddings? I would rather die." She stopped for a light at Florida Avenue, reached into the back seat for a rag, and handed it to Michael. "Would you wipe off your window, I can't see a thing on that side."

"Why do you always think of the most unappealing prospect?" He twisted in his seat, he cleared the window. "What about Imogen Cunningham? What about Stieglitz's portraits of Georgia O'Keeffe? You have postcards of them taped up all over the kitchen, and all you can think about is second-rate graduation portraits."

She turned right on S Street and started looking for a place to park. She was not thinking about second-rate graduation portraits. She was listening to rain against the car. She was thinking about having a brand-new pair of roller skates, a brand-new key. About how fast she could go. When she would get there. What excuse she would give Michael.

"Esme."

"What."

"Say something."

She spoke calmly, quietly. "Did I ever tell you this? For Christmas when I was eleven, my mother gave me the autobiography of Sammy Davis, Jr., because he's Jewish. He's the only famous Jewish person she knows about, except Barry Goldwater."

Michael began to laugh, and his laughter made her laugh too, made her see the absurd good intention in her mother's gift.

When they stopped laughing, Esme said in the same calm voice the thought that had just come to her, the alibi to end all alibis, "I just decided what to do with the money my mother gave me."

"What's that?"

"I think I'm going to visit my father."

"Your father?"

"Yes."

"In Houston?"

"That's where he lives. At least last time I heard."

"You haven't mentioned him in ages."

"That doesn't mean I haven't been thinking about him."

"I must say, I'm a bit surprised."

"By what?"

"Your sudden interest in seeing him."

"Blood is thicker than water, and all that. Is that a parking space on the right?"

"It's a hydrant."

"I hate this street. I hate this neighborhood. There's never anywhere to park."

"We'll find something. We always do."

When she arrived in San Miguel, she would be irresistible. She would say to Rory, *I'm a woman, you're a man. Why waste the afternoon?* And now it would mean something entirely different, it would mean that their love was adult love, that their passion was unbridled.

"Maybe I'll leave next week," she said, "when my courses are over. I'm sure I can get a ride from the ride board. Probably lots of people going out west next week when school's out, don't you think? It'll be dirt cheap to get there sharing expenses. I'll have enough money left over to take the train back. Or maybe I can find another ride board in Houston, at one of the colleges."

"You're really serious?"

"I'm really serious."

"It's so far away."

"No, it's not." A lot farther than Michael knew, than he would ever know.

"Well, I guess it's a good thing that you're going. Confronting your father. It's very brave." He draped his arm around her shoulder. She would get a ride to Houston from the ride board and then take a bus to Mexico. On her way, she would read that book Rory had mentioned in one of his letters, a famous book about Mexico called *The Labyrinth of Solitude*, and she would tell him when she got there what a fascinating book it was. "Just don't be gone long," Michael said, "because I'll miss you to pieces."

The Labyrinth of Solitude

THE PLEASURES OF all the unwasted afternoons in the world to contemplate and the infinite pleasure of this moment, as the old bus lurched through the pitch-dark night, took hairpin turns on roads it was too dark to see. They might have been driving through space, it was that dark. She sat in the back and smoked Mexican cigarettes she had bought when the bus stopped for fifteen minutes in Monterrey eight or nine hours ago. She had been sitting for hours, for days. Hadn't talked to anyone since the couple who had given her a ride from Washington to Houston had let her off there last night, at the Trailways terminal. A paperback copy of *The Labyrinth of Solitude* sat on the seat beside her, wedged between her camera bag and the armrest. She had read only bits and pieces of it; reading on the bus made her nauseated. It was too dark to read now anyway—there were no lights above the seats. Too noisy to sleep. The bus clanged and belched and roared with every shift of the gears. The driver kept a radio on a shelf behind his seat—you saw it as you went on and off the bus—with the volume turned way up. The disc jockey's strange, insistent voice, Spanish too fast, too colloquial for her to comprehend, carried throughout the bus. It sounded like it was being broadcast from an echo chamber.

When she saw Rory tomorrow, she would tell him that logistics had kept them apart all this time. She would tell him that love needs direction sometimes, the way an orchestra does. Now and then, she would whisper in his ear, love needs a hand.

On the radio, a brass band began a squeaky instrumental rendition of "Honky Tonk Women," and Esme wanted to tell someone how happy she was right this minute, alone in the dark on this bus. There was no one in the world, no one, who knew where she was. A different sort of thrill entirely from the thrill that awaited her in San Miguel.

They would arrive at dawn.

. . .

The landscape was marked with cupolas and crucifixes, narrow cobblestone streets that wound to the top of the hills and vanished, rust-colored Spanish tiled roofs, buildings made of stone, buildings painted white, pale pink, the color of salmon, the colors of the earth. Early morning in San Miguel.

The hotel at the foot of the hills that her student guidebook had shown her to—two hundred years ago it had been a convent. Now, the guidebook said, it catered to the art students in town, Mexican tourists, hippies on a splurge. The rates were low, breakfast was included. Bedroom doors opened to the outside. Cloistered walkways, beautiful blue tiles on the walls, fluted dark wood molding, the way the sunlight fell through the open roof. Up a narrow flight of stairs and across a short bridge were more rooms, unexpected patios, hidden staircases, shifting streams of sunlight and shade, her room. Eight dollars a night.

This is where she would take him, in the room with a patio just outside, this room with this view of San Miguel. This is where she would have him.

She examined the street map spread out on the dresser. The Instituto Allende, where he taught, was eight blocks away. She could not find the name of the street where he lived. The rest of the map: there was nothing else she had come to see. She looked up, to the mirror above the dresser. Her hair fanned out over her back. It was almost dry. She was going to pull it back from her face for him, pin it up in a loose bun that she had been practicing for weeks. She would take the pins out for him later, let her hair tumble down her back. Or the furor of their passion would undo her hair in its own time, in the heat and deshabille of their love.

She imagined her hands, these hands, held out to him, and when he took them, her fingers would curl around his and she would not let go.

———

"Rory Dean? Someone in the school office should know where he is. It's over there, the far side of the courtyard." The majestic courtyard of the Instituto Allende, a jungle of palms, banana trees, jacarandas in bloom, the wild purples and pinks, the scent of jasmine.

It was astonishing to think—she crossed the courtyard as she might a cemetery or private property, a feeling of curiosity and fear—that this was the air he breathed every day, this was where he worked, in this arboretum, this paradise. *This single picture is a whole story in itself.*

Another picture—the way she looked right now. In dark glasses and a cheap straw hat bought on her way over, so she would be able to slink around unnoticed, so she would be able to see him without his noticing her, at least until she could collect herself, until she was ready to be seen. She had come all this way. She clutched her camera bag and entered a door marked OFICINA. She was breathless, she was terrified.

"Rory Dean?" the woman behind the counter said, an older woman with long gray hair, a turquoise blouse, silver rings, an American. She turned to a man sitting at a desk. "Is Rory back yet?"

"I didn't know he was away."

"He went up to Guanajuato a few days ago. Some assignment or other. Hasn't Inez been teaching his class?"

"Check the signout board."

How casual they were about him, how unimpressed. It was not possible that his life was so banal, so ordinary.

"Rory Dean never signs in *or* out," the woman said and looked at Esme. "Was he expecting you?"

"Not really, I was just . . ."

"Here's someone who ought to know." A woman had just walked into the office. She was petite, had short black hair, olive skin, a handful of keys, like a hotel maid, a janitor. "Inez, dear, this young lady's looking for Rory."

"He'll be back here tomorrow. Something I can help you with?"

Esme shook her head. "About what time should I come?"

"His first class is at eleven. He's usually around shortly before then. I'll be seeing him late tonight, if there's something you—"

"That's okay." Esme turned and walked out the door, through the archway that led to the lush courtyard, the leaves of the banana trees the size of the wings of small airplanes. "I'll be back, don't tell him I came," she mumbled, even though they did not know enough about her to tell him any-thing, even though they could not possibly have heard what she said.

She headed up the hill toward the *zócalo,* the winding cobble-stone streets, pastel-colored houses covered with bougainvillaea, shops that sold ashtrays, etchings, street scenes of San Miguel, street scenes before her eyes, an old man leading a mule down the road, saddled with bundles of wood, a Mexican boy with a ghetto blaster, a little girl with a baby in her arms. There were a hundred reasons why this Inez might be seeing Rory later tonight. She might be staying in his house while he's gone, taking care of his cats. Maybe he had cats. Maybe this Inez had to tell him some-thing about his students, the classes she had been teaching. They were friends, just friends. The important thing was that he was going to be here tomorrow, and Esme was too. The rest, the rest would be easy, the rest would be a snap. Her hair would tumble down her shoulders, her back. They would talk for hours. There were so many things she had to tell him.

She began to take pictures of people around the *zócalo.* Tourists, the old women who sold tamales on the corner, the children, children were everywhere, selling Chiclets, selling ices, holding out their hands for money. They smiled when she took their pictures. In English they said, "Give me a peso." She gave them pesos. One of them, a boy, moved to sit at the feet of a fruit vendor and Esme took pictures of the two of them. The child, conscious of her camera and her interest, kept moving from stall to stall, posing for her. Esme followed him. It was easy to take pictures of children. Easy to sneak pictures of the adults nearby. Then she lost the kid, he ran into a store and did not come out. Esme kept up the same rhythm on her own, with no one to guide her, no kid to act as her shill. She pressed the shutter and dashed away, down to the next block, the next vendor. She had read that Cartier-Bresson had great reflexes, that he was like an athlete, the way he could set up his shots in a few seconds, take the pictures and be off. The invisible man. She took a picture of an old man on the steps of the *Parroquia*, the fake Gothic church designed, it said in her guidebook, by a Mexican said to have learned the architecture by studying French postcards of Gothic cathedrals. She took pictures of a woman carrying a basket of mangos on her head, a man deftly cutting up a pineapple and spreading the pieces across a slab of ice.

Here was a transformation she could feel, put her finger on: she was becoming the photographer she had always wanted to be, the one who was not afraid to take pictures. It was the air, the crowd, it was her proximity to Rory, it was all the possibilities that had emerged since she had left her old life, that awful life she had lived back there. She took two rolls of film, three rolls of film. She walked with no thought to where she was going or how she would get back to where she had started.

But at every street corner, on the steps of every church, every time a tall man with black hair turned his face toward her, she expected it to be Rory Dean. And every time, she felt her heart sink and then spring back in relief when it was not.

The swings of love, the contractions of love. Moments of peace, terror, unbearable longing; they made her dizzy, lightheaded. Or maybe it was the altitude, the six thousand feet. Or the fact that this was the first foreign country she had ever been to. Or that she hadn't had a good night's sleep in three or four days. When she found her hotel again—it was down the hill, a few blocks that way—she would go to sleep. Sleep straight through until tomorrow morning, when her life would start all over again.

Eight o'clock that night—she did not sleep through the night after all—the sky was dark blue, growing darker, the color of sapphire, a photograph that could not be taken, if you were the sort of photographer who took color pictures, which she was not. But if you were, you would never get the color right. You would never be able to convey the way it felt to be sitting here tonight, this view from this table, an outdoor café overlooking the *zócalo*, counting down the hours until you saw the love of your life. The crowd and commotion on the square, roving musicians, a stage being set up across the narrow street from the café. The moon, a sliver tonight, an arc of gold against the sapphire sky. She chain-smoked Mexican cigarettes and watched the plumes of smoke sail over the wrought-iron bannister and vanish into the night.

She would have to tell Rory how she came to be in Mexico. She had gone to visit her father in Houston, she'd say, her crazy father, and after a few days with him, she'd thought, what the hell, it isn't that far from Houston to Mexico, when you consider how far it is from Washington to Houston. Never mind that she was no Jack Kerouac, someone who headed for the road whenever the urge struck. Maybe Rory thought that she was. Maybe he would think that now. Now. Then. Tomorrow. Fifteen hours from now. *You must visit San Miguel*, he had written in his letters to her. I took you at your word, she would tell him. Here I am.

"*¿Más café?*" the waiter said.

"*No, gracias.*"

"We have many festivals in San Miguel," he said in almost perfect English and tipped his head toward the street. A crowd had gathered around the makeshift stage not thirty feet from her seat. They began to applaud as a man crossed the stage, picked up a microphone and spoke. It did not work. He tapped it three or four times. Then it worked. The stage lit up, it was as bright as day. He held out his arm, welcoming a woman in a bright red dress and a band of six mariachi players, including a little boy of nine or ten. They crossed the stage and took their places in a line. Bright green uniforms, black hats with curled brims, embroidered with shiny gold thread, trumpets at their sides. One carried a guitar. The woman in red—her dress had a tight waist, a full skirt with layers of white petticoats. The music began, a blare of trumpets, a hoot, a holler. The woman danced among the musicians, slapping her heels against the stage as fast as she hammered castanets between her fingers. She spun and spun and the folds of her petticoats rose and fell like waves.

If Esme got up closer, there might be enough light to take pictures. She paid her bill, headed down the stairs of the café, unzipped her camera case, and took out the camera. She stood near the back of the crowd and looked through the viewfinder; she was tall enough to see over most of the heads in the audience. Almost enough light for this shot. She moved closer. The stage was flooded with light. There was a crescendo of trumpets, the end of a song, great applause.

The lead trumpet player sidled up to the little boy in the band and presented him to the audience, hand outstretched. "¡Este es mi hijo!" he shouted to the crowd and grinned. In his difficult English, for the sake of the gringos, he translated, with that same grin on his face, "Dees ees my sonn!" Esme took a picture, took three or four pictures, of the father beaming at his son, boasting in Spanish and English and in the language of his eyes, and perhaps it was because of her own proximity to the consummation of a great love that she thought, with a fullness of feeling that surprised her, That is pride, the way that man talked about his son. That is love. Maybe that would come through in the photograph, all of the man's feelings for his son, and Esme's feelings for them. If she could make all of that happen in one photograph, that picture would be the good one, the one that stood out in the pile. She had never taken one like that, not yet, even though she had taken more than two hundred pictures. She took a few more shots of the stage, but by this time the band had begun a new song. These were tourist shots, postcard shots, the quaint mariachi players in the town square. No big deal.

She stepped back from the noise and the crowd and lit a

cigarette. Out of the corner of her eye, she saw a tall figure off to the left. She spotted him and froze. At the foot of the steps of the *Parroquia*, walking this way, in a pool of light cast by one of the stage lights, there he was. Not a man who looked like him but the man himself. He had a large canvas bag slung over one shoulder, a camera bag over the other. Coming this way, but looking down, not looking at her. He was fifteen feet in front of her, he would have to look up any second now, or walk right into her. Unless she walked away. She could walk away, but she had come so far, she had come all this way. She could not move.

His head down, he came closer and closer, the ideal subject in the center of your zoom lens. Rory Dean. There was no time to escape, to think of what to say, to remember all of the speeches she had rehearsed.

He lifted his head and saw her, saw a figure he did not yet recognize as her. Then he did a double take. "Esme?" She nodded. This was the moment she had been waiting for. This was why she had come. If she held out her arm, she could touch him, they were that close. "Is that really you?" She nodded. "What are you doing here?" He threw his arms around her, but when she tried to hold him, she felt his heavy bags as they slid down his shoulders.

He let go and stepped back. "What a surprise. What an incredible surprise." He smiled and stood close to her. There were scores of people around, trumpets whining, the smell of spiced beef. "When did you get here?"

"This morning."

"You're going to have to cancel all your plans and come have a drink with me. I just got back from a fantastic trip to Guanajuato and I'm— But before I get into that, where have you been? How did you get here?"

"I was in Texas," she said, "visiting my father."

He tipped his head toward the hill beyond the *zócalo* and began walking. He wore jeans and a beige Mexican shirt, he walked with a bounce in his step as he led the way through the crowd.

"So I was in Texas," she said, "and I thought I'd—" she laughed, she was delirious, in love— "well, I thought I'd make the most of it and come on down."

"What a terrific idea. I thought it would be just another dull Thursday night."

"It doesn't seem dull here. I mean, all this—"

"That?" He pointed back to the *zócalo*. "That's regulation San Miguel. They've got a saint to honor every other day of the year. The sidewalk's very narrow up here." He touched her arm. "Let's stay on the street. There's a restaurant up a few blocks where we can sit down and talk. I just got off the bus from Guanajuato. I was on my way home when I saw you. If I'd taken my car, I'd have missed you. You got in this morning, isn't that what you said?"

"Yeah. And I got a great room at a hotel right down the street. Eight dollars a night. I couldn't believe it. Even I can afford that."

"Here we are." He led the way through a plain door, it could have been the entrance to a house. They were in a small dimly lit room with three or four dinette tables, plastic chairs, a flowered linoleum floor. "Have a seat." Rory put his bags down by the table. "Would you like a beer?"

"I'd love one." She took out her cigarettes, she looked around the room, expecting a waiter, expecting to see someone besides the two of them. She had never had her own beer. She had had three or four sips of Michael's once and had not liked it enough to drink more. But what the hell, she had never been in love like this before, and she had never taken a bus to Mexico either. "Kind of quiet, isn't it?"

"Things are slow at night. They're mobbed at lunchtime."

A man came out from behind a gauzy curtain in the corner. A stout man with a square face, a gold tooth, a belly that hung over his pants. Rory ordered two beers.

"I went by your school this morning," she said, "to see if you were around. They said you wouldn't be back until late tonight.

I was going to go back to the school tomorrow." She smiled. "It looks like I saved myself the trip."

"I'm sorry I wasn't there this morning."

"Oh." She put the back of her hand to her forehead, mock suffering. "It was difficult, but I survived."

"I knew you would."

The waiter put their beers on the table, two long-necked bottles, two short plain water glasses. A still-life, she thought. But how could you ever convey in a photograph all that it meant, how many miles she had traveled to drink this beer with this man?

"A toast," Rory said and raised his glass. "To your travels. To your stay in Mexico." They touched glasses and drank. "Tell me how you got here. Did you—"

"I started in Washington about a week ago." She was right, it was just logistics that had kept them apart. All love needed sometimes was a hand. "I got a ride on the ride board at school with a couple who go to G.W. and live in Houston. We drove straight through, the three of us. Saw some incredible sunrises and sunsets, I think they were in Oklahoma and northern Texas, big-sky kind of stuff. Made me want to take color pictures—" she held up her hand—"but just fleetingly. I waited for the urge to pass, and thank god it did." She drank some more beer, she tried to swig it down like Rory was doing, but she did not like the taste at all. "Then I saw my father in Houston for a few days, and—"

"Wait a second, this is the one you never see, right?"

She nodded. "Until a few days ago."

"How was that?"

She took another sip of beer and waited for the right word to come to her. "Uneventful. I think that's the ideal visit with a parent. Kind of like the ideal plane ride. Anyway, since I got to San Miguel, I've been taking just *heaps* of pictures."

"I know the feeling. I think I took forty rolls of film in the last four days."

"I guess it's different for you, because you've been here for a while, but I feel like I'm *seeing* for the first time, because there's so much to see here. It makes Washington look like—Washington never looked like much to me. So it's not really a contest. It's so beautiful here. Don't you think so? My god, I haven't even asked you how you like it here. I mean, you've said you liked it in your letters, but it's never the same, talking versus writing. People always *say* different things than they write, don't you think? I'm talking a lot, aren't I? I haven't really talked to anyone in days."

"How did you get from Houston to here?"

"Bus."

"Are you serious? How long did it take, three days?"

"Not quite." She laughed. "But I do have a few bed sores."

"I bet you do. Jesus. I drove when I came down here from Washington. Those fucking roads through the mountains. You can't see a thing at night. You can barely see the white lines, when there are any." He shook his head. "Enough travel talk. People spend most of their time when they're traveling talking about traveling. Tell me how your work is going."

"You mean my work-work or my—"

"I mean your photography."

"I told you, I've been taking zillions of pictures since I got here. I was very brave today. I just walked up to people and took pictures. I wasn't my usual quivering self. And tonight, right before I ran into you, I was watching the mariachi players, and I took a picture of this father and son, and something good happened. If it comes out, if there was enough light, I think it'll be good. I don't think that about too many of my pictures. It kind of gave me an idea, it's still very vague, I'm pretty much making this up as I go along, I mean, right now. The idea has something to do with taking pictures of kids and their parents. Then maybe following the kids around when they're older, when they're on their own. You know those studies psychologists and sociologists do that go on forever? They check in with their subjects every few years and find out if they're still neurotic or still fat or still afraid to change the tires on their cars, and then they publish the results in some journal that nobody reads? What I'm thinking of—actually, this just came to me—is a photo essay of a kid growing up, and first you see him with his parents and all the people around him, because all of them define his identity at that point. Then I would take pictures of him as he got older, at different stages, and all those people would be on the sidelines. Maybe they wouldn't even be there at all. It would just be him. But there would have to be some kind of visual theme that connected them, or a mood, or a place, so that they wouldn't be just a group of disparate photographs. I don't know how it could be done."

"Why a man? Why not a woman?"

"I don't know, I hadn't thought it through entirely, I—"

"You know me, I always think people should start with an experience that's close to them."

"Is that why you did a book about female junkies?"

He laughed.

"Or is that just the advice you give your students?" she said.

He threw up his hands. "You caught me. I give up. What can I say? Your project sounds very ambitious. I don't know how you'd do it, but it sounds like something you could do."

"You mean, unlike the Washington ghetto?"

"I never said you *couldn't* do that. What I said was that it was too far afield for—"

"I know. I remember."

"What do you say, want another beer? Want something to eat?"

"I had dinner about an hour ago. Sitting out there. It's so beautiful here."

"If you like San Miguel, you really should see Guanajuato while you're here. It's just about an hour on the bus."

"That's nothing to me," she laughed. "It's like one stop on the subway."

"That's right, after your trek across the Himalayas. You look a little wiped out."

"I am. What about you?"

"Me too. I've been away for four days. Four long days." He took a long swig of beer, finished what was in his glass.

This was the place in her script where he should reach over and touch her hand, look into her eyes, invite her to come home with him. "So," he said and rolled his empty glass between his palms. This was the place in the script— "How long are you planning to stay in San Miguel?"

"I don't know." He was shy, he was not going to just come out and invite her home. "It depends. What are your plans?"

"I'm here for the duration." He smiled.

She looked down at the table, the cigarette butts in the ashtray, the plastic rose in the plastic vase. She was afraid to look at him, afraid he would see all of her longing, her frailty.

"If you don't have any plans for where to go after San Miguel," he said, "I'd recommend Mexico City, Puebla, Oaxaca, a hundred places, depending on what you want to see. Are you interested in ruins?"

"Ruins?" She had not written ruins into the script. "Well. I guess I am, sure."

"It depends how avid you are on the subject. You can do the deluxe ruin tour and go to the Yucatán, do Uxmal and Chichen-Itzá, or you can go to Palenque and see the jungle or you can do more selective trips, just a day or two—"

"I came here to see you," she interrupted.

"Hey, I'm a goldmine of information. And it's always helpful to know someone in the towns where you're traveling. If you want the names of some friends of mine in other places—"

"You told me in your letters that I should come to San Miguel."

"Everyone who visits Mexico should come to San Miguel. And you did. It's fabulous. I never thought you'd go so far out of your way to—"

"Rory. I came here to see you. I think about you all the time. I adore you. I . . . " Her voice trailed off as she saw the expression on his face take shape and freeze.

His eyes were open wide, they did not move, they looked

right at her. He did not say anything for a moment. Then he said, "Esme, I live with someone."

"I thought you and she—"

"I don't live with Franca anymore, I live with someone else."

"Inez?"

"How do you know Inez?"

"She was at your school when I went there this morning. She said she was going to see you later tonight. I thought she was your friend."

"She is my friend."

"But that's not all?"

"No, it's not all. That doesn't mean you and I can't be friends. You know that I care about you. You know that I think you're terrific, don't you? You should know that. There shouldn't be any doubt about that."

"Why didn't you tell me about Inez in one of your letters?"

"If you had told me you were coming, I would have. I would have invited you to stay with us."

"I'd have told you but I didn't know I was going to come until—" She bit her bottom lip, perhaps to keep herself from speaking again, from telling another lie, yet another lie in this long train of lies that had begun— She did not know anymore when it had started, how many lies she had told and to whom. But just now she had told him the truth and look where it got her. "It was very sudden."

"Can you come see me tomorrow at school?"

"What for?"

"To talk some more."

"About what?"

"I don't know right this minute. Whatever comes up, whatever—I think I should be on my way. It's getting late and I'm exhausted."

"What time should I come?"

"My class ends at two. Come at two." He took a wallet from his back pocket. "Will you be all right until then?"

She nodded.

"Are you sure?"

She nodded.

"What hotel are you at?"

"The Posada de las Monjas. It's down the hill a few blocks."

"Do you want me to walk you there?" He stood and tossed a few bills on the table.

"I can find it."

"Are you sure?" He picked up his bags, swung them over his shoulders.

"Yeah."

"We're just three blocks from the square now. Straight down. I live up the hill a few more blocks."

"Good. I mean, okay."

He touched her shoulder, ran his fingers down her arm and clasped her hand for a few seconds. "Are you sure you're going to be all right?"

"Yeah."

The street was dark. Up the block, up the steep hill, she saw a tiny orange light from the end of a cigarette. She remembered her mother's stories about blackouts during the war, how you couldn't even smoke a cigarette outside at night because the Japanese could fly over and see the speck of light from thousands of feet up, and that would be it, bombs away, the end.

"You go straight down this street for three blocks and you'll run into the zócalo. Then you know where you are?"

She nodded.

"I'll see you tomorrow," he said. "At two. Come to the photography studio." He held out his hand and took hers and shook it. He held it for another few seconds, rubbed his thumb against her skin, the prelude to something more. But it was not. "Good night," he said. "Get home safely."

"Okay."

Colors, lights, sounds, scents, they were all at the periphery of her senses. She walked down the hill in a haze, like someone who had just seen a collision, had come this close to being hit herself. Her knees were weak, she could feel her heart in her chest, it beat like that woman's castanets tonight, it was working so hard it might give out. She went three blocks, four blocks, she walked through the crowded *zócalo* to a street near her hotel. She kept walking down the hill, she almost lost her balance on a slippery cobblestone. When she turned a corner, she saw a tall church tower. Her hotel, the hotel that used to be a convent, was right next door. Get this, she said to herself, I come to Mexico for a man and end up in a convent. But not for long.

There was no plan, but there were no hesitations, not a moment in which she lingered. She checked out of her hotel as soon as she packed and walked the four or five blocks farther down the hill to the bus station, past the cemetery, past a few burros tied to a lamppost, past the corner store. A chicken squawked at her feet.

Six or seven buses were parked on the wide, cordoned-off street. This was the bus station. In the dark between the buses, on tables and blankets, women were selling baskets and ash-trays and cold sodas and *gorditas*. The air was heavy with exhaust fumes.

She went from the front of one bus to another, looking for one that said LAREDO or MONTERREY. She asked a driver. Only one bus a day to Monterrey, he said, it left at noon. Laredo? He shook his head. "*No hay aquí, no hay.*" His bus was going to Celaya, but she had no idea where that was.

The other buses, the other towns: León, Morelia, Irapuato. She had never heard of them. She saw a young woman, a hippie, about to board another bus whose headlights had just gone on. "Where's that bus going?" Esme called out.

"Mexico City."

"Where do I buy a ticket?"

"Over there." The woman pointed across the road to a

lighted storefront with a red-and-white sign over the door that said DISFRUTE COCA-COLA.

She boarded the bus, took a seat on the aisle next to an old Indian woman. It was dark, it was hot, there was not enough room for her legs. She swung them into the aisle, clasped her camera bag on her lap. She did not know how she was going to live in her own skin, in her own body, for the rest of the night, for the rest of her life. Why waste the afternoon, when she had the rest of her life to throw away? She had just thrown away half of it, three-quarters of it. She might have had a chance, if she had not told him everything so soon, so eagerly. If she had given him time to come around on his own. He might have walked her to her hotel and kissed her the way he had done that night in Washington. The driver turned on a radio as the bus set off. They must all have radios, the same tinny radio, the same disc jockey, broadcasting from the same tunnel. It was dark inside the bus, dark outside. You could feel every bump in the road, every crevice; you might as well be in a school bus. She could have invited him up to her hotel room, very blasé, very nonchalant. She could have had him, if she had pretended that it didn't matter. Men ran the other way if you let on that you needed them.

When she got to Mexico City— She did not know what she was going to do. It would be after midnight. She had enough money to stay in Mexico City that night. Enough to leave that night, pick another destination, hop on another bus, throw in her lot with Jack Kerouac. Enough to buy twenty rolls of film. At thirty-six exposures a roll, that's seven hundred and twenty pictures. That's three and a half really good pictures. Of Mexico. Of Mexicans. Parents and children. Fathers and sons. Fathers and daughters. What was it she had told Rory a long time ago? She would have to be a magician to take a picture of her father. Or go to Houston. Take this bus to Mexico City and head back north, back through Laredo, the way she had come, those fucking roads through the mountains, you can't see a thing at night, Rory hadn't even seen the white lines on the road when he had driven down from Washington. Esme hadn't seen the white lines on the road herself, and had ignored the ones that were everywhere else. Ignored Inez, who had as much as said that she and Rory were lovers. Ignored the truth of Rory's letters to her, two typed letters from San Miguel. Two of them, yes, but they were only half a page long. They were all about the geography in San Miguel, and the weather, and *The Labyrinth of Solitude*, which she had not read. Let's face it, they were not love letters, even though he had signed the second one "Love, Rory."

The bus rumbled, picked up speed, made hissing sounds as it climbed a steep hill and began a slow descent. The driver turned up his radio and the bus was filled with a Muzak version of "Hello, Dolly!" The lights of San Miguel disappeared over the hill.

It might run in the family, consulting *Ripley's Believe It or Not* when you're trying to figure out what to do with your life. So forget taking pictures of her father. Forget Houston. Scratch Texas. No telling what effect another dose of her father might have on her. She might end up thinking that if she flapped her arms hard enough she would take flight.

The Beginner's Book of Dreams

FOR THE HUNDREDTH time, she thought of turning back, turning around, getting on the next bus to the next place, pick a place, anyplace, any town but this town, anywhere but where she was right this second, it just so happened to be Houston, just so happened to be the front door of the garden apartment where Meyer Singer lived, a three-dollar-and-eighty-five-cent cab ride from the Trailways terminal downtown, just so happened to be two-thirty in the morning, and he was not expecting visitors. "Who's there?" he called out from behind the door, and she thought, if I turn around right now, he'll never know it was me. "Who is it?" he said.

Before she could decide whether to answer him or run, the door swung open and there was a short man in a bathrobe, squinting up at her. "It's Esme," she said.

"Esme! My god. For Christ's sake, come on in." He flipped on a light switch and she looked away from him, looked around at this place where he lived, yellow stucco walls, chintzy furniture. "Am I dreaming or what?" he said and shook his head. "Half the country is looking for you, and they all think you're here. I've been trying to convince them for days that you're not, and here you are. Here you are. I must be dreaming. I'm sound asleep, I hear the bell, I think I'm having a dream that the doorbell's ringing. I get up, I open the door, and here you are. Jesus Christ." He kept shaking his head and looking at her. She had come all this way and she had nothing to say to him. "Sit down, would you? Where the hell have you been?" He pulled out a chair from the table in the foyer, a chintzy table, metal chairs with plastic-covered padding, things you put no money down on, and pay off month by month. "Sit down. You look like— Hiya, Magoo. What a treat to see you." He smiled as she sat down. "You look terrific. You look like a real girl. A gorgeous, skinny girl. You want something to drink? You want something to eat?

You wouldn't believe who's been calling. Three times a day. The police. The FBI. You got to give them a call. You got to tell them you're not— No one knew what the hell had happened to you. They said you were supposed to be here. I told them, I said, I haven't seen her, I haven't heard word one from her, she never told *me* she was coming."

"If you have some cold water, I'd like that, please."

"No problem." He bounded the five or six feet into the tiny kitchen. "Coming right up."

"Who else has called?" There was a painting on the wall above the table, a cheap landscape in a cheap frame. The place had the look of a motel room, someplace you would stay for a night. Unless it was where you lived.

"A fellow named Michael. A gal named Georgia. Some old folks who live in a little town called New Haven." She looked into the kitchen and saw him open the refrigerator and peer down into it. "The cupboard is a little bare tonight, pumpkin. How do you feel about a peanut-butter sandwich? Let's see, there's peanut butter and grape jelly or peanut butter and—"

"That's fine."

He stood up and spoke to her over the open door of the refrigerator. He was old himself now. His hair, what was left of it, a rim along the edge of his scalp, was gray, the skin under his eyes was wrinkled. She did not know why she had come to see an old man she did not even care about. "If you don't mind my asking," he said, "where were you?"

"Mexico."

"Mexico?"

She nodded.

"Where in Mexico?"

"San Miguel de Allende. It's northwest of Mexico City. About three hours."

He turned his back to her and opened a cabinet door, began to take out utensils, plates, glasses. "Any particular reason?"

"I went to see someone who lives there."

"This fellow Michael called here a few days ago looking for

you. Said you were supposed to be here. I said I haven't heard word one from you." He unscrewed the lid on the jar of peanut butter and began to spread it over a slice of bread. "An hour later your mother calls. An hour after that, your grandmother, your grandfather. The next day, the police come by. Your mother is hysterical. She thinks you were kidnapped or murdered or god knows what. Your grandmother is hysterical. Your grandfather is hysterical. That fellow Michael—"

"What about you?"

He turned around. "Me?"

"Yeah. What about you?"

"At the moment, I'm standing here looking at you, and you look fabulous. You look like a million bucks."

"You weren't worried?"

"Of course I was worried. Here." He carried in a plate and glass of water to the table. "You want anything else?"

"No." She began to eat the sandwich, made with soft white bread, jelly that was sickly sweet.

He sat down across from her, pulled a pack of cigarettes from the pocket of his bathrobe. "I had this feeling—" he stopped to light a cigarette—"don't ask me where it came from, that you were all right. And you know what?"

"What?"

"I was right." He smiled and smoke came out of his mouth. "Not only was I right but you came *here*. Just like they said you were going to. How's the sandwich?"

"It's fine. It's good."

"Want another?"

"I don't think so."

"You don't mind my asking, how did you get here?"

"Bus from Mexico. A taxi from the bus terminal in Houston."

"How long's it take to get from San Marco to Houston?"

"San Miguel. It takes about twenty hours. But I came from Mexico City. So it took longer."

"That's a hell of a ride."

"Yeah. I guess so. But you get kind of used to being so uncomfortable."

"Let me get this straight. You told your mother you were coming to see me—"

"I didn't tell her anything. I told Michael I was—"

"Who exactly is Michael?"

"This guy I . . . I live with him. I told *him* I was coming here. But I really went to Mexico."

"He said you got a ride from Washington to Houston."

"I did. As soon as we got here, the people I was with drove me to the bus station."

"And you couldn't tell Michael because you were going to see another fellow. Am I right?"

She nodded and drank down half the glass of water.

"Look at it this way," Meyer said. "The apples don't fall far from trees."

"What do you mean?"

"The gal used to live here with me, she was a nurse over at the Medical Center, you must have gone by it on your way here. She and I were having some problems, she got pretty upset that I was always—"

"I don't think that I want to hear about this," Esme interrupted.

"No problem. No one's going to make you listen to something you don't want to listen to. This ain't that kind of household, Magoo. You sure I can't get you something else? You look like you're bushed. You look like you been sitting in a bus for a day or two. You want to make any phone calls?" He pointed to the phone that sat on the far end of the table, up against the wall.

"It's pretty late."

"It's even later over there—" he held his thumb— "back East. But honest to god, I don't think anyone would mind hearing from you. I assume you know your grandparents' news."

"What news?"

"They sold their house."

"When?"

"They called to tell me a few weeks ago. They're moving to an apartment in Branford or West Haven, some godforsaken place. Christ, I've talked to them three or four times in the last three days. Every time they call, it's the same thing. 'Have you heard from Esme? What are the police doing? They're not doing enough.' Your grandfather thinks if he came down here and talked to the police himself they would find you. He thinks the Houston police have nothing better to do than listen to him. He thinks the world's got to stop because his granddaughter didn't want to tell her boyfriend that she's got her eye on another guy. He's got to make everything a federal case. But what do I know?" He held up his hands and shrugged.

"Why did they sell the house?"

"What they *said* was that it was too big, too many stairs, they didn't need the aggravation. But if you listen closely, you get the truth, not the bullshit. You know what it is?"

Esme shook her head.

" 'The *shvartzes*' are moving in and the property values are going down. It's that simple. But some people need to think the world is more complicated than it is. Your grandmother is a classic case. She tells me twenty-seven reasons why they've got to sell the house, including 'the *shvartzes*,' but if you're really listening, with both ears, you hear that that's the *real* complaint. But if people want to believe their own lies, what can you do?"

"I guess not much."

"So how's the picture-taking business?"

"It's not much of a business at this point."

"How's the art school working out?"

"It's fine. The semester ended the week before last. I guess it's all right. It's not the best art school around, but it's cheap. I mean, I can afford it, almost." She drank down the water in her glass, held the glass to her mouth, even when it was empty, and wondered when she had stopped believing that her father

would come through for her. Whether there was a precise
moment when she understood it, or whether it had taken a long
time to sink in.

"I've got some deals cooking myself. When they come
through, two things." He spoke with his hands, held up his forefinger. "One, send you some bread, so you can go to whatever
school you want. Two—" his forefinger and his middle finger—
"I'm heading back to L.A. I've had it with the heat and all the
redneck, cowboy crap. And the goddam one-horse towns. I could
have stayed in New Haven if I'd wanted to pack it in early. You
know what?"

"What?"

"You look like you're about to fall asleep."

"I think I am."

"Why don't you turn in. Take the bedroom. I'll sleep on
the couch."

"It's all right. I'll sleep on the couch."

"No one who's spent twenty-four hours on a bus is allowed
to sleep on the couch. It's in the lease. The bathroom's over
there." He pointed. "The next door over is the bedroom."

"Thanks."

"Leave the dishes. I'll get them."

"Okay. Thanks." She stood and picked up her bags, and with
her head down, she began walking toward the bathroom.

"Magoo?"

She stopped, stood with her back to him. "What?"

"It's great to see you."

"Yeah," she mumbled.

"Go to Mexico more often. Stop here on your way back.
But next time, don't get the police mixed up in it. Or the
FBI."

She was afraid to turn around and look at him, or maybe
afraid to be seen by him. "Yeah." She spoke a little louder, loud
enough so he could hear her. "That's a good idea."

"I'll be up by eight, eight-thirty. I'll take you out to breakfast. Unless you want another peanut-butter sandwich."

"No. I mean, sure." She turned a half turn, the least she could do. "That'd be fine. Breakfast out. Well. Goodnight."

"Have any idea how long you're going to stay?"

She shook her head.

"Stay as long as you want."

"Okay."

" 'Night, Magoo."

" 'Night."

She sat at the foot of the bed and smoked cigarettes until there were no more noises coming from the other rooms. The bedroom was crowded with cartons, scattered papers, clothes strewn on the floor, socks in the corner. There was a long shelf mounted on the wall jammed with books, files, magazines standing upright. Above the dresser, a painting of a pouting clown with huge eyes. Her eyes dropped to the top of the dresser, to stacks of cards and papers. She got up and riffled through them. A bill from Texaco, a notice from a bank, an envelope addressed to Meyer from his father, postmarked five or six days before. Inside was a note, in Goody's tentative, uneven script.

> Meyer,
>   I hope this is enough. Don't forget mothers birthday June 12.
>   Love,
>   Dad

Enough what? Probably money. What else would her grandfather send? What else would Meyer ask him for? What else did Meyer need? Esme examined the books in the bookshelf mounted on the wall. *Making Your First Million, Think and Grow Rich, The Power of Positive Thinking, The Magic of Self-Confidence, How to Do Your Own Divorce, The Businessman's Book of Dreams.* She pulled that book from the end of the row, wedged against a flimsy metal bookend. The inside cover was stamped PROPERTY OF THE SEATTLE PUBLIC LIBRARY. She pulled out the card from the pocket. The due date—January, 1968.

At the other end of the bookshelf were three or four shoe-boxes. She lifted the top to one of them and poked around inside it. Notices from collection agencies. A bill from a Houston management company for this month's rent. A check Meyer had made out two months ago to the same company and that had been returned, unpaid, by the bank. A letter from an attorney in Las Vegas, dated two years ago and addressed to Meyer at a post-office box in El Paso. The lawyer intended, he said, to file an appeal in "the case" but had learned that the tax returns could be used as evidence. He did not need to tell Meyer what that might mean. Meyer should get in touch with him immediately.

There were letters with no return addresses sent in care of motels in Arizona towns she had never heard of, newsletters from outfits called Sweepstakes, Inc., Contest Newz, Business Bonanza, and Success Alive, Ltd. Brochures for assemble-it-yourself unpainted furniture, desk-top calculators, radar detectors.

In the next shoebox were socks and handkerchiefs. In the next were road maps. She stepped back from the wall and looked around the room. She spotted a row of liquor cartons pushed against the wall under the window.

She knelt in front of the first carton, ACCOUNTS scrawled in black marking pen on each surface, and reached forward to pull it from the wall, expecting resistance, expecting to haul a box of paper. She could lift it with one hand. She tore open the flaps held down with masking tape. There were towels inside. Beneath the towels were men's undershirts, handkerchiefs, more road maps, a library book called *How to Be Your Own Lawyer*.

At the bottom of the carton was a small picture frame face down. She turned it over slowly. He had framed a letter.

Dear DADDY. *This is Esme, July, 3, 1961. How are you Stu? Palms Springs is very pretty and dry being the dessert. Dru and Ted and Lucy are also here. Quinn boght me candy today, that looks like rocks, but isn't. Love. Esme.*

The trip to Palm Springs when Georgia had cried in the cab going to the airport, and Dru had lied about why Georgia was crying, and Esme had known that she was lying. But she had not known that she would grow up to tell her own lies, that she would lie so thoroughly to the man she lived with that she did not even want to call him on the phone to tell him that she had not been kidnapped or murdered. This was not the person she had intended to grow up to be. Someone who could not be trusted. Someone like My, My Meyer. Your crazy father. Who keeps towels and road maps in a carton marked ACCOUNTS. Someone like her mother, who lives with men she can't stand but believes in the knight in shining armor. Someone like herself who traveled three thousand miles when she thought she'd found him.

She pulled out another carton and yanked open the taped flaps. It was almost empty, the junk you throw into the last carton after you have packed everything that has a proper place. Loose batteries, pencils, a corkscrew, paper clips, a few passbooks from savings accounts. She flipped through them, the pages all stamped CLOSED. They were from banks in Southern California, they were twelve, fifteen, eighteen years old. At the top of each page was typed: "MEYER SINGER in trust for ESME SINGER."

Under the passbooks, face down, was another picture frame. She turned it over: her parents and Billy Maxwell and a woman, Billy's first wife, in bathing suits, standing on a beach. A five-by-seven black-and-white in a velvety gray mat. Their honeymoon. "Sheraton-Acapulco" was printed in script at an angle on the bottom corner of the mat, like a star's signature on a publicity photograph. It was the same photograph that Georgia had, the same one Winky had shown her years ago in Southampton. Esme was astonished now by her mother's beauty, her mother at twenty-two, the look of a starlet, a woman you could not help falling in love with. *Just think. If your mother had been wearing a different dress that night.*

Just think. Her parents had once been in love.

Georgia had picked *him,* the skinny guy in the bathing suit with the receding hairline standing in sand that covers his feet, standing with his arm around Georgia's shoulder. The short Jew and the tall, striking girl from Redondo. He is young, tan, full of energy. The world is his oyster, the world exists for him to conquer it. *That's why I fell in love with your father,* Georgia had once told Esme, *because there wasn't anything he couldn't do. He had me convinced that he had the world on a string. Just think.*

Esme unfolded a wad of papers wedged into the corner of the carton. They were yellowed copies of official pieces of paper. TITLE TO PROPERTY was printed on the top page. It was difficult to read, to decipher. The property was in someplace called Reseda, California. It had been purchased by Meyer in 1953 and sold in 1962. Printed at the top of the second page was TRUST AGREEMENT. It looked like a printed contract, dense paragraphs with a few blank spaces. Reseda, California. Contents of Trust: Four acres: Lots 452, 453, 454. And near the bottom, her name: Property Held in Trust for ESME SINGER. Beneath it were signatures, dates, seals.

Reseda, California. She had never heard of it. She would have to look at a map. As she stuffed papers back into the side of the box, she realized where it was. The San Fernando Valley. That was the property Meyer had bought, the trailer park that was going to make him a real-estate baron.

The next carton in the row, marked PLANS, was heavier than the others. Inside she found the Houston yellow pages from three years ago, the Greater Phoenix white pages, the Salt Lake City yellow pages. She was about to push the carton aside and go to the next one when she spotted something wrapped in newspaper pressed against the side. Another picture frame. She unwrapped it, expecting another honeymoon, another wife, a trip to Bermuda. Instead she found a note in her mother's handwriting that covered most of the glass: "Meyer, Her friend's father took this. Georgia."

She lifted her mother's note from the glass and her eyes widened. She stared at the black-and-white of herself in the black hat she used to wear with her nine-dollar muskrat coat. She remembered Don Marks's having taken the picture, when she was fourteen or fifteen. She and Leah had been coming into the house one afternoon as he was leaving, with his camera around his neck. He liked Esme's hat and took a few pictures of her in front of the house, almost on the run. She could not believe what she saw now. Her mother, at twenty-two, with long hair and a black hat. High cheekbones, eyes that looked straight into the camera, lips that did not curl up into a smile; she had not wanted Don to think that she was frivolous, so she had not smiled. She did not need to, she saw now. She was sultry, she was stunning. She did not look anything like the girl she had despised, the girl she could not stand looking at in the mirror for all those years.

She propped the photograph up against the bed frame behind her and began to push the carton back against the wall. There was a manila envelope wedged into the bottom of it, under the phone books. She eased it out and looked into the mouth of the envelope. Loose papers and index cards. She dumped them out.

Typed in faint, uneven letters, on the card that landed on top: *THE BOOK OF DREAMS (For Beginners) by Meyer Singer* © 1971. She sat cross-legged on the floor and thumbed the stack of cards. The rest of the cards were blank, except three or four on which this line had been typed, in the same faint typeface: *A QUITTER NEVER WINS AND A WINNER NEVER QUITS.*

She set the cards aside and picked up the stack of loose-leaf paper. A paragraph cut out from a book had been taped to the first page:

> *"You may as well know, right here, that you can never have riches in great quantities unless you can work yourself into a white heat of desire for money, and actually believe you will possess it."*

On the page beneath it, there were two more paragraphs, cut out from the same book.

"Henry Ford met with temporary defeat, not only at the beginning of his automobile career, but after he had gone far toward the top. He created new plans, and went marching on to financial victory."

"A burning desire to be and to do is the starting point from which the dreamer must take off. Dreams are not born of indifference, laziness, or lack of ambition."

There was typewriting on the next page, the same old typewriter as the one used on the index cards.

Book of Dreams: Introduction by the Author, Meyer Singer
MONEY MAGIC: FROM DREAMS TO DOLLARS

The best place to begin is at the beginning. Try this. Can you imagine yourself a millionaire? If the answer to that question is no, stop reading right here. But if its yes you are holding the key to your dreams in your hands right this minute. What you need is to believe in your powers of perseverence. And experience feeling the white heat of desire!!!

Take Henry Ford, one of the most successful businessmen of all times. Don't think for a minute that he didn't have his share of failure along the path to fabulous wealth. And even when he reached the top, he wasn't immuned from defeat. But he saw every setback as a challenge and he bounced back from failure with victory over

She found eight or ten more pages like this one, filled with typos, blank spaces, sentences that had never been finished, paragraphs cut out of books and taped between typewritten paragraphs.

She gathered up the pieces of paper and shoved them back into the manila envelope, dropped the envelope and the old photograph of herself back into the carton, pushed it back against the wall. She had seen enough. Seen too much. It was time to get out of here. End this little experiment in family life.

All the other experiments had failed, she didn't know why she had thought this one would be different. The time he'd shown up in a Rolls-Royce with that woman and her kids, all the times he was supposed to show up and didn't, the plane tickets that never arrived. What had she expected to find in there? Henry Ford's letters? Walter Cronkite's engagement calendar?

The clock on the night table said it was four. It was pitch dark out. She would never be able to get a cab, unless she called one. She looked around the room. No phone. If she went out there and used the phone, she would wake him. And she was so tired. If she took a nap for a few hours, she could leave when it was light out and he would still be asleep. She set the clock for six. Pulled out a button on the back that had a picture of a cowbell with an arrow next to it. In the morning, in two hours, she'd count her money again and figure out how far she could go with it. She was going to sleep with the lights on. She had read that people who knew they were going to die slept with the lights on. Because death enters stealthily, and if the light is on, there is nowhere for death to hide before it overtakes you. Right now she was just going to put her head down, put her head down for a little while on this pillow, it had been a long time since she'd put her head on a pillow. A long time since she'd slept in a bed. You never really get used to discomfort. She had told her father that you do, but you don't. You never get used to being so tired, so tired that you couldn't open your eyes now if Rory Dean were standing next to the bed, and he were everything you had hoped he would be.

She was eight and a half, she was fifteen, she was almost nineteen. She was stepping out of a cab in a yellow chiffon dress, a man had paid the fare on the meter, he was holding the door to the restaurant open for her. She was calling the Sign of the Dove looking for her mother. She told them Georgia looked like Lauren Bacall and she was found instantly. There were black-and-blue marks on her arms that she tried to hide from Esme. There was a black eye she could not hide. Then it was dark out in Mexico, and Esme, Georgia, and Meyer were on a bus. It went faster and faster down a steep hill. There were no brakes, the bus could not stop, in seconds it would drive off the side of the mountain.

"Magoo!"

Her eyes popped open. She was out of breath, her heart was racing. She was dressed. She did not know where she was.

"Magoo! Breakfast is ready!"

The room was filled with sunlight, so light that it was a moment before she realized that the overhead light was on too. She was here, at Meyer's, and she had slept with the lights on. The clock on the night table said four. She had slept for twelve hours, she had slept all day.

"Magoo!" Meyer called from the other room. "Are you awake?" She smelled something cooking, something pungent and smoky.

"I'll be right there." Her voice was hoarse, her mouth felt like it was coated with sawdust. That smell was sausage or bacon. As she opened the door to the bedroom, she heard a sizzling sound in the other room.

Meyer peeked his head into the hallway. "Got anything against bacon?"

She shook her head.

"What about eggs?"

She shook her head.

"Then come on out here and have a seat." There was a newspaper on the dinette table in the foyer. "How do you like your coffee?"

"A little milk."

He returned to the kitchen, a few feet from the narrow foyer. "Coming right up."

She sat down and reached for the newspaper. "What time is it?"

"About nine. Nine-fifteen." He started whistling, moving plates and pans around the small kitchen.

"How come the clock in your room says four?"

"It's broken. I tried to fix it a few times. I'm going to get a new one, one of these days." He whistled on and on, a tune she did not know, or maybe it was no tune at all. "I tell you, your grandmother would have a fit if she knew I was cooking bacon for you."

"I won't tell her," Esme mumbled and noticed the date at the top of the front page.

"What'd you say?"

"I said tomorrow is your mother's birthday. June twelfth. Don't forget to call her."

"How could I forget? I been reminded a hundred and seven times. Every time I talk to my old man, that's all I hear. Here it comes, a breakfast special."

"Where did all the food come from?"

He put a plate of scrambled eggs, bacon, and English muffins down in front of her. "I took a walk over to the U-Totem. It's open all night. I woke up about six, couldn't get back to sleep. You sleep all right?"

"Yeah."

"If you told your grandmother I made bacon for you, you'd never hear the end of it."

He went back to the kitchen and returned with a saucepan of hot coffee and two mugs. They were beige plastic, there was something printed on them in bright red letters: THE BEST CUP OF JAVA IN TEXAS AND THAT'S NO B.S.!

"By the way," Meyer said, "I gave your mother and your grandparents a call this morning, to tell them you're alive and kicking. Eat, before it gets too cold. Georgia said she'd phone your friend Michael."

"Thanks." She took a bite of eggs, a bite of the muffin. "Thanks for calling them."

"Needless to say they wanted to talk to you, but I said you were out like a light. How's the breakfast?"

"Great. Aren't you eating?"

"I ate a few hours ago. I didn't know when you'd get up. I been up for a few hours. I was hungry. Let me heat up some more coffee." He picked up his mug and went back, whistling, to the kitchen. He took the plastic lid off a container of coffee, poured what was in it into the saucepan and turned on the flame. "The U-Totem people make a pretty good cup of coffee, don't they?"

"Yeah. Pretty good. Where did you get the mugs?"

"What do you think of them?"

"I guess they're all right."

"One of my buddies had a few thousand made. He's trying to get a gimmick going. He's talking to the companies that run the concessions at the sports stadiums. You wouldn't believe the empire those folks have got. Would you believe they sell two million hot dogs a year?"

Esme shook her head and finished the eggs on her plate.

"When I move back to L.A., after this deal comes through—"

"You mean the coffee cups?"

"No, that's my buddy's. I give him some pointers now and then, but the deal I'm working on is a whole different bag." He poured steaming coffee into his mug. "The way I see it, when I move back to L.A., I'll have a bigger place. Maybe something out by the beach. I'll send you a plane ticket. It'll be just like the old days."

She turned and looked at her father, standing in the kitchen, sipping hot coffee from a cup that said THE BEST CUP OF JAVA IN TEXAS AND THAT'S NO B.S.! She looked down at her plate and remembered that in the old days she believed her father would never lie to her. She would have put money on that proposition when she was eight or nine or thirteen. "What old days are you talking about?"

"When we lived in L.A. Before you and your mom took off for New York."

"Oh, I thought you meant—" She stopped in the middle of her sentence, the middle of her thought. She had thought he meant the days when he used to promise to send her plane tickets.

Or maybe he had delusions of having sent plane tickets he had never sent. She would not put it past him, what with the cartons of delusions in the other room.

"I'll never forget the day your mom called and told me you were moving East." He stood leaning against the counter and lit a cigarette. She could see his profile.

"Do you have a phone book?"

"Sure do, Magoo. Coming right up." He reached down into the cabinet next to the stove. "No extra charge." He put the phone book on the table and sat down across from her. "I don't know if I ever mentioned this to you, but I was working on a deal or three back then that would have gotten me to New York as a regular-type thing. Who you calling?"

She opened the phone book and began flipping through it. She wanted to get out of here. She did not want to hear any more about deals that never came through. Deals he had probably just made up, because if he had been scheming to move to New York back then he could have told her about it before now. "The bus station."

"That sure took the wind out of my sails, when your mother took you to New York. I thought she really had it made." He paused. "Because she'd be able to watch you grow up." He stopped again. "Did you say the bus station? Don't tell me you're heading back to Mexico. Here, here's a pencil."

"Thanks."

"So where you heading?"

"Home," Esme said without thinking, because she was thinking about what he had just said, because all these years she had thought that her presence had not mattered to him one way or the other.

"New York?"

"What?" She raised her eyes to look at him.

"Home to New York?" he said.

"Washington."

"Any idea when?"

"The next bus."

"Why so soon? You just got here. Don't tell me the sheriff's on your trail."

"The sheriff?"

"You're not under orders to get out of town by sundown, are you?"

She shook her head and lowered her eyes. She could hear the surprise in his voice, because he had told her last night that she could stay as long as she wanted, and this was it.

The number for Greyhound was the last listing on the page. Esme wrote it on a napkin. She did not know why it was so important to leave right now, except that she always walked out when there was struggle or strife or something like this, whatever this was between them.

"At least stick around for lunch. I know a great Tex-Mex place. The best chili in the world. You like Tex-Mex?"

She nodded faintly and flipped ahead through the phone book. She slowed as she reached the *T*'s.

"I bet you don't get much of that in Washington. Ribs. Chili that'll burn the roof off your mouth."

She found the listing for Trailways and stared at it. She could get on the next bus and be done with the struggle or strife or whatever it was. Or she could stick around a while longer.

"If Tex-Mex isn't your thing, we've got some terrific burger joints."

She wrote down the Trailways number on the napkin, then the address. Then she began to doodle. She was fooling around, stalling for time. Anything not to look at her father, to see on his face, not three feet from her, the disappointment she heard in his voice.

"Ever had a chili burger?"

She nodded.

"We've got some of the best burger joints this side of the Mississippi. Ever hear of an outfit called Floyd's?"

She shook her head and stared at the napkin, covered now with interlocking circles, spirals that went nowhere, and remembered her name on the documents in cartons in the other room, everything he owned in trust for her, and the wind she had taken out of his sails without even knowing it for all these years, and she thought, I have to go home, but I might, I might be able to stay for lunch.

"What do you say, Magoo? If you play your cards right, lunch won't cost you a nickel."

"I'm going home but I . . . " She stopped and thought about the home she wanted to go to, not her mother's place or her father's but her own, a place she would have to create. There would be quiet rooms with high ceilings, the sunlight streaming in, people visiting, talking about art. Tall bookshelves, a light breeze, walls of paintings, photographs she and her friends had taken. Among them would be the photographs she had taken in Mexico, the one still in her camera, of the mariachi player and his son. That was pride, the way that man had looked at his son, that was love. Love that had embarrassed no one, that had made no one want to recoil or flee, the way Esme wanted to flee right now.

"What I mean is that I'm going home but . . . " She reached for the phone on the far end of the table and remembered the letter that began, Dear Daddy, Hi Stu, This is Esme. " . . . but if there's a bus that leaves late this afternoon—" careful to lower her eyes as she spoke, as she dialed the number for Greyhound— "you might have yourself a deal."

"Fantastic!" Meyer jumped up and picked up the plates and mugs from the table. "Finished?" Esme nodded. "Now we start the clean-up procedure. It's one of the little things we have to do on the maid's day off." Meyer began to whistle and sauntered the few steps into the kitchen. "If that isn't dynamite," he said almost to himself and turned his back to her and began to wash the dishes.

She watched him. She knew it was not fantastic, that she might stay for lunch, it was not exactly dynamite. Not much of a deal, if you ask Esme. Her father was wearing pale yellow pants, a striped shirt with short sleeves, cheap clothes that were per- haps a size too big for him. She was thinking about Henry Ford's fabulous wealth, about the white heat of her father's desire for money, about how badly she used to miss him when Georgia took her to New York and they lived in the apartment with the black walls and lit candles every Sunday in St. Patrick's.

Her father whistled "Yankee Doodle Dandy" over the sound of running water and Esme got a busy signal from Greyhound. She dialed the number for Trailways. Make a wish, her mother used to say in the beautiful eerie dark of the cathedral, and hand her a quarter, never enough quarters for everything she wanted, the things money could buy, and the things it could not. Make a wish, Georgia used to tell her, say a prayer, light a candle to remember someone you love.

Esme knows it is not much of a deal, that she might stay for lunch. But if you ask her, if you turn around and ask her, there's a chance she'll look you in the eye and tell you that it's a deal she can deliver on, and that that is as good a place as any to begin.

Permissions Acknowledgments

A NOTE ON THE TYPE

The text of this book was set in Electra, a Linotype
face designed by W. A. Dwiggins (1880–1956). This
face cannot be classified as either modern or old style.
It is not based on any historical model; nor does it
echo any particular period or style. It avoids the extreme
contrasts between thick and thin elements that mark
most modern faces and attempts to give a feeling of
fluidity, power, and speed.

Composed by
Maryland Linotype Composition Company
Baltimore, Maryland
Printed and bound by
R. R. Donnelley & Sons
Harrisonburg, Virginia

DESIGNED BY JULIE DUQUET